EMBRACING THE SKULL

EMBRACING THE SKULL

Martine Jardin/Diana Kemp-Jones

Copyright © 2001 Martine Jardin/Diana Kemp-Jones
All rights reserved.

This book is a work of fiction. Names, characters, places, and incidents either are products of the author's imagination or are used fictitiously. Any resemblance to actual events or locales or persons, living or dead, is entirely coincidental

EMBRACING THE SKULL

The skull glowed with ruby brilliance...

Green mist filled the hallway. Dark shapes materialized within it and roiled above them with menacing intent. They lunged for the two figures clutching the glowing skull but were hurled back with a tremendous force.

A harrowing roar like a thundering locomotive deafened them. Destiny's eyes were large luminous pools. She stared at a monstrous entity bearing down on them. Her body began to tremble as she sank into a trance-like state. A wave of distortion emanated from her flesh and snaked toward the creatures like a vengeful wraith. The force lunged and encompassed the malevolent entity with a shimmering white light. As it inhaled the pure light it howled in agony. It screamed and hurdled through the hallway where it disintegrated before their eyes.

To our fathers and those who believed

CHAPTER ONE

December 1983

Dr. Allan removed his glasses and placed them on the open file before him. He leaned back in his worn leather chair and gazed thoughtfully at the woman sitting on the side of the examination table. "Why don't you go and get dressed, Sarah? Come back here when you're finished. I'd like to talk to you."

Noticing the worried frown darkening her expression he sent her a reassuring smile.

"Is it something else besides menopause?" Sarah asked.

"No. Don't worry about a thing. You're not ill and you're not going through menopause. Now hurry up and get dressed."

"But—"

"In a few moments, Sarah. I need to test your urine before we talk."

Sarah slid off the table and hurried to the changing cubicle. Alarmed by Dr. Allan's mysterious attitude, she pondered a variety of possible scenarios while she slipped on her socks, slacks and sweater. *Could it be that new flu virus I've read about in the papers?* she thought. Hurriedly, she pulled her boots on and brushed her hair.

When she opened the door of the cubicle, Dr. Allan was seated at his desk. She walked slowly toward the gleaming, antique cherry wood desk and sank into a comfortable chair facing it. Finding the silence unnerving, she fidgeted impatiently and let her gaze roam around the cozy office, while the doctor made some notes in the file. An antique clock, silver letter opener and framed family photos added a homely touch to the neatly arranged desk. On the pale papered walls, a series of handsomely framed diplomas attested to a long and distinguished medical career. Each was familiar, their text memorized from years of visits. The office spoke of a man who was more than a face in a white coat; it breathed the essence of a man who was a caring, compassionate human being.

She watched him adjust his wire-rimmed glasses. His keen hazel eyes peered at her from behind thick lenses, his gaze so penetrating it triggered a new bout of anxiety. "Did the urine test show something, Dr. Allan?" she asked.

"Yes, it did."

She moved forward to the edge of the seat, her feet tapping anxiously on the floor, almost wishing to yank the words from his mouth yet at the same time fearing them. She waited. His hand habitually smoothed back hair that had long ago disappeared. Once, he sported a full head of wheat colored hair. Now, all that remained was a silver band hugging the bottom of his head.

"When did you say you had your last period?"

"Five or six months ago. I didn't worry about it because I'm at that point in life when these things happen. My mother went through menopause quite early in life. I believe she was only thirty-nine."

"And you've experienced bouts of nausea all this time?"

"Yes. At first I thought it was just that new bug going around, but lately I've also been quite fatigued and have suffered bouts of depression. All the symptoms point to menopause. The books say—"

"Never mind the books, Sarah," he said with an indulgent smile. "And perhaps you could leave the diagnosis up to me, please?"

He looked at her expectant face. He'd known Sarah and Chris van Kampen for so long he considered them family. His practice was in its infancy when the newlyweds became his patients. For the first ten years of their marriage they desperately tried to have a baby. After enduring a gamut of tests that revealed nothing amiss, he sent them to a renown fertility clinic. The specialist suggested fertility drugs, but because of the possibility of multiple births, they decided against that option. Further tests produced no viable reason for their inability to produce a child. Sarah and Chris were heartbroken. Finally, they registered with a number of adoption agencies. However, the lists were discouragingly long. When Sarah turned forty and Chris forty-one, they voluntarily withdrew their names before they received the letter from the agencies disqualifying them from adoption due to their ages.

Sarah could not help but wonder what was so important in her file. "Dr. Allan?" she asked hesitantly.

He grimaced. "I'm sorry. I was lost in thought for a moment. How old are you now, Sarah? Let me see," he said, and flipped through the papers in her file.

She answered him before he found the notation.

"I'm forty-one."

"I see. Sarah, how would you feel about having a baby?" Carefully he watched the expression on her face. Her eyes widened, betraying her surprise. He had always found her an attractive woman and the years had been kind to her. Her fair skin was virtually unlined and was complemented by a delicate mouth and well-formed lips. A cascade of auburn curls framed her oval face; her china blue eyes a startling contrast.

"What a strange question," she said. "Has the adoption agency been in touch with you? I thought we were considered too old to raise a child. I told you that when we withdrew our names."

"I'm talking about a baby of your own, Sarah. You're pregnant."

He might as well have pronounced a death sentence. She half rose from her chair then slowly sank down again. She felt the blood drain from her face, her hands fluttering like birds in her lap. "You mean—" she started, but couldn't finish the question.

A wave of dizziness momentarily attacked her when the import of his words sank in. The doctor's face wavered before her eyes. She closed them, his words penetrating her fogged mind. Faint music drifted around her, the sound a jubilant chorus. Her mind slowly cleared as the spectral serenade restored her. She opened her eyes and stared at him.

"What wonderful music," she murmured. "I'm really going to have a baby?"

"Music? You probably heard your singing heart," the doctor

quipped. "Yes, Sarah. It has finally happened. I would guess you to be about five months pregnant."

The dizziness passed. Focusing on the doctor, she shook her head vehemently. "I don't believe it. After all this time—it's impossible."

The haunting melody disappeared along with the giddiness. For a moment she thought she had been hallucinating. She watched the doctor's kindly round shiny face crinkle with merriment.

"My dear, haven't you and Chris been sexually active these last years?"

Sarah felt the blood rise to her face. "Well, yes, but—"

"And you've used no precaution?"

"No, of course not. Why should we? I mean—"

"Okay. I've made my point."

She quietly pondered his words. "I can't believe I'm going to have a baby after all these years," she said, her voice shaky with emotion.

"Well, you are, Sarah. I must warn you though that having a baby at your age will not be easy. And there's always the chance that the baby—"

"Could have birth defects because of my age," she interrupted him. "I know. I've read countless books on the subject."

"I think I should refer you to an obstetrician, Sarah."

"No. I want you to look after my pregnancy. Oh, Lord, what is Chris going to say about this?" As she voiced the question, she tried to picture Chris's face when she told him the news. She knew he had always harbored a deep disappointment about their inability to have children, but conversely, he had not been willing to consider putting her through grueling infertility treatments. She hoped he would not think she had tried some new drug or procedure without his knowledge.

"Knowing Chris as well as I do, I'd say he'd be delighted at this news. I'd like to at least run a number of tests on you. And we have to put you on a special diet and vitamin supplement. It's strange you never noticed any of the usual symptoms. You've gained weight. Your waist has thickened. Didn't that strike you as strange? You've always been a slip of a woman."

"Aren't those characteristic of middle age? Since I figured that

I was going through menopause I didn't worry about the weight gain. I thought it was normal."

"And normal you are, in every sense of the word. I'd like you to go and get your blood tests done now and I want you to get these vitamins." Quickly he scribbled a name on his notepad, tore the page off and handed it to her. "See the receptionist before you leave. She'll give you some necessary information and a diet sheet. And then you'd better hurry home because the snow is sticking to the ground," he said as he glanced out of the window. "I'd like you back here in two weeks, young lady," he added with a grin.

Sarah returned the smile. "You know, you're right. Suddenly I feel quite young!" she said as she rose and walked toward the door. "I still don't know how Chris will react to this," she called over her shoulder while closing the door behind her.

For a moment she leaned against it to absorb it all. *I'm pregnant—I'm going to have a baby—*The thought, after waiting so long and finally accepting that motherhood was not to be, now filled her with a mix of disbelief, joy and apprehension. Her feet automatically found their way to the laboratory. *A baby—*the words echoed through her mind accompanied by the loud rhythm of her heartbeat—

***

Sarah drove along the snow-covered driveway of the property she and her husband owned. Stately evergreens flanked the driveway, their feathery branches already laden with a veil of white. The small farm just outside Chilliwack was nestled on a ten-acre parcel of land, so the driveway was quite long. She and Chris bought the old farm soon after they got married and over the years it became their safe haven. It was a peaceful spot that they could call their own, away from the world and its hectic pace.

Something moved among the trees, its fleeting form barely visible against the pristine white snow. She slowed the car to a crawl and peered through the window. A fluffy white wolf cub stood beside the road, its tail wagging. "Oh, poor little thing," she said softly. "What is he doing out here all alone?" She stopped the car meaning to fetch the cub and bring it home. As she stepped from the car and slowly approached, the cub yelped. He frolicked joyfully, nipped at the drifting snowflakes and then scampered off into the trees.

She gazed after it, his chubby form swallowed by the wind-sculpted snow. *After all this time — a white wolf cub* she mused. *Could it be there are still some wolves left in the area?* She searched for a while hoping to glimpse the pup. Starting to feel the cold she reluctantly got back into the car and continued the drive toward the farm.

Long ago she and Chris made plans to expand. They spent hours drawing up plans for restoration and additions to the house. With a sense of anticipation, they spoke of their dreams to raise their children on the farm and eventually divide the land among them. Unfortunately, those were dreams that were never fully realized because of their inability to have children. Though they had painted, renovated the kitchen and made the house comfortable, the blueprints for the additional rooms and remaining restoration were eventually stuffed into a box and relegated to a neglected corner of the hallway closet.

Until now.

Slowly she approached the ramshackle farmhouse. Critically, she surveyed their home, her long forgotten dreams surfacing. It needed painting and a new roof was long overdue. Sagging shutters and neglected window boxes reinforced a general air of disrepair. She realized the house had become just a place to come home to. Gradually, over the years, their lives had descended into a mundane existence. Though she and Chris loved each other deeply, the early fire that ignited their relationship receded with their dreams until each passing day became an uneventful blur.

Now, she felt that old spark rise with a burst of enthusiasm. A rekindling of the passion they once shared and a vision of the house restored, caused her to eagerly scan the property for Chris. She knew he would be watching for her.

Sure enough, just as she pulled through the last gates, he emerged from the barn. She slowly applied the brakes to avoid a skid and watched him approach, still holding his rake.

Her heart overflowed with love as she observed him. Working outside in the elements had weathered his skin and aged him beyond his years. But in her eyes he was still the dashing young man with laughing brown eyes who won her heart. His hair, sandy blond but leaning toward silver, was still thick. He pulled off his cap and ran his fingers through his hair. It was an old, familiar gesture causing her to smile. Aching to shout out her news, her cold fingers fumbled with the handle to wind the car window down, but she decided that this wasn't the right moment to tell him about the baby. She wanted to make the moment special, memorable.

"Are you quitting for the day, Chris?"

"What are you bringing me, honey? Good news or bad?" he said with a welcoming grin.

She hesitated. "I'm not quite sure." Instantly his smile disappeared and his brown eyes mirrored concern.

"What did the doctor say?"

She didn't know at that point whether to blurt it out or just to wait. She hesitated and then asked him, "Chris, why don't you put that rake away and come inside. We need to talk."

Her response darkened his eyes with alarm and quickly she tried to put his mind at ease. "Honey, don't worry. I'm fine. But I do need to talk to you."

"Okay, I'll go and finish up in the barn," he grumbled but threw her a suspicious look as he turned.

She quickly wound up the window and felt guilty that she hadn't told him right away. While she drove the car into the garage happiness and anxiety simultaneously gnawed at her. She felt happy, but would Chris feel the same? Since they had withdrawn their names from the adoption lists, they had not mentioned the topic of children. However, she often glimpsed a hint of sadness in his brown eyes and knew that he still longed for a son or daughter. Their dream faded with time, but now it was reborn along with her hope. Why should she fear his reaction? It was after all only two years ago that they still hoped for adoption.

"Okay, I've finished the chores. Now how about telling me what the doctor said?" Chris asked while pulling out a chair and plopping down on it.

"Later. I have a surprise for you," she replied. Somehow she wanted this night to be different. Though she cherished their rural lifestyle she longed for this evening to be more like the old romantic times they used to share and not the routine of daily life. "Why don't you go shower and maybe relax for a while? I'll get dinner started and will serve it in the dining room tonight. I'll call you when it's ready."

His eyebrows shot up into half moons. "Since when do we eat in the dining room when it's just the two of us?" he muttered, but did as she asked.

Sarah took great care in setting the beautiful mahogany table. Pleased that she had recently polished her silverware she stood back to admire the finished effect. Carefully she lit the three ivory candles. The graceful candelabrum was a wedding gift. Its freshly polished silver gleamed and reflected the flickering flames. The sparkling crystal ice bucket that contained the bottle of aged Burgundy she had been saving for a special occasion completed the picture. Satisfied with her efforts, she called to Chris from the bottom of the stairs. "Chris, are you finished? Dinner is ready!"

Before she even returned to the dining room, she heard his feet fly down the stairs. Straightening a chair, she waited for him. When he walked through the door, his face registered incredulity as he scanned the elaborately set table. Amusement tickled her when she spotted a blob of shaving cream just beneath his ear. Giggling, she approached him. "I don't think this will taste too good with dinner," she quipped while removing the white blob and placing it on the tip of his nose.

Chris laughed and wiped the cream off with his shirtsleeve. "Guess I was in a hurry. I could smell that roast beef in the bathroom. Honey, what is all this? Here I was worried that something was wrong and all I get from you is that you have a surprise. I didn't forget our anniversary, it's not your birthday or—"

"Just sit down," she said with a smile. "The mystery will be revealed shortly." Though she acted lighthearted, she felt a touch of unease regarding his reaction to the news.

Chris opened the bottle of wine and reached out to pour it into her glass but she covered it quickly with her hand. "I don't want any, honey. I'll drink water instead." Promptly she filled her glass with water from a crystal decanter.

He frowned. "Now this is a first. You never refuse a good glass of wine with dinner. Why all the cloak and dagger? We're hardly discussing military secrets," he said while he sliced the succulent roast and served himself a generous helping.

She waited until he helped himself to vegetables and mashed potatoes. As he started to eat she blurted out her news. "Chris, I'm going to have a baby."

He had his fork poised to enter his mouth. His mouth hung half-open. The fork clattered onto the plate and the food on it splattered over the fine linen tablecloth.

For several moments he sat frozen, just staring at her. Then he smiled widely. His fingers trembled noticeably as he picked up his glass and gulped down his wine. "You're not joking. I can tell by your face," he said while putting the nearly drained glass down.

"Sweetheart, I wouldn't joke about something as serious as this. We've waited a long time, but it seems it's finally happened," she said softly while searching his eyes. Her anxiety evaporated when she read the joy in them. They glistened with the promise of tears that she had never seen during their marriage. Only then did she completely understand how much their inability to have a child had affected him.

Suddenly he jumped up. The dining chair crashed unnoticed to the floor as he grabbed her hands and pulled her into his arms. He hugged her tightly. "Honey, you've just made me the happiest man in the world," he shouted in a jubilant voice.

"You're not worried about our age?" she asked carefully.

"Hell, no! Why should I worry about our age? You said that as if we're retired already. We're still young, Sarah. Is everything all right? What did the doctor say?" He looked down at her upturned face worriedly, the thought that something could be wrong with her pregnancy now replacing his happiness.

"Dr. Allan said everything was fine. I have to take extra vitamins and watch my diet, but I'm healthy. The baby is due in April, Chris." She did not voice the concerns she had about having a baby at her age. There was no need to worry him unnecessarily.

"April? You mean you've been pregnant all this time?"

"Yes. It seems I'm already five months gone."

He held her for a moment, allowing her happy announcement to sink in, then gently eased her back onto her chair. "I have noticed you were gaining a bit of weight, but I never expected—"

Still holding his hand, she squeezed it and smiled. "Yes, my waist has thickened, but I just thought it was caused by changing hormones. After all, this isn't uncommon at my age."

He grinned, let go of her hand and tackled his dinner with gusto. "I didn't mind. The extra weight becomes you. You look more beautiful than ever. And now, you look positively radiant."

They finished dinner and spent the rest of the evening making plans for the baby's arrival and the changes to the house they would make. Sarah dug up the old blueprints from the hallway closet and ignored the dishes. It was an action completely out of character because she always cleaned up after dinner, but now she pushed them aside, unrolled the drawings and placed them on the table. They pored excitedly over them, and made enthusiastic changes to the old plans.

After they went to bed, she gazed at her husband for a few moments before turning off the lights. It was as if the news of his impending fatherhood had erased years from his face. His happiness warmed her heart and banished the fears and doubts lurking within her. She pulled the cord to switch off the light and crawled into his waiting arms. Together they prayed, as they always had, but this time their prayer was filled with extra thankfulness.

***

Sarah woke from a deep, dreamless sleep, unsure of what had disturbed her. Glancing at the glowing clock on the nightstand, she saw that it was only four. With a grimace, she started to pull the blankets up to go back to sleep until she heard a sound resembling bells. Suddenly the room filled with a delightfully jingling chorus that formed a distinctive, lilting tune. It sounded like the serenade she heard in the doctor's office that day, except clearer. Wonderingly, her eyes searched the room but she saw nothing.

A glance at Chris showed her that he was still in a deep sleep. His soft snoring confirmed it. Convinced that she was still asleep and this was just a dream, she was about to snuggle into the pillow and blankets when the room lit up with kaleidoscopic colors. They bounced off the walls, onto the ceilings and pooled across the bed until the room was immersed in a spectral light show. Startled, she sat up. Without taking her eyes away from the strange phenomenon she reached out and gently shook Chris to wake him. He didn't stir, his soft snore a droning lullaby. She shook him harder but to no avail.

"Chris, wake up," she said softly. Then a little louder, "Chris, honey, you have to see this! There's something in the room."

He didn't move.

Clutching the blankets high against her chest, she edged toward the headboard. Though the song of the bells was soft and melodious and the colors danced like fluttering rainbow veils, she felt afraid. Several vague and misty shapes appeared among the colors and small round spheres danced around the bed. Her eyes widened as they approached and hovered over her, terror invading her body. With shaking hands she tried to wake Chris again. Her lips trembled and her throat was so constricted no sound escaped.

"Sarah, do not be afraid," a gentle male voice spoke close to her. "We are not here to harm you. Please listen carefully." Other voices joined the gentle voice until they harmonized.

Sarah bit her lip to make sure she wasn't dreaming. Somehow she found speech. "Who are you?" she asked tremulously.

"Please still your fear, Sarah. We mean you no harm. We are those who watch over mankind and the folly it rushes toward."

"Why are you here?" she asked. Somehow, the fear drained away. A warm glow stole over her body and infused her with a sense of well-being. "What do you want?"

"We want nothing except to tell you that we will watch over your family. You and your husband will not see us, but we will be with you all the time and we will protect your daughter."

"Are you angels?" Sarah asked wonderingly.

"We are the Antiquitas, the ancient ones, the keepers of knowledge. Long ago we planted a seed of influence on this world. This influence will culminate in the birth of your child. Destiny will be your daughter and the daughter of a new Earth. Your fates are intertwined in ways that will change the very essence of humanity."

Sarah frowned. "I don't understand. We're just ordinary people."

"Not so ordinary," whispered the voices. "In time you will understand. For now, it is only important that you understand that you are the harbingers of our Earth child. Rest easy, Sarah. Now, we must go now."

"Wait!" she cried. "What do you mean? What else do you know about my daughter?"

She looked expectantly around the room, but heard only the fading sibilance of the voices. Disturbed, she was unable to go back to sleep, her thoughts racing from her encounter with the strange phenomenon. Only when dawn finally filtered through the curtains did she drift into uneasy slumber.

***

The next morning at breakfast, Sarah told Chris about her experience. "What do you think it meant, Chris? And what did they mean by Earth-child?"

"I don't know, honey," he said while pouring milk into his oatmeal. "Maybe it was your subconscious dealing with the news about your pregnancy. It's been quite an emotional experience for us both."

She nodded without conviction, her thoughts drifting to the mysterious voices. "I suppose so. But it was so real. I could have sworn I was awake when it happened. This wasn't like any dream I've had before. Usually I forget them or remember only fragments."

"Some dreams seem very realistic," he said reassuringly and patted her on the hand. "I've had a few like that myself. But somehow I don't think we were visited by supernatural beings. Dreams are often a means to settle the turmoil of the conscious mind. With the unexpected news you had, I'm not surprised you had such a vivid one."

"They said Destiny was our daughter—so we will have a girl."

Chris took a sip of his coffee. "Look, honey, it was just an unusually intense dream brought on by your excitement. I wouldn't put too much stock on the mystical elements. And frankly, I wouldn't discuss this with anyone else. You know how people think about that mumbo jumbo. Before you know it, they'll have you committed. Anyway, I assume you're not going to work today?"

"No, I called in sick." She flashed him a beaming smile. "Matter of fact, when I go into town today I'm going to hand in my notice.

We've missed so much all these years. I don't really want to be a working mother. I'd much rather stay at home and look after our child."

"Good idea. I don't want you working anymore either and there's really no need for it. The income we receive from our crops is more than enough to support us. In fact, I'd rather you didn't drive today. The roads are treacherous. I have to go into town anyway as we're almost out of chicken feed. Write your letter of resignation and I'll take it in for you," he told her, leaning forward to kiss her on the cheek. He looked into her radiant eyes for a moment, noted her glowing cheeks, and thought how young she looked.

"I wanted to go shopping," she said hesitantly.

"I know, honey, but you've got four months to get ready for the baby. It can wait."

"Okay. I've got some wool I bought to knit stuff for the church bazaar. I can start knitting and if you bring back wallpaper samples and paint charts I can—" She stopped for a moment to catch her breath. "Oh, and don't forget to pick up a new Sears catalogue."

Chris smiled at his wife's enthusiasm. Her face glowed with a joy he had not seen in years. Suddenly, she was once again that beautiful young girl who captured his heart. Her happiness radiated toward him like a tonic, its afterglow seeping into his heart and revitalizing his long-forgotten dreams. "Yes, I'll do all that. Matter of fact, I'll go and see Tony Hansen about renovations."

"I guess I can finally get around to catching up with my canning and preserves," she said with a grin. "Looks like I'm about to become a true farmer's wife."

***

CHAPTER TWO

April 15th, 1984

Kaleidoscopic colors swirled before Sarah's eyes. She tossed and turned, the prismatic abyss expanding and contracting until it consumed her. Like a drowning swimmer whose strength finally faded, she let go and merged with rainbow brilliance. It swept her along a spectral tide. Buoyantly, she drifted toward a light that shone with solar intensity.

As she reached out to touch the light, a piercing pain shattered her tranquil state. It startled her, shocking her into awareness. She opened her eyes and glanced at the glowing numbers on the alarm clock. It was just past midnight. She licked her lips and swallowed. For some reason, she felt incredibly thirsty.

A faint humming sound resonated throughout the house as she went downstairs to the kitchen. Frowning, she glanced around, listening, trying to pinpoint the unusual sound that gradually grew louder. Suddenly, it was accompanied by singing, a beautiful chorus unlike any she had ever heard before.

Feeling faint, she stumbled to the kitchen table and leaned on it. The voices rose with ethereal jubilance, as if portending a miraculous event. Thinking that she was once again dreaming, she fought off the dizziness and walked to the fridge. Just as she was about to open it, wetness gushed down her legs.

Her heart skipped a beat when she looked at the small pool of fluid on the kitchen floor. "It's time," she murmured and quickly hurried back upstairs to their bedroom.

"Chris, wake up!" she called out and shook him gently.

He opened his eyes and blinked at the light. "What's the matter?"

"My water just broke."

That woke him up in a hurry. "Oh my God. You'd better get dressed. I'll get your bag," he said nervously as he sat on the side of the bed and started to put on his socks and groped hurriedly for his jeans.

Sarah laughed. "Chris, I haven't got any contractions yet. There's no rush."

He stopped dressing to look at her. "Are you sure?"

"Yes. I wouldn't have woken you yet, but you'd never forgive me if I left it till the last minute. I'll go and have a shower. You go back to sleep for a while."

"I don't think—" he started nervously.

"Honey, labor may not start for a while. You might as well get some rest."

But after she had her shower and walked out of the bathroom Chris was fully dressed and sat on the side of the bed waiting for her.

"Has it started yet?"

"No. I'm going to crawl back into bed for a bit," she said. "You might as well join me."

He lay on the bed beside her with his clothes on. Sarah grinned. She felt nervous too, but they'd read enough books and attended a few Lamaze meetings. As this was her first pregnancy, she knew it could take quite a while before labor seriously began.

Neither of them could sleep. Finally she suggested they go downstairs for a glass of warm milk.

Chris looked at her nervously. "No, I want you to lie down and take it easy. I'll go and get the milk. Are you okay?"

"Yes, not a twinge so far and I'm fine. How about we play cards for a while? That will take your mind off things." Awkwardly, cradling her belly with her hands, she got off the bed and groped for her gown.

"Hell, how can you think of playing cards at a time like this?" He walked around the bed and took her by the arm, supporting her.

She allowed his tender concern though she didn't need physical support right now. "Just a minute, I want to look at the nursery," she said while opening the door next to their bedroom.

Chris put his arms around her and they stood in silence, gazing at the nursery they had so lovingly prepared. Because of her dreams, Sarah had decorated it in pastel rainbow colors. The wall behind the crib displayed an arcing rainbow—constellations and cherubs against a dreamy, pale blue sky scattered with puffy clouds. She had painted the mural herself; her artistic endeavors a work of art. The white crib was ready for its occupant. Sarah looked down at the lacy bumper pad, the matching comforter and sheets and smiled. "Tomorrow or the day after, our son or daughter will occupy it," she said while imagining a tiny face peeking above the comforter.

"I wonder if it will be a girl," Chris said. "Isn't that what those voices supposedly told you?"

Sarah smiled but said nothing, her conviction that she would have a daughter stronger than ever.

At her insistence they played cards, but Chris could not concentrate on the game. He fumbled with the deck, dropped the cards on the floor several times and kept asking her if she felt anything, any twinge at all.

"Chris, I had another strange dream. And when I went downstairs to the kitchen I also heard that music again, only this time it was much louder."

"Well, it's almost time. Your subconscious—"

"No, Chris," she said indulgently. "This was no dream caused by excitement, my subconscious, or whatever logical nametag you want to place on it. It was a vision, beautiful and reassuring. The kaleidoscopic—" but she had to stop because the first contraction suddenly attacked. It didn't feel bad, almost like the cramps she experienced with her periods. "It's started," she told him.

He jumped up. "Okay, I'll go start the car."

"No, Chris, we have to wait until the contractions are closer together. Sit down for goodness sake."

"It's frosty. I don't want you to catch cold."

"I've got to time the contractions, honey." She was amazed at her own calmness. The last seven days she'd felt nervous, expectant, feeling every twinge, and Chris reassuring her each time she thought that labor had started. Now that the time had finally come, a peaceful serenity possessed her.

They played cards though she could tell Chris's mind was not on their game. Each time she had a contraction he kept worriedly glancing at her face and at the clock. Finally, at three in the morning the contractions were five minutes apart. "I think we should go to the hospital now, Chris. Doctor Allan said when they're five minutes apart we—"

He didn't need to be told twice. Within minutes he had his jacket on, ran to the garage and started the car. Rushing back into the house, he grabbed her bag, loaded it, and waited for her impatiently while she checked the doors to make sure everything was locked. He hustled her into the car and pulled the seatbelt around her, struggling to get it across her enormous belly. Normally, he managed it easily. Now, he fumbled with the catch and muttered under his breath. Finally it clicked into place.

After he strapped himself in, he clicked the remote control to open the garage doors. "Shit, I don't believe it. It's April for God's sake."

A dun blanket of snow greeted them. Lacy flakes plastered the windshield as he drove slowly out of the garage.

"We've had snow in April before," Sarah said.

"I know. But this is a special day."

"So our baby will be greeted by a white world. Snow is beautiful, Chris. Look how fresh and clean everything looks."

He carefully navigated the driveway because he had already changed the snow tires for summer tires. "I don't have time to look," he said nervously.

Sarah gazed out the window. As they approached the gates, she saw something move. Pressing her nose against the side window, she peered out. "My God, it's that cub again. Chris, stop the car!"

"Are you mad? You're in labor and you want to stop to look at a cub?"

"This one is special. It's that wolf cub I told you about before. Maybe it's lost its mother."

"We can look for the cub after the baby is born, honey. Honestly, I've heard of pregnant women having strange notions, but this beats them all. I'm sure they'd appreciate us arriving at the hospital with a wolf cub."

As Chris drove through the gates, she reluctantly turned to watch the cub. For a moment, their glances locked, the cub's head bobbing as if in acknowledgment.

***

"How come Doc Allan isn't here yet?" Chris asked, anxiously pacing the floor.

"They'll call him when it's time, honey. Sit down. You're making me nervous."

She'd been in labor all day, Chris becoming more edgy by the minute. The contractions were quite close together now, so close that she hardly had time to take a breath. "It won't be long now. Did you call our parents?"

"Yes. They're all here in the waiting room."

"Ooooh," she cried when another contraction tore at her.

Watching her face contort in pain, he rushed to her side. "Breathe, honey. Remember?" He started to puff with her as she clasped his hand and squeezed hard.

"Call the nurse. I think this is it," she panted between breaths.

Within minutes they rushed her into the delivery room. Nurses flitted about while two other nurses transferred her to the delivery table and prepared her. They pulled up her gown and draped a green sheet over her. "You're fully dilated, dear. It won't be long now but I don't want you to push just yet," a nurse told her.

Doctor Allan arrived already gowned and masked. "Well, Sarah, this is the big day!"

By his twinkling eyes she knew he was smiling underneath the mask. "Yes," she panted. "Big is the word. I want to push."

"Don't push just yet. Only when we tell you to."

Chris stood behind her and held both her hands. When Dr Allan finally told her to push, the pain was so bad she almost pulled Chris down. "Give me that shot!" she shouted in between spasms.

"Too late now," a nurse said. "You should have taken it when we offered it to you."

After an hour she'd still not given birth. Sarah felt exhausted—the will to push almost gone. The pains were so severe she felt as if she were on the rack.

Chris left his wife's side for a moment and whispered to Dr. Allan, "What's going on? Why is it taking so long?"

"We might have to do a caesarian, Chris," his voice still audible. "If nothing happens within the next few minutes, we'll take her up to OR."

"No way in hell are you cutting me open!" Sarah screamed, giving a mighty push almost in defiance of the doctor's words.

Dr. Allan shoved Chris aside. "Look! There's the head! That's it, Sarah! You're doing great! One more push now!"

Chris watched in wonder as he saw the crowning. "Sarah, she's got beautiful hair, like spun silk!" he shouted excitedly.

She hardly heard him. The urge to push was now so great that all the sound in the delivery room receded to a distant din, the blood roaring in her ears as she pushed with all her strength.

Relief.

Now that the baby's head was out, the small body slithered out easily. Sarah fell back onto the pillow, her hair drenched, rivulets of perspiration running down her face. Her ordeal was over and the pain vanished though her body shook as if in protest at what it had just endured. She looked at the infant between her legs and watched the doctor and nurses working on the baby, cutting the cord, suctioning the little mouth and cleaning the nostrils of mucus.

"It's a girl, honey. You were right all along," Chris murmured.

She didn't answer. Her pain forgotten, she was focused on the silent infant.

"Damn, she's not breathing," muttered Dr. Allan while grabbing the baby by the feet and holding her upside down. He slapped the small buttocks. Once. Twice. Still no cry. He lay the baby between Sarah's legs and desperately suctioned more mucus from the tiny mouth.

Chris watched, his heart throbbing painfully. He moved to Sarah's side and held her hand, squeezing it tightly.

"Chris—" she said in a tremulous voice.

"She'll be fine," he reassured her trying not to show his own fear.

The baby lay like a limp doll as if reluctant to enter the world, her eyes tightly shut.

Without realizing it, Sarah held her breath. Her heart contracted in pain at the thought that her baby wouldn't live.

Stillborn—

The word echoed in her mind, stabbing relentlessly at her heart.

Suddenly, a shimmering rainbow mist filled the room and surrounded the baby. In the midst of it floated a large bubble, a fragile dome that gleamed with a gossamer sheen. It pulsed like a living entity and filled the air with a gentle buzz. Suddenly it burst, releasing thousands of sparkling particles. Spheres danced around the delivery table, their music hauntingly joyful.

She recognized the spheres as the same ones she had seen the night after she learned she was pregnant. Immediately, peaceful warmth entered her body and erased her fear. The particles formed a diaphanous mist that funneled and seemed to enter the infant. Within a moment a soft wail filled the delivery room.

Dr. Allan raised the snuffling baby in his arms.

Sarah let out her breath and gazed up at Chris. His face was pale, drawn. His voice was laced with deep emotion as he ineffectually wiped a tear rolling down his cheek. "We have a daughter, Sarah," he said, bending to kiss her on the forehead.

A nurse swaddled the baby and placed her in Sarah's arms. She hardly felt the doctor stitching her as she gazed down at the cherubic face and the crown of pale, downy hair. "Look at her, she's so beautiful. She is going to be blond, like you."

Chris merely nodded. He was too overcome by emotion to speak as he gazed down at his daughter and reached out to clasp a tiny fist.

"We'll call her Destiny. What do you think, Chris?" In the background she heard joyful singing, an indescribable song that no one but she seemed to hear. She almost asked him if he could hear it, too, but for some reason stopped herself. It was a strange phenomenon, one only she could witness. *The angels—*she thought. *They were here all the time—*

"Yes, honey. Whatever you want," he said hoarsely. He cleared his throat and bent down to kiss his daughter. "Destiny is a beautiful name. After all, it's a miracle we had her. I guess God plotted that it was our destiny to have this lovely little girl. Yes, Destiny it is—"

***

CHAPTER THREE
ROME
December 2008

The weeping city was shrouded in a leaden pall of smoke. Above the cries of the wounded and dying, a tolling bell solemnly lamented man's legacy; now crushed and broken between the dust and rubble that had become the domain of vermin. Scuttling from the shadows, the creatures openly mocked the scourge-ridden populace for whom neither cures nor hope were to be found.

The streets were shattered. Fires raged from gaping asphalt crevasses and the bowels of once proud monuments and buildings. Churning rivers of blood wound through the blighted land, the fallen drifting on its surface like scattered autumn leaves.

Temporary Red Cross camps served as hospitals. Makeshift tents were crowded around flickering bonfires; the flames illuminating the gaunt haunted faces of the homeless. Volunteers tended the wounded, the sick and dying as best they could. Without sufficient medical supplies or hope of adequate treatment, their efforts were almost futile, their main task to comfort the dying. A tangible essence of fear and desperation tainted the air.

As the dirge of the tolling bell faded the frightened voice of a reporter bleated from a static-ridden radio transmission.

"Without time for recuperation after the brief but catastrophic third world war, it is as though the world has been pummeled by a mighty fist. Great cities have tumbled liked dominoes. Earthquakes, tidal waves, firestorms and typhoons have devastated entire countries and have left others crippled. Survivors face pandemic famine and disease while desperate refugees pour into the few remaining havens on Earth."

The reporter became emotional, almost hysterical as she described the widespread destruction.

"It's like a vision from hell," she told whatever audience could still receive the transmission. "But one I never thought humanity would witness. Everything we knew, all we have accomplished has been swept aside. All over the world, the signature of humanity is being erased. The Great Wall of China lays toppled like a child's discarded building blocks; the once mighty pyramids are nothing but mounds of dust. The Statue of Liberty gazes not at the sky but at the murky bottom of New York Harbor, nor will we ever again hear the resonant chimes of Big Ben—"

Static shattered and finally silenced the transmission. Almost as if in response a flurry of bats rose like a malevolent cloud from the Basilica of St. Peters, the hands of its clock permanently stopped on midnight, the bell silent as it gazed over the devastated city. Though Michelangelo's great dome was damaged, the apses, facade statues and columns crumbling and showering a hail of debris, the Basilica stood like an eternal symbol of hope among the ruins. Holy fire shone through broken windows and its massive doors hung askew.

The fiery light beamed through the intact stained glass image of the Holy Spirit; the dove a shining symbol above the miraculously undamaged altar. A faint whisper of organ music resonated through the rubble-strewn interior and toppled monuments to fade to the sound of a child softly singing. Huddled by the altar below the Chair of St. Peter, a little girl gazed at the beatific light as it embraced her. Her dirt-caked face and tangled blond hair could not conceal her angelic beauty. She resembled a cherub incarnate. Suddenly she stopped singing and listened intently.

"Angelica," a soft female voice said. "There is something for you beneath the rubble. Take it and keep it safe."

The warm, gentle resonance of the voice soothed away her fear.

Her eyes darted to the pile of rubble beside her. Something glinted in between the rocks and she quickly dug to reach the gleaming object. Her deep blue eyes glowed in rapture as she pulled out a golden candlestick and tucked it into the pocket of her tattered coat.

An injured priest stumbled from an annex, his bloodied vestments torn. Though weak and emaciated he bore no sign of the scourge. His dark, sunken eyes darted in search of the source of the melodic voice. Finally his gaze fell to the altar. Father Claudio walked slowly toward the child and babbled incoherently before he picked her up and cradled her in his arms. "Povero bambina. Padre Claudio li aiuterà," he said while trying to cover the child with his torn habit. The girl did not resist. Floundering through the debris, clutching the little girl tight against his chest, the glow of holy fire bathed them in benevolent light as they fled the Basilica.

The ravaged streets were almost impassable. More than once, Father Claudio and the child had to hide from marauders who would kill for a scrap of bread. Vermin squealed mockingly from alleys and gutters, their eyes feral pinpoints in the darkness. The priest eventually found an emergency Red Cross shelter and left the little girl with a nurse and a small group of orphaned children.

She sat silently among the group of crying children. Quietly, she waited until a volunteer approached her.

"What is your name, little girl?" Greg Collins, a British volunteer, asked softly. She didn't answer. Her eyes were large and unafraid as she gazed at him solemnly. "Nome? Come ti chiami?" he asked in Italian. He felt spellbound by her direct gaze and then he implicitly understood that something had led him to this child. She was different from the other children. At all cost, she had to be on the next mercy flight. All sound around them ceased as their minds touched. Without speaking she conveyed a message to him.

"Il mio nome e Angelica Peragine. Sono la sorella di Destino. Fra poco, la mia sorella ed io saremmo insiema di nuovo."

Greg's Italian was limited, but he understood the words that whispered in his mind. Her name was Angelica and soon she would be together again with her sister. *Destiny*, he thought. He had dreamed about this woman so often, the visions always affirming that his path would lead him to Italy for an important purpose. Now he understood why.

He nodded and gazed deeply into Angelica's fathomless blue eyes. The cries of the other children faded as the young man and the child shared a moment of peace, understanding and hope. For a moment the passage of time was suspended as tranquility descended.

Slowly the surrounding noise encroached. The spell was finally shattered as a nurse tapped him on the shoulder requesting his help. Reluctantly he released the child's small hand and turned away to help with the other children.

Angelica Peragine sat quietly in a corner. Unlike the other children, she wasn't afraid. While huddled near the altar she had heard the voice and suddenly, like a bad dream, all insecurity and fear vanished. The voice continued talking to her while the spheres serenaded her. She listened enthralled to the words. The voice was sweet, warm, almost like her mother's, but she knew it wasn't. Her mother was gone forever, swallowed by a violent earthquake that had shaken their village. And the voice was with her now.

"Soon, my child, you will be with your sister. We will lead you to her."

Her father was also gone—as were all the people she loved. The violence and terror that ravaged the land had consumed them. But she was still not alone. She had the voice, a guardian no one could see, but one that lulled her fear and dried her tears. The voice instructed her to take the candlestick and bring it to Destino.

Destino—she thought, the name filling her with anticipation.

She fingered the candlestick hidden inside her coat pocket and watched Greg tending the other children. They had spoken to each other through their thoughts and she understood they would meet again.

Now she heard the voice again and luminous balls of light danced around her.

"Angelica, we are with you," chanted a mellifluous chorus. "Do not be afraid, child. We are the Antiquitas. We are your friends and will travel with you. Soon, you will be with the chosen ones. Take good care of the talisman. It is the key to the future. Destino, you sister, awaits you."

The voices receded but the rainbow lights remained,

surrounding her with song and music. Mesmerized, she listened, comforted by their presence and a sense of recognition.

Waiting—

Later, as a forbidding mantle of cloud pressed against the city, a Red Cross team escorted the children on the hazardous journey to the airport. A solitary transport plane waited with revving engines amidst the ruined terminals. It was the last flight to leave for Vancouver, Canada, one of the few remaining cities capable of accepting refugees. The team hurriedly boarded the children on the mercy flight, their backs hunched against a bitterly cold wind.

A mighty rumble shook the earth as the plane taxied toward the crumbing runway. The land swayed, toppling the remaining buildings into the maw of a great crevice bisecting the airport. With shrieking engines the last mercy flight from Rome lifted off, its rising tires barely avoiding the magma that gushed forth from the wounded earth like geysers consuming everything in sight.

Unafraid, Angelica gazed out of the grimy window at the surging clouds. Lightning scythed the darkness, momentarily illuminating an insectoid shape hovering beyond. Turbulence buffeted the plane eliciting cries of fear from the other passengers. She clasped her hands tightly and closed her eyes, shutting out the image of the ominous shadow. Suddenly she dared to look again when radiant color shimmered through her closed eyelids. The sublime glow of a diffused rainbow appeared outside her window. The sound of crying children faded as she regarded the hovering sphere that floated alongside the plane as if in protection.

"Destino, sto venendo," she whispered.

"She is coming—" echoed the voices softly.

***

CHAPTER FOUR
December 17, 2008

Destiny van Kampen hurried out of the decrepit sky train station. Though the rail network sustained a degree of earthquake damage, retrofitting had at least kept the system functional and provided the only viable means of travel for most able to do so. A few flickering lights barely illuminated the graffiti marred walls, the frigid air not quite banishing the rank odor permeating the building.

Hunched protectively inside her heavy down jacket, only Destiny's face was visible beneath the fur-trimmed hood. Her breath emerged in a stream of white puffs as she dodged the human chattel in makeshift camps infesting every available space.

As always, the homeless inhabited the station. Security guards had long ago given up on removing them since there was no place for them to go. They understood the need for shelter as many of their own families and friends were in the same predicament. She tried to ignore the begging hands, the heartrending pleas for food and the echoes of bawling children. Often, she gave one or two of the more wretched a food stamp but the need was too great, she didn't have enough stamps to go around. It broke her heart to witness such misery each time she traveled to work and despite her efforts she could never harden herself to the sight.

A bitterly cold wind raked her face as she exited the boarded-up doors. Clutching her purse tightly against her chest, she walked briskly up the hill to Carnarvon Street and turned the corner to her apartment building. Her breath puffed like a locomotive, the frosty evening air biting into her cheeks. Though there was little traffic in the street, her eyes were alert and watchful as she glanced at the reflection of bonfires and trashcan fires flickering from surrounding damaged or abandoned buildings. A child wailed in the distance and silenced abruptly, the sound swallowed by an oppressive bank of cloud cloaking the city. Immersed in an unnatural twilight, the late afternoon felt more like the depths of a winter night.

The eternal rumble of bulldozers greeted her when she approached her apartment building. Impatiently she waited for them to move from her path. Ensuing dust clouds mixed with drifting smoke to taint the air with an acrid aroma. The machines and crews labored steadily to clear the rubble from the streets and repair cracks and holes to the best of their abilities. Most of the work was temporary, as the scope of damage throughout the city and Lower Mainland belied any hope of complete restoration. Nevertheless, Carnarvon Street was not as badly damaged as other areas of the city where many of the older buildings had virtually disintegrated.

Automatically, she glanced behind her but saw no one, though in the uncertain glow of randomly functioning streetlights shadows seemed to stretch menacingly toward her. For the last several days she had the feeling that someone was following her. Though she stopped to try and catch her suspected stalker, and had even hidden inside a surviving Government Issue store and peeked through the window, she never spotted anyone.

A raucous whisper of heavy metal music drifted to her ears. She shuddered and paused to glance at the decrepit bar cross the street. Hunkered amidst two derelict buildings, the squat building bore the scars of its violent history in the guise of boarded up windows, bullet-raked flanks and rusted metal outer doors. Street people infested the adjoining alleys, their gauntness highlighted by the flickering flames of oil drum fires. The music momentarily blared as shadowy figures entered and emerged from the entrance and melted into the shadows. As if sensing her scrutiny, one heavily clad figure stopped to gaze her way before moving on.

"I've got to move to another apartment," she muttered while

quickly turning away. She watched an armada of bulldozers lumber toward the partially collapsed building next door. Though her own workday was over, the crews of workmen put in twelve to fifteen hour days six days a week.

A group of homeless sheltering within the ruins scattered, their meager belongings clutched in their hands. The bulldozers' mighty treads extinguished a scattering of bonfires, some still bearing the meals of the hapless itinerants. She felt a pang of compassion as she watched them scurry like displaced rats. Dismally, she wondered where they would go. So many people had been left homeless that the resources of rescue agencies were hopelessly stretched. Men, women and children sheltered wherever they could, survival dependent on what they scavenged from the ruins.

Bursting from a makeshift hovel, a little boy clad in dirty, ragged clothing screamed when his harried young mother struggled to drag him and a bundle of belongings from the path of an advancing bulldozer. She swore when the machine flattened their shelter. The child stubbornly resisted her efforts to yank him out of the bulldozer's path, a battered stuffed animal his target. Recognizing the symptoms of the scourge, the mottled appearance of the child's face sent a shiver through Destiny. A testament to the horrors wrought by a tainted environment, the lethal, chameleon-like virus attacked the body and triggered any genetic flaws or hereditary predisposition to disease.

She unconsciously stepped back. Technically, everyone was prey to the virus, though it was known that those with weakened immune systems were most prone. No cure had been found yet, the virus mutating so quickly that antidotes quickly became obsolete. Coupled with almost nonexistent funding and lack of researchers, the hope of a cure was indeed as distant as the hope for a peaceful world.

The haunted look in the little boy's eyes reflected a pain that had no place in an innocent child. Destiny stared with pity at the exhausted mother, her face aged beyond her years by hardship. As the mother coughed up blood and stumbled across the ruins, Destiny could only wonder whether the little boy would survive long enough to join the growing ranks of orphans. Though Vancouver no longer maintained orphanages, over the last few years the city had requisitioned some abandoned buildings and converted them into temporary shelters until homes could be found for the growing numbers of destitute children.

Disheartened, she turned away. She glanced up at the damaged flanks of her apartment building. *They've been working on this building forever though I suppose I shouldn't complain. At least I have a roof over my head*, she mused.

Though her building, the College Tower, had suffered some damage, it had survived fairly intact much to the surprise and gratification of its tenants. Repairs were taking a long time to complete, and took even longer for buildings not considered in danger of collapse, but under the circumstances, she was grateful to have a place to stay at all.

She had lived in apartment 1501 of the College Tower ever since she left her parents' farm and moved to the city. Though the neighborhood was decent enough, the seedy bar across the street almost deterred her from renting the apartment but lack of funds and the reasonable rent for a one-bedroom suite were a higher priority. The fifteenth floor felt safe and she had installed extra locks on her front door as a precaution.

Unfortunately, the bar's illicit activities increased over the past few years, especially since it was virtually the only one left intact in the area. The police, their meager resources already overtaxed by escalating crime and public relief duties, were often slow to respond to calls despite the fact that unruly drunks and bar room brawls were replaced by screams and the sinister sound of gunshots.

Often, in the early hours of the morning, she awoke to the piercing sound of sirens and the staccato rhythm of automatic gunfire. Though disturbances had become familiar to her since the war, the bar's proximity was a constant source of concern. Just recently, the apartment manager found a body surrounded by used syringes in the underground parking lot of her building. She often wondered where the people, a great many of whom were homeless or unemployed, obtained the money to spend in the bar or buy drugs. She suspected that bartering on the black market was heavy. That people even under such appalling circumstances still peddled drugs never ceased to amaze her.

It was because of the bar and its unsavory clientele that

she never accepted overtime at work. Employed as an emergency services relief coordinator, she witnessed the staff at her company gradually reduced to almost half and those that remained had to take on extra duties simply to retain their jobs. She preferred to take work home with her and get to her apartment at a decent hour.

It's as if the world has gone mad, she thought and noticed that she could now approach the front entrance without having to negotiate precarious piles of rubble. *But then, it has.* She paused at the lobby entrance to gaze at a teenager and baby huddled in a corner of the entrance. The young girl clearly looked diseased, her face a jaundiced yellow. The emaciated infant in her arms squirmed and wailed as she feebly attempted to feed it from an empty breast.

Destiny quickly dug in her purse and tore off one of her food stamps. The young girl uttered a garbled cry and yanked a tattered blanket over her face when Destiny approached with the stamp. The hand that clutched the blanket was covered in sores; the ragged nails almost black. She dropped the stamp on the ground close to the girl and headed to the apartment entrance, but not before the sharp report of a gun rose above the noise of the droning bulldozers.

With a gasp, she swiveled toward the bar, but could hear only an angry chorus of voices concealed within the shadowy depths of the alley. The workers paused to scan the area before continuing their work, the constant threat of violence something they faced on a daily basis. The wretched young girl had eyes only for the food stamp and quickly snatched it from the ground. Feeling vulnerable in the open, Destiny poised the apartment key in her fingers and hurried to the door as an approaching siren wailed in the frigid air.

***

CHAPTER FIVE

The squad car turned into Carnarvon Street barely a moment after Destiny reached the apartment entrance. Battered and weatherbeaten, the vehicle's headlights blazed behind a protective grill, its beefy tires flanked by chains. The flashing light on the roof strobed drunkenly from its remaining bulbs as the car pulled up outside the bar.

As the whooping siren silenced, Brett Young glanced at his partner and driver, Phillip Cheetham, before keying in the radio.

"Unit 17 responding to disturbance at Outrigger Bar."

"Roger," came a static-shattered response. "Status on callout at food distribution center?"

"Couple of tweakers got out of hand. Situation's under control."

"Roger. Captain wants you back at the station ASAP. Gunderson's been taken ill and we need cover for the downtown area."

Young glanced at the bulldozers flanking a relatively intact apartment building across the street.

"We're at the Outrigger now. Give us five. Young out."

Cheetham's brow cocked as he unstrapped his seat harness. "What's the deal, Brett? A disturbance at the Outrigger isn't exactly a priority call. We could have let another unit take it."

Young checked his weapon and stepped outside the squad car.

His breath frosted in the air like a puff of white smoke. He hesitated before turning to his partner. "We were in the area. No point in leaving it. If Gunderson's ill, he's out of action. A few minutes won't make any difference."

Cheetham frowned at Young's distracted expression. Following the direction of his gaze, he noticed his partner focused on the apartment building rising beyond the contingent of bulldozers.

"You feeling okay, Brett?"

Brett stared at the tall apartment building, his eyes scouring the mostly darkened windows until they stopped on a street-facing apartment. Something within him urged him to cross the street but he fought it. Puzzled by his inexplicable compulsion, he turned to his partner. He noticed the concern in his Cheetham's eyes. Frost clung to the older man's black moustache in silver streaks, his lips chapped from the cold. Though they had been partners and friends for years, Young somehow could not bring himself to discuss why he felt so compelled to answer this call or why the building across the street intrigued him so much.

The sound of a muffled scream echoed from the alley.

"I'm fine," he finally said. "Let's go. It's colder than hell out here."

They hurried into the alley, the dirty snow crunching beneath their boots. Two men, their features barely distinguishable beneath a coating of filth, stumbled around in a bear hug. The larger man struggled to reach a gun clutched by his smaller adversary. His mouth dropped to reveal a toothless maw as he spotted the approaching officers. Muttering an obscenity, he pulled away abruptly and bolted down the alley. The second man grunted, blinked at the officers and after ineffectually waving his gun at them, staggered off into the shadows.

Young started to follow, but Cheetham held him back.

"Forget it. They're just a couple of lurkers. Don't waste your energy. They're long gone by now."

As they returned to the squad car, they heard another call come in. Brett climbed in and reached for the radio.

"Let it go, Brett. We've got to get back to the station."

But Brett stubbornly answered the call.

"Let someone else take it," Cheetham insisted. "Jesus, what's with you tonight?"

"Break-in in that apartment building across the street. Won't take long to check out. You stay here. I'll be back in a minute."

"Low priority, Brett. The captain will bust a gut if we don't get back soon."

"Look, we're right here. This won't take long," Brett said, the words strange even as he spoke them. It was unusual for him to argue with his partner. Usually they agreed on everything, but a stubborn premonition urged him to take the call and his instincts were never wrong. Without waiting for Cheetham's response, he hurried across the street and skirted the bulldozers.

Cheetham sighed and shook his head. "Cap's going to chew us out big time for this," he muttered as he locked the car and followed Brett.

***

CHAPTER SIX

With the sound of the siren resonant in her ears, Destiny's gloved hands trembled as she unlocked the entrance door and made sure it clicked shut behind her before she hurried to the elevator. She glanced at Jake, a former security guard hired by the landlord to keep out trespassers. He watched her progress with a typically stony expression. To Destiny, his presence seemed almost ludicrous, but if the landlord wanted to spend precious cash to protect a damaged, half empty building, that was his privilege. Certainly, there were enough jobless to make earning even a pittance desirable.

"Evening, Miss van Kampen," he said gruffly.

She noticed the direction of his gaze, his steely eyes hardening. "It's okay, Jake," she said. "The girl didn't bother me. She'll probably move on now." She heard Jake grunt noncommittally and sighed. As she jabbed the elevator button she knew that once she was out of sight, Jake would undoubtedly harass the girl for the hell of it, but something about his subtly menacing demeanor prevented her from being brusquer.

The elevator pinged as it arrived. Just before she stepped inside, she glanced out once again toward the lobby doors but saw nothing. *My imagination's working overtime,* she thought while the elevator rattled to the fifteenth floor. *Got to keep a cool head.* Out of habit, she gazed at the numbers. They no longer lit up as the elevator ascended, so she never knew where she was until it stopped on her floor.

Suddenly, the elevator jerked and came to an abrupt halt. The dull interior light flickered and winked out. She took a deep breath to stop the pounding of her heart, the air cloying and warm. Her fingers felt for the panel and jabbed at the buttons hoping to find the alarm button, but nothing seemed to work. "It's just another power outage," she murmured, trying to squelch the fear that yet another earthquake had hit.

The light flickered. The elevator juddered, only to come to a halt again. Inky blackness surrounded her, accentuating the distant creaks and groans emanating from the elevator shaft. She tried not to envision the cavernous drop below. Holding her breath, she waiting for the inevitable shaking and rumbling of the heaving earth, but nothing happened.

When the light flickered on again, the elevator proceeded normally. She exhaled slowly as it stopped on her floor and when the doors slid open, she hurried out on unsteady legs.

Her key ready, she quickly walked down the hallway. The threadbare, somewhat soiled red carpet attested to the lack of all but necessary maintenance, the light fixtures lightly caked with dust. She could not remember the last time the windows had been cleaned or the peeling paper on the walls reglued. Distractedly she inserted the key into the lock, only to discover it was already unlocked.

Filled with apprehension she slowly turned the knob. Without stepping inside she kicked the door. It flew open, struck the wall, and swung back toward her. Carefully she used her foot to push it open. Her eyes widened in shock when she surveyed the disorder in her bedroom. The room was opposite the entrance. Out of habit she always left the door open. Her breath caught in her throat as she rushed down the hallway back to the elevator and frantically stabbed the button. It lit up, flickered off, and lit up again. She glanced at the stairwell but the thought that someone could be lurking there stopped her.

The elevator finally arrived on her floor. She catapulted inside and hastily jabbed the button to close the doors. The sound of her pounding heartbeat resonated in her ears as the elevator descended with agonizing slowness. A disturbing cadence of creaks and groans rose from the shaft. She began to imagine the elevator grinding to a halt between floors or suddenly plunging into total darkness again.

As soon as the elevator stopped on the second floor, she squeezed through the opening doors and sprinted down the hallway to the manager's apartment.

"Mr. Simmons, please open the door!" she cried while banging the door with her fist. "Mr. Simmons!"

Simmons, a pudgy, balding man in his late fifties, cautiously opened the door. His face was lathered with shaving cream and he held a towel in his hand and a razor.

"Hold it, young lady. It's after hours and—"

"You've got to come with me! Quickly! Someone's broken into my apartment," Destiny panted.

This spurred Simmons into action. Quickly he wiped the shaving cream off his face, stuffed the razor in his pocket and followed her to the elevator. She could barely contain her impatience while it crawled to her floor. Simmons plodded after her as she bolted through the opening doors and was already puffing by the time he reached her apartment. Destiny stood to the side, her emotions a mixture of fear and concern.

Gingerly Simmons took a step into her apartment and glanced at the chaos in her bedroom. He turned around and joined her in the hallway. "I'm calling the police. We don't know if the crashers are gone. They can't very well jump off the fifteenth floor."

Destiny waited anxiously while Simmons returned to his apartment to call the police. He was out of breath when he returned. "How the hell did they get in?" she asked. "I always lock my doors and I certainly wasn't expecting anyone."

Simmons averted his eyes when he answered. "A young man buzzed me today and said he was your brother from out of town. I'm sorry. I let him in. He sort of resembled you, so I—"

She felt anger overpower her fear. "You let a total stranger into my apartment? Don't you remember that when I applied for this apartment I put on the forms that my only relatives were my parents? For God's sake! You've seen the kind of people hanging around the neighborhood. What were you thinking?"

Simmons bristled. "Young lady, I've got over a hundred apartments in this building. Jake and I have our hands full keeping squatters off the property while repairs drag on. I can't remember everyone's particulars."

"What time did this supposed brother buzz you?"

"I guess it was around three or so," Simmons said resignedly. "I remember because I was in the boiler room trying to fix a leak and the wife came down to tell me that my tea was ready."

The buzzer rang in her apartment. "One of us has to go in and let the police inside," Destiny said, relieved that they had even responded at all.

When Simmons hesitated, she darted into the foyer and pushed the button on a wall panel to admit them. She bolted from the apartment and rushed toward the elevator. Impatiently she paced until two patrolmen emerged.

One was quite tall and attractive, the other swarthy and heavy-set. The heavy-set officer nodded to Destiny. "Ms. van Kampen, I'm Officer Cheetham and this is my partner, Officer Young."

Destiny nodded to the officers. Her gaze lingered on Young for a moment. He seemed to watch her intently.

"You were lucky we happened to be called out to a shooting in the bar across the street," Cheetham continued. "Is anyone in the apartment now?"

"I didn't hear anyone. Whoever broke in is probably long gone by now."

"You're probably right, though I suggest you wait here while we take a look around."

It took only a moment for the officers to inspect her apartment. As Young walked past the living room window, he paused to stare at the squad car parked across the street.

Cheetham approached him and touched his shoulder. Young started at the contact. "No one here," Cheetham said. "Including you, by the looks of it."

Young cleared his throat and moved away, disturbed by the unsettled feelings battling within him. He stepped into the hallway acutely aware of Cheetham's scrutiny. "Are you the manager?" he asked Simmons, who was nervously loitering.

"Yes, I am."

"Would you come in? We'd like to ask you some questions." He hesitated as he turned to Destiny. "Ms. van Kampen, we'd like you to check your apartment carefully and tell us if anything is missing," he said while still trying to figure out what had drawn him to this building. Confused about his sense of urgency, he turned back and watched the young woman inspect her apartment.

Her eyes locked briefly with his before she broke the contact. An unnerving sensation crept down her spine as she reluctantly walked into the living room and eyed the chaos. It only took a glance to see that the stereo, television, computer and CD player were still all there. It was strange that the crasher had not taken them because she knew they would fetch a good price on the black market. The entire couch had been slashed right down to the base and lay in a miserable heap of stuffing and springs. Lamps lay shattered on the floor. Paintings were mutilated and hung in tattered ribbons. Even the back of the television was ripped off and the innards of the computer strewn amidst the mess.

When she inspected the bedroom she found nothing missing. Her meager jewelry sat in a pile on the floor. The jewelry box was flattened as if someone had stomped on it and discarded it in a corner. The mattress of her futon bed had been yanked off and perched drunkenly against the wall. It was slashed from top to bottom on both sides and the stuffing protruded like misshapen warts. An explosion of feathers was all that remained of her pillows.

Surveying the wanton destruction, she swallowed the knot forming in her throat and tried to stem the tears blurring her vision. Throughout the troubles, her little apartment had been a refuge from the madness outside. It was a retreat, a place of comfort that allowed her to retain a shred of identity in a world where people had become nothing more than statistics.

Wiping her eyes, she stared at the cracked living room window. Not even the drapes had been spared as they lay in a shredded heap on the floor. She toed the fabric listlessly with her foot, her gaze wandering out the window past the squad car parked in front of the bar. In the adjoining alley, lurkers huddled around an oil drum fire piled with ragged tire fragments. One man in particular, his emaciation evident even from a distance, groveled on the street as though searching for something.

Despite the numbing cold he was dressed only in a baggy

sweatshirt and torn jeans, his overclothes probably sold to feed his drug habit. Clumps of matted hair concealed his haggard face. From the obsessive behavior that could only identify a crack addict, she realized he was tweaking, the chunk of crack cocaine he desperately sought missing only in his warped mind.

Unwilling to further witness the depths to which humanity had descended she returned to her inspection of the apartment. Her heart sank at the sight of the ravaged kitchen. Water pooled beneath the open refrigerator door. Jars of her mother's preserves and pickles were open and had been emptied, their contents congealing on the counters and floor. The large wooden spoon that had obviously been used to empty the jars stood upright in a sludgy pile of peanut butter like some perverse monument.

Her throat constricted when she looked inside the freezer. The compartment was stripped of its contents. Her modest store of meat lay strewn half-defrosted on the floor. Flour was dumped into the sink together with coffee, tea and other dry cooking items. Rations of milk and juice had been poured over them to form a disgusting gruel and the empty containers tossed into the dining room.

She eyed the mess with mounting outrage. The loss of food, such a precious commodity when millions starved and rationing was strictly enforced, was more devastating than the destruction of her other possessions. It would take months of ration coupons to restock the food, if some could be replaced at all, and her trips home to visit her parents were limited to twice a year. Without a car, Chilliwack was almost impossible to reach, the overtaxed busses only running once a week and costly. She knew she could take food home from her mother's larder at Christmas but the loss of what she had so painstakingly bartered for crushed her.

Her gaze fell to the mound of peanut butter. Angrily she yanked the wooden spoon from it and hurled it across the kitchen. The miserly four-ounce jar of crunchy unsalted peanut butter had cost her an old coat and a pair of boots on the black market. Surveying the ruins of her home, she realized there was precious little left to barter with now. She felt close to tears as she joined the officers. "Nothing's missing," she said, her trembling voice betraying the agitation she felt. "Except maybe my sanity—"

"Ms. van Kampen, perhaps it would be better if you wait in the manager's apartment for now until we're finished here," Cheetham suggested. "We'll come down later to ask you both some more questions."

Simmons nodded and without a word took Destiny's arm and led her to the elevator. In silence they descended to the second floor. Numbly she allowed herself to be guided into the manager's apartment and led to a chair. Only a few oil lamps were lit, their flickering flames casting the room in eerie shadow. A clutter of heavy antique furniture added to the gloomy atmosphere. A tiny, battery operated television displayed the snowy images of a newscast.

Destiny sank down into an overstuffed armchair and leaned her head back to ease the pounding in her temples. Stunned by the plundering of her home, she had been unable to utter a single word. She still felt too shocked to speak to anyone and would have preferred that Simmons kept his mouth shut.

Mrs. Simmons, a motherly little woman with a shock of black hair barely showing a strand of gray, handed her a cup of tea that she accepted with trembling hands. "Thank you, Mrs. Simmons," she managed.

"You take it easy now, dear," said Mrs. Simmons as she retreated to the kitchen. "You've had a terrible shock."

Destiny forced a wan smile. The cup shook as she raised it to her lips and sipped the hot liquid. Slowly she felt her nerves settle and her mind regained a semblance of sanity. She looked Simmons in the eyes and asked brusquely, "Can you describe the man you let into my apartment?"

"Yes, I can," he said, somewhat uncomfortably. " Like I told you, he kind of looked like you. That's why he fooled me I guess. He was tall with similar features to yours, blond and blue-eyed. About thirty. Do you know anyone who looks like that?"

She shook her head. Her silken mane of platinum hair swung gracefully with the movement. "No, I'm afraid not. I certainly don't have any enemies or vengeful ex boyfriends. I don't understand who would do this to me and even less, why."

As promised, the officers arrived at the Simmons apartment for questioning. Mrs. Simmons offered everyone tea, which was politely declined. Simmons described the young man he had let into

Destiny's apartment. Destiny told them everything she knew, but could give them no real answers.

Young smiled sympathetically. "Ms. van Kampen, it's almost as if the crasher was searching for something. Do you have any idea what that could be?"

"No. I'm just an employee at an emergency service relief center. I coordinate the delivery of supplies throughout the city using the government computer uplink. It's not as if I work with top-secret material or anything. Perhaps the crasher mistook me for someone else?"

"Still, it doesn't fit the usual profile. Do you have any friends who might have hidden something in your apartment?"

She thought about her two closest friends, Chantelle and Krista, and shook her head. Both had recently moved to a quieter neighborhood after a violent food riot closed down their street and left them prisoners in their apartment complex. "I only have two close friends and they don't live nearby. It's not like I can pop out for a meal and movie anymore. I live a very quiet life."

"How about male friends?" he asked carefully.

"No male friends. Not at the moment."

"I see. Normally, crashers will grab what they can as fast as possible and run. They certainly wouldn't leave behind food and valuables they could use for bartering. It doesn't fit the usual pattern."

"I can imagine," she said thoughtfully. "The amount of food destroyed alone would have fetched a fortune on the black market." She shook her head. "Honestly, I can't imagine what the crasher would have been searching for. I'm still convinced that it's a case of mistaken identity. It can't be anything else."

"Will you be all right, Ms. van Kampen? Do you need some ration vouchers? We could drop you off somewhere for the night if you like."

Destiny considered the suggestion. "No. I want to stay in my own place." She added impulsively, "It needs tidying! Dammit! I'm sick and tired of living under these conditions. I feel like a rat in the darkness, forever afraid, forever a potential victim. When will it ever change?"

Young smiled. "You're fortunate they only vandalized the place and didn't really take anything. Some of your stuff can be salvaged. Perhaps the crasher was interrupted. I noticed you have a safety lock on your door. Please make sure you use it and don't let anyone in that you don't know."

"I never do."

"I really don't think it's a good idea for you to be alone this evening," he said solicitously.

Gazing into his eyes, she felt comforted by the concern she saw in them. "Officer—I'm sorry, what was your name? I didn't catch it," she said, embarrassed that she had forgotten the officer's name.

He handed her a card with a smile. "That's understandable. My name is Brett Young. My pager number's on that card and you can call me any time of the day or night if you need anything. I'm on duty until midnight, but a colleague has been taken ill, so I'll probably be working a double shift. If you insist on staying in the apartment please promise you'll call if anything happens?"

His eyes were an earnest brown. She had taken very little notice of the officers, their faces little more than talking blurs. Her mind was too busy with the ransacking of her place. Now, she let her eyes rest on the younger officer's face and liked what she saw. He had a square jaw, an angular face that showed strength. His eyes were honest and filled with concern for her plight, his blond hair clipped very short. She imagined it would curl if he wore it longer. His lips were just right, not thin, neither too full and his nose was slightly tilted giving his face a boyish appearance.

"Thank you. I will," she said. Can I go back to my apartment now?"

Cheetham started to rise, but Young beat him to it. "I'll go with you," he said.

Rising from the armchair she turned to the manager and his wife. "Thank you for the tea, Mrs. Simmons, and for letting me wait here. Mr. Simmons, I'll talk to you later."

"I hope we won't lose you as a tenant, Destiny," Simmons said with an anxious frown. "You've been with us a long time and good renters are almost impossible to find."

"Mr. Simmons, I'll be honest, I can't really say at the moment. Too much has happened and I need time to think things over. Thanks again."

Young glanced at Cheetham. "I'll meet you outside."

Cheetham nodded. "I'll finish up here."

Brett escorted Destiny back to her apartment. Standing amidst the disorder he looked around helplessly. "If I weren't on duty, I'd offer to help you clean up. Is there any hope of replacing your belongings?"

"Unlikely. I've always been somewhat of a pack-rat, like my mother," she said tiredly as she wondered how she would, or even could, replace her computer. She had purchased it at a substantial discount after the older models at work were upgraded. The few bootleg machines available on the black market were priced well beyond her reach.

She shook her head. "I used to have insurance ages ago, but the company went bankrupt with all the others. Maybe I should go Japanese and just decorate the place with mats and a few bamboo shades. If I could even find those—"

Young was momentarily silent. He looked at Destiny and felt admiration for the way she had handled the crisis. Many of the women he encountered after a crime were hysterical or depressed, their mental states affected by the scourge. He recalled one such unfortunate woman who committed suicide shortly after being robbed by a tweaker. Though the woman was unharmed, she descended into such a state of paranoia that she could no longer leave her home and eventually slit her wrists.

He sighed inwardly. This call had been one where there was little he could do for the victim, yet in this instance, he instinctively felt that his presence provided Destiny with a modicum of support and reassurance. Outwardly she appeared remarkably calm and healthy. He knew that for a woman alone things could not be easy for her. As he was on duty, it was inappropriate for him to ask her out, but it had been a long time since he felt so attracted to a woman. Her eyes intrigued him most of all. They were the color of sapphires and provided a startling contrast to her creamy skin and platinum hair. Her nose was small and finely chiseled, giving her a beguiling look interestingly offset by a rather full mouth. She possessed an ethereal beauty he'd never seen in any woman. He studied her closely for a moment as she inspected the shambles of her apartment. Her fragile appearance belied the inner strength she displayed. He noticed that her head just reached his chest.

On impulse, he wrote his home phone number on the back of another card. "This is my home number. I've got a Jeep and I'd be glad to help you. Just call me when you're ready."

His disarming grin was infectious. She smiled and nodded. "Thank you. I might just take you up on that. That's if my phone still works," she said while searching for it. She found the remnants buried beneath a pile of couch stuffing, the back ripped off the base, the portable in two pieces. "Guess I won't be able to call you," she said as she held the demolished phone up for him to see.

"Let me look at it. I'm quite handy with stuff like that," Brett said and took the phone from her hand. "I see. This wire clips in here, and the red one goes—" He screwed the covers back on and tackled the base. After clicking the button a few times, he listened and grinned. "There, you have a working phone again. Now, I'd better go and rescue my waiting partner."

"Thanks for your help," Destiny said as he walked to the door and opened it.

"Be careful," Young said while stepping into the corridor.

"Don't worry, I'm not about to break that habit now."

After she closed the door behind him, she double locked it and leaned against it for a moment with her eyes closed. "Why did this have to happen?" she murmured. "I work so hard to make the best of things. I don't ask for much. Who even knows I live here except for my friends?" She thought about her past boyfriends, Jack and Trevor. Her last date was two years ago before the downtown club district was firebombed. Since then there had been no one in her life and she couldn't imagine any of her friends involved in something like this. Getting by on a day-to-day basis was difficult enough.

Shaking her head, she walked into the living room and stared at the destruction. Her plants, her beautiful potted plants that she painstakingly nurtured from precious cuttings lay in ravaged heaps. Black soil and pottery shards soiled the carpet. A solitary tear ran down her cheek as she picked up a trampled spider plant offshoot and clutched it to her face for a moment. The loss of her plants pained her the most, the comforting presence of green living things vanquishing the loneliness of her existence and offering a glimmer of joy to her heart.

Quickly she scooped up some dirt and put it in an unbroken cup that lay among the debris. Carefully she pushed the little shoot into the dirt and gazed at it with loving eyes before setting it on the floor. A new shoot—new beginnings. Undoubtedly she would have to move and start over again. She stretched out on an uncluttered space next to the cup and gazed at it for a little while, then placed her hands beneath her head and stared up at the ceiling.

A familiar jingling sound slowly echoed around the room. She smiled at the welcome tune that had accompanied her all her life and had comforted her many times. The tinkling bells became louder and played their enigmatic song for her until she felt their music lull her shattered nerves. She opened her eyes, knowing what would come next and waited in anticipation.

Within moments, the room filled with color. The spheres pirouetted around her, over her, hiding all the destruction and suffusing her with a sense of tranquility. A warm, fragrant breeze tousled her hair. The room filled with familiar scents and rainbow colors. Flowers—roses, violets and lilacs—she knew them all so well. She felt warm, safe and loved as the voices started to hum softly. They were her voices, the voices that had serenaded her for as long as she could remember—

***

CHAPTER SEVEN

Destiny sat up with a start, her senses alert to a disturbance in the chain of events. The spheres were somehow different from the comforting companions she had known all her life, the atmosphere in the room charged with an unpleasant buzz of static.

Once, not long after she started school, she talked to her mother about the spheres and the voices that became her companions. Her mother listened quietly, then explained in a very serious voice that she could trust the spheres and the voices but she must never discuss them with anyone because people wouldn't believe her. From the tone of her mother's voice Destiny understood the import of her experiences. Though she discreetly questioned her friends about their dreams, none ever described anything resembling what she had almost come to take for granted.

By the time she reached college she had accepted that her experiences were extraordinary events that defied explanation and that most people would not be able to understand them, let alone sympathize with them. The knowledge made her circumspect in her choice of friends and the extent to which she would consider discussing the phenomenon.

A harsh green shaft suddenly burst from the ceiling and aggressively chased the playful lights into the corners of the room. They lurked silently in the shadows as if fearful of the hostile presence. The peaceful serenade was replaced by a series of staccato clicking noises and a high-pitched whine that forced her to cover her ears. Before she could move away, the green shaft engulfed her with a bone chilling cold. Her teeth chattered from the contact, her skin pimpling with gooseflesh. Suddenly, a resonant humming pierced the silence. It rose from the dancing spheres that merged into one and formed a sinuous glowing orb. Pulsing like a spectral heartbeat, it hurdled toward her and surrounded her with a halo of pure, benevolent light.

Feeling safe once more, she removed her hands from her ears. The green beam reared abruptly and emitted a guttural hiss. Slowly it retreated as the orb forced it from the room. The dancing spheres converged joyfully on her. They whirled around her, touched her arms, face and legs, and then gradually reformed into the orb. It writhed sinuously as it transformed into a vaguely human shape.

She watched in awe. Never before had anything like this happened whenever the spheres appeared. Now that she thought about it, the spheres had always been there whenever she was upset or in distress. Their dancing antics and soothing serenade was all she ever experienced. They never appeared when she was calm and everything was fine. Now that she was in distress, it seemed as though her ordeal had disturbed her trusted companions as well.

The form materialized into a human silhouette. She watched transfixed and peered at the luminous shape. *They must be angels*, she thought. *All this time I've been surrounded by heavenly bodies and never realized to what extent they influenced my life.*

"Who are you?" she whispered.

A voice filled the room. Deep and vibrant, its warmth enveloped her and filled her with loving trust.

"Destiny—bearer of the light—"

"I don't understand. Who are you? Are you angels?"

"If humanity could see us, they might conceive us as such. We are the Antiquitas, the ancient keepers of knowledge. Angels inhabit the realm beyond the living. We are not from there but from a place well known to you."

She reached to touch the apparition and grasped nothing but shifting air. A soft tingling sensation crept up her arm. It enveloped her hand and traveled through her body like a series of electrical impulses. "Why haven't you shown yourself before?"

"It was not necessary and we did not want to frighten you. Now, the time has come when we must appear and prepare you for the task ahead."

"Prepare me for what task?"

"Destiny, you must leave this place. It is unsafe. The elementals who would stop the fulfillment of your task will do anything to obtain that which you carry."

"Wait a minute. Now you're talking in riddles."

The apparition shimmered with ethereal light. "When you were born, a very special knowledge was implanted in your mind. Soon, it will become known to you, and then you must carry it to safety. In the meantime, you must flee from the legion of darkness known as the elementals. They are spawned by a race from a region bordering the galaxy known as the Eletarii. Intent on expanding their empire these hostile creatures scan the stars in search of vulnerable worlds to dominate. When their scouts visited Earth during one of the great wars of the last century, we became aware of their intentions to turn legions of humanity to their purpose. The elementals have embraced the ways of the enemy and will stop at nothing to prevent you from accomplishing your mission."

"How can things get worse than they already are?" she murmured. "And how can I possibly battle something like this when I can't even protect my own home?"

"You are not of this world, Destiny. Your heritage stems from an ancient race. You were chosen to become our Earth child and have had our companionship all these years to protect you. You know us. When your mind opens to the knowledge, you will remember and fully understand why you came here."

"Remember? You make it sound like I come from some place else than my mother's womb."

"You did, Destiny. You are one of our children."

"How is that possible?"

"Everything will become clear at the appropriate time. For now, you must leave this place."

Destiny shook her head, the import of their enigmatic words difficult to accept. "I don't understand. And now you want me to leave my apartment? But, where will I go? I could give up my job and go back to the farm, to my parents."

"No. The farm is known to the elementals. There is no sanctuary there."

"Are my parents in danger, too?" she asked as apprehension and concern for her parents now filled her.

"No, the elementals do not seek your parents. Only you. You must leave here immediately."

"But if they're that powerful, they'll find me wherever I go."

"Your powers are greater and we will guide you. The young policeman will be of help. Contact him now and ask his assistance."

"Brett?"

"Yes. He is a good man and is surrounded by an aura of benevolent light. He, too, was chosen and is our Earth son. When the call reporting your break-in was received at the police station we made sure that it was radioed through to his squad car. We knew he would respond because the time was right for you to meet. Your long forgotten feelings for each other are returning. That is important because you belong together and he will be very useful and a powerful ally."

Destiny giggled. "That's an odd way of putting it considering we just met, though I do like him. I don't understand—how can we be your Earth children?"

"As we said, you will eventually understand. Brett will be a vital part of your quest and your developing powers."

"Forgive me if I feel overwhelmed," she said. "This is starting to sound a bit too much like the *Twilight Zone*. You're telling me I'm from another world and I have powers?"

The apparition wavered. "We must go now, Destiny. Our ability to communicate with you is weakening, but we will contact you again. Leave tonight. You are not safe. Contact Brett Young—leave this place—"

The voice faded and the apparition dispersed into a constellation of shimmering spheres.

She watched as they slowly winked out. Her mind filled with dozens of unanswered questions. The phenomenon had not frightened her; in fact, it had calmed her and filled her with a sense of safety. Now she realized that it was a false sense of security because the voice had warned her she was in danger. The threat to Earth came from the Eletarii and their legions of elementals. She shuddered. *So all those rumors of UFO sightings must have been true all along—*

She thought about Brett and made up her mind. The spheres had been her faithful companions for so long and she had to trust them now. Hesitantly she picked up the phone and glanced at the card that lay next to it. He told her she could call him any time. But what would she tell him?

The dialing tone connected to the exchange operator. "Good evening. You have fifteen minutes left on your monthly allocation. Please try—" Destiny slammed the receiver down and shook her head. "This is ridiculous. If I had such powers, I surely could have used them to my advantage before now!"

The warnings churned inside her mind. She trusted the spheres and the voice that had materialized from them. Quickly, she dialed again and gave the exchange operator Brett's pager number. As soon as she was connected, she left him a message to call her.

While she waited for his response, she thought about the hardworking crews who toiled day and night to restore power and telephone lines to the city. The frequent blackouts immediately after the earthquakes were frightening, forcing her to huddle behind locked doors with only candle and dim lantern light to chase the shadows. The spheres helped her through that difficult period, and she realized with a grim sense of foreboding that the darkness of the past might be nothing compared to what she now faced.

The ringing phone interrupted her reverie. Quickly she grabbed the receiver. "Brett? I'm sorry to disturb you. I know you're still on duty, but I've changed my mind. I don't want to stay here tonight."

"Hey, that's okay," he replied, the pleasure at her call evident in his voice. "I told you to call me. Can you hang on until I find someone to trade my double shift?"

"Sure. I'll pack some things. Perhaps you could drive me to a motel? I think there are still a couple open around here."

"No problem. Look, I've got to answer a call so I'd better get off the phone. Keep an eye out for anything suspicious. I'll be there as soon as I can."

Quickly, she searched through her wardrobe strewn all over the bedroom floor and packed some casual clothes in a battered gym bag lying nearby. She paused as she unearthed a long evening gown from a pile of office clothes still on their hangers. The silky black fabric and delicate spaghetti straps harkened to a long ago New Year Eve's party at work. Somewhere there would be a pair of matching shoes with diamante bows on the heels and a tiny clutch bag barely large enough to hold a lipstick.

She sighed and tossed the dress away almost angrily. She had spent a week's wages on the designer dress and had worn it to attend the millennium celebrations with her parents. Ironically, the festivities were only lightly attended due to fears of unrest; the magnificent fireworks and expense incurred worldwide a somehow fitting swan song for humanity. Nothing catastrophic happened at the stroke of midnight, and those who attended without fear were able to enjoy the last jubilation on Earth.

"Lipstick, Christmas and millennium celebrations," she muttered. "Where the hell did all that get us?"

She zipped up the gym bag and got to her feet. With a grimace, she glanced at the computer and thought about the disc in her purse that she had brought home from work. "Guess work will have to wait. At least until I find another place to live."

***

Brett arrived just after eleven-thirty. He gave her a disarming grin as he took the bag from her hand and waited while she locked the door.

"Brett, what if they come back tonight?" she asked while they walked to the elevator. They stopped and Brett pushed the button. Before he answered, she appraised him silently. He had changed from his uniform into jeans and dark blue jacket. Without his uniform, he looked younger, more boyish and the attraction for him deepened as she studied his face. He must have felt her gaze because suddenly he turned to look directly into her eyes. His response, and the deep timbre of his voice, triggered a long forgotten shiver of excitement within her.

"Then all they'll find is an empty apartment. I'm glad you changed your mind. I was rather worried about you. We often can't respond at all if there's a lot going on in the area," he said.

Once inside his Jeep, a jacked up fortress with oversized tires fog lamps and heavy front and rear grills, he suggested casually, "Destiny, you could stay at my place for the night. I have a guestroom set up. It would save you a fortune. What motels are left certainly aren't cheap and probably aren't that safe, either."

"I don't know," she hesitated.

"You don't have to worry. I'm a cop, after all. Unless of course you can't stand a bachelor's messy place—"

A voice spoke suddenly. She didn't know if it was inside her head or if she really heard it.

"Yes, Destiny. Go with him. You have nothing to fear."

She made up her mind then and looked Brett in the eyes. "Are you sure it wouldn't be an imposition?"

"No trouble at all. I don't live far from here. I'm only around the corner, in Burnaby. If you like we can search for a new apartment for you tomorrow. I'm working afternoon shift so I'm available to drive you around most of the day."

Though he lived nearby, he drove cautiously, his eyes constantly scanning the sparse traffic on the street. Due to electricity rationing, few lights shone from the surviving buildings, the darkened windows sightless eyes. Homeless people and children milled like displaced souls, herds of youngsters listlessly combing litter-strewn gutters for scraps. A woman shuffled painfully along the street, her body so severely twisted by rheumatoid arthritis, she could barely see the broken pavement ahead of her.

Destiny shuddered as she watched the wretched woman hobble along. Even the other homeless drew away from her, the revulsion in their haggard faces clear. The scourge was a living damnation; a curse that plundered the core of the genes themselves to unleash dormant horrors onto weakened bodies. Clearly, the scourge had unleashed a condition in the woman that until a few years ago would have been easily treated.

Brett followed her gaze and glanced at her. "Do you ever wonder about it all?"

"Who doesn't?" she said. "I know my parents are from healthy stock—but still, there may be genetic throwbacks we may not be aware of."

"I had to pass a pretty exhaustive physical to join the force," Brett said. "But there's no testing available to pinpoint any genetic dormancy. At least, none that I know of. It wouldn't do me any good anyway."

An angry honk distracted them. Cars with even license plate numbers lined up at a solitary, heavily guarded gas station, the cost of running a car and the exorbitant price of fuel relegating vehicle ownership to the wealthy or high-level government workers. Despite the late hour the haphazard availability of fuel often mandated bizarre hours of operation.

Destiny stared at the faces within the stationary cars; the engines switched off to conserve precious fuel. Most of the patrons were older and probably relied on income sources that younger people would not have had the opportunity to amass. Her parents had a car, albeit an older model, and although she had a driver's license she had never been able to qualify either for purchase or for the requisite ownership permits.

Staring at a point beyond the gas station, her gaze blurred. Pages out of time danced through her mind, fleeting images of a happier past, of blue skies and a childhood free from worry and fear. The memories seemed as distant as the stars that had once graced the night.

Brett glanced at her with concern and gently shook her arm. "You okay? You looked like you were a million miles away."

She started and turned to him. "I wish I were," she said wistfully. "I wish I could be anywhere but in this dark place."

He squeezed her hand, his handsome features caught in a frown. "I know how you feel. Sometimes I wonder how much more of this I can take. I mean, I knew joining the police force wasn't going to be a vacation, but since all this shit started—" his words trailed away as he too was caught up in a distant memory. "Well, you know what I mean."

The dull glow of a few functioning streetlights gave both of them a moment to reflect as it shone upon a shabby soup kitchen operating from a converted lunch truck. Bagged garbage lay in mountainous heaps on derelict lots; the flimsy barbed wire screens little deterrent to aggressive vermin.

Brett continued to drive a couple more blocks before pulling into the security gates of a modest apartment complex relatively undamaged compared to most of the buildings on the street. Only a few vehicles occupied the underground garage, the cavernous concrete structure loudly echoing the Jeep's approach. As he pulled into his parking space a large mangy rat squirmed from a vent and scuttled past with baleful eyes.

Destiny shuddered and climbed out of the vehicle. "God, I hate those things."

He shrugged and pulled her gym bag from the back. "We've tried everything to get rid of the rats, but as you know, it's a losing battle. Back in the days of the Black Death, at least the cats turned the tide." He paused. "Now there aren't any cats—and fire isn't an option because the scourge isn't caused by vermin."

Silently, she followed him to a first floor suite, the overgrown shrubbery and empty severely cracked pool attesting to longstanding neglect. Only a few outdoor lights shone, the pathways and stairs cloaked in weeds and shadow. A discarded birdcage lay half-concealed by a scraggly bush.

"Did you ever have a pet?" she asked.

When she saw a fleeting shadow darkening his eyes, she instantly regretted her question. "Sorry, Brett, I didn't mean—"

He raised his hand. "No, it's okay. It's been a long time since I thought about Murphy."

"Murphy was your dog?"

He nodded. "He was my best friend, a Jack Russell Terrier." His eyes glistened. "He—it was after the vets started closing down. He broke away from his leash one day and fell through the floor of a demolished building. I tried to—"

She gently squeezed his arm. "Don't say any more," she said, her own eyes blurring from incipient tears. "We've suffered enough pain. It wasn't my intention to cause you more."

Mustering a weak smile, he fumbled for his door key.

Destiny took a few deep breaths to ease the sudden emotional attack and almost grimaced when she stepped inside. Even in the flattering glow of subdued lights, it was clear that Brett had not exaggerated that his place was a mess. She glanced around and noticed the pile of dishes rising from the sink of the cramped kitchen. "I guess you don't like doing dishes?"

"Don't say I didn't warn you," he said sheepishly. He rummaged through the tiny fridge and offered her a beer. With an apologetic tone, he said, "That's all I've got. If I'd known that I was going to have female company I'd have asked my friend for a bottle of wine instead of beer."

She stared at the beer can as though it was a magnum of champagne. "This is lovely, Brett. Thank you! Beer—my God, it must have cost you a fortune!"

"I also managed to get a sausage and some cheddar cheese on the black market. How about I throw a pizza together?"

Her stomach suddenly rumbled when she realized she hadn't eaten anything since lunch. The thought of pizza, a treat she had not enjoyed in years, made her mouth water. Even her mother's well-stocked larder had been bare of cheese for some time.

Brett smiled at her, his upbeat mood returning. "As a cop, I often stumble across lucrative propositions. Nothing illegal, mind you. For instance, the liquor store in Middlegate Mall got raided not long ago. They only sell beer and a few spirits, of course, but enough to justify the small business surcharge. The manager asked me to maintain extra vigilance for them as a favor. He gives me a six-pack of beer each week. He's a friend of mine so he doesn't charge me the regular price." He winked conspiratorially. "And he even promised me a bottle of wine for Christmas."

Destiny's brows shot up. "Wine? I thought the vineyards were withered?"

"Some surviving strains are apparently being grown in greenhouses. Though I can't imagine where."

She turned to stare at the kitchen. "Well, I guess we'd better not keep the chef waiting. Why don't I clean up and you can get started on the pizza?" She glanced at the small oven. "Will your electricity ration cover the cooking time?"

Brett nodded. "Law enforcement personnel are allowed extra rations. And frankly, I don't cook all that often, so I've got a surplus."

The evening passed quickly, the simple pleasure of cooking and conversation nurturing a sense of connection to Brett. While she tackled the stack of dirty dishes, his antics while making the pizza dough and applying the toppings with a flourish brought long dormant laughter to her heart.

Later, when he removed the golden bubbling pizza from the

oven, the two descended on it like starving vultures and promptly devoured it. Perched on the breakfast barstools, they giggled like children as they guzzled their beer and wiped their sauce-stained chins with napkins.

When they were finished and Destiny had licked the last crumbs from her plate, he showed her to the guestroom and set her gym bag on a cozy armchair. "The bathroom's right across the hall. Feel free to take a shower. I've got a surplus on water usage as well as I tend to shower a lot at the station."

"That would be wonderful," Destiny said.

"And don't worry about the kitchen. I'll clean that up later. I know you must be tired after such a stressful day."

Stifling a yawn, she said, "It was stressful earlier, but you pretty much compensated for it."

"Then I'll see you in the morning. Hopefully, tomorrow will be a better day."

"Goodnight, Brett. Thanks for being a friend."

"My pleasure."

Destiny closed the door. She was pleasantly surprised at the simple but comfortable furnishings and the general tidiness of the room. Warmth gushed from the central heating vent near the ceiling; no doubt another luxury allotted Brett. Feeling a leaden fatigue overwhelm her, she quickly brushed her teeth and changed into pajamas, the tempting shower something she would leave for the morning. The bed was cozy and the feather down quilt invitingly warm as she snuggled beneath it and closed her eyes. Only some of the spheres appeared when a delicious drowsiness overtook her. They hovered near her while softly humming their song.

The events of that evening had exhausted her more than she realized but sleep did not come easily. She tossed and turned most of the night, her mind churning from the ordeal of the break-in and what the voices had told her about her mission on Earth and her connection to Brett.

Powers—she had no idea what they meant, or even if she wanted to know—

***

CHAPTER EIGHT
December 18, 2008

Destiny struggled awake. Her sleep had been filled with wondrous dreams of an idyllic landscape filled with blooming meadows and verdant trees. Birds chittered from branches laden with blossoms, the warm sunshine glistening on a clear gurgling stream. The air was heavy with the heady fragrance of flowers and the distant drone of bees. An untainted azure sky merged into a serene horizon of gently rolling hills. She felt completely at peace, the drowsy warmth filling her with a delightful sense of safety. When she opened her eyes, she felt momentarily disoriented until realization crept in of the previous day's events.

Listening for sounds indicating that Brett was up, she jumped out of bed and shivered. The chill that invaded her bones foretold snow. Her premonition never failed. Quickly she turned on the light and glanced at her watch to see that it was still very early.

Wide-awake now, she stood on the bed to look out of the long narrow window near the top of the wall. She wiped the foggy surface clean with her arm and pressed her nose against the cold glass. The dim glow of a solitary streetlight barely illuminated the fresh snow blanketing the road outside. In the distance, bonfires created a false dawn. Misshapen snowflakes resembling gray tufts of cotton candy rained a dismal veil. It seemed somehow ironic that the frosty blanket would soon smother the drought-scorched land, the grim aftermath of the hottest summer in history. The only consolation was that the snow would melt next spring and give the thirsty soil some relief.

Yet, there had been no sun, the days eternally shrouded in a humid pall of cloud and smoke caused by distant volcanic eruptions. The muggy heat was a misery as emergency services struggled to clear the dead and dying before more new cases of the scourge ravaged Vancouver. Without enough electricity to spare for fans or air conditioning, the death toll soared and scores of businesses closed down. Vermin flourished, and for a while, the city was brought to a virtual standstill. Destiny still shuddered at the recollection of those hellish weeks, the isolation tempered by the relentless diminishing of her supplies.

And then, virtually overnight, the temperatures plunged to well below zero. The unexpected cold ushered its own brand of hardship, and again, the death toll rose as the sick and homeless bore the brunt of the premature winter. Curfews kept the city imprisoned by fear, the darkness pressing at the windows almost more frightening than even the nightmarish legacy of the scourge. And each year it got worse, the summers hotter and dryer and the winters brutally cold. The melting snow was tainted and no more drinkable than the murky tap water, though there was no guarantee that even the purified bottled drinking water was completely safe. She longed for a patch of blue sky—a ray of sunlight, a single blossom to appear somewhere, anywhere—or perhaps to glimpse a green leaf or even a single blade of pristine grass—but they existed only in her memories.

Once, she took it all for granted. Rumors of war and predictions of devastating natural disasters became such a routine they lost all meaning and were rapidly relegated to the rhetoric of cults, soothsayers and the tabloids. She viewed the world as an innocent, cocooning herself in her cozy working girl existence until suddenly, barely a few years into the new millennium, some absurd border skirmish in a country she could barely pronounce escalated into a global incursion that brought the Earth to its knees. Vancouver was nuclear free, so it was spared much of the devastation of war, but no country was immune from the ensuing natural disasters that swept cities asunder like God's vengeful broom.

It was still dark outside. Wistfully, she gazed at the falling snow. The drifting flakes should have been white, but they were tainted a dun gray by the pollution that permanently cloaked the city. Nevertheless, it was still snow. This time of the year was her favorite, and somehow snow gave the Christmas season a more festive feeling and at least temporarily concealed a lot of the destruction.

She shuddered from the chill. Jumping off the bed, she rummaged through her gym bag for some clothes. The apartment was cloaked in silence, so she assumed Brett was still asleep. After pulling on her sweats she ventured out into the living room and noticed that Brett had indeed cleaned up the kitchen, if not the rest of the apartment. In the dim glow of the lights, she noticed a computer on a desk in the corner and quickly cleared the stack of files and paperwork concealing the keyboard. When she tried to turn the machine on, she discovered it was password protected. Not wanting to waste Brett's electricity ration, she decided to wait until he got up to ask if she could use it.

Feeling the need to be occupied, she started to tidy the living room. She piled his discarded clothes on the couch and tried to straighten things as best she could. The furnishings were a hodgepodge mix of contemporary interspersed with southwestern. While she cleared the mess, elements of Brett's personality emerged in the guise of a dusty guitar perched in the corner. Tucked in the other corner stood a tall bamboo screen painted with delicate Chinese flowers. In front of it, a large trunk, its top littered with magazines. Books on travel lay scattered below a modern glass and metal coffee table, and she even found a snorkel and mask partially wedged beneath an armchair.

Thoughtfully she fingered the cracked mask. A faint smile crossed her lips as she recalled her years in the university swim team. After graduation she had continued to participate in meets until the war broke out. Never again did she have the opportunity to venture into the water. Fortunately, she had moved to the city by then and had found a job. *Or not so fortunately*, she thought. So many times she wondered if she should simply go home.

With a weary sigh, she tossed the mask and snorkel into a nearby closet. After she finished tidying the living room, she ventured into the kitchen and rummaged around for some breakfast goods. Drawing the dusty blinds on the single window, the sight of a tiny succulent cutting rooting in a glass of water on the sill stopped her cold.

Her hand trembled as she carefully picked up the glass. The Christmas cactus was merely an inch high cutting, a wispy filament of a root tentatively probing the water. She stared at it as though it was an apparition before reverently returning it to its spot on the windowsill.

The growling of her stomach prompted her to continue searching the cupboards. They were quite literally bare, and the miserly jar of powdered coffee she discovered was so solidified, she doubted she could chisel it out.

"You might want to give that a miss unless you like really aged coffee."

Destiny almost dropped the jar. She stared at Brett rather sheepishly and stuck the jar back in the cupboard. "Morning. I was just going to make some."

"I usually grab something at the station, but thanks anyway," he said with a grin while he stretched. "I see it's snowing. Do you like snow?"

"Even though it's tainted, I love it, except when it turns into a slushy mess. This certainly isn't the fluffy white stuff I used to play in."

He sauntered over to the fridge and opened it. "I'm afraid there isn't much I can offer you in the way of breakfast. How about I take you out? I know a place that's still open and serves up surprisingly good chow," he said while he produced a carton of milk and held it out to her. "My weekly ration. I never cared much for it so it lasts me quite a while."

Destiny found herself staring at Brett. She tried to suppress the strange sensation that flowed through her veins. It had been a long time since she felt even remotely attracted to a man. After her last relationship had fizzled out, she made the decision to avoid involvement for a while. At least, until she met the right man. Opportunities were few and not many were prepared to commit to someone else when their own existence was threatened. As he handed her the milk, their hands touched briefly. A snapshot image of Brett flashed through her mind, the features familiar but somehow different. She hesitated, momentarily confused.

"Breakfast—that would be wonderful. Do you have an arrangement with the owner there as well? But afterward I really have to look for another place to live."

He smiled. "No arrangements with the owner, but their subsidized meals are quite reasonable. We'll pick up a paper on the way. The Vancouver Sun still prints rental listings once a week. Do you have any idea where you want to look for a place?"

Destiny gulped down the last of the milk and pulled a face. She did not particularly care for it either but for the lack of anything else to drink, she forced it down. "I don't know. Something not too far from the sky train. I work downtown."

"Okay, let's get dressed. You can have a shower first. The automatic shutoff is set for five minutes, but that should give you enough time."

She nodded. "That's fine," she said with a smile. "In this weather, I'm not likely to get hot and sweaty."

He grew pensive as she rinsed out her glass. "Destiny, have you given any more thought to what the crasher could have been searching for?"

"Honestly, I don't have a clue," she said, unwilling to discuss the subject further. "I'll go take that shower now."

As she walked to the small bathroom, she thought, *but I do have a clue. The voices told me that I've got something the crasher wanted. But if it's something I carry in my subconscious, then ransacking my apartment doesn't get them what they want. But if it were in my mind, then why wouldn't I know it?*

***

Eerie silence cloaked the apartment complex while they made their way to the garage. Snow blanketed the path and muffled their steps, their breath misting in the frosty air. Though a few lights shone feebly through drawn curtains, there was none of the typical bustle of the morning commute. Her head swiveled as she sniffed the air. "Is that coffee I smell?"

He nodded. "Wish I knew where it was coming from. Smells

like the real thing as well. Remember those bean grinders they used to have in the supermarkets? Man, what I'd do for a cup of Vienna Roast—"

Following Brett through the rusted security gate, she smiled. "Don't feel bad. I fantasize about eggs—scrambled and fried eggs and mushroom omelets. I hate that powdered stuff. Tastes like reconstituted chalk. Whenever I visit my parents, Mom usually makes me some real eggs. Their chickens still lay the odd egg and she uses them to barter with, but if she knows I'm coming, she saves some for me and spoils me."

"Well, if it's any consolation," Brett said, "we hardly see eggs at the station. Poultry products in general are practically on the endangered species list. They never did solve that bacteria problem in the egg yolks."

"Dad built a veritable fortress in the barn to keep the chickens safe and somehow, he manages to keep them alive. I think they feed them scraps from the table and whatever feed he can lay his hands on. Can you imagine what would happen if people knew about them?"

"They would be in someone's pot before the feathers settled."

Their footsteps echoed as they walked through the cavernous garage. In the distance, bulldozers coughed to life, drowning the jarring clang of sirens. The few vehicles Destiny noticed the previous evening were still there. She rubbed her gloved hands together while she waited for Brett to unlock the Jeep and heaved herself into the seat. The vehicle started with a hearty roar.

"Don't see many of these on the road," she said, her eyes habitually scanning the sparse traffic as they pulled into the street. Smoke rose from endless bonfires glimpsed from alleys and abandoned buildings, the scorched odor of rubber and garbage something she could never get used to. Construction crews assembled in the predawn gloom to start their grueling workdays and tackle an endless route of demolition, restoration, and repair.

"Actually, the Jeep belonged to my father," Brett said, his voice rising above the mechanical roar. "He's in the force as well, but decided to take a senior posting in Calgary and left the vehicle here for me. My mother was more than happy when he accepted the post because we were originally from that area."

"That was generous of him," Destiny said. "I saved enough money for a car and was on a waiting list for three years but finally pulled out after I failed to qualify for ownership."

"You're not missing much. The ownership surcharges make owning a car more expensive than property these days."

Destiny grimaced as she noticed a hand painted Red Cross symbol atop a large army surplus tent occupying a vacant lot. Volunteers ladled soup to a coiled line of homeless and helped those clearly too ill or too debilitated inside the tent. To the side, an ominous lineup of bagged bodies awaited pickup by the coroner's van. The grim sight reminded her of the old animal control trucks that used to collect road kill.

"When did they set that one up?"

"The Sisters of Mercy shelter had to be closed down. Some paranoid schizophrenic went berserk and started attacking the health care workers."

"My God, were they infected?"

He nodded. "Even someone in good health can't resist a direct infusion of the virus into the bloodstream."

"Sometimes I wonder whether anyone's even bothering to search for a cure," she said with a deep sigh. "All the homeless—all the sick—I'm sure the powers that be feel it would be a lot more cost effective just to let them die."

He cast her a concerned look. "You don't really believe that, do you?"

"I'd like to say no, but sometimes I find it hard to believe in the goodness of man anymore."

"Don't let anger cloud your judgment, Destiny. Otherwise it consumes you just as thoroughly as the scourge itself."

While they waited for their pancakes, Brett purchased a newspaper. He scanned the lengthy classifieds and marked several possibilities for her. Between those so desperate for income they were willing to rent almost any livable space and the gougers, who practically extorted from renters on the guise of providing security, finding suitable accommodation was a precarious venture. Ironically, the fee for ad placements supported Vancouver's only surviving newspaper. He handed her his selections. "I've marked a few that I know are in decent areas. Of course, I don't know your budget so you'll have to tell me which ones you'd like to see."

"Thanks, Brett. I really appreciate everything you're doing for me. To do this without a car would take forever."

"The pleasure is all mine. I have to be honest, though, and tell you that I have ulterior motives," he said with a grin.

Fighting a sudden urge to giggle, she quickly buried her face behind the newspaper. "A couple of them look interesting and fall within my budget."

"I have another suggestion but I don't know if you'll go for it."

She lowered the paper and looked him in the eyes. "And that is?" she asked while her heart fluttered and crept up to her throat at the warmth blazing from his brown eyes.

"How do you feel about sharing a place with a friend? A male friend? Most of your stuff is ruined anyway, and I've been looking to share with someone for a while now. It's hard to find someone you can trust, and I haven't managed to find anyone suitable yet."

Destiny felt a peculiar sensation spread through her body. "I don't know. This is all kind of sudden—"

Brett paused. "Maybe not so sudden. I have a rather strange confession to make. Last night, before we got the call about your break-in, we were supposed to report back to the station. Well, I did something I never did before—disobey an order from a superior. I insisted on answering your call because I felt I had to. In fact, it was almost like a premonition. I can't really explain why."

He hesitated as he noted the strange look in Destiny's eyes. "Well, anyway, you'd be much safer if you shared my place. Wouldn't you feel better with someone around?"

Her thoughts churning from what the voices had told her about Brett, she tried to remain nonchalant. "Actually, I would, but I hardly know you."

"Well, maybe we can take the time to get to know each other better," he said and reached across the table to take her hand. "I know you feel the same way, Destiny."

"Yes. I mean, no—well, I really haven't had time to think." She stopped for a moment. His revelation had shaken her more than she was willing to admit. "I do like you, Brett, but I don't want to rush into anything."

He chuckled. "Okay. I won't pressure you. But I really would like to get to know you better and since I'd like a roommate and you're looking for a place—"

She made up her mind. Heeding the voices, she decided it was probably a good idea for the time being. This way no one could easily discover where she lived. Brett was also a police officer, which offered a sense of security she had not felt for some time. "Yes, I think I'd like that. It's probably not a great idea to be alone right now, at least for a while."

He clasped her hand firmly within his own. "I'm glad. That saves us a lot of running around. We can spend the time sorting out your apartment."

"I'd better phone the landlord first," she said. "He's probably going to raise a stink because I'm not giving proper notice."

"I left my cell phone in the car," he offered. "I'll go and get it for you."

"No, I can use a pay phone. I'm sure they have a working one here."

"There's a pay phone near the cashier. Why don't you go and make your call? By the time you're done breakfast should be here."

She was surprised when Mr. Simmons or at least his wife didn't answer the phone. Somewhat guiltily she listened to the recording on his crackling answering machine and left a brief message. She hoped he wouldn't give her too much aggravation about moving out so quickly. Rehearsing in her mind what she would say if they ran into him at the apartment she started to walk back to the table, only to stop in her tracks. Brett was reading the paper, totally unaware of her fixed gaze on him. He was surrounded by an aura of such mauve brilliance that she had to blink a few times. *The voices told me about his aura,* she thought. *It's amazing.*

Her gaze traveled over the other customers. The combined auras transformed the restaurant into a spectral glow. All sound was momentarily blocked as she inspected a shimmering veil of color comprising various shades of mauve and green. Vaguely she wondered what it all meant and remembered that the voices said that the mauve was good. But only Brett's aura possessed a deep shade of mauve. Some of the others were a lighter tone fading to a barely tinted mist. She felt a tendril of unease as she stared at the greenish auras, their colder tones reminiscent of the entity she had seen after the break-in.

The phenomenon faded and the bustle of the restaurant penetrated again. As she walked back to their table she warily eyed the customers who displayed the green auras. Outwardly they looked no different from anyone else. She shuddered and quickly brushed past a solitary male diner whose aura displayed the brightest green in the restaurant. Throughout the years the spheres had been her trusted companions, an accepted part of her life. But now, everything was changing. Never before had she witnessed anything like this. First the voice, and now the ability to see auras. She struggled to find a meaning, but knew instinctively only the voices would have the answer.

Brett looked at her curiously while he wolfed down his huge pancake. "What's wrong, Destiny? You're very quiet."

She pasted on a smile. "I suppose yesterday's events were just a bit overwhelming."

"Did you reach the landlord? You weren't gone long."

She shook her head. "No, I had to leave a message. I hope he doesn't get too upset at me."

Brett shrugged. "Under the circumstances you have every right to be concerned about your safety. Is there anything you want in particular from your place?"

"I guess anything salvageable. What I need is my computer, but I don't think there's much left of that. I tried yours this morning but it's password protected."

"If you need to use it I can give you the password when we get back," he said. "I know now what it must be like without one. Since the postal service's last round of cutbacks, it's about the only way I can keep in touch with anyone. One of my friends sold it to me in exchange for a case of beer. I also thought it might come in handy in my search for my birth parents. I wanted to find out about them so I could obtain information about my health history, but I know there's no chance of locating them now. Unfortunately my adoptive parents had no information about them. My online allocation is only an hour a day through the police network. I haven't had any mail from my family for some time."

"Do you have any brothers or sisters?" she asked.

"Yes—well, I mean, they're not blood relatives. I don't know if my natural parents had any other children. What about you?"

"I'm an only child. I've always wished for a brother or sister, but my parents were already in their forties when they had me. I was what you call unplanned. They tried for years to have children and it never happened. Then suddenly I came along."

"Where do your parents live?"

"Near Chilliwack. We own a farm there. I lived there all my life until I went to university. After graduation, I found a job in the city. Sometimes I wonder if I would have been better off going back."

"I can imagine your parents worry about you. Do they still work the farm? If they were in their forties when they had you, they'd have to be close to seventy now."

"My Dad is sixty-eight and my mother sixty-seven. Dad is still active, yes. But not like the old days. I guess he's sort of semi-retired. He's been busy trying to clean up the volcano ash. It hasn't been easy for them lately. They lost a lot of their cash crops because of the tainted soil and there's no hired labor to be found out there." She sighed. "I wish I could tell them about what happened, and about the—" She stopped herself just in time. "But I don't want to worry them."

"About the what?" Brett asked, curious why she had cut off the sentence midstream.

"Oh, about the break-in." Desperately she wanted to tell someone about her experiences, about the spheres that had accompanied her throughout her life and now her ability to see auras. But what would Brett think? That she was delusional, or worse, that she was showing the first signs of the scourge? He had clearly been directed to her, but how would he react if she confided her deepest secret to him?

"Are you close to your family, Brett?" she asked, quickly changing the subject.

"Reasonably close. I was closest to my adoptive grandmother, but she's gone now. Like I said, I haven't had any e-mail from them in a while. I haven't been back to Calgary since the airports closed. Still, they're all I've got so I do try to keep in touch."

"How old were you when they adopted you?"

"I was about twelve. Before that I lived in a number of foster homes."

"I'm sorry. Your childhood must have been somewhat insecure."

"I suppose it was until I was fostered into the Young home and later adopted by them. It's hard to fit into a brand-new family when you're already an adolescent. The other kids teased me a lot."

"I guess it would be difficult," she commented. "That's a shame, really. I've always been close to my parents, though I would have loved to have brothers and sisters. Being an only child can be quite lonely at times."

Brett sighed. "Maybe it's different for a man."

"I doubt that applies anymore, Brett. Nowadays we've achieved true equality. Every man, woman and child for themselves in the true sense of the word." She glanced at her half-eaten pancakes. "These are delicious, but I can't finish them. I'm stuffed," she said with a smile and set her knife and fork on the plate.

"Hey, even I'm stuffed and I can manage quite a plate full. They're filling, aren't they? At least food isn't thrown away anymore, so it won't go to waste. There's usually a lineup of homeless waiting by the back door for leftovers." He glanced at his watch. "If we're going to move stuff from your apartment we'd better get going. The snow is starting to pile up. It'll be slow going down the hill."

She carefully piled the pancakes onto one plate and signaled to the waitress. "Let them give this to the hungry." The waitress nodded. Destiny slung her purse over her shoulder and followed Brett to the cashier and waited for him to pay the check.

Traffic was only slightly heavier as they drove to her apartment. Wan daylight filtered from a cloudy sky, the atmosphere dull and oppressive. Bonfires glowered from alleys and derelict buildings. Sunken faces peered through thin tendrils of smoke, the bolder homeless venturing to the streets to beg. Brett stopped to allow a coroner's van to cross at an intersection without lights.

Destiny recoiled as a scabrous man of indeterminate age stopped rummaging through an overflowing trashcan and raised his weather-beaten face to stare at her. His rheumy eyes never blinked—the darkness within them a fathomless pit. A leering smile revealed a toothless maw. Suddenly he bolted toward the Jeep with a lopsided gait. Yanking a rusted wrench from his pocket he raised his arms and bore down on the vehicle's window.

"Brett! Move!" she screamed, her mind barely registering the sickly green haze surrounding the man like a noxious fog.

Brett floored the gas. The Jeep lurched away from the descending weapon and fishtailed around the coroner's van. Destiny clutched the armrest with white knuckles when their vehicle skidded. It bounced off the curb but Brett managed to regain control, his eyes alternately flicking to the rearview mirror and the street ahead. Destiny peered around and shuddered as the tramp stood in the middle of the road, the wrench still raised in a defiant salute.

"My God—" she whispered. "Did you see him? Did you see his eyes?"

Brett shook his head. "No time. By the tone of your voice I knew we had to get our asses out of there." He glanced once more into the rearview mirror before turning into a road partially blocked by a demolition in progress. Crews signaled him on after a pair of bulldozers trundled across the street.

"A number of incidents lately have forced us to reassign security patrols to protect crews and other essential services," he said tightly. "But for this to happen during the day—" He shook his head in disgust. "I'll have to speak to the captain about this. If violence reaches a point where no one can venture out at all then we're finished as a society."

Destiny stared blankly at a ragtag group of children in an abandoned parking lot fighting over the skeletal remains of a tennis racket. A few battered campers and trailers formed a dejected caravan beyond; the adults huddled silently around a communal bonfire.

"Aren't we finished already?" she murmured. "It's only a matter of time before we all end up like this."

Her mood did not improve as they approached her apartment building. Brett parked in the underground lot, but this time removed his weapon before they headed for the lobby. She glanced at the barricaded elevator and stairwells to the building. Thanks to Jake there were no squatters camping out but their recent presence was more than evident by the graffiti and urine stained walls.

Brett squeezed her hand. "You okay? You've hardly spoken a word."

Destiny nodded. "I guess I'm still bit shaken up by that run-in with the tramp."

Jake was talking on the lobby phone as they walked in. He instantly lowered his voice and gave them a curt nod, his gaze never leaving Brett as they waited for the elevator. Something sparked in Jake's eyes. Destiny shuddered. Though it was no more than the momentary afterimage of a flashbulb, the sensation left her with a lingering sense of foreboding. The elevators doors slid open. She felt reluctant to go up to her apartment, her rising apprehension borne of something more sinister than her fear of being trapped in the elevator.

Swallowing her unease, she stepped inside. The elevator bumped and rattled to the fifteenth floor. She started at the ping and reluctantly followed Brett into the corridor. As they walked toward her apartment, she spotted a tall man with blond hair lurking near the stairwell. The lurid green aura surrounding him reminded her of the aura that enveloped the tramp.

The man's eyes suddenly riveted onto her and she felt writhing fingers invading her mind. She tried to speak but found the words frozen in her throat. The evil emanating from the man sent an arctic shudder through her body. Panic seized her as she tried to fight off a pervasive sense of unease.

Brett turned to see why she stopped. "Destiny? What's wrong? You look like you've seen a—" He followed her gaze and barely glimpsed the man slipping through the stairwell door.

"Shit!" he cried, sprinting in pursuit.

She leaned against the wall for a moment to regain her composure. Brett had broken the spell and now she felt drained. Faced with the danger the voices had described, she hoped the man's mental probe had not picked up any thoughts about her situation with Brett. In that case, she wouldn't be safe at his apartment. But, would she be safe anywhere? At least with a man in the house she had some protection.

He returned a moment later. "He's gone. Why didn't you say something? Do you think it was the crasher who broke into your apartment?"

She could still picture the dead expression in the man's eyes. "I'm almost positive. Why else would he have taken off like that?"

"Are you sure you don't know who it could be?"

"Absolutely," she said, slipping the key into the lock. She opened the door and walked into the apartment. "Honestly, Brett, I couldn't be more invisible to the world outside if I tried. There's no way I'd be involved in anything dangerous."

Everything looked the same as they left it the night before. Though it was clear the crasher had not had been in her apartment, Destiny still felt uncomfortable. She shivered, partly from apprehension, partly from the chill of the unheated apartment.

"Would you rather leave it another time?"

"No—let's get this over with. I don't want to come back here again. This isn't my place anymore."

Brett surveyed the shambles. "Where do you want to start?"

Destiny shrugged. "There's not much left to retrieve. Clothes, any unbroken valuables we could use for bartering—"

Barely five minutes had elapsed before Mr. Simmons appeared at the door. His face assumed an almost petulant appearance as he watched them rummage through the mess.

"What's all this?" he said.

Destiny turned toward the man and steeled herself against his arguments. Her anger at the landlord's negligence in letting the crasher into her apartment finally surfaced and she snapped, "What does it look like? A Tupperware party? I'm leaving. I'm sure you got my message I left on your machine."

"But, but—" he spluttered. "You can't! You haven't given a proper month's notice!"

Brett stepped forward, his body towering over the indignant landlord. "I hardly think you're in a position to dictate terms, Mr. Simmons, considering it was you who allowed the crasher access to Ms van Kampen's apartment. Seems you've also become a bit slack with security. We spotted the crasher again only a few minutes ago."

Simmons stepped back, fear replacing his bravado. "The tenancy act—"

"The tenancy act is no longer in force. You know that quite well and so do we. Arbitration is no longer an issue," Brett said calmly. "Destiny is moving out."

Destiny reached for Brett's arm. "It's okay, Brett. Mr. Simmons can take whatever I leave behind as compensation. Neither of us is in much of a position to haggle."

Simmons turned florid. "Very well," he shouted. "You have half an hour to vacate the building. I'll be back, and if you're not gone, I'll call the cops!"

Brett chuckled. "You seem to forget something. I *am* the police."

Simmons almost choked on his next words. "Yes—well—just get the hell out of my building. Both of you!" He turned and marched toward the elevator, his muttering not quite comprehensible as Brett slammed the door.

"Arrogant little bastard. It amazes me to see how selfish people continue to be. One of these days he may find himself out on the street. He should appreciate what he has."

"Yes. It's not as if I'm skipping out without paying the rent. I've paid up till the end of the month. Anyway, let's forget about him and get started. I'd really like to get out of here."

Trying to suppress her fury at Simmons and the sudden upheaval in her life, Destiny tackled her wardrobe and personal belongings. What little was salvageable fit into a couple of cardboard boxes she had stored in her hallway closet. Last of all she grabbed the cup with the spider plant shoot she planted the night of the break-in. Carefully, she placed it in her jacket pocket.

"You want to take another look around before we go?" Brett asked. "What about your computer? We might be able to sell the parts."

She shook her head, the shattered remnants of her apartment now a meaningless jumble. "Leave it. Let's go before Simmons comes back with his hired thug. I have a feeling that he or at least Jake is in on this. Why would he let a stranger into the building a second time?"

"I can give you a good guess; money, goods, protection. Look, after we get you settled I'll call the station. It might be a good idea to bring Simmons and Jake in for questioning."

As they carried the boxes to the elevator, Destiny thought about the apprehension she experienced when they entered the building. Somehow she had sensed the crasher's aura. Now his face was forever embedded in her memory. She would recognize him anywhere.

Brett had her wait in the Jeep while he loaded the boxes. The tires squealed as he spun around and roared out of the underground parking lot.

Destiny's eyes roamed the street for any sign of the crasher, but she saw nothing until they approached an intersection. Suddenly, out of the corner of her eye, she spotted a suspicious green haze in the narrow alley between two boarded up businesses.

"Brett, over there! He's in the alley!" she shouted.

Brett hit the brakes so hard the Jeep slid onto the sidewalk. Weapon drawn and ready, he jumped out of the vehicle and dashed into the alley but came back moments later. "He's gone again! Who the hell is this guy, some kind of magician? The bastard appears and disappears at will."

Carefully, he edged the vehicle off the sidewalk and drove slowly down Carnarvon Street. When he turned the corner they noticed two cars had collided. Street people converged from nowhere to comb for pickings. Some of the bolder approached the vehicles, but none moved to help the dazed victims sitting inside. They both appeared to be older men. A man's body was wedged beneath the wheels of the first car.

Brett braked and dialed the police emergency code on his cell phone. "I've got to report this. Looks like a casualty." He pulled up close to the accident and got out. Loitering street people hastily dispersed when he approached.

Destiny didn't want to look but somehow her eyes were drawn to the body wedged beneath the wheels as Brett knelt beside it to check for a pulse. The awkwardly angled limbs indicated that they were broken. A shock of blond hair caught her attention. Slowly, the green mist surrounding the body dissipated. She knew it was the crasher and that he was dead.

An enormous sense of relief overwhelmed her. Though she felt sorry for the man at having met such a violent end, she was thankful that he was gone.

Brett returned to the Jeep and got in. He rubbed his hands to warm them and gently reached for hers. "The drivers of both cars are okay, just a little shaken. They said the guy ran out into the street right in front of them. They couldn't stop because of the slippery road. He was killed instantly."

"It's the crasher," she said, relishing the reassuring grip of his hands and the comforting sensation it sent through her body.

"Are you sure?"

She nodded. "Yes. I'm sure."

"Well then, it's over." With a hint of disappointment he added, "So what are you going to do now that he's out of the way? Do you want to move back into your apartment?"

She was about to say something when a voice sounded close to her ear.

"No, Destiny. It is not over. It has only just begun. There will be others. Go with Brett."

A soft rosy light hovered before her eyes for a moment and she nodded.

Brett felt somewhat confused at her nod. "I—would you still consider being my roommate or do you have other plans?"

"I'm sorry. I was thinking of something else. No, I'd like nothing more than to be your roommate."

"Great, let's go home," he grinned, his attention turning to an approaching, heavily reinforced squad car. "Hold on. I know them. Let me have a quick word to explain that this was the crasher we were after. We didn't actually witness the accident, so we shouldn't have to hang around."

She nodded and smiled. Home—it sounded good. It felt right. A feeling of security suffused her as she watched Brett converse with his fellow officers.

A voice spoke over her shoulder. "Be careful, Destiny. Their eyes see everything."

Her flesh crawled. *Whose eyes?* she asked silently.

But the voice did not reply. Weighing the words carefully in her mind, she felt a powerful sense of apprehension. If the crasher had not been an isolated incident, how many were among the ranks of the elementals? Were they linked like a communal hive mind, able to track her wherever she went? She considered the population of Vancouver alone and wondered how many more she would have to face.

***

CHAPTER NINE
December 24th, 2008

Destiny waded through the filthy slush toward Edmonds sky train station. Around her, a smattering of commuters grimly plodded on like automatons, their eyes fixed to the slippery ground. The dull black, grays and browns of their heavy clothing reflected the somber tones of the city. There was no conversation, no sound beyond the distant roar of heavy machinery and the occasional shrill wail of a siren. She glanced at her watch, her concern in missing the last of the few operating trains quelled by the need for caution as she plodded through the sludge. Nearby, a heavily wrapped middle-aged woman slipped and barely kept herself from falling. Her frustrated curse seemed to echo the general mood of futility permeating the population.

A man wearing spiked boots shuffled past and left a trail of indentations in the slush. The removal crews could hardly keep up with the continuing onslaught. Almost as soon as the weather warmed a little, another cold front would arrive and yet more snow and ice would choke the beleaguered city. It hampered restoration and cleanup to the point where it seemed like winter had become an eternal season.

She glanced up at the sky. A thick, leaden cloud front hung ominously low, indicating yet another storm. She kicked up her pace, her thoughts already drifting to the workload awaiting her at the office. The scourge had shut down two food distribution points, forcing her to reroute an already overtaxed delivery crew. She was aware of rumors of a rudimentary vaccine for the ever-mutating virus, but doubted it existed because those in power continued to succumb as easily as the homeless on the streets did. Her only hope was to avoid as much contact as possible with the infected and to keep herself reasonably healthy.

Some consolation, she thought to herself.

Though her rubber boots were sturdy and fitted with anti slip soles she often had to steady herself. She took care in crossing the street. A solitary bus packed with passengers, its battered appearance evidence of the stringent public transport budget, slowly wheezed toward her. As she glanced at it something compelled her to turn and look behind. A thin gangly man stood huddled by a lamppost. Her pace quickened instinctively when she noticed a faint but familiar green haze surrounding him. She stepped onto the curb and looked behind her again. The man was still there, the greenish aura now starkly visible. It reminded her strongly of the aura of the crasher who had invaded the sanctuary of her apartment.

Fear constricted her throat as she tried to run. The slush impeded her progress but her awareness of the footsteps behind her prodded her on. She took her purse from her shoulder and wound the long strap tightly around her hand. If the man tried anything, she would use her purse as a weapon.

The escalator to the platform, switched off to conserve electricity, loomed before her. She mounted the rubberized steps and wound her way around the commuters. A glance over her shoulder confirmed the man had followed her, his glowing aura writhing malevolently.

Pushing her way through to the platform, scaling two steps at a time, she tried to ignore the irritated remarks of commuters as she shoved them aside. A train was about to pull out. She dove through the closing doors of the nearest carriage and landed heavily on the floor. Rubbing the aching shoulder that had borne the brunt of the impact, she scrambled to her feet and glanced out of the misted window. The man, his hat now askew above his unkempt greasy hair, frantically tried to pry open the door. The train gathered speed.

Tensely, she watched him jog beside the carriage until he realized the futility of his effort and finally stopped. His dead blue eyes followed the speeding train, his lips working furiously.

Each detail of his countenance was etched into Destiny's mind, from his crumpled hat down to his threadbare coat and scuffed cowboy boots. This man was older than the one who had ravaged her apartment. He was at least in his forties. With his lean and wearied appearance he hardly looked fit enough to pursue anyone, let alone her, but now she couldn't be sure what or who to watch for. She shuddered and mopped the perspiration beading her forehead.

"Are you okay?"

Destiny whirled to face a pretty teenager wearing a backpack. "Yes, I'm fine. Thank you," she said noting with relief the faint mauve aura surrounding the girl. Automatically, she scanned the other passengers and saw a veil of pale to dark mauve auras, some among them a faint green. She wondered whether they were elementals or whether they were future recruits.

"That man was chasing you," the young girl said. "You should call the police."

"Don't worry, I will. My boyfriend is a cop," Destiny said, at the same time thinking, *what possessed me to call Brett my boyfriend? Is that how I already think of him?*

"Did you know him?" the girl asked curiously.

"No. Never met him before," Destiny told her while keeping a careful watch on the passengers displaying green auras. Some of them stared at her. The directness of their gaze sent an unpleasant chill through her body.

"You'd better get off at the next station and call the police immediately," the girl said. "There are enough street freaks running around out there."

Destiny nodded in agreement, though she knew her pursuer was no street freak. "Don't worry. I'll report it as soon as I get to work. Thanks for your thoughtfulness," she told the girl.

"Not a problem," the girl replied with a grin. "Where do you get off? I'll walk you to work if you like. You look quite shaken."

"I'll be fine, but thanks anyway," Destiny answered, but deep down she was uncertain. If her pursuers knew her route to work, someone could easily be waiting for her there.

She got off the sky train at Burrard station. Her eyes scoured the crowds but she couldn't see anyone suspicious. Mingling with the throng spilling from the train, she headed for the stairs. Even now, Burrard Street was busy. Commuters hurried to get to work, and cars, whose privileged drivers had dared to brave the icy roads, honked impatiently. For a moment, Destiny could almost imagine the rush hour before the war, when traffic and congestion were part of the daily routine. She longed for the chaotic normalcy of those days.

Banishing the nostalgic vision she glanced around and hurried to her partially damaged office building. The upper floors had collapsed, but the lower half remained intact and had been certified by the public safety division as safe for occupation. Once in her cramped cluttered office she threw her purse on the desk and called Brett. He would still be asleep and she felt guilty waking him, but she had no choice.

"Destiny? What's wrong?" he asked sleepily.

"A man followed me to the sky train. I managed to lose him but if he knows my route, then he probably knows where I live and work."

"Are you sure?" he asked, stifling a yawn. "The crasher who broke into your apartment is dead. Maybe this was another street freak like the one who tried to attack us yesterday."

"Dammit, Brett, I'm not the kind to imagine things. You should know that by now."

"I'm sorry. I do know that. I wasn't thinking. Can you describe the man?"

"In detail. Brett, I'm scared."

"I'd like to know why these people are after you. What is it that you've got, or they think you have? I haven't even seen black marketeers hassled like this."

Destiny hesitated. She wanted to tell Brett the truth, the need to talk about her experiences overwhelming. This would also be the ultimate test of his obvious interest in her. "Brett, I need to talk to you. There's something I need to tell you."

"I agree," he said quietly.

"No. It's not what you think. I'm not involved in anything illegal. This is something that's beyond my ability to comprehend.

Anyway, I can't tell you over the phone. Let's talk about it tonight."

"Are you going to be all right? Maybe you should come home."

She heard the concern lacing his voice and smiled wanly. "I can't. This is my last day before the holidays and I have to finish the distribution roster by tonight."

"Well, I'm off today. I'll come and pick you up. What are you doing for lunch? I don't like the idea of you venturing out."

"There's a little coffee shop next door where all the office people go. I'll be fine there."

"Okay. I'll phone the police station and tell them about your stalker. They'll send someone over to question you."

"Really, Brett, don't bother. They have better things to do. Besides, it won't do any good. Please don't phone them until after we've talked?"

"Destiny, I don't—" he started but she interrupted him.

"Brett, I'll explain everything tonight and then you can tell me what you think."

"This doesn't make any sense," he said in a puzzled tone. "Why wouldn't you want the police involved?"

"I know it doesn't make sense," she agreed with a sigh. "That's why we need to talk. Look, my boss is here, I have to go."

"Okay. Be careful, Destiny."

She hung up. His concern warmed her in a pleasant way. They had formed quite a friendship over the past few days and she knew that what she felt for him was now beginning to stray beyond that. It was a sensation she couldn't describe, a feeling that seemed almost out of place in the current atmosphere of fear and uncertainty. She never felt anything like it before with her previous boyfriends. It was almost as if she'd known him all her life, as if they were related somehow—but maybe they were. The voices told her that Brett had been chosen, too, that he was an Earth child just like her.

Since she moved in with Brett, the voices were silent because of her tranquil state. Now that she was in turmoil she knew they would come to her. Could she ask them questions this time? Would they give her answers?

But the voices didn't come. Only the spheres appeared briefly, their soft music instantly calming her.

The day crept by with numbing slowness. A series of brownouts caused the computer to crash several times, losing the updated roster information and putting her behind schedule. Her thoughts constantly drifted to the auras that she now saw displayed everywhere, even in the office.

With some concern she noted that her boss was surrounded by a faint green aura. She eyed him suspiciously each time he approached her. Only a few of her associates sported faint mauve auras. Feeling threatened, even in her place of work, the chore of completing the roster became more difficult. After she finally finished it she was tempted to ask her boss if she could leave early, but the last hour of the workday was designated for the staff Christmas gathering.

She spent half an hour tidying her office and thinking about her new stalker. What had he planned? Would he have accosted her in broad daylight? Did he think she was carrying the information he was after? Or was he just supposed to keep an eye on her? Questions tumbled through her mind while she sorted out piles of printouts.

The staff gathered in the break room and exchanged gifts. Someone had decorated with a few balloons and some limp party streamers. Refreshments were limited to a jug of reconstituted tropical fruit punch and a miserly tray of imitation sugar cookies. The boss had given them a ballpark figure of ten dollars for gifts. She had drawn his name and soon discovered that buying for a man was almost impossible as almost every store in Vancouver was out of business. Nevertheless, he seemed pleased with the tie she had bargained for at a local flea market.

Stacy, one of her colleagues, had drawn Destiny's name. Her gift was a lovely crystal statuette of an angel. Destiny thought nothing could have been more appropriate at that very moment. Noticing the pale mauve aura surrounding Stacy's face, she felt a surge of relief.

"Do you like it, Destiny? I bought it in that small antique shop just down from us."

"I love it," Destiny said while tracing the delicate outline of the angel's wings. "It's beautiful. I didn't know there were such lovely things in that shop. I always thought it was just a junk store. I should go and browse around there some time."

Stacy drew closer and took a sip from her punch. "You should have seen this crystal skull they had! Somebody asked to see it and the dealer brought it out. I tell you, it looked so real it was eerie, but the price was sky high. The dealer said he's had it for a long time and there are only a few like it in the world. No one knows how they were made or who made them."

Destiny's eyes glowed with interest. "Really? I remember seeing documentaries about the crystal skulls. There are several in existence, nearly all flawed. The narrator suspected them to be copies of the original. This one woman had the only perfect skull. It was beautiful. Wouldn't it be something to own one? It would be a great conversation piece to display on the coffee table. Just out of curiosity, how much is he asking?"

"Five-thousand dollars."

"Wow! Sky high isn't the word for it."

"Tell me about it. He said it was very rare."

"If it's real, then it's very rare indeed," Destiny mused. She wondered briefly what it would be like to own such a treasure, but immediately shrugged it off. The way the world was at the moment, a loaf of bread was far more precious.

The crystal skull still on her mind, Destiny left the Christmas gathering early. As she stepped from the building, she scanned the sidewalk but saw no sign of the pursuer or of Brett. Quickly, she walked to the antique shop. Filled with last minute holiday shoppers, she actually had to negotiate around the cluttered displays. The friendly glow from twinkling candles in the store window and the joyful sound of Christmas carols infused her with a festive spirit she had not felt in years.

She was glad she bought gifts for her parents some time ago and that they had remained undamaged in a corner of her closet. Quietly she roamed the shop admiring antique furniture and unusual ornaments. She spotted an ornately carved music box that could serve as a man's trinket box. She had not yet bought Brett a gift; her thoughts of Christmas pushed aside since the break-in. Carefully, she lifted the box off the shelf and wound it. When she opened the lid, a haunting tune greeted her. She listened mesmerized to the same melody that the spheres often hummed. It startled her to hear the lifelong tune that had pacified her many times as a child. She closed it and opened it again, listening, lost in time.

The antique dealer startled her.

"Can I help you? That little box comes from an old English castle. It dates back to early twelfth century. At least, as far as I can tell. I think it could be much older, but I have to go by the date the original owners gave me. It's made of a very rare material, none like I've ever seen before."

"It resembles some kind of ivory or pearl," Destiny said while inspecting the box. Its glow reflected different pastel shades. When she turned it, the colors transformed from creamy shades of blue to shell pink and pale yellow. The effect was that of pearls crushed and blended together to create the box. "How much is it?" she asked, wondering at the same time how the dealer managed to even find such rare antiques.

"For you? Let me see," he said thoughtfully while he took the box from her fingers and closed the lid. "I can let you have it for a hundred."

"How about eighty?"

He ran his fingers through sparse gray hair. "Sorry. I already dropped the price for you. I have a feeling that the box belongs with you, or perhaps someone you know, but I'm not going any lower than what I paid for it. I've had it for quite some time," he said firmly as he placed the box back on the glass shelf.

"I'll take it," Destiny said impulsively. "I heard you have a crystal skull. Is it available for viewing?"

The dealer regarded her curiously, his faded hazel eyes boring into her. For a moment, she wondered about him until she noticed a faint mauve aura flare and envelop him in ethereal light. When she focused on the other customers she clearly saw all their auras. They formed a vibrant mist of pastel shades, some faint, others more brilliant, but none of them green.

"The skull is in the safe. I've already put it away since no one is willing to pay such a high price for it."

"Can I see it?" she asked, driven by an urgent desire to see the skull, to touch it.

"Yes, if you're really interested."

"I am." She had no idea why she said that and felt immediately guilty. The price was beyond anything she could afford yet a powerful impulse compelled her to want to see the skull.

She followed him to the counter and inspected the antique jewelry in the display case while he disappeared through a rear door. He promptly returned carrying a glass case. Several people stopped him to admire the contents. Some tried to touch the case, but the dealer maneuvered it away from their hands. It was obvious the skull was his prized possession and no one was allowed to get close to it.

The dealer finally broke away from the customers and placed the case carefully on the counter. Destiny gazed at the smooth crystalline perfection of the skull. Its beauty overwhelmed her for a moment. "It's magnificent. May I hold it?"

Within seconds people crowded around Destiny and waited for the dealer to open the case. He hesitated and glanced at the other customers. "I don't really like people handling it," he said, then took a small key from his pocket and unlocked the case. "But I feel I must allow you. Would you all step back please?"

The skull was approximately the size of a baby's head and shone with mystical brilliance. She stuck her hands inside the glass case and placed both her hands on either side of the skull and felt its power surge through her body. For a very brief moment, the spheres appeared and hovered around the glass case as if to convey a message.

Destiny watched one of the spheres hover over the case while another hummed around her head. She nodded—the message in her mind suddenly clear. She looked at the dealer. "I want to buy it."

He ran a hand through his hair, the gesture betraying his uncertainty. He glanced at the skull almost as though seeking approval. "Young lady, I have other customers waiting. The price is—"

"I know the price. You want five thousand dollars for it. I want it." She had no idea why she wanted the skull so badly and thought of her savings, which would be eaten up by such a foolish extravagance.

"I'll agree only if you can pay cash or by approved debit card," he told her hesitantly. "And that's providing I'm able to reach the verification center. The service only operates a few hours a week."

She nodded—her determination to buy the skull overriding any other consideration. "I can pay with my debit card for both items," she said, removing the card from her wallet and handing it to him. The dealer paused before lifting the phone to call for approval. She had the distinct impression that he didn't really want to sell the skull.

The dealer inspected her signature on the card. "You know, I almost hate to let it go. It's been my friend for many years."

"How did you come by it?" she asked.

"An old woman left it to me. She was a very dear friend."

"Then why do you have it on display?"

"I'm getting on in age and have no family. I hoped the skull would point me to the rightful future owner."

"How could it tell you that?"

"It can. Would you please place your hands around the skull again?"

She complied and gasped when she noticed her hands glow and become almost transparent. It was almost as if a torch illuminated the flesh from beneath.

The dealer stepped back as light enveloped her and gasped. "It seems I've found the rightful owner. You may have the skull. I will not sell it."

Heated whispering rose from behind her. The other customers were awed by what they had just witnessed. Destiny looked at him in astonishment. "But the cost—"

"Never mind the cost," he said, his eyes betraying a mix of hope and recognition. "I've been waiting a long time for this moment. Let me wrap it for you."

Amazed at such a precious gift, she watched while he canceled the debit card transaction and waited while he wrapped the case in lengths of tissue paper and then produced a box to pack it in. After wrapping the music box he returned her debit card.

"Are you sure you don't want me to pay for the skull?" she asked, noticing the hint of tears in the old man's eyes. She wondered why he would want to part with it and felt a pang of regret as she put the card back inside her wallet.

"I'm very sure," he finally said. "The skull can't be sold. That's why I priced it so high."

"But I told you I wanted to buy it. What if you hadn't felt sure that you wanted me to have it? And suppose another customer had come in and told you they wanted to buy it?"

"An unlikely scenario. No one has ever wanted to pay the asking price. Sometimes, if people looked like they had money, I made the price so outrageous that they'd drop the matter immediately. And if you had insisted on buying it, I would have told you nicely that I changed my mind. But now the skull has spoken and shown me the rightful owner. Legend has it that there is only one such person, and whoever that is, will be immortal and never suffer illness."

"But why not keep it for yourself?"

"I'm tired, my dear. This dark world has aged me before my time. And I always knew that it didn't quite belong to me, or even to the dear friend who gave it to me. We were just its guardians. We both knew that some day the skull's rightful owner would come. And now she has."

"How could you know that?" she asked.

"We were told."

"Told? I don't understand."

"The skull's original owner, Madame Marie LeVanier, found the skull in a small antique shop in France not long after the Second World War. She was able to purchase it for a few francs because the dealer thought it was glass. Shortly after she immigrated to Canada, she had a dream in which she was told she must safeguard the skull until the rightful owner came to claim it. When she became ill a few years ago, she had another dream in which she was told I would be the next guardian. Only when she entrusted the skull to me did I come to understand its unique powers, and like her, I also had the dream. Now the person we were told to expect has finally come to claim the skull."

"I don't know what to say," Destiny said, her thoughts churning from the phenomenon that occurred when she had cradled the skull.

"Well, hurry up and say something so the man can help us," someone behind her grumbled. "We all want to get home and enjoy Christmas Eve."

The dealer carefully gave her the box. "Can I have your name? Perhaps your phone-number as well? I'd like to keep in touch," he said while he handed her a business card.

"Of course." Destiny wrote Brett's phone number on the notepad he pushed toward her. "My name is Destiny van Kampen.

Look, are you sure you won't let me pay for the music box at least?"

He ignored her question. "My name is Bill Laguna. And no, I won't charge you for the box. The skull and the box belong together."

"Together? I don't understand. You were willing to sell me the box a moment ago. And if I hadn't bought it, surely someone else would have?"

"I already sensed the music box belonged to you. I wouldn't have sold it to anyone else. It was just a matter of waiting to see if you communed with the skull the way I expected you to."

She shook her head. "I find it hard to believe I'm some kind of messiah."

The dealer gave her an enigmatic look. "In time you will understand. Guard them well, Destiny, and have a blessed Christmas."

Destiny felt the impatient stares around her. She smiled at the dealer. "Very well. Thank you, Bill, and have a merry Christmas," she said and walked out of the store carrying the box with her precious gifts. She pondered his words and considered how appropriately they tied in with recent events.

Quickly she hurried back to the office building, the stalker forgotten for the moment. Just a few doors down from the antique shop, an agitated crowd blocked her path. Carefully she stepped off the sidewalk and grimaced as she sank into a pile of slushy snow. A short, dumpy woman blundered from across the street and bumped into her so roughly she almost fell. Angrily Destiny turned with a retort on her lips, but when she saw the woman immersed in a sickly green aura she spun around and hurried back to the office as quickly as possible through the treacherous slush.

The unruly crowd enveloped her, impeding her progress. A noxious green fog writhed against her, its acrid stench choking her with every breath. Through a gap in the crowd she suddenly glimpsed the cause of the commotion. In the center a bedraggled man dressed in filthy rags and a tattered poncho sat on a splintered crate, a battered box of mangy red apples before him. A crudely scrawled sign priced them at fifty dollars each.

Destiny's eyes widened at the sight of the fruit and the people scrabbling to buy them. Where the man had gotten the apples, she had no idea, but more importantly, he sat surrounded by a shifting green mist. His rheumy eyes suspiciously regarded the growing crowd as he made his hasty sales, one shaking gnarled hand snatching money while the other held a gun, which he occasionally waved at those he felt might be tempted to snatch an apple without paying. Destiny could feel the growing tension of the spectators circling the box of fruit like a pack of hungry predators. At any moment pandemonium could erupt if someone attempted to steal the fruit and the man started firing.

Clutching the cardboard box protectively to her chest she barged through the crowd, wincing as an elbow made painful contact with her ribs. People, aggravated at her passage, complained and swore, but she refused to make eye contact. Finally she managed to escape. She paused to brush the snow off her legs and hurried away from the crowd.

As she suspected, Brett sat waiting in his Jeep, the engine running. Exhaust formed a spectral cloud behind it. He jumped out to open the door for her. When he reached to take the parcel from her hands, she said, "No. I'll keep this on my lap. It's very fragile."

"Where have you been?" he grumbled. "I thought I told you to stay put in your office?"

"I'm sorry. I needed to get another gift and I guess I just lost track of the time. Then I got caught in that crowd back there. A street person has some apples and is trying to sell them for fifty bucks apiece. The people are going crazy to get them."

He continued to mutter as he jumped into the Jeep and pulled into the street. "Well, just don't worry me like that in the future. The last thing you want to do is get caught in a crowd. Never mind what they're selling. All day long we've had reports of muggings and—" He noticed Destiny's distracted expression and softened his tone. "Look—would you like to go somewhere tonight? I know a theater that's still open. The prices are extortionate, but they show some of the old classics."

"No thanks, Brett. I think I'd rather spend the evening quietly at home with you. Unless of course you have other plans?"

"No other plans. I'd like that, too," he said while he honked at a car that shot out of nowhere and almost sideswiped them. He angrily shook his head. "You can have only one other car on the road but you can bet some asshole won't—"

She looked out the window and glimpsed a man on the sidewalk. Dressed in heavy weather gear, it was impossible to distinguish his features. Surrounded by a brilliant green aura, he gazed intently at the car that had almost struck them. Spitting into the snow, a puff of smoke emanated from the tiny puddle and snaked toward the vehicle like a spectral finger. It funneled and siphoned into the exhaust until a shower of sparks belched out. Frozen in her seat, she watched as the car began to fishtail. Steam billowed from the engine, obscuring the driver's view. The car spun violently on the icy road and struck a power pole. She shuddered, the voice's warning once again coming to mind. The darkness it had warned about was becoming more apparent.

Trying to put the chilling incident out of her mind, she said, "Brett, you're off over Christmas. Would you like to come with me to my parents' farm tomorrow morning and have Christmas dinner with us? If you're with me I'll feel safe and I can stay a little longer, at least until after Boxing Day."

"I'd like that," he said and reached to squeeze her hand.

"Good. I'll call Mom tonight and tell her to expect an extra guest for dinner."

"How about the man who followed you? Have you seen any more of him? And why won't you talk to the police?"

"Brett, you *are* the police and we can talk about it tonight."

His eyes danced as he made a mock salute. "Yes, Ma'am!"

Destiny smiled. Brett's appearance in her life had begun to foster long forgotten feelings. Being with Brett was making a difference in her life that she could barely comprehend. How long had it been since she had enjoyed such companionship with another human being? Reluctantly, her thoughts drifted to the evening. She hoped that once he heard what she had to say, his feelings for her would remain the same.

***

CHAPTER TEN

As Brett unlocked the door to the apartment, he paused and gave Destiny a sheepish look. "Say," he said, "would you give me a minute to tidy up? I left a bit of mess this morning."

Smiling, Destiny cast a glance to the closed living room door. "That bad? I thought I had you trained."

"Well, I had a bit of a relapse."

"Okay, I'll wait in the hallway," she said, amusement shining from her eyes as Brett quickly removed his jacket and boots and disappeared into the living room. Shrugging her shoulders, she removed her overclothes and waited until he called out. She shook her head at his peculiar behavior and braced herself to find organized disarray.

Instead, delicious warmth and soft guitar music greeted her when she stepped into the living room. She stopped for a moment to listen to his baritone voice and the familiar tune of a Christmas carol. *Silent Night, Holy Night* —

To her surprise, a fireplace glowed from the corner that had been concealed by the bamboo screen and trunk. Fragrant candles and a small artificial Christmas tree decorated with tiny glass baubles and strings of golden tinsel presented a cozy festive scene. She approached the tree and gently touched a shiny red ornament. A golden star crowned the top and winked in the flickering firelight.

Contentment flooded her at the welcoming atmosphere and the sound of his voice singing in the background. She stood admiring the tree until the last notes drifted through the room. "Brett, this is a wonderful surprise. Did you do all this today?" she asked, turning to face him.

"Obviously," he said with a satisfied smile. "Did you see any Christmas decorations when you left this morning?"

She laughed. "I didn't even see a fireplace when I left this morning. Matter of fact, I never looked behind that screen. I thought you'd put it there to hide some cracks in the wall or something."

Brett beamed. "Let's say you inspired me to do some long overdue housecleaning. Guess you can tell I've lived alone for a while. I don't use the fireplace because this place is really just a place to sleep. But now that you're here, well, it's just nice to be able to enjoy the company of another person."

Her eyes momentarily pooled as she stared at the bayberry candle. Quickly, she joined him before the fireplace and tried to stem the onslaught of emotion his thoughtfulness caused. "Thanks for going to all this trouble, Brett. It's been a long time since the holidays have meant anything to me. You've got a wonderful voice."

"Thanks for the compliment. It's been a long time since I've played or even felt like singing, but having you here has become an inspiration for me. Besides, I think we both needed a little Christmas spirit."

An appetizing aroma wafted through the air. She sniffed and turned to him with questioning eyes. "You've also cooked? This truly is the season of miracles."

"Hmmm—should I claim the credit for this? Actually, I went and bought food for us at a Chinese restaurant. Ding Ho Wong was—"

"Let me guess, another one of your special contacts?"

He smiled engagingly. "Being in the police force does have its advantages. And, I think you've already determined that my cooking skills aren't exactly Cordon Bleu. Still, it's mainly rice and a few vegetables," he added apologetically. "Ding Ho's spices make up for the missing ingredients."

"You're full of surprises, Brett. Though I wouldn't knock your pizza. It was pretty good."

"Who can't make pizza? I think even a child can."

"Provided that child can get sausage and cheese on the black market. Even bread is a luxury for some," she said and stood up. She picked up the box and the smaller parcel. "Anyway, I still need to wrap a gift. I'll just be a minute."

"What's in the large box?"

"It was something I wanted to buy. Instead, it was given to me. I'll show it to you shortly. It's really quite extraordinary."

Once in her room, Destiny rummaged through one of the boxes of salvaged items from her apartment until she found some wrapping paper she had saved from past Christmas celebrations. She wrapped the music box in a cheerful piece of red tinfoil paper. After putting the finishing touches on a fancy bow, she searched for a suitable card. The few she retrieved from her apartment were an odd assortment of leftovers, mainly just for friends. She found one that she bought for her last boyfriend but had never given to him. Somehow, it hardly seemed appropriate to give Brett a card intended for another man.

Instead, she decided on a simple gift tag. While pondering what to write on the card she heard Brett strike up the chords for 'O Little Town of Bethlehem.' A glow suffused her as his rich voice drifted throughout the apartment and embraced her with its warmth. She felt a strange sensation of remembrance—a feeling of love she recognized as though it was a long lost companion. She wrote on the card, *To a new friend who is not a friend anymore, but has become someone very special in my life.* She didn't know what else to say. The feelings she had for Brett were mixed, and as yet she couldn't define them.

When she returned to the living room, Brett had a nacho platter waiting on the coffee table along with a bottle of champagne. She placed the small gift under the tree and sat down beside him on the couch. "Now I must be hallucinating," she said with raised eyebrows. "Champagne?"

"I want tonight to be extra special, Destiny. Don't worry, I didn't call in all my favors. The liquor store manager offered me this instead of the bottle of wine he promised me for Christmas. Of course, I couldn't resist."

Destiny started munching on the nachos. "Did he give you these, too? God, they're delicious." She laughed and brushed the crumbs from her lap. "You've put a lot of effort into making this evening special. I appreciate it, even if I appear to have the table manners of a goat."

He laughed. "Well, you're in good company," he said, helping himself to a fistful of chips. "The nachos and cheese I picked up on the black market." He reached for a pair of simple champagne glasses on the coffee table and filled them with the sparkling liquid. Destiny accepted the offered glass and raised it in a salute. "To better days and friendship."

"To better days together," Brett said as he softly clinked his glass against hers.

She sipped the champagne and savored the taste. Bubbles tickled her nose. "I can't remember the last time I drank champagne. I think it was after I graduated from college."

"When I was accepted into the force, my parents gave me a bottle of champagne. We celebrated together. I still have the cork somewhere around here."

They sat quietly before the fireplace sipping their champagne until Brett finally asked, "Destiny, what did you want to talk to me about?"

"I almost hate to spoil the moment."

"I think it's time you leveled with me. Something's obviously troubling you and I'd like to help."

"Well, first there's something you need to know about me."

"So the lady has dark secrets after all," he said with a smile.

Destiny took another sip of her champagne. "No dark secrets, but something that does border on darkness. Brett, do you believe in psychic phenomenon?"

"Why do you think I always watch the old *X-Files* reruns?"

She laughed. "That's if you can even see anything through the static. Okay, so you have an open mind. If I told you that I've experienced strange phenomenon ever since childhood, you wouldn't laugh at me?"

Brett set his glass down on the coffee table and turned to her with interest. "You've got me intrigued. Don't stop now."

Gratified that he didn't dismiss her confession as nonsense, she started to tell him about the spheres and the voices. She talked for a long time and noted with satisfaction that he listened quietly without judging her.

"And now I can see auras, too," she concluded, "both good and bad. The voices are speaking to me and becoming much clearer. Sometimes apparitions accompany them as well. It's almost beyond my ability to describe it all to someone who's never seen them." She stopped and waited for him to comment.

Brett refilled their champagne glasses. "You said the Eletarii have infiltrated certain people. How is that possible? Through some kind of mind control?"

"It would have to be to control so many. I clearly saw a green aura around the crasher at my apartment, the vagrant who tried to attack us the Jeep and the man who followed me to the station today. And now that I can see these auras, I've been spotting various shades of green around quite a few people. They're the elementals."

"So you think that these people are part of a conspiracy to overtake our planet and they're after something hidden in your mind, but you don't know what?"

She hesitated. The words sounded unbelievable even as Brett spoke them. "Apparently. That's what the voices told me anyway."

"And what's my role in all this?"

Destiny shrugged and reached for the nacho platter. She nibbled thoughtfully. "I don't know that yet. I was afraid to tell you for fear that you'd think me certifiable, or worse, infected by the scourge. My God, I still have a hard time believing it all myself. The voice told me that I'm not of this world, that neither of us are of this world. You were chosen and we were meant to meet."

Brett nodded thoughtfully. "I can believe that. My partner must have thought I lost it when I insisted on answering the call to your apartment building that night. But all I knew was that I had to do it. Something urged me to that building."

Destiny stopped for a moment to sip her champagne, then looked him in the eyes. "Brett, I'm scared. I don't know who I am anymore. If we're both from another place, another time, what does that make us?"

"Well, even if it turns out that both of us are really little green men, it wouldn't change my feelings for you," he said. "Though I have to wonder if that recent spate of UFO sightings has anything to do with the Eletarii."

"Sightings? When was this?"

"Just recently. The government tried to keep it quiet, as they always do. There was a brief segment about the sightings on the news a couple of months ago, but with everything else going on I doubt it held much interest. Now, though, I doubt it's a coincidence."

"Were any reported in this area?"

"Apparently sightings were reported all over the world. I remember we had quite a few calls at the station from people who claimed they saw strange lights in the sky. Some even said they heard things. Of course, at the time, we dismissed it as hysteria or ravings from delusional cranks. Now I have to wonder if they're connected with what your voices told you, or even if they sent you the spheres and the messages."

Destiny adamantly shook her head. "No. Whatever this is has nothing to do with the voices. These sightings are definitely the Eletarii. They don't need a show of force because they have a ready-made army here on Earth. What easier way to conquer a world?"

"And they're doing all this to stop you?"

She sighed wearily. "I only know what the voices have told me, Brett. We've seen for ourselves evidence of that evil. I suppose it would have been too much to expect aliens to drop in for coffee and a friendly chat."

He nodded thoughtfully. "Well, predators exist on our world. Look at the sharks and other carnivores. Hell, look at our fellow man. Who's to say extraterrestrial life is any different?"

"I'm amazed you're taking this all so calmly. At least you don't think I've lost it."

He smiled wryly. "I see a lot of horrors on the streets, more than you want to know about. These days, nothing would surprise me. Believe me, you're the most normal woman I've met in a long time." He paused to sip his champagne. "Exactly how are you supposed to fight these forces, Destiny?"

"I wish I knew. What I do know is, the voices told me I have powers that have not yet fully surfaced. I suppose they'll guide me. My psychic abilities are becoming stronger every day."

"From what you've told me, they seemed to have started

increasing after the break-in. Did you ever tell your parents about your experiences?"

"When I was a little girl I talked to my mother about it. She also experienced the same phenomenon during her pregnancy, but they stopped after she had me. I remember she warned me never to speak about it because people wouldn't understand. You're the first one I've discussed it with."

"I feel honored. It can't have been easy keeping such a thing to yourself. What prompted you to tell me now?"

"Because you wanted me to go to the police and tell them about the man who followed me. I don't think we're dealing with ordinary crashers or stalkers, Brett. I think we're dealing with the supernatural or at least forces beyond human comprehension. It's something the police wouldn't understand."

"Yes, you're probably right. Most of my colleagues aren't into supernatural phenomenon. They're too busy with the horrors of reality."

"So what makes you so different, Brett?"

He shrugged. "Even as a boy I was always interested in ghosts and usually looked for books with a supernatural angle. Then as I got older, I started getting into psychic phenomenon. I've read books by Nostradamus, Cayce, Montgomery, and many other noted psychics. The subject always fascinated me and still does."

She sighed. "Am I glad to hear it. I was afraid you'd throw me out after hearing all this."

Brett drew closer to her. "That's the last thing I'd do. Being with you these past few days has made me realize how lonely my life has become."

"Is this what they call a whirlwind courtship?" she asked in an attempt to keep the mood light.

"You confessed your secret, now I'm confessing mine."

A heavy silence ensued as he searched her face. "You know, it's funny. For the longest time I used to envy the officers with wives and families. Despite the hardships, they at least had the support of people who loved them. I always felt so isolated, especially after losing Murphy and—"

Destiny watched his eyes mist. "You don't have to—" she started to say.

"No, I need to say it. I've kept the pain inside far too long. You talked earlier about losing your faith in humanity, but I did, too. It seemed nothing I did mattered, that I didn't count as a human being. I started to believe that God had finally had enough of all of us and that this was his way of saying to hell with you all—until I met you."

A soft smile played on Destiny's lips. "Maybe it takes something like this to wake us all up. At least this is a start." She reached out and squeezed Brett's hand. "Would you like to see what's in the box now?"

"Yes, why don't you go and get it and I'll set the table."

Brett picked up the almost empty nacho platter and returned to the kitchen. *Easy,* he thought, *don't rush her. She's gone through a lot. The last thing she needs is more stress in her life.*

Before he set the table he added another piece of wood to the fire and watched until the flames engulfed the log in a scarlet glow. Just as he placed the cutlery on the place mats, Destiny returned. He stopped what he was doing when he saw the glass case she carried and set carefully on the coffee table. "What the hell is that? It looks like a skull."

She grinned, produced a small key and opened the case. Reaching inside, she cupped her hands around the skull and held it for a moment. She felt its warmth surge through her body and closed her eyes.

Brett watched in amazement as her hands lit up and glowed a suffused pink. The flesh became transparent, revealing the network of veins and bones beneath. "Destiny, what—"

"Ssshh," she whispered. "This is so amazing. I wish you could feel this."

"Well, even though we're supposedly from the same world, I don't seem to possess your abilities. How did you do that?"

In response to his question she slowly lifted the skull from its bed. Still cradling it in her hands she held it out to him.

Brett looked at the meditative expression on her face. Her eyes shone with a fathomless luminosity that seemed to pierce through him. Whatever doubts he had about her experiences immediately evaporated.

"Brett, come here and hold it."

Hesitantly he stepped forward and reached out to her with both hands. Carefully, she placed the skull within his grasp and watched his fingers close around it. "Don't drop it. It's nothing to be afraid of. Let its essence flow through your body."

"I don't feel anything," he said.

"Here, let me help," she said and moved toward him. She placed her hands over his. Slowly the luminous glow appeared. Both their hands became transparent now.

At that moment, Brett felt a powerful vibration like electrical impulses coursing through his body. He reeled as he sensed the melding of their minds. It was as if they had fused into a single entity, their thoughts commingling in a web of brilliant energy.

His voice locked in his throat. Gazing into the liquid depths of Destiny's eyes, a sense of recognition, or perhaps, precognition, filled his heart. He knew without doubt that they had known each other before, in a time and place locked in their subconscious minds. The skull and its mystical powers had revealed some of the mysteries of their origins and the task awaiting them.

Destiny gasped as she felt the power surge through her body. The connection with Brett became an infinite dimension of energy that writhed and crackled like lightning. She stared in awe at the spectacle.

The wondrous moment ceased when the telephone rang. Contact was broken and slowly their hands returned to normal. Destiny removed her hands and watched while Brett placed the skull carefully in its case. "Aren't you going to answer the phone?"

Brett shook his head. "I don't want to talk to anyone just now." He took a step toward her and touched her face. "Who are you? What happened to us just now? I know what I saw, I know what I felt, but is it possible that—?"

"Don't try to explain it, Brett. Just try to embrace it. If we were meant to find each other, there must be a reason. All I know is that there's something important we have to do, not just for us, but for the world."

Each lost in their own thoughts they barely spoke as they ate dinner. The phone rang again, but this time, Brett answered. He motioned to Destiny and put his hand over the mouthpiece. "Do you know a Bill Laguna?"

She jumped up and took the phone from Brett. "That's the antique dealer," she whispered as he returned to the couch.

"Hello, Bill. What can I do for you?"

"I'm sorry to call so late, Destiny. I just wanted to know if you made it home safely with your precious possessions."

Destiny smiled. "Thanks for your concern, Bill. The skull and I are just fine. I'm staying with a good friend."

"Yes, I know him well," Bill said so softly that she thought she misunderstood him. "Brett's a fine man. His strength will help you in the battle ahead."

"You know him? But how? I didn't even mention his name."

"Learn to trust, Destiny. Open your mind. The answers you seek are waiting for you there. There's no longer reason to doubt. Have a blessed Christmas, child."

She was about to answer when he hung up. Her expression reflected her astonishment as she listened to the dial tone.

"What's wrong?" Brett asked.

"He—Bill just wanted to make sure I got home okay. It's the strangest thing. He seemed to know—"

"Know what?"

"It's as if the man is psychic. He said he knew you. I'm sure I didn't mention your name when I bought the—"

"Maybe he is psychic. I believe in that sort of thing. What did you buy?" Brett probed.

"Actually, I didn't buy anything. I have a gift for you but Bill wouldn't take any money from me. Anyway, it's not Christmas yet," she said and sat beside him. "You'll see tomorrow."

"Talking about tomorrow, we have a long drive ahead of us and the roads are bad. You may not have noticed, but it's a hell of a blizzard out there."

Destiny stared at the crackling fire. "I know. Hopefully the storm will have eased by tomorrow."

Brett glanced at the skull. "Yes, I hope so too," he said and got to his feet. "How about some coffee? I managed to get an ounce on the black market."

She nodded. "That would be great." She snuggled against the couch and continued to stare at the hypnotic flames dancing in the fireplace until her eyes grew heavy. A musical voice whispered close to her ear, the words drifting through her mind like a gentle lullaby.

"The journey begins tomorrow, Destiny. The skull and music box must always be with you. They will be your guides, your lanterns in the darkness—"

***

CHAPTER ELEVEN
Christmas Day, 25th December 2008

Destiny gazed out of the Jeep's window at the passing countryside. A dun gray blanket of snow gave the landscape the stark appearance of a black and white photograph. In the distance, the horizon merged with a murky vista of monochromatic tones. The rusted hulks of abandoned cars lay like fallen soldiers in ditches bordering the highway and in the center divider. More than once a suspiciously prone shape in the snow attested to a foolhardy victim bent on scavenging the derelict vehicles. She shivered and wrung her hands together to warm them. Even with the heating on maximum the frozen air penetrated her clothing and nipped her flesh.

After they left the more populated areas the landscape transformed into a barren wasteland. Skeletal trees that had once been lush orchards rose like gnarled arthritic hands from the depleted soil. Distant farms were scattered on the horizon, the only sign of life a paltry finger of smoke spiraling up from the chimneys. Lush fields that had once grown hop, corn, or other crops, lay wasted.

Nevertheless, dark figures trudged along the fouled snow, bags slung over their shoulders. Oblivious to the harsh elements they knelt to dig deep into the frozen dirt in the hopes of finding a stray root that had survived, perhaps a leaf or a shriveled potato, anything that would still their hunger.

Brett was forced to drive very slowly, not only because of the hazardous conditions but because the snow hid a myriad of cracks and potholes deforming the asphalt. The snow also concealed patches of black ice and even though it had stopped falling for now the temperatures were still well below zero. On the other side of the highway, a lonely salt truck sprinkled its cargo. Only half the trucks were out, because it was Christmas day, and they were working four hours shifts to give each worker the opportunity to celebrate the holiday with their families. Their side of the road had not been salted yet.

"Look at Mount Baker, Brett," Destiny said as they neared Chilliwack.

Brett eyed the ominous fingers of smoke coiling from the mountain. Its angry black threads were visible even through the thick cloud-bed. "Looks like it's about to erupt again."

"The valley is still reeling from the aftermath of the last eruption."

"It wasn't just the volcano that took lives, Destiny."

"I know," she said. Silently she considered the war, the earthquakes and the scourge, all of which seemed to comprise Earth's swan song. "It's just that the volcano was just so close to home. I was visiting my parents the last time it erupted. Fireballs rained onto the land like a meteor shower. It was terrifying. Dad was out there with his army helmet on and a hose trying to stop the house from catching fire. Mom and I were trying to herd the animals to safety. And the choking layer of dust after it was all over was unbelievable. We had to wear masks for days. I took time off work and stayed with my parents for a week to help them clean up."

"Were you afraid?"

"The spheres were with me all the time, so no, I wasn't afraid. I knew we were safe."

"Are the spheres with us now?"

"No. I haven't seen them. You know, now that I know they're my guardians, why do I keep calling them the spheres?"

"Probably because you've lived with them all your life. I imagine whatever the spheres are, they were created as an illusion for you as sort of a comfort, almost like a child's imaginary faerie world. They did it to make you feel secure."

"I never thought of it that way." She watched an angry plume of black smoke belch from Mt. Baker and boil into the sky. A dismal gray haze obscured the base of the mountain. Even under the snowy conditions and low hanging clouds, they could easily see it. She knew that behind that haze the mountain and miles of surrounding countryside were stripped of life and vegetation.

"How much farther, Destiny?"

"We're almost at the turn-off. Just a few more miles."

"I wonder how many more catastrophes the world will have to endure," Brett said as he surveyed the devastated countryside.

"I doubt the world will last much longer, Brett. Only a third of the global population survives and half of those are dying of the scourge. I think it will only be a matter of time before we all succumb one way or another."

"I still have hope, Destiny. Especially now that I've met you."

"Hope? I barely recognize the word."

He squeezed her hand. "What do you say we drop this morbid subject for now and celebrate Christmas," he said with a forced air of cheerfulness. "So what's in the small parcel with my name on it? I thought you said you'd tell me today?"

"The day has just begun," she joked. "You're just like an impatient little boy."

"Mm, now let me see. What exotic treasure awaits me? Soap? Shaving cream? Aftershave lotion?"

"You'll never guess so don't bother trying. And give me some credit for originality." She pointed to a barely visible side road. "You have to take this turn-off."

Brett braked a bit abruptly and almost went into a skid. "A little more notice would have been nice."

"Got to keep your attention on the road," she said with a grin and glanced at the back seat to make sure her valuable cargo was safe.

They passed a group of homeless trudging slowly to the fields. One of them pushed a rusted old shopping card that kept getting stuck in the snow. "Brett, stop the car. Surely those people are aware that the remaining churches are always open to the homeless?"

Brett stopped, but when she opened the window, the group

furtively glanced toward the vehicle before scattering like startled rabbits.

"Leave them alone," he said. "They probably think of us as rivals." He shook his head and drove past the retreating group. "It's amazing how many of them survive despite their circumstances. I'll say that much for the human spirit."

Destiny sudden lurched upright. "Brett! Up there! In the sky!"

"Don't startle me like that," he muttered while slowing to a crawl. He followed her gaze but saw nothing beyond the dun blanket of cloud. "I don't see anything."

"I thought I saw a metallic flash. It moved so quickly—"

"You're still thinking about our conversation last night. It would be too much of a coincidence to spot a UFO now. Maybe it was a plane."

"No—it was there for a moment and then it darted out of sight. No plane could do that."

Brett remained silent. Though he did not want to admit it, he had been one of the many who had seen the strange lights. Seized by a sudden sense of unease he drove on, his mind unwilling to accept a possible alien invasion of Earth.

"It was probably lightning behind the clouds."

"Maybe," she said, though they both knew otherwise.

***

A delicious aroma of roasting turkey greeted Brett and Destiny when her mother opened the front door. Sarah beamed with delight, her heavy silver hair twisted up beneath a woolen hat. Her petite form was bundled in a thick home-knitted sweater and thermal pants. Extending her arms she embraced Destiny in a bear hug. Destiny instantly relaxed when she sniffed the mouthwatering aroma of apple pie spice on her mother's clothing.

"I'm so glad to see you!" Sarah said. "We've heard so many horrible things lately. I wish you'd consider coming to live at home, sweetheart. Dad and I do worry about you."

Destiny momentarily gazed at the shimmering mauve aura around her mother and kissed her on the cheek. Eagerly she searched the hallway for her father. "Is my nose deceiving me? Mom, after seeing nothing but devastation on our journey, I can't believe what you're cooking. It makes me feel guilty when I think of all the hunger in the world."

Sarah nodded. "Well, you know I've always been a hoarder. Somehow it seemed the practical thing to do out here because you never could tell when bad weather would strike. And, I've always had a feeling that some day it would be necessary. But, we share our good fortune and donate as much as we can to the church."

"Where's Dad?"

"Out in the barn feeding the chickens," Sarah said, her gaze drifting to Brett. "And this is your friend?"

"I'm sorry," Destiny said with a rueful grin, regretting her lack of manners. "Mom, this is Brett Young."

Brett was surprised at the surprisingly firm grip of Sarah's hand. Outwardly, she appeared frail, but he suspected that it was strictly superficial. Strength shone from her eyes and spoke from the firm handshake.

Sarah glanced at Destiny and considered the different expression in her daughter's eyes. Had she finally found someone? A look at the young man's face revealed why Destiny appeared so happy. Brett exuded warmth, strength, and his eyes mirrored kindness. "Pleased to meet you, Brett. Welcome to our home. It isn't often we get visitors these days."

"Thank you, Mrs. van Kampen."

"Please, call me Sarah. I was never one for formality."

Destiny turned to him. "Brett, can you fetch the gifts from the car, please? And don't forget the box."

He understood what she meant. She told him that morning what the voice had said about always keeping the skull close.

"Come, you're letting all the warmth out of the house," Sarah urged, tugging at Destiny's arm. She pointed to a forced air vent. "Dad's done wonders with the boiler, but we still have to conserve energy."

A buzzer rang from the kitchen. "Excuse me a moment, sweetheart. The pie's done."

Brett sprinted to the car while Destiny waited by the door. Sniffing the wonderful aroma of the apple pie made from her mother's store of dried apples, she held her breath while watching him through the triangular window. He carried the box containing the precious skull nonchalantly underneath one arm. His other hand gripped the bag containing the Christmas gifts. Though her father had cleared a path to the house, it was still slippery.

As soon as Brett entered the house she took the box from him and placed it carefully in the hallway closet.

"Aren't you going to show it to your parents?" he asked, following her.

"No. I'm not sure they'd appreciate something like that. People around here don't have time for mystical nonsense."

The cheerful sound of Christmas music and voices emanated from the living room. Her mother appeared from the kitchen busily wiping her hands on a checkered apron. Destiny looked at her with raised eyebrows. "Who's in there?"

"Oh, your father and I decided to open our house to some of the homeless. We felt it unfair that we should enjoy so much while others scrape for what they can get in the fields and garbage piles. We took in a single mother, Lisa, and her little girl, Candy. Lisa isn't that well and I'm not sure about the child. We also took in two elderly members of the church. You remember Mr. Mead and Mr. Cheltam?"

"Yes, I remember them. I'm surprised they survived. That's just like you, Mom," Destiny said while briefly hugging her mother. "Too bad we couldn't clone more like you."

Sarah smiled. "Well, I didn't give them your room. The two elderly men are quite fragile. I fear for them, though I do my best to nourish them back to health."

"I wouldn't have minded if you gave them my room. You could have packed up my belongings. I can always sleep on the couch whenever I visit."

"No, sweetheart. That room is yours," Sarah said stubbornly while leading the way to the kitchen.

"Brett and I will go and say hello to everyone first and then I'll come help you in the kitchen," Destiny said as she and Brett entered the living room.

Lisa, a pretty, if gaunt, young brunette instantly rose from an armchair and smiled. Her daughter, a curly haired moppet of about three, quietly played with a patched doll. The elderly men set down their cups of herbal tea and stood to greet them. Destiny barely controlled her dismay at the sight of the emaciated parishioners. Though she had seen worse in the city, it galled her to see how the elderly suffered.

"Hello, Destiny," Lisa said timidly. "Sarah's told us so much about you."

"Pleased to meet you," echoed Brett and Destiny as they shook her frail hand. The little girl looked up briefly and smiled shyly, but said nothing as she returned her attention to her battered doll.

Mr. Mead and Mr. Cheltam were more vociferous in the greetings, their gratitude in having a warm shelter and the basic necessities evident in their eyes. "Your mother is truly an angel," Mr. Mead said, enthusiastically pumping Destiny's hand. "God bless you all." Mr. Cheltam nodded in agreement as he shook Brett's hand. "Angels, all of you," he echoed.

Noticing only the palest mauve auras around the guests, Destiny inwardly sighed with relief. She glanced around at the crackling fire and the sparse but cheerful Christmas decorations. Her gaze rested on the artificial tree. Years ago, Sarah bought it at a yard sale, but Chris put up a fuss about having an artificial tree so he stored it in the attic. The live potted Christmas tree they used for years had not survived. Now, with so many trees destroyed, the artificial tree finally became useful. Each ornament gracing the tree bore special meaning. It had been a family tradition to buy Christmas decorations for each other every year. Destiny smiled at the angel she made when she was in kindergarten. Its fluffy, blue tulle dress was now faded—its smiling face barely visible beneath wispy strands of blond doll's hair.

"Destiny!" Chris cried out, his voice resonant as he stepped into the living room and fiercely hugged his daughter. "It's been far too long since I've seen my little girl."

A shimmering mauve aura embraced her father. Destiny gazed into his weather-beaten but still handsome face and noticed an incipient tear in his eye. "I've missed you, too, Dad. But I'm home now."

Chris turned to Brett and offered his hand. "Nice to meet you. I'm Chris."

"Dad, this is a friend of mine, Brett Young." Seeing a chance to slip away into the kitchen, she suggested, "Look, why don't you two get acquainted while I go help Mom? Dad, Brett can update you with what's going on in the city."

She kissed her father on the cheek and turned to go to the kitchen. Lisa rose and offered to help, but Destiny declined. "Today is meant for all of us to enjoy," she said noting Lisa's grateful smile. The woman looked far from well, the dark smudges beneath her eyes accentuating her pallor. Destiny nodded to the elderly men and slipped out to the kitchen. She needed to be alone with her mother for just a little while and preparing the meal gave her that opportunity.

She paused to smile at her mother's expertise while Sarah simultaneously busied herself with a vegetable casserole and a pot of mulled cider. "Mom, I can see why you took those people in. They look terribly undernourished."

"Yes, we felt it was time we opened up our home. Will you peel the potatoes?"

Destiny took the peeler and worked her way through a pile of scrubbed potatoes. Never once did Sarah pause in her preparations. "I wish you could bottle your energy and give me some," Destiny said. "Honestly, Mom, I don't know how you do it."

Sarah stirred the cider bubbling in the pot. The aroma was almost narcotic and Destiny found her mouth watering at the prospect of enjoying a steaming mug.

"The minute you stop fighting is when it's over," Sarah said.

"Don't you ever get tired of it all? I mean the constant struggle, the worsening conditions that—"

Sarah smoothed back a stray lock of hair. "We do all right here, Destiny. And I never was one for quitting. No matter how difficult things get, you can never think of giving up."

Destiny glanced at the golden brown turkey roasting in the oven of her mother's wood burning stove. "Mom, I can't believe you managed to get a turkey. I heard on the news that the government was allocating four hundred on a lottery basis."

Sarah smiled conspiratorially.

"No way—"

"Hey, before it stopped, I played the lottery for years," Sarah said, "and won some respectable little prizes to boot."

"You could have butchered a couple of our chickens."

Sarah's eyebrows shot up. "Never. We raised those chickens from the day they were hatched and have kept them alive against all the odds. They're still supplying us with a few odd eggs. We also use some of the eggs for barter, as you know. I hope that soon they'll start laying regularly again and we'll have at least one good source of protein."

Destiny stared wistfully at her mother's well-stocked kitchen cupboards. "Rationing has relegated the joy of eating to memory, at least in the city. You can spend half a day in line and there's not much to find. The black market is a little better, but without goods to barter, there's no way anyone can afford the prices."

"Well, things aren't so easy here, either," Sarah said. "But I think we enjoy a better standard of living thanks to our past efforts. Before you leave I'll pack up a box of supplies for you." She paused to wash her hands.

Destiny noted the hot water bubbling from the tap and smiled at her father's ingenuity.

"I'll be glad when we can work the land again," Sarah said. "Then I'll be able to can and freeze more vegetables for us. It's a good thing I've got plenty of my preserves and dried vegetables and your father's smoked sausages and bacon, but if the soil doesn't clear soon, we'll run out, especially with more mouths to feed."

"You still can't work the land? Even after Dad's endless efforts to till it?

"No," Sarah said with a sad smile. "The ashes have soured the soil so much that all your father's efforts to till it and fertilize have been in vain. Dad broke up part of the cement floor in the basement and cultivated the soil beneath. He installed some fluorescent lights but the soil still won't grow much produce. Anyway, enough of that. She cast an appraising glance at her daughter. "This young man you've brought home, is it serious, Destiny?"

She smiled. "We only just met, but for the first time I feel—I don't know. He's different. He actually cares about me. I honestly never expected to find that in the city." She fought the urge to say more.

"Grab what you can, sweetheart. If you find any chance of happiness, then guard it with everything you have. It's a precious commodity few are able to enjoy anymore. He seems like a very nice young man. I read a lot of strength in his eyes."

"It's still early days, Mom, but I've got my fingers crossed."

"Well, I understand your concern. Meeting people can't be easy these days. But at least Brett's in the force. That in itself is good security. And he should at least earn enough to support a family."

"Mom, let's be realistic here. It's a dangerous job. And as for children—honestly, you can't be serious. I hardly think I want to bring children into this world. Look at it—people everywhere are dying from the scourge. Resources are running out, social infrastructures are collapsing—"

"The good will be saved, Destiny," Sarah interrupted. "You have a good heart. You always did. Whatever stray or injured animal you found always ended up here. As long as you care, you'll survive."

"And what kind of a future would be left for my children? If there is any future at all— If no cure is found for the scourge, it could be merely a matter of time for all of us. No. A family is far from my mind."

"Destiny, soon we will experience a thousand years of peace. We will see a new world and a new Heaven. The Bible tells us so."

"I'll believe that when I see it," Destiny said tightly. "Now, do you want me to take the bird out of the oven?"

"Yes. And then you can go and set the table."

Brett jumped up when he saw her putting the red Christmas cloth on the table. "I'll help," he offered.

Destiny handed him a bundle of silverware. "Sure, you can set. I'll get the plates."

"When do we open gifts?"

"After dinner. It's always been a tradition because first we'd go to church and then the afternoon was always too busy preparing the meal."

Brett noticed her reserved mood, but said nothing as he helped set the table. Chris lit the candles and invited everyone to sit, then went to help Sarah serve the meal.

During dinner, conversation revolved mostly around the recent spate of natural disasters plaguing the countryside. Wearied of the depressing subject, Destiny kept silent. She paid attention to little Candy instead, the child responding with smiles but little conversation. It occurred to her that the child might be suffering from some kind of ailment and she wondered grimly whether the little girl would also fall victim to the scourge.

Suddenly, a soft rumble shook the house. Sarah's fork and knife dropped on her plate. "Another quake," she said, rising quickly. "Is everything secure?" she asked, glancing at Chris.

Chris nodded. "I'll turn on the news," he said as he got up to turn on the tiny black and white television.

Candy started to cry. Lisa picked up the distressed child. "It's okay, baby," she cooed. "Remember what Mommy taught you. Let's go down to the basement."

Brett helped the two elderly men as the group headed for the basement door.

Chris snorted impatiently while he waited for a picture to appear on the television. Static shattered the screen and cleared to reveal the snowy image of a male newscaster. Anxious to hear the report, he muttered beneath his breath. Though the house shook again with enough force to rattle the dishes, there was nothing on the news. Another tremor shook the house, this one more violent than the last.

"Hurry, get into the basement!" Chris shouted and headed toward the basement door behind the others. The door slammed shut behind Lisa, leaving Brett, Destiny, Sarah and Chris outside. Brett struggled with it, but it would not open. Chris tried as well, but found it jammed. Desperately he pounded on the door. Footsteps sounded on the wooden stairs on the other side. The doorknob turned and they could hear someone pushing and banging, but it would not budge.

"It's jammed!" Lisa yelled from behind the door. "We can't get it open!"

"Quickly, let's find some shelter!" Chris shouted.

A powerful gale rocked the house. The glass rattled as if every window had been smashed and the doors strained inside their frames, but the windows were intact and the doors closed. Destiny had to grip the stair railing to steady herself. Sarah and Chris stumbled to the living room clinging to the walls and doorframes. "Get under the table!" Brett yelled at the older couple.

He grabbed Destiny and pulled her toward a storage closet.

"What the hell's going on?" he shouted. "This is no ordinary earthquake."

"I shouldn't have come here. The voices warned me but I didn't listen!"

"What is it?" he yelled, to overpower the howling wind.

"The elementals have followed us! Get the skull!"

"What does the skull have to do with this?"

"Never mind! Just get it!" How could she explain that she felt instinctively that the skull could help?

Brett lunged for the hallway closet. He tried to yank it open but it remained firmly shut.

"Smash it!" Destiny shouted. "Hurry, before it's too late!" She heard a din rising in the living room and kitchen area. It sounded as if every piece of china was hurled against the walls. A chair came flying through the open door and smashed against the wall of the hallway.

Brett wedged his back against the opposite wall and with all his strength slammed both feet against the closet. He punched through the door and crawled to the gaping hole. The lights went out, forcing him to grope for the box. His fingers encountered it and he pulled it toward him. Hanging onto the jagged edge of the hole with one hand he opened the box with the other and tried to lift out the glass case, but he couldn't manage it single-handedly.

He painstakingly maneuvered the box toward Destiny. Holding onto anything he could grasp he joined her and wedged his feet between the spokes of the stair railing. He tried to lift the glass case out but it seemed to weigh more than his own body weight. "I can't get it out!"

"Tear the box!" she screamed.

His fingers tore at the cardboard until he saw the small key sticking from the lock. He was relieved she left it in place and fumbled with it until the door to the case swung open. Destiny laboriously edged toward the box. She let go of the spokes and lunged for the skull and plunged both her hands into the glass case to cradle it. With a mighty heave, she pulled and withdrew the skull. "Help me! Place your hands over mine!"

He hardly had time to comprehend that the skull glowed with ruby brilliance as he placed his hands over hers. Green mist filled the hallway. Dark shapes materialized within it and roiled above them with menacing intent. They lunged for the two figures clutching the glowing skull but were hurled back with a tremendous force.

A harrowing roar like a thundering locomotive deafened them. Destiny's eyes were large luminous pools. She stared at a monstrous entity bearing down on them. Her body began to tremble as she sank into a trance-like state. A wave of distortion emanated from her flesh and snaked toward the creatures like a vengeful wraith. The force lunged and encompassed the entity with a shimmering white light. As it inhaled the pure light it howled in agony. It screamed and hurdled through the hallway where it disintegrated before their eyes.

Slowly, all became silent.

Destiny collapsed in an exhausted heap.

Brett slowly withdrew his hands and scrambled up. "Destiny? Are you okay?"

"Yes," she murmured as she struggled to sit, her hands clutching the skull. "I'm fine. My parents—"

"I'll go and check," he said and hurried to the living room.

She sat and cradled the skull on her lap. Once again a transparent crystal it gazed up at her with vacant eye sockets. She stroked it before she placed it back into the glass case that stood unharmed in the torn box.

Her limbs felt leaden as she stood up, put the box in the closet, and walked to the living room. She found her parents sitting on the chesterfield. They surveyed the devastated living room with a dazed expression. The turkey lay dismembered in the corner of the room, while the overturned dining table sat among a pile of shattered china and spilled food. Except for the couch most of the furniture was displaced. Broken glass lay everywhere.

"Mom, Dad, are you okay?" Destiny asked worriedly.

"Yes, we're fine," Sarah said. "That was some earthquake."

"I wonder why the news didn't warn us," Chris said. "That had to be a good sixer at least."

Destiny threw Brett a warning glance. "Yes, it's very strange. Maybe there wasn't time." The questions would come soon enough when her parents found out that there was no quake.

The others cautiously emerged from the basement door. Gasps

of astonishment rose when they saw the chaos in the living room. "Strange, we didn't feel much down there," Lisa said, tightly clutching a pale-faced Candy. "We heard all the racket upstairs though. The basement must be very solid."

Brett and Destiny toiled for several hours to clean up the mess. Her parents insisted on helping as well, but Lisa was occupied with her clearly distraught daughter and the two elderly men were too overwhelmed and upset. Brett escorted Lisa, Candy and the two men to their rooms so they could recover from their ordeal.

After the house was back in order and the men busy disposing of the debris, Destiny turned to her mother who was quietly sipping a cup of herb tea on the couch. "Mom, why don't we open the presents now? We need a break."

Sarah looked up at her. "Good thinking. Shame we never finished dinner, though. I was quite enjoying it."

Destiny had to smile. "I think we basically missed the apple pie, that's all. We'll stay an hour or so and then we have to head home. Brett got a call. He was summoned to work unexpectedly."

"Oh? What a pity. Your father and I were hoping you'd spend a few days with us."

Destiny didn't like the white lie, but she had no choice. Her parents would never understand if she told them that danger had come with her.

A moment later, Chris and Brett returned.

"Time to open the gifts, now," Sarah said cheerfully. "The others can open their gifts in the morning."

The ritual helped to raise everyone's spirits, but Destiny still sensed an air of tension. Carefully, everyone removed the wrapping so it could be used again. She had discreetly asked Brett not to open his gift from her, as she wanted him to open it later in private. She felt the box was special, the moment to give it to him spoiled by the invasion of the entity.

Chris exclaimed in delight when he opened a pack of bootleg tobacco Destiny had bartered for on the black market. "I won't even ask how you got this," he said with a broad grin. "But I've dreamed about this for a long time."

Sarah beamed as she withdrew a set of stainless steel kitchen utensils. "Destiny, these are wonderful."

A home knitted scarf, toque and gloves pleasantly surprised Brett. "Sarah, I haven't had a home made gift in a long time. I really appreciate this," he grinned, pulling the toque over his head.

Destiny fingered a thick royal blue sweater. "Mom, this is almost identical to one I wore years ago. It was my favorite and I wore it to pieces. You remembered—"

"Yes, of course I did. I pulled apart your old one and some of my old knitted sweaters and copied the pattern. The color always looked so good on you. I knew you'd like it."

"I guess it's time we packed up now," Destiny sighed. "Time passes too quickly. I wish we could stay longer."

"I'll go and pack you some food to take along. Promise me you and Brett will visit again soon?"

Sarah packed a box of homemade jams, fresh bread, apple pie and canned goods for them. The turkey sat like a ruined monument on the counter where Destiny had put it after she rescued it off the floor. Sarah gazed at it. "Destiny, please throw that thing in the garbage. The way it behaved at the table and flew through the room makes me think the thing is still alive. It's as if it's hexed."

Destiny grinned. She knew her mother would not touch the bird. "I'll take part of it home with us, Mom. Don't ask Dad to throw out the rest. I'm sure Lisa will divide it for the others. It would be a shame to waste it," she said while plucking chunks of meat off the bird and putting it into a container. "Brett and I don't mind eating this hexed meat."

They said their good-byes and got into the Jeep. While driving slowly down the icy driveway, Brett turned to her. "Destiny, that was one hell of an experience. Is this what we're facing?"

"Seems that way."

"What will you tell your parents when they find out there was no earthquake?"

"I haven't figured that out yet. I should have listened to the voices. They told me not to go to the farm because it was known to the elementals."

"I wish they had a face. Not knowing what to expect is the most unnerving part of all this."

"I imagine, it, they, or whatever they are, soon will," she said as she stared into the gathering twilight.

"How did you know to use the skull? I've never seen such power. It glowed like a coal, and that trance you went into was like something from a sci-fi movie."

She shook her head and leaned it wearily against the headrest. "I don't understand it myself. Something urged me to use the skull, voices in my head. I guess it will become clear to us eventually. At least, I hope it will. I could do without more surprises like this though. I'm absolutely exhausted."

"I can imagine. Why don't you close your eyes for a while," he suggested, giving her hand a quick squeeze. "I'm sorry it turned out this way, Destiny. I know how much you looked forward to this day."

She didn't respond. To Brett's surprise, she was fast asleep. He returned his attention to the road and continued to drive hoping he would find the way back to the highway in the drifting snow. Focused on the hazardous conditions, he did not notice a group of shadowy figures watching from a barren field, their eyes fixed on the retreating vehicle.

***

A scrawny, pockmarked man standing at the head of the group watched the hunted ones drive away. "Damn," he muttered. "We were so close—" He suddenly turned and sniffed the air like an animal scenting its prey. His rheumy eyes narrowed and fixed on a trio scavenging in the snowy field. Spittle drooled from his lips as they turned up in a malicious smile.

"Go," he muttered to the others. They grunted in response and lumbered off through the snow. Moments later, they fell upon the hapless trio, their screams of terror drowned by a feral cacophony of whoops, shouts and cries.

The man scratched at a pustular scab on his face. Uttering a phlegmy chuckle, he watched the green auras of his followers strengthen with the flow of their victims' blood. "Soon—soon we will feast upon them all—"

***

CHAPTER TWELVE

Brett waited impatiently for the security gates to trundle open. They groaned and creaked, the ill-maintained mechanism faltering on more than one occasion. If they failed, the gates would have to be left permanently open, leaving the building vulnerable. He sighed and hoped this would not become yet another problem to deal with.

The Jeep echoed loudly in the cavernous garage as he drove in and approached his parking spot. Weary from the hazardous drive home, he nudged Destiny gently. She had not once moved during the lengthy journey. "Destiny, we're home."

She opened her eyes and sat up with a start. "Good Lord, I feel like someone beat me up."

"I'm not surprised. You were twisted like a pretzel for quite a while but I didn't want to wake you."

She blinked and looked around the dimly lit garage. "Are we home already? What time is it?"

"Close to midnight." He saw her shiver. "Why don't you go in and I'll bring the stuff inside?"

Fatigue spurred her as she hurried to Brett's apartment. An arctic chill permeated the air and stung the exposed skin of her face. She had experienced many frigid winters, but the bitter cold embracing her now like a spectral lover chilled her to the point of numbness. Her fingers fumbled with the door key.

When she entered the living room she noticed the glow of the smoldering embers in the fireplace. She crumpled some papers and threw them in with a couple of logs. The wood ignited quickly; the gently crackling flames warm and cheerful.

"Now there's a welcome sight," Brett said, setting the bag containing their gifts on the coffee table. "It's a good thing there's so much wood around. Since rationing, it's almost like living in the olden days. I've collected quite a few oil lamps as well. The only thing missing are the horses and carts."

"I think I would have preferred the days of horses and carts to this," Destiny said.

Brett stared at the fire for a moment. She could almost see the memory playing before his eyes. "Well, I've got to get the box yet. I'll be back in a minute."

When he brought the tattered box back inside, Destiny noticed he was handling it with care this time. He placed it beside the bag of gifts and removed his jacket. "It's snowing again," he said, tossing it on a chair. He caught her glance and smiling, picked it up and brought it to the closet. "See what a good influence you are," he said with a grin.

"I didn't say anything."

"You didn't have to. Your eyes said it all. By the way, we have some champagne left. Would you like a glass?"

She nodded while intent on removing the glass case from the box. Placing it beside her on the couch she gazed at the skull.

"What are you trying to do? Hypnotize it?" Brett joked when he saw her concentrate.

"Mm? No. I was trying to figure out why the skull seems to have such extraordinary powers."

"Perhaps it's not just the skull. It could be a combination of your powers and the skull's," he said as he handed her a bubbling glass of champagne.

"Don't count yourself out, Brett," she said while sipping. "You're part of this as well. Anyway, I don't know if I can cope with this kind of responsibility. I'm just one woman. Even with such power, how can I possibly fend off the elementals?"

"The skull is special," Brett said. "It's clear that it's critical to whatever our mission is supposed to be. Anyway, after what happened today, I think we've gone past the point of debate."

She nodded.

He sat down beside her and pulled her into his arms. The warmth of his embrace felt comfortingly familiar and she felt a chink of resistance slide away.

"Would you like my gift now, Destiny?"

"You bought me something? I didn't see anything left under the tree."

He smiled. "That's because it was in my pocket all the time. I wanted to give it to you in private at your parents' place but I never had the right opportunity." While he spoke he dug deep in his pants pocket, produced a small velvet box and opened it.

She gasped when she saw the ring. A constellation of deep blue sapphires embraced a spray of diamonds set in an unusual crescent shape. Pinpoints of light sparkled like miniature fireworks. A golden hollow rested in the center, almost as if a stone were missing. The unique design was unlike anything she had ever seen and seemed to pulse with a life of its own. "It's beautiful, Brett. But jewelry costs a fortune. How on earth did you—"

"No strings," he said, placing his finger on her lips. "Just a special gift for a special woman. I know what we're both facing. Though I can't explain what's happening to us, I wanted you to have it as a token of my feelings for you. I can't claim to have bought this on the black market or anywhere else. My adoptive grandmother was a wonderful woman. We bonded immediately. She cared for me as if I was her real grandson. I was with her just before she died and she gave me this ring. It had apparently been in the family for longer than anyone could remember. When her own mother gave her the ring, she was told she would instinctively know who to give it to. Not long before she died, she had a dream that the ring belonged to me rather than her other grandchildren. She said that it was meant for only one special person, that this person would be the woman I was going to marry."

"But you hardly know me—" she murmured as conflicting emotions roiled within. Hope, hesitation and fear supplanted the usual emptiness she had trained herself to feel. "I mean, we don't even know if any of us have a future."

"I don't believe that. If we can just get through the present, the future holds many promises. The more I'm with you, the more I feel this sense of familiarity, of recognition. I can see it in your eyes as well. We both know our meeting was more than coincidence. And as for the future—whatever is left of it, I'd like to spend with you. You've restored my faith in a way I can't even explain."

"Yes," she admitted. "I knew there was something different about you, but I thought it was simply because it's been so long since anyone has taken an interest in me. Frankly, I'd given up on the thought of ever meeting anyone. The love that my parents shared for decades seemed something out of a fairy tale. I didn't think it had a place in this world anymore."

"Well, maybe it does after all," he said. He pulled the ring from the box and placed it on her finger. "I can't guarantee what tomorrow will bring, if anything. But at least to share what time we have left will make the darkness more bearable."

Leaning forward, she kissed him softly on the lips. The contact was brief but electric. "Thank you, for more than you can imagine." As she kissed him she felt a peculiar tingling in her finger. She leaned back and gazed at her hand. The gems shimmied in the light of the fire, the midnight blue of the sapphires twinkling in concert with the brilliant diamonds. For a moment, she glimpsed a starlit sky and knew that the ring belonged to her.

He smiled. "I'd still like to see my gift."

She laughed. "Of course, the aftershave lotion."

"Why the mystery anyway?"

"After what happened at dinner I felt the moment was lost so I decided to give you the gift when we were alone." She stood up to retrieve the small parcel from the bag of gifts and handed it to him. "I don't know why, but when I saw it I felt compelled to get it for you."

He tore the wrapping off and gazed at the delicately carved ivory box. "It's beautiful." He ran his finger along the intricate design. "Someone put a lot of love into the making of this box."

"Open the lid, Brett."

He lifted the lid. A haunting melody, resembling the tinkling of bells, filled the room. Though he did not immediately recognize the tune, somehow it seemed so familiar. He listened to it intently until she spoke.

"Brett, look at the skull."

He glanced at the skull and saw it glowing softly. "I hope it doesn't mean another episode like tonight," he said and closed the lid of the box. Immediately, the glow disappeared.

"It started to glow when you opened the music box. It stopped as soon as you closed it."

"You don't think—"

"I don't know. Open the lid again and see what happens."

He tried it and as soon as the haunting melody floated from the box, the skull glowed. "What do you think it means?"

"I wish the voices would come so I could ask them to explain. Brett, if we join hands, maybe our combined power will summon them."

"Let's give it a try. Sit with me by the fire," he said.

She sat cross-legged across from him and firmly gripped his hands.

"Now what do we do?" he asked.

"I don't know. I've never consciously contacted the spheres or voices before. They've always appeared at random. Maybe we should concentrate." She closed her eyes and forced her mind to go blank.

"It's not working," he said and was about to pull his hands away when a gentle humming filled the room. "Listen—do you hear that?"

She smiled. "Yes, it's them. They're here."

Within seconds, the room filled with diaphanous veils of color. Brett looked around in wonderment at the phenomenon. He realized he should have been able to experience the same as Destiny, but his troubled childhood and the demands of the physical world had left him little time to hone his abilities.

"Can you smell the flowers? It reminds me of meadows in the spring. And the mountains—they were such a glory to behold with their evergreen forests."

"Yes, I can smell them. And I can envision the trees—" Brett said reverently.

All but a few spheres gradually disappeared. Instead, translucent forms pirouetted throughout the room and hovered like spectral clouds around the seated pair. Their song was haunting, ethereal and vaguely familiar. It dimmed to a whispered susurration and finally a solitary voice. Destiny recognized it as the one that had addressed her before.

"My children, the time has come to give you knowledge of the path that lies ahead. Your memories must surface. You were both sent to this plane to fulfill an important mission."

"Sent from where?" Brett asked.

"You were chosen from those who inhabit your home. By agreeing to go to Earth, you were obliged to live among humanity until you could return to us. That time will soon come. But first, you must complete your mission."

"What knowledge do I possess that the elementals will stop at nothing to get?" Destiny asked.

"You have the knowledge that will ultimately defeat them. However, they will learn of this too late. You need not fear. You and your loved ones will not be harmed. The Antiquitas are with you at all times and you will instinctively know when and how to use your powers. They are now as natural to you as breathing."

"Was last evening an example of those powers?"

"It was a lesson in channeling and directing your power. The skull merely served to help you nurture your abilities."

"What exactly is our mission?" Brett asked.

"You must open the celestial portal so Altithronus, emissary of the Antiquitas, can complete the final stage of your mission. You must pack sufficient food and be prepared to travel. Take the skull and the music box. The portal must be opened at the stroke of midnight on December thirty-first."

"Why? What's so important about that date?" Destiny asked.

A powerful solar flare predicated around that time will have a tremendous impact on Earth. The mission must be completed before then."

Destiny frowned. "It sounds like you're asking us to risk our lives for this Altithronus. Is he that important?"

"Altithronus is the liaison between our people and the Antiquitas. You will not be risking your lives. In fact, you will save them. You must open the portal to the future and fulfill your destiny. Do not doubt, child. All your questions will be answered when you open the portal."

"Not too much to ask—" she murmured, her emotions a mixture

of anxiety, apprehension and uncertainty.

"Do not feel discouraged. Trust your own power. You will know what to do when the time comes. You must leave tomorrow and seek a Chinese merchant in Vancouver. He can be found—"

The voice faded. Neither Brett nor Destiny could distinguish the last words.

"Their ability to communicate with us has weakened," she explained to Brett. "It's kind of like a radio transmission. Sometimes it's clear, other times it fades quickly. It's never the same twice."

"Well, that gives us some idea of what we're up against. Altithronus—somehow the name is familiar—" He reached for the poker and stoked the fire. "How are we supposed to find this Chinese merchant without an address? Chinatown seems the logical choice, but there are still quite a few shops open in the district of Vancouver."

Destiny placed the skull back in the glass case and locked it. "I have no idea. Obviously, I was meant to have the skull. Perhaps it will lead us to the merchant." She shook her head. "I'm still finding it difficult to take this all in. Of all the people in the world, why are we so special? We're from another place? Another time? I can't imagine we would have made such a choice."

"According to the voices, we agreed to follow this path when we were chosen, Destiny. We can't deny what we've seen and heard."

She sighed. "It takes a leap of faith to just pack up and go, especially under these circumstances."

"Well, I can't just leave the force without notice. The department is short staffed as it is."

"I know. It worries me that the voice would ask us to leave our jobs. I don't know what to do."

The voice echoed through the room with a sudden burst of energy. It was so loud that it startled them both.

"Trust your path. If you do not seek the keys, all will be lost. Your journey will be difficult, but there is no other way."

She jumped up while Brett sat spellbound on the floor. "Well, I guess it's settled," she said.

Brett suddenly lurched over and slapped his hands to his ears. His expression grew agitated as he shook his head. Though his lips moved, no sound emerged. "Images are entering my mind," he finally said with tightly closed eyes. "I see mobs of frightened, panicking people. I hear screams of such magnitude that it seems the whole world is in agony." He paused, his grimace betraying atrocities beyond description. Tears streamed from his eyes, his breath panting with each word. "God—I see it so clearly now. The skies are alive with a fleet of ships—they remind of me locusts descending on a field of grain. It goes beyond the scourge or anything we've witnessed so far. We truly are humanity's only hope."

"What else do you see?" she asked, her eyes never leaving his face.

He opened his eyes and removed his hands from his ears, his expression troubled as he struggled to compose himself. "I—I saw the last days. It was frighteningly clear. I know now that we have no choice. He rose and pulled her into his arms. "I saw things too appalling to put into words—the suffering—the misery—"

"So then it's true," she said, clutching him. "Oh, God, I can't believe it's come to this. Despite everything, I somehow hoped we'd get through it." Her gaze drifted to the cheerfully crackling flames. "As long as you're with me, then I know everything will be all right. If you can just hold me in your arms for a little while, maybe the world will disappear."

"Come," he said and pulled her close to him on the couch. "Don't be afraid," he murmured against her cheek. "I'll be with you. Together we can make it. The only way we can go is forward."

"I was afraid, but now I'm just confused about what we face."

"You've always trusted the spheres and the voices. You can trust them now."

"Yes. I know." She snuggled deeper into his arms. "And now I feel I can trust you," she said, memories of another existence surfacing from the depths of her mind. "Because somewhere in the past, I know I loved you." The words came naturally now that she admitted her feelings for him.

Brett kissed her, his words merely a whisper as he spoke against her lips. "And I know that I loved you then, Destiny, and I love you now. More than anything, I want us to be together. No matter what we face, promise me we will be together?"

She stroked his hair. "We will. If we were brought together for a purpose, then there can be no other path for us."

He searched her eyes. "Now I understand why I always felt my life was so incomplete. I felt more like an observer than a participant. All this time, you were the missing piece to the puzzle of my heart. When all this is over we'll—"

"We'll have tomorrow, and all the days after that," she finished.

Clasped in their embrace, they silently watched the dancing fire and nurtured the hope that blossomed in their hearts.

***

CHAPTER THIRTEEN

Boxing Day, December 26th 2008

"I made turkey sandwiches, Brett," Destiny called out to him from the kitchen. "I'm glad I decided to salvage the bird. Mom was ready to throw it away. She figured it was hexed."

Brett emerged from the bathroom. His hair still spiked from his shower, he quickly rubbed it dry with a towel. He grinned. "The fowl from hell? If I think about the price of turkeys I would have tried to at least exorcise it before throwing it out. Well, maybe it'll take the cardboard taste away from the bread."

She giggled. "Yes, I can imagine you advancing on a stuffed turkey with a cross and holy water—just like that old film—what was it called now?"

Brett shivered and slipped into his room for a sweater. When he returned, he turned on the heating thermostat control. "Too cold to think. I know the one you mean. We should get about half an hour of heat. You'd better dress extra warmly. Even with chains, I don't even know if the Jeep will get through the snow. Hopefully, they've cleared the main roads."

"What if we can't get through?"

"Then it will have to wait. Have you looked out the window?"

"Yes. We had at least three feet last night."

"Need I say more?"

Voices suddenly resonated through the apartment. The air crackled with static electricity and smelled faintly of ozone. Destiny's flesh crawled as the voices echoed around them.

"Nothing must impede your journey. There can be no turning back. You must leave today."

A half-finished sandwich dropped from her hand and plopped onto the plate.

"Did you hear them?" Brett asked.

"Yes," she said, quietly surprised at her own acceptance of their exodus. She should be angry, questioning the voices about this upheaval of her life. Instead, she felt nothing but a sense of tranquility. "I guess we go to Vancouver, come what may."

"Fine. Let's hope they provide us with a snow blower," he grumbled and returned to the bathroom to finish dressing.

Destiny finished packing a supply of food and a thermos of coffee. Under such severe weather conditions, stranding was always a possibility and she didn't want to take chances. Longingly she glanced around the cozy apartment and felt a pang of regret. It would have been so easy just to shut out the world and make a better life for the two of them here, but she knew they were no longer in the domain of the everyday world.

Her gaze rested on the cactus and spider plant cuttings on the windowsill. The withered bush outside effectively cut what little light filtered through the clouds. On impulse, she reached for the tiny plants and stroked them before reluctantly returning them to the windowsill. She sighed and went into her room to put on her overclothes. When she emerged, Brett was busy packing their supplies. Both were dressed in warm jackets, toques, scarves and gloves.

"Don't forget we have to take the skull and the music box," she said, her voice muffled behind the thick woolen toque.

"The music box? Why?"

"I was told we always need to bring them both with us."

He sighed impatiently. "The cardboard box is broken and it's ridiculous to carry that glass case everywhere. What if I wrap them in a towel and you carry them in your bag?"

"Good idea. But the skull's pretty heavy, so we'll have to take turns carrying it if we need to leave the Jeep."

While Brett gathered their gear, Destiny noted his weapon clipped securely to his belt. He locked the front door and strode quickly along the snowbound path. She almost had to scramble to keep up with him, his distracted expression reflecting the thoughts churning through his mind. Glancing at the street through the high metal railing, she noticed that even though the street had evidently been plowed, fresh snow was already starting to accumulate.

They quickly loaded the Jeep. Destiny climbed in and waited impatiently while Brett fitted the chains. When he started the vehicle, it coughed explosively and filled the air with noxious exhaust.

"Damned low grade fuel," he muttered. "I'm surprised the engine hasn't completely seized up. At least the super has cleared the driveway somewhat. That's one bonus. I doubt if we'd have even gotten through the gates."

He rubbed his hands for a moment before he put the vehicle into four-wheel-drive and emerged into the street. For once, the dismal streets were virtually silent as the Boxing Day holiday gave city workers a well-deserved break. Even the homeless were scarce, the bitter cold keeping them under cover. Occasionally they encountered a salt truck or a snowplow, but the eerie stillness cloaking the city was almost disconcerting.

Destiny's attention remained fixed on passing landmarks that she instinctively felt she would never see again. The soup kitchens and shelters operated as they always did, but stores and businesses were all closed. Beyond rose St. Andrews' steeple, once not visible from this distance. It now soared above the destruction and appeared as an icon of hope for the many homeless and desperate. Though she had not been to church in years, its undamaged spires and serene stained glass windows offered some solace to her spirit.

Brett spoke very little. Despite the deserted streets, what should have been a twenty-minute journey turned into a painful crawl as he negotiated the hazardous road conditions.

He drove slowly down Granville Street. Huge piles of rubble, once beautiful, stately homes or modern offices and department stores, were blanketed in snow. The grim scenery was more reminiscent of mountainous terrain rather than the city as they continued to pass hillocks of snow-covered debris.

When they entered downtown Vancouver they were at a loss where to go. Once, the city had teemed with life on Boxing Day—shoppers returning or exchanging gifts, hunting for terrific bargains, but such activity was nothing more than a memory. Destiny stared glumly at the boarded windows of once thriving department stores. Faded signs advertising sales harkened to the days when supplies still made it to the cities, but the gradual closure of industry forced prices sky high so that even ordinary merchandise was beyond the reach of all but the government and black marketeers.

Looting and riots had become so commonplace that a curfew was set and martial law enforced. Out of desperation many took to eating pet food and at one point there was a marked decrease of small animals. Even though a semblance of order had since been restored and the curfew lifted, pets had become virtually extinct, the vacant veterinary offices and pet supply stores a poignant reminder of how the innocent once again suffered.

Destiny glanced at Brett and wondered about the sad fate of his dog. If a vet had tended the animal in time, could he have been saved? As her mother had pointed out, every stray or injured animal had always ended up as her new pet. She always hoped to have a pet when she moved to the city, the joys of companionship and unconditional love something she had come to cherish, but the idea joined all her other discarded dreams when even the possibility of owning a goldfish vanished in the funeral pyre of civilization.

"I guess our only option is to go to Chinatown," he said. "There's nothing here. Where are the voices to guide us?"

"That sounds like a good place to start," she said. "Maybe if I touch the skull it can help us." Quickly, she pulled off her gloves and stuck her hands inside her large canvas bag and unwrapped the skull. She pulled it onto her lap and held it between her hands. Its warmth immediately flowed through her fingers, radiated up her arms and seemed to center in her mind. Within moments, a voice spoke in her mind giving her directions. "Turn left here, Brett."

"Okay, we turn on Davie Street. And then?"

"I don't know. That's all I heard, to turn left on Davie. Davie Street isn't anywhere near Chinatown. We're heading toward the ocean. Just drive and let the skull lead us."

The Jeep crept down Davie Street behind a battered, solitary van. It looked to be a good thirty years old. Brett tensed and tried to keep a safe distance, not an easy task as they were driving downhill. By the condition of the van's bald, unchained tires, he was not surprised when it lost control and started to spin. He cursed and veered to avoid the fishtailing vehicle. "Damned idiot!" he cried as it wedged itself against the curb. "Even now, some people have no sense."

A dark, heavyset man emerging from the van snared Destiny's gaze. A faint greenish aura shimmered around him. He looked directly at her with narrowed eyes and trudged toward them with a deliberate pace.

"Brett, let's go!" She cried while protectively grasping the skull. "The driver—look at him!"

He immediately veered to give the driver a wide berth. The man scowled and started chasing the Jeep.

"Another one of your friends?" he asked tersely as he tried to steer.

She frowned when the man slipped on the icy street. He struggled to his feet and began to shout in a guttural foreign language.

"Just go! He was one of them."

"How the hell did he know we'd be heading down this road?"

"Maybe walkie talkies—how should I know? If we hear voices, maybe they hear them too."

Brett muttered under his breath and took a couple of turns to lose the man.

The urgent voice in her mind confirmed they were close. She peered through the snow-dusted window. Suddenly she seized his arm. "Brett, stop!"

"Dammit, don't startle me like that! I can't brake quickly on these icy roads. What is it?"

She plastered her face to the window and pointed. "Look at that little shop. It's almost hidden by rubble and snow."

Brett slowed and stopped. A modest shop front peeked from between a gap in the ruins. Its grimy window was covered with red Chinese lettering. In smaller English letters beneath, a sign read, Liung Zhang Li, Chinese Herbalist. A large sign on a partially boarded glass door showed that it was open.

"That must be him!" she said. "The voice was right."

"What's the skull doing?"

"It's warm," she said, gazing at its soft amber glow. "I'm sure we're at the right place." Feeling a tingling in her hand she paused to remove her left glove. A shivery sensation coursed through her fingers and trailed up her arm. Almost in response, the skull shone with golden radiance.

Brett took his eyes off the road for a moment and glanced at Destiny. "What's wrong?"

"The ring— it feels almost alive."

"My God, Nana never told me anything about this."

"She probably didn't know. I think it was waiting for me," Destiny said.

"I wonder what else is?" Brett murmured as he carefully maneuvered the Jeep onto a relatively flat portion of the pavement. He had trouble opening his door and shoved against it hard to move the snow out of the way. Quickly, he jumped out and sank knee deep into cold wetness. He waded around to the other side and removed some of the snow so that the passenger door would open easier.

Destiny carefully wrapped the skull in the towel and after putting it back into the bag handed it to him and jumped out of the Jeep. "Look, someone's actually shoveled a path to the front door. I can't believe anyone would be open on a day like this."

"Maybe he lives above the shop. See the windows up there?" He pointed at some windows crudely covered with pieces of plywood.

"Yes," she murmured, then fixed her attention on the choppy, murky waters of English Bay. Huge waves pummeled a wrecked freighter smashed ashore by an angry sea; the distant roar of the surging water the only sound in the dismal landscape. The beach, once teeming with sunbathers or people enjoying a stroll in the bracing sea air, was strewn with boulders, rubble, debris and dead waterfowl. Further down the beach lay the shattered remains of several boats. The stench of rotting fish and soured seawater permeated the air.

Shading her eyes against the driving snow, she peered at the shoreline. Makeshift tents dotted the soiled sand like a dismal refugee camp, the homeless enduring the bitter cold. She shuddered as a blanket draped figure crawled through the debris searching for food. In her mind she recalled the families and groups of young people that long ago crowded the beach, the odor of suntan lotion and happy laughter a distant memory. The high-rise buildings facing the sea had toppled—the once famous seawall no longer there for people to stroll, skate or bike. It had not been able to withstand the tidal wave that lashed the coast and the seawall had crumbled under the heavy impact.

"Destiny, what are you doing? Come on. You'll freeze to death standing there gazing into space," Brett urged her.

"Look at the beach, Brett."

"I know. I used to live in the West End and rollerbladed along the seawall all the time. The stench became really bad after the fish started dying. Since I was stationed in Burnaby anyway, I looked for an apartment there and was lucky enough to find one." He shook his head. "Look at those wretched people scrounging for food among that garbage. Come on. Let's go inside. It's freezing out here."

They gingerly negotiated the slippery path. Loud chimes jingled as they opened a creaking door and stepped into a warm but dimly lit interior. A pot bellied stove stood in the center of the store. Atop a small burner, a brass kettle puffed and spat. The poky shop reeked of ginger and exotic herbs, the pungency not quite concealing the musty odor of age and dust. A rattling ceiling fan circulated the warm air and shifted the cobwebs lacing the store like paper doilies.

It took a moment for their eyes to become accustomed to the obscure surroundings. The shop's interior was lined with sagging shelves of dust-caked bottles and potions. A door creaked open somewhere in the back and a wizened old man with stooped shoulders shuffled toward them. Brett tensed, but Destiny immediately noticed his glowing mauve aura and knew the man meant them no harm. The tiny figure barely reached her shoulders and regarded her with bright button eyes.

"Ah," he said in heavily accented English. "You have arrived. This is good. Very good." He extended his gnarled hands in welcome. "Welcome to Li's shop. Li waited long time for you." He bowed several times.

Destiny smiled. She almost had the inclination to bow too as Li kept bobbing up and down. He was dressed in vivid red Mandarin robes embroidered with gold-threaded symbols and dragons. A small gold embroidered skullcap sat on his head. From beneath it a long gray braid hung down his back. A carefully trimmed pointed silvery beard reached his narrow waist. His exquisite robes looked grossly out of place amidst the decrepit shop. She gazed at the symbols—they seemed somehow familiar. After they shook Li's hand, his hands disappeared inside his voluminous brocade sleeves. He shuffled to an antique wooden counter and stood behind it.

"You knew we were coming?" Brett asked.

The man nodded vigorously. "Yes. Li know. The woman, she is chosen one. Now, Li must give—"

The loudly jangling door chimes interrupted his words. Li's eyes darted to the door.

"Quickly," he hissed with a frown. "This not good. Not customers. You must leave. Come back when—"

Brett and Destiny spun around to face five male youths. Threadbare coats and tattered jeans did little to conceal their emaciated frames, their unkempt beards and greasy hair rendering them a savage look. It was almost impossible to determine their race beneath their gaunt, dirt-crusted faces. Only the tremor in their hands and their bloodshot unevenly dilated eyes betrayed evidence of the scourge.

Destiny swallowed hard as she stared at the youths through a green aura so intense it almost hurt her eyes. *Neurological disorder,* she thought dispassionately. *Or perhaps brain damage from overdosing.* If the youths had used drugs, the scourge would have augmented any existing damage.

Brett glanced at their weapons. The one he assumed to be the leader carried a sawed off shotgun, three others had pistols and the fifth one brandished a vicious gutting knife. His hand crept toward his gun.

The leader snapped the shotgun toward Brett with surprisingly agility. He grinned displaying a few remaining blackened teeth.

"Welcome to my shop," Li rasped.

"Shut up, old man," snarled the leader. "We're not interested in your shitty little shop. We just want these two, so disappear!"

The shotgun veered toward the old man. Before Brett could react, one of the three bearing a pistol turned toward him with a leering smile. "Go ahead, fucker, give me a reason."

Destiny gasped. Brett's hand rested on his weapon, his jaw twitching with anger, but he remained motionless.

Li stepped back and shuffled to the end of the counter. The leader continued to aim the shotgun at his back. "That's right. Fuck off, you old bastard. We've got some business to finish up here."

Destiny watched his finger move to pull the trigger. A blinding white anger surged through and around her body like an electrical current. The vortex increased until all she could hear was a spectral wind. Her eyes flashed. "Don't," she started to say with a voice that was hers but wasn't.

The leader ignored her and continued to press the trigger.

Brett turned and stared in astonishment as her eyes rolled until only the whites showed. Her head sagged and she slipped into a trance-like state. Suddenly, an infernal glow emanated from the canvas bag slung over her shoulder. The energy channeled into her body and distorted the air around her. It writhed and shimmied toward the thug aiming the shotgun and enveloped the weapon. A sizzling noise rose as it transformed into a molten blob and dripped gelatinously onto the wooden floor. Steam hissed, the wood buckling from the intense heat. The thug screamed in agony and uselessly tried to extricate his seared hand from the molten metal.

"What the fuck's going on here?" one of the others shouted. He waved his pistol at Destiny and moved threateningly toward her.

Brett tried once again to reach for his weapon, but the thug covering him jammed his pistol against his head. "Don't move," he said, "or the bitch eats it."

Destiny's body convulsed, her eyes continued to roll back. Her hair haloed around her as static electricity charged the air. The energy swirled around her body, its wraith-like form lurching toward the advancing thug and hurling him like a missile through the glass door. It shattered explosively, showering the snow with vicious shards. The remaining three thugs backed in terror toward the door.

The leader lurched drunkenly toward Brett and Destiny, his eyes glazed with pain and hate. He clung to his wounded hand, the flesh raw and oozing. "What the hell's the matter with you?" he shouted to the others. "Take the bitch! Just make sure you don't mess her up too much!" He pointed at Brett. "We don't need him."

Destiny groaned. The energy flared and spun like a vortex from her body. A pungent odor of ozone filled the air. Vials exploded. Bottles fell off the violently rattling shelves. The small shop trembled under her power. All the weapons glowed and transformed into molten masses. The thugs screamed as they struggled to rub the scalding metal from their hands. Despite their agony they advanced like mindless automatons, a steady stream of obscenities spewing from their mouths.

"Whore! You'll suffer for this! You'll tell us what we want to know and then we'll rip you apart one piece at a time," the leader growled. He lunged for her but was seized in mid-stride and repeatedly battered against the floor. Screaming, he grabbed his head. "Stop! Stop her! The bitch is killing me!"

The others were helplessly rooted to the floor, unable to look away when their companion's head exploded. "Oh my God," one of them uttered. "She's a fucking demon!" Spurred by the grisly sight, they tried to advance toward Destiny. A wave of energy engulfed them. They yelped like wounded dogs as it scalded their flesh. Enraged, they lunged for Destiny. Brett moved to protect her, but she broke abruptly from her trance and glared at them with terrible intensity.

The attackers struggled to outpace the pursuing energy but the force was too powerful. One after another they were hurled through the shattered door, the jagged shards of glass still embedded in the frame shredding their battered flesh. Mortally wounded, they struggled to rise and crawl to safety, but finally collapsed onto the crimson-stained snow.

Brett found his voice and embraced Destiny. "My God, Destiny, are you okay?"

She struggled out of the trance that had overwhelmed her. Almost immediately the energy dissipated, leaving a swathe of destruction in its wake. Horror filled her eyes and her stomach lurched as she gazed at the mutilated body on the blood-soaked floor. "Brett—what the hell happened here?"

"You don't know?"

"No. I only remember being very angry. I've never felt such fury in my life. Then everything went dark. I felt something flow from me, something very powerful, but that was all—" She glanced once more at the body. "He was going to kill Li."

"He was going to kill all of us except you. You saved our lives, Destiny."

"I—wish I could remember—"

"Maybe it's better that you don't. Now I understand the powers you possess."

She felt the blood drain from her face as she surveyed the carnage. "My God. This is unbelievable—I did all this? I could barely kill a rat let alone a human being. No, I couldn't have done this—"

Concerned at the shock and terror that filled her eyes, Brett said in a soothing voice, "We'll talk about it later. We'd better get out of here in case more of them come." He called out to Li. "Li, are you okay?"

Li, disheveled but unhurt, shuffled from the back room. "Li fine. No worry about Li. Woman much power. Li know. Now you must go. Li must go. Time is come. Portal must open."

"You know about the portal?" Brett asked.

"Yes. Li know. It written in ancient Chinese legend. Li give woman medicine to make calm." Quickly he turned and after rummaging through the broken bottles on the shelves behind him he removed an intact bottle and sighed with satisfaction. He poured some of its contents into a delicate porcelain teacup and walked to the stove that had somehow survived the psychic onslaught. After pouring some of the brewing herbal tea into the cup he held it to Destiny's lips. "Drink. You must drink."

She gazed at Li's benevolent mauve aura. He was a chosen one and she knew she could trust him. Sipping the soothingly warm liquid, her eyes half closed as it slipped down her throat and calmed her trembling body. "I'm sorry. I don't know what happened. I would never kill anyone." She didn't know what Li had given her to drink, but whatever it was eased her shattered nerves.

"We'd better get out of here," Brett said. "If they knew we were coming here, others may be on their way."

"You must have this," Li said and reached under the counter. He handed Destiny an ancient, beautifully filigreed vial inlaid with silver. "This much old. Do not open. Very important."

"Thank you," she mumbled, clasping the vial in her hand.

"You take bottle, too. Ten drops in tea and she be fine," Li said and handed Brett the brown bottle of herbal elixir.

"Thanks. Can we give you a ride?" he asked while he stuck the bottle into his jacket pocket.

"No. Li must leave for final journey. Go now. We meet again soon."

Brett led Destiny from the shop. She gasped when she spotted the mutilated bodies sprawled in the snow.

"They were scum," he said while placing a protective arm around her and pulling her tight against him. "Don't even waste your thoughts on them."

"I know," she murmured, "but to massacre them like this—"

They hurried to the Jeep. Brett had barely pulled away when he noticed Destiny's eyelids droop. He pulled over and gently checked her eyes but she was not in shock. He figured the elixir was probably an herbal sleeping draught. With a sigh, he turned back. "All fun and games," he muttered.

The drive back to Burnaby was long and tedious. Snow rained a dull curtain and created a dismal twilight that seemed to suck the very spirit from him. Rather than plod along surface roads, he decided to chance the freeway. It was surprisingly in better shape, though he still made painfully slow progress. He kept his eye on the gauges. Once it was realized that he had defected from the force without notice, his gasoline privileges would be revoked. He felt a pang of guilt for his actions and knew his overtaxed colleagues would sorely feel his absence, but after witnessing the harrowing events at Li's, he realized Destiny's mission had to take precedence.

She was still fast asleep when finally he pulled into the garage of his apartment complex. He lifted her from the seat and carried her inside to the couch. Not even the removal of her jacket and boots woke her. Quickly he covered her with blankets and returned to the Jeep to fetch their gear.

After he removed his own snow gear he stoked a fire and sat beside Destiny, protectively placing his arms around her. Thoughtfully he gazed down at her sleeping form.

"This is not the last of it," a voice spoke near his ear.

He swiveled to see the speaker but saw nothing.

"Take good care of her," the voice said.

"I wasn't much use today," he answered. "She took care of us all."

"Yes, but soon she will need you. For now, we will erase the memory of the horror from her mind while she sleeps. Please do not speak of it again until she is ready to accept the responsibility of her powers."

"Thanks," he mumbled, his gaze fixed on the crackling fire. Though fatigue sapped him, he could not clear his mind of the disturbing events at Li's. For a long time, he communed with the flames as though seeking answers in their ever-shifting depths—

***

CHAPTER FOURTEEN

Chris put his empty cup on the sink. "That was delicious coffee, honey. I heard you up and about last night. What happened?"

"Lisa is very ill and so are the two men. I don't know, Chris," Sarah said. "It doesn't look good. I'm beginning to fear the worst."

"Maybe you should call Dr Allan."

She shook her head. "He does his best, but a man his age can't cope with all the sick. Don't forget he's even older than we are. He only came out of retirement because there's such a shortage of doctors."

"What about the other surviving doctor? You could try him."

"Well, we have to do something. I'll call him," she said while wiping her hands on her apron. She walked into the living room and as she picked up the phone heard a vehicle pull up outside. Anticipating a visit from Destiny, she quickly ran to the window. She wiped the pane with her sleeve and peered through the frosty glass. As soon as she withdrew new frost formed on the small patch.

"Good Lord, why would Father Delaney venture out in this weather, Chris?" she called out to Chris who was busy pottering in the kitchen.

Chris hurried into the living room and scraped at the frost on the windows. "I don't know. It must be something urgent. I'll go let him in," he said, rushing to the foyer.

A few minutes later Father Delaney came in. Tall and imposing in his heavy winter coat, his weathered face flushed from the bitter cold, sharp blue eyes echoed the smile on his face. In his arms he carried what looked like a bundle of blankets. "Morning, Sarah."

"Morning, Father. You're up and about early. What brings you out on a day like this?" she asked as she placed a mug of steaming coffee on a side table for him.

"This," he answered and gently set the bundle of blankets on the couch. Kneeling before it, he opened up the top of the blanket to reveal a cherubic little face framed by silvery blond hair.

Sarah eyed the priest questioningly. "She's precious, Father." She knelt by the couch and lovingly stroked the little girl's cool cheek. Chris approached and stood behind Sarah while she murmured to the child. "Hi, sweetheart, what's your name?"

Two china blue eyes gazed back at her. She smiled faintly but did not respond.

"She doesn't speak English, Sarah," Father Delaney said, pausing to sip the coffee. "We know her name is Angelica Peragine. She arrived on a refugee flight from Italy just two days ago. I placed her with Bob and Annie Gill, but Annie has since fallen ill from the scourge."

Sarah's fingers tightened against the blanket. "Is Annie going to be all right?"

The spark faded from Father Delaney's eyes as he shook his head. "Breast cancer. I pray for her recovery, but it appears she has a familial history—"

Sarah felt lightheaded for a moment but said nothing as she thought of the three ill people upstairs. Lisa was in bed with a raging fever and the two elderly men had been up all night vomiting blood.

"I'm afraid I've run out of younger foster families willing to take in a child," Delaney continued. "I know this is an imposition, but do you think you could temporarily take care of Angelica?"

Without hesitating Sarah said, "Of course. She'll make a wonderful companion for Candy. Need you even ask?"

Chris nodded his agreement. "Sarah's still pretty chirpy for her age, Father. After all, the little girl isn't a baby anymore. She'll certainly brighten up our lives some."

Delaney nodded. "Good. Annie sent some clothes along. We have donated clothing at the church so when the weather clears perhaps you can come and look through the bags and find some more clothing and toys for her."

Sarah clasped Angelica's hand. The child's grip was surprisingly firm, the intensity in her fathomless blue eyes almost hypnotic. She felt a pleasant warmth trickle into her flesh and answered distractedly, "That's no problem, Father. I kept all of Destiny's old things in the attic." She reluctantly disengaged her hand from Angelica's grasp and rose. "You look exhausted, Father. Have you eaten today?"

The old priest sighed and set down his empty cup. "Thanks for asking, Sarah. I've eaten but so many are in need of help and food that I almost feel guilty when I have a meal. I'm busy from morning till late at night. He shook his head wearily. "It never ends. New faces appear at the church doors each morning and the look of hopelessness and despair in their eyes always moves me to tears. There are times I wonder how I can cope with all the needy."

Chris nodded knowingly. "Sometimes I wonder why the innocent must suffer. It doesn't seem right. Even now, I imagine those of power and privilege are riding through this with relative ease."

"It isn't right," said Father Delaney. "Who are those responsible? Have they also reaped what they've sown? Does justice even exist anymore? I am almost ashamed to admit that there have been times when I've questioned my own faith."

"We all have, Father," Chris said. "I don't think we'd be human if we didn't."

Sarah gazed tenderly at Angelica. "Our home is quite large and we have another bedroom so if you need shelter for someone, please let us know? We're always happy to help. And there's always the attic—"

"I appreciate that, Sarah. I'll keep your kind offer in mind. If only the younger generation would understand the need of the homeless."

"Many of them are too wrapped up in their own lives and haven't thought about tomorrow. Those in the city who live alone like our Destiny are afraid to take anyone in. As for the younger generation out here in the country, well, what can I say? For most, surviving another day is all that matters. I'm thankful my larder is well stocked. We'll be fine for quite a while. And now my guests and Angelica, too," she said knowing full well that her young protégée would probably stay longer than just a few weeks. "If you need any canned goods you'll tell me, won't you?"

"We always need food, Sarah. The church basement is overflowing with the homeless and my staff can hardly keep up with meal preparation. Soup is the main nourishment at the moment. The church must abide by the rationing laws like everyone else."

Without a word, Sarah disappeared to the kitchen. Quickly, she unlocked the door to the basement stairs leading to her huge pantry. The shelves were double stacked with canned, dried and preserved goods. Large plastic bins piled with potatoes and root vegetables lined the sturdy walls. Bags of flour, rice, cornmeal and beans were neatly stacked beneath the shelves. From the ceiling hung dried herbs and slabs of home smoked bacon, hams and sausages that filled the pantry with a delectable aroma.

She filled a large paper bag with food items she thought the church could use and brought it upstairs to the living room. "Father, here are some things for you. I'll do some baking this week and Chris will bring it to the church. I suppose bread is what's mainly needed?"

Delaney glanced into the bag. "Yes. Bread and jams but also items we can use to make soup, chili, stews and such. At least one warm meal a day is critical in weather like this." His eyes glowed with gratitude as he tugged at a smoked ham and sniffed it. "Sarah, this smells delicious. I can't remember the last time I— Thank you, my dear. You have a kind heart. Most people can't spare anything. This ham will make the best soup anyone's had for a long time."

She shook her head in amazement. "Well, you can thank Chris for that food dehydrator he bought me for Christmas years ago. I protested at the time because I thought I'd never use it, but I started playing with it. I dried anything and everything I could possibly think of, and now we're reaping the benefits of all the fruit and soup vegetables I dried before all this started. And Chris went overboard with the smokehouse he built." She paused, her gaze momentarily distant. "You see, we had a premonition about these times. So, shortly after the war, he butchered most of our pigs. He salted and smoked enough sausages, bacon and ham to feed an army.

I got mad at him because I thought we'd never eat it all. I must warn you, though, they're heavily salted or they'd never have lasted this long."

"Besides," Chris said, "shouldn't we stand by each other in times like these? I don't understand how we could be the only ones with food to spare. What about the other farmers in the community? I'm sure their larders are filled, like ours."

Father Delaney nodded. "I agree, Chris. And yes, I know quite a few farmers with overflowing larders. But I'm afraid under such circumstances it quickly becomes every man for himself. Selfishness rages as badly as the scourge and is probably just as impossible to eradicate. As for the salt content—I think it hardly matters. Even salt has become a rare commodity." He turned to Sarah. "How is Destiny? I've heard such horrors about the city—all that looting and unrest, people breaking into homes and killing for food. It's become dangerous just to walk the streets anymore."

Sarah sighed. "I worry about her all the time, Father, but she seems to be doing fine, considering. Destiny has met a young man and it looks serious. Maybe some day we'll even have a wedding," she said with a smile.

"Now that would be nice," Father Delaney said wistfully. "I haven't presided over a wedding in longer than I care to remember."

Sarah's attention was drawn to Angelica lying quietly on the couch. Though the child remained motionless, she could not help but flinch from the aura of peace that emanated from the child.

"By the way, Father, did the church receive any damage yesterday from the earthquake?"

Delaney's eyebrows shot up. "Earthquake? I didn't feel anything, nor has anyone reported one."

"That's strange," Chris said. "Our house almost shook off its foundations. We haven't had such a strong quake in quite a while. There was nothing on the news about it."

"With everything going on at the church, I probably didn't even notice a tremor," Father Delaney said. "Maybe you're right on top of a fault line. Well, I must be off. Chris and Sarah, I thank you from the bottom of my heart. May God bless you."

Chris saw the priest to the door while Sarah approached Angelica. The child scrambled out of the blankets and suddenly sat up, her hair cascading in a shimmering veil down her back. Sarah gasped at her ethereal beauty and extended her hand. "She could be Destiny's younger sister," she murmured. Without a word, Angelica slipped off the couch and firmly grasped her fingers. The contact was pleasantly warm and electric. As they walked to the kitchen, Sarah tried to talk to her. "Angelica, after you've had something to eat we'll give you a nice hot bath and go up to the attic to find you some of Destiny's old clothes and toys. Would you like that?"

The child gazed at her with large luminous eyes. Sarah thought she heard the whisper of a voice, but could not be sure. "I must call Destiny and tell her about you. She's my daughter and has pretty blond hair, just like you," she told Angelica while she reconstituted some powdered milk. "I know she'll be delighted to meet you."

When Sarah mentioned her daughter's name again, Angelica's eyes lit up. A broad smile transformed her lovely face and her actions became animated. "Si. Destino!" she said as she accepted the glass of milk. "Destino—Lei Puo salvaci noi."

"I don't understand Italian, but I'd swear she just said Destiny's name," Sarah said. "How odd."

***

CHAPTER FIFTEEN

The constant ringing of the phone jarred them both awake. Destiny sat up with a start and looked around the shadowy room lit only by dying embers and a single table lamp. Brett bolted upright, his muscles stiff from having slept on the couch in an awkward fetal position. He grabbed the phone and stifled a yawn.

"Hello?"

"Brett? This is Sarah, Destiny's mother. Is she there?"

"Yes, I'll get her for you. How are you doing?"

"We're just fine. We haven't had another tremor, thank goodness! Though I'm really surprised the news never reported it."

"Well, you know how understaffed the radio station is," Brett said guardedly. "Probably too much going on at once." As he handed the phone to Destiny, he remembered the voices and realized they had probably erased the worst memories of the event from her parents' minds as well.

"Hi, Mom," Destiny said sleepily.

"Hi, honey. Look, I've got something to tell you. Father Delaney came round yesterday with one of the refugee orphans the church was able to place. Well, it seems that the foster family can't take her in now. You remember Mrs. Gill? I'm sorry to say she's come down with the scourge." She paused at Destiny's sharp intake of breath. "Father Delaney asked if we would take her in instead. Well, after one look at her you'd understand our reasons. If I've ever seen an angel incarnate it's in the form of that little girl. Now, she's an Italian refugee, so she doesn't speak any English. When the roads are cleared is it possible for you and Brett to come and visit?"

Destiny smiled at the enthusiasm in her mother's voice. "I can't say I'm surprised you took her in, Mom. What's she like?"

"She's about seven or eight, and absolutely the sweetest thing you've ever seen. The child is the absolute image of you at that age. Very shy and quiet, but those eyes—it's like she looks into your soul. I've never met a child like her."

A shudder suddenly coursed through Destiny as a startlingly clear image of the child popped into her head. "Yes—she's indeed special. Well, at least she'll be company for little Candy. Children manage to play together no matter what language they speak."

She heard Sarah's frustrated sigh.

"I'm sorry to say Candy hasn't been well, Destiny. I'm not sure if the little girl is pining for her mother, or if she's manifesting symptoms of the scourge. Lisa's quite ill and bedridden. In fact, it seems that all our guests are showing signs of the scourge. Your father and I are doing everything possible but it's a losing battle. Maybe this little girl will brighten Candy's days. Her name is Angelica. It quite suits her, but you'll see for yourself. Do you think you can make it?"

"We'll try, Mom, but I can't guarantee anything. The roads are horrendous at the moment and according to the weather forecast, they're expecting more snow."

"I know. But try, will you? There's something about this child. I can't explain it, but somehow I feel she belongs with us."

Destiny wanted to agree but kept silent. "Okay. We'll see how it goes. How are you and Dad doing?"

"Well, yesterday was a bit of an ordeal but we've been through worse. Thanks for helping us clean up. I certainly hope we don't have any more tremors or I'll have to get a potter's wheel and start making some new crockery."

Destiny couldn't help but smile at her mother's indomitable spirit. Despite what must have been a frightening experience for her, Sarah never let adversity get her down.

"You were always good with your hands," Destiny said. "Oh, by the way, the turkey's been behaving. The sandwiches were delicious."

Sarah chuckled. "What an odd thing to say. What about your young man? Has he been behaving?"

Destiny found herself caught off-guard by her mother's candor.

"He's different from the rest, you know," Sarah said. "Your father and I both realized it the moment we met him. Hang onto this one, Destiny. You may not find another like him."

"Ah—yes. I will. I mean—I guess I, too, realize he's special, not to mention handsome, good-natured and considerate. I suppose when you're alone so much, you stop looking after a while and get used to your own company. I just wasn't expecting to meet anyone."

"Well, don't let this one slip away. The two of you belong together. I've never been so sure of anything before."

Destiny considered what the voices had told her. "Don't worry, Mom. I won't. Anyway, I've got to go. Give Dad a kiss for me."

She said good-bye and hung up. Thoughtfully, she turned to Brett. "Strange, Mom doesn't remember too much about yesterday."

"Probably just as well."

Destiny turned to the bag on the coffee table and dug through it. The silver inlaid vial gleamed in her hand as she fingered the delicate filigree. "At least we found Li. That's a start."

"I wonder what the vial is for," Brett said, recalling the voice's assurance about erasing the memory of yesterday. "It certainly looks valuable. What did your mother have to say?"

"She and Dad have taken in an Italian orphan. Her name is Angelica. She doesn't speak English. Mom wants us to come and meet her."

"Is that a good idea? Next time someone could get hurt."

"I know. I was thinking the same thing, but—"

Vigorous knocking at the door interrupted them. "Are you expecting anyone?" she asked.

Brett shook his head. "You're the first visitor I've had in quite a while." He rose and started toward the door.

Destiny watched his movements slow to an almost dreamlike crawl. Suddenly an overwhelming sense of danger surged through her. She bolted from the couch and ran toward him. "Brett, don't open it!" she cried. "It's not—"

Her warning came too late as he opened the door. He turned to her with a smile. "It's okay, Destiny. Just some of my colleagues who dropped by to celebrate Christmas with us."

She stared at the five officers hustling through the door. All were engulfed in a shimmering green haze, the coldness in their eyes soulless like a shark's. She tried to catch Brett's gaze, but he did not notice her frown and slight shake of her head.

"Destiny, I'd like you to meet Roger. We attended the police academy together. And this is Martin. He works street patrol. He and I have gone through—"

The door slammed shut behind the last officer. Brett cast the culprit a surprised look. "Easy on the noise, Dave. The walls are like paper in this place."

Martin pulled his gun from the holster and leveled it at Brett. "Okay, enough small talk. Where is it?"

Brett's smile faded as the weapon gleamed in the subdued light. "Okay, guys, a joke's a joke, but this is going too far. You know better than to pull a prank like that."

"Shut up and sit down," Roger barked. He withdrew his weapon and aimed it at Destiny. "Where is it?"

"I don't know what you're talking about," she said, edging toward Brett. "I'm just visiting."

"Don't fuck with me, pretty lady," Roger hissed. "You know damn well what I'm talking about. Now hand it over!"

Flushed with anger, Brett approached his friends. "Roger, Martin, what the hell's the matter with you guys? You're on duty. Surely you haven't been dipping into—"

"Shut up, Brett," Roger said, brutally slamming the revolver into Brett's ribs. Brett winced but said nothing. "If you have any feelings for your girlfriend here, I suggest you tell her to give us what we want. Now!"

Brett moved to seize the gun but instantly froze when Roger cocked the weapon. The others closed formation around them and raised their weapons. Brett felt confused and angrily gazed at each of the faces he thought he knew.

Destiny's eyes glittered as she faced Roger. His angular face shone an unhealthy ruddy glow; his pale eyes wide and distended. Unruly strands of sandy hair poked from the hood of his soiled blue parka. Her nostrils quivered at the rank odor emanating from his stocky body. "I told you I don't know what you're talking about," she said calmly. "What could I possibly have? I don't even have a place to call my own."

Brett glanced sideways at her. "Christ, I'm sorry, Destiny," he whispered. "I know these men well and this isn't—"

"It's okay, Brett. You don't have to apologize. I know who they are." She watched his eyes widen as realization sunk in.

Roger poked the weapon deeper into Brett's ribs and turned to face Destiny. "Your mouth is still spewing crap. Be cooperative and hand over the information or you can kiss your boyfriend here goodnight. Where's the fucking disc?"

Brett flinched. Roger turned on him with a rabid expression not unlike the men in Li's shop. "Be smart and stay out of this, okay? We have no quarrel with you. All we want is the disc with the information. Convince the bitch to give it to us and we'll get the hell out of here."

"Brett, don't listen to him. He'll kill you no matter what I do."

Brett turned to face Roger. He looked into his friend's eyes and saw only darkness. Whatever humanity had existed within them had been devoured. He swallowed as an unpleasant chill emanated from Roger. "Destiny, give them the disc."

"But—"

"Just give it to them and that'll be the end of it."

She grasped his meaning and rose from the couch. Roger kept his gun trained on her while she walked to the computer and ejected the disc from the drive. Gratified now that she had not yet labeled it, she held it out to him. Roger snatched the disc and held it out to Martin.

"Put it in the computer and check it out. The bitch could be giving you a list of porno websites for all you know."

"Okay," Martin snapped. "Keep your gun on them."

Roger waved Destiny aside as Martin slipped the disc into the drive but the computer wouldn't start.

Gesturing impatiently, Roger cocked the gun and pressed it against Brett's temple. "What's the password to start the computer?" When Brett didn't answer, he pulled a switchblade from his pocket and waved it toward Destiny. "I'll carve her face like a jack o'lantern if you don't tell me the—"

Brett hesitated until Roger moved a step closer to Destiny

while keeping the gun trained on Brett. "The dog's name. He died a long time ago — I can't remember it right now," he told Roger.

"Murphy," Martin said. He sank onto the chair, typed the password and stared at the flashing screen. "I remember the damn mutt. Always barked his face off when we stopped by. He scowled at the unresponsive screen. "What's the password for the disc?"

"It doesn't have one," Destiny answered.

Roger cursed under his breath. "Are you fucking stupid, man? Type in a-colon-slash. That will bring it up."

"Oh, yeah," Martin said and typed it. Within seconds the screen displayed a window filled with programming language. "Is this it?"

"Does it have a symbol?" Roger asked, his bloodshot eyes straying to the screen, searching for a sign, a symbol, anything that would indicate they had the correct program. "Damn, I don't see anything. If only I knew what to look for — I don't even know if it's a disc we need. She has the information so it has to be somewhere. They told me she carries it—"

Brett took advantage of the moment. His foot shot out and kicked the gun from Roger's hand. At the same time he lunged for Martin, his eye on the other officers who stood vacantly watching like mannequins. He hoped Destiny was wrong about his friends and that they would assist him, but they merely scrambled to Martin and Roger's aid and within moments had Brett face down on the floor with his wrists and ankles securely cuffed.

"Wrong disc, bitch!" Roger snarled when he didn't see anything unusual on the screen. " Now where's the right one?"

Destiny hardly heard his words. When she saw one of the men kick Brett and punch him hard in the stomach until he doubled over in pain a red haze floated before her eyes. She moaned and felt her body go limp. In her mind she saw the energy flare from the skull and engulf her. As her eyes rolled back to reveal the whites a roiling aura of energy shot from her convulsing body and tossed the men like feathers. Two of them knocked heads while the others rolled around the room. They landed heavily, toppling furniture and ornaments.

Cursing and shouting, oblivious to their injuries, they scrambled for their fallen guns only to pull back as the weapons glowed white hot and disintegrated into a powdery ash. Their faces were so distorted by the darkness that had subjugated them they no longer looked human.

A wraith of pure energy surged toward the men and penetrated their foreheads. They fell to the floor in agony as their eyes bulged from their sockets and their tongues protruded. Writhing, they grasped their necks to prevent from strangling. Blood seeped from their orifices, bones cracked and the air stank of scorched flesh. Though only minutes had elapsed, it seemed more like an eternity to Brett before the room was finally quiet.

Destiny's body convulsed as she emerged from her trance. She sank onto the couch, exhausted and deathly pale, unable to stem a flow of tears. The sight spurred Brett into action. Pleased that the men had cuffed his hands in front, he rolled toward one of the bodies and maneuvered the keys from his belt clip. After he removed the cuffs he quickly rushed to Destiny who stared listlessly at the carnage.

"Destiny, lie down. I'll get you something to drink," he said while he eased her back onto the couch. It would take too long to make the tea Li had given them so he quickly fetched a cup of milk from the kitchen and added a few drops of the potion from the bottle of herbal elixir. He held the cup against her pale lips. When she didn't drink, he held her head back and poured a small amount of liquid into her mouth. She swallowed unresistingly while her eyes focused on a point beyond his shoulder. Within seconds she fell into a sound sleep.

Gently, he kissed her on the forehead and stood to survey the five bodies. His apartment resembled a slaughterhouse and the reek of tainted blood was nauseating. He frowned at the thought that men he considered his friends could become so corrupt. *Where will this all end?* he thought grimly. *How much more will we have to endure?*

"This is only the beginning," the voice said.

Brett angrily turned in the direction of the voice. "Why do we have to be subjected to these attacks? Can't you protect us?"

"No harm will come to you. Destiny has all the powers necessary to protect you both."

"But the killing—those men were my colleagues, my friends. I can't believe they would do something like this."

"They were your friends once, Brett. But they were never your true friends. When the Eletarii came, they found many willing recruits among humanity simply by exploiting the darkness within their minds. Your friends became eager servants and took orders from their superiors just as we instruct you and Destiny."

"Orders from who? Or what? I don't understand who the players are in this crazy game!"

"Soon you will understand. Now you must leave this place and never return. It is time to start your journey."

"In this weather? You've got to be crazy! We'll never make it through the snow."

"Pack whatever provisions are necessary for Destiny and yourself. Take the bag that contains the skull, the music box and the vial. Keep it with you at all times. Do not let it out of your sight. Dress warmly, for tomorrow you must begin your journey. There will be nothing where you will travel. Go now. It is no longer safe here."

"Where do we go?" Brett asked. "Where is it safe? Is there such a place anymore? Will we be hunted like animals?"

"It is not safe anywhere. That is why you must move on and never stay overly long in one place until you reach your destination. We will accompany you. Please hurry. We must leave you now. Our energy fades—"

"Come back! Dammit, I want to know more!"

"Hurry," the voice echoed as it faded to silence.

Frustrated, Brett glanced at Destiny. "Well, Destiny, what do we do now? Do I pack, put you in the car and go?" He ran his fingers through his hair. "Where? How far can we drive in this weather?"

Indecisively, he paced the floor. He wished she would wake, but realized that she would probably sleep for hours and awaken with no memory of the incident.

"The farm—we could at least hide there for a few hours until she wakes and then we can talk," he mused. "No, we can't go there. Look what happened the last time when we—"

"Go to the farm," the voice told him. "You will be safe there for the time being."

"Wait a minute. Earlier you told us—"

"Learn to trust, Brett."

Exasperated and confused, he walked to the bedroom and

tore off his blood-splattered clothes. He changed into thermal underwear, clean jeans and sweater and quickly packed whatever provisions he thought they would need. He looked around the apartment a last time and knelt to stroke the dusty neck of his guitar. "Well, I guess this is it. I wonder if I'll ever see you again."

After checking on Destiny, he loaded the luggage into the Jeep, started it and turned the heat to maximum. Aware that others might be waiting to hear from the officers, he rushed back to the apartment. Destiny slept soundly as he pulled off her soiled sweatshirt and pants. For a moment he gazed down at her slender body. She looked so fragile and vulnerable, unaware for the moment of the past or future.

Feeling a tremendous surge of protectiveness, he quickly dressed her in clean sweats and a warm sweater, slipped on her jacket and boots and wrapped her in some blankets. He slung the canvas bag over his shoulder, picked her up and carried her out to the Jeep. After fastening the seat belt around her, he jumped into the driver's seat and roared off. Even though he was tempted to look back as the garage doors that painfully rattled closed behind him, he resisted the urge.

Snow drifted in desultory sheets as he pulled into the street. A permanent twilight had settled in and leeched every element of life from the surrounding landscape. Apart from the muffled drone of road crews, the city seemed little more than a corpse shrouded beneath a veil of silent despair.

He shook his head and headed down the deserted street toward the highway.

***

CHAPTER SIXTEEN

Though the highway had been repeatedly plowed and salted, the relentless snow soon piled up and even with chains on the tires, driving was almost impossible. Brett had given up glancing in the rearview mirror to check if they were being followed, as it seemed the elementals found them wherever they were. He wondered if, like Destiny, they had a talisman to help them, like the skull, and almost smiled at the irony of how his life had so dramatically changed within a matter of days.

"As if things could possibly get worse," he murmured.

Destiny did not sleep as long as he expected. After about an hour on the highway, she stirred and suddenly sat up. "How did I get in the car? Where are we going?" she asked, groggily staring at the lifeless scenery.

He smiled grimly without taking his eyes off the road. "You were asleep. The voice told me to leave and never return to my place. For lack of a better place to go, I'm taking you to the farm."

Destiny struggled out of the blankets. "God, it's warm. Why did I fall asleep? I don't remember being that tired. Did your friends go?"

Brett pretended to check the mirrors. "Yes—I persuaded them to think about what they were getting into. I—figured common sense would prevail in the end. Guess it's just a policeman's training. You must have been exhausted from your ordeal at the shop yesterday and you drifted off on the couch."

"But why did the voice tell us to leave?"

Brett hesitated. "Because—others would find us there."

She shuddered. "Those men were evil incarnate. I sensed it even before I saw them."

"It's hard for me to imagine such a thing," he said. "Those men were once my friends. We attended the police academy together. I would have trusted each one of them with my life. I couldn't believe how much they've changed. They were like strangers—I barely recognized them."

"I'm sorry," she said with a sigh. "It must be hard for you to accept such a betrayal. I suppose we can't trust anyone anymore. I'm wondering about my own friends now. I haven't heard from them in a while. Then again, I never called to let them know I moved to your apartment. At one time I never would have considered my girlfriends capable of evil, but now—who really knows? The world isn't the same anymore. Values we used to consider important are meaningless."

"Not all meaningless," he said, squeezing her hand. "You've certainly restored my faith in love and friendship."

Destiny smiled. "And hope."

As Brett drove, she silently pondered recent events. "You know, I should be terrified. The voices told you that we would be pursued. How can I feel so calm after everything that's happened?"

"I don't know. I feel apprehensive, but not really terrified. I found it all difficult to accept but the voice told me to concentrate and remember and everything would become clear. I just haven't had time to focus yet."

"What do you think is going to happen to us? I find it difficult to imagine what this mission is all about, let alone that we're some kind of messiahs."

"I wish I knew, Destiny. The best we can do is take one day at a time. I guess we're street people now—out of a job and no place to go. We can't stay at the farm for long. It's too dangerous."

"I was thinking the same. Look what happened on Christmas day." She sat upright suddenly. "Did you remember to bring the skull and the music box?"

"Yes, and the vial."

"Good," she sighed and leaned her head against the window. "You know, I really don't think it's a good idea to go to the farm. Maybe we should stop at a motel. I don't want to endanger my parents. It's too risky. The elementals will find us."

"No!" a firm voice said clearly drowning out the drone of the engine. "You must go to the farm. Where there are three, the legion of light can enter and protect you from the threat of evil."

Startled, Brett pulled over to the shoulder. "Three?"

"Yes. The pure and innocent are most powerful. You must visit the farm and remain there until we contact you again. Go now. Your path is clear."

The voice faded. Brett took Destiny in his arms for a moment. "We'll have to trust them," he said while cradling her head against his cheek. "God knows I'd rather keep on driving and never look back, but there's nothing else we can do."

She stared pensively at the dismal scenery. "I didn't think it could get any worse, but if the voices are right, then the worst is yet to come. It seems we have no choice. Then again, if there's even a hint of a better future for us somewhere, anywhere — I'm willing to try."

Brett pulled away. "There's no turning back for either of us now. We'd better drive on. It's starting to snow again. It never stops, does it?"

"Humanity's tears," she said, looking at the leaden flakes drifting from the sky.

***

Twilight had already descended when they drove through the farm gates. The Jeep crept along the driveway, an occasional rattle of protest rising from beneath the hood. Destiny noticed that her father had plowed the winding drive but snow was already settling and another foot had accumulated. Brett's nose was almost pressed against the windshield in as he tried to peer through the ice that caked it like sugar frosting, the overworked wipers doing little more than reducing it to slush. The snowfall was deteriorating into a blizzard, reducing visibility to inches and buffeting the vehicle like a toy. Only the beckoning lights from the farm guided them through the snow.

A sigh of relief escaped his lips when he pulled up near the barn. "We need a Snow Cat for this kind of weather."

"Let's get inside," Destiny said. "I can feel the cold already. Why don't you park inside the barn before it gets snowed in?"

"Okay, you go into the house and I'll take care of it."

"No. I'll help you. The doors will be hard to open." She jumped out before he could protest.

Their faces numbed as they fought against the freezing gale to open the barn doors. To prop them open, they had to pile snow against them. Brett quickly drove into the barn. A generator buzzed softly in the corner for the heat lamps in the chicken pen. "Let's unload the Jeep now," he said. Carrying their belongings, they hurried through the doors and kicked aside the snow they had piled against them and laboriously pulled them shut.

***

Sarah glanced up from her knitting as the knocker pounded against the front door several times. "Who on earth could that be, Chris? No one in their right mind would venture out in this storm."

Seated in an armchair by the cheerfully crackling fire Chris set his book down reluctantly. "I'll go and see," he said and left the room to answer the door. "My God!" he exclaimed when he saw his daughter and Brett huddled by the door, their teeth chattering as they dusted snow and ice from their parkas. "Get inside, you two!" He ushered them inside and slammed the door shut. "Sarah, come and see what the storm blew in!"

Heedless of the ice that mantled her daughter's parka, Sarah embraced Destiny. "I'm so glad to see you, but why on earth didn't you wait until the storm was over? It was madness to travel in these conditions."

Brett helped Destiny out of her parka. Even though she wore ski gloves, her hands were numb from the cold as she stiffly removed them. He rubbed them between his own.

"When we left Burnaby the storm hadn't begun yet. It took us by surprise," Destiny said.

"Well, come on in and warm yourselves by the fire. What a

shame Angelica's in bed now," Sarah said as she vanished into the kitchen. "I've got some hot barley soup to warm you up," she called out to them.

"That sounds good," Brett replied. He crouched by the fireplace and vigorously rubbed his hands.

Chris returned to his armchair, his old corncob pipe resting on a dish beside him. He picked it up and lit it. A pleasant aroma of herbal tobacco wafted around the room. "How long are you staying?"

"I don't know, Dad. Not that long, I'm afraid," Destiny said while she joined Brett. "Where is everybody?"

Sarah returned to the knitting she had left on the couch. "In bed. The two men haven't been able to keep any food down and Lisa has a high fever. Little Candy's losing weight."

Destiny's head pivoted sharply toward Sarah. "She's not—"

Sarah didn't miss a stitch as her knitting needles busily clicked. "Dr. Allan's assistant, Dr. Moran, managed to stop by after I placed an emergency call. I'm afraid the diagnosis wasn't very good, Destiny. She is manifesting the scourge—the autism I always suspected the child suffered from is worsening. She is so withdrawn and listless I have to spoon-feed her. If that isn't enough, Lisa's stubborn fever could leave her brain damaged and the two gentlemen appear to have a serious intestinal disorder. I dread to think what might happen if Lisa goes before Candy."

The implications lingered heavily in the air. A heavy silence ensued. Destiny sipped the aromatic soup and listened to the needles clicking. The comforting sound, the cozy image of it all, made her acutely nostalgic. Memories burst to the surface of her mind like rising bubbles as she recalled the happy child she had once been. When sanity still ruled the world during her teen years, she would often come home from dates to find her mother knitting and her father reading and smoking his pipe, waiting for her. During the winter, the fireplace would always be lit. In the warmer seasons, her mother would use the fireplace to display for her wonderful dried flower arrangements.

The recollection almost made her gasp, as she briefly tasted the freedom she so long ago enjoyed. Somehow it seemed incredible that her only worries had revolved around what to wear and whether a boyfriend would call her again. She sighed.

They had just finished the warming soup when a musical voice rose from the doorway.

"Buona sera, Destino."

Chris's pipe almost fell from his lips as he gazed at the child in the doorway. "I'll be damned. It almost sounds like your name, Destiny. She's hardly spoken a word since she's been here."

Destiny gazed transfixed at the little girl. She recognized the long, white nightie as one of her old ones and smiled that her mother had kept her childhood clothes. An angelic vision gazed back at her. Large innocent blue eyes complemented an ethereal face framed by silver blond hair. It cascaded in thick, glossy waves over her petite shoulders and down her back. Destiny smiled and was surprised when Angelica ran toward her and hurled herself into her arms. She had recognized the greeting and whispered in response, "Buona sera, Angelica."

Two delicate arms wound around Destiny's neck and hugged her tightly. Rosebud lips pressed a kiss on her cheek and Angelica rested her face against Destiny's.

Destiny suddenly felt intense warmth, a powerful maternal bonding, as if she'd known this child before. The sensation was almost electric and raised gooseflesh all over her body. Suddenly a vision entered her mind. It rose from a forgotten place in her memory and stunned her with its clarity. For seconds she felt their souls touch, their minds melding together. She knew with certainty that they had once been together. Before—in a different place—

Angelica reached out to Brett and placed her hand in his. He held the delicate hand within both his own and he too felt the contact, the closeness and the knowledge of a different time and place. *What had brought this child to the Van Kampen home?* he wondered. *Why?*

"Well, I'll be," Sarah said softly. "Seeing the two of you together I'd swear you were sisters. I felt a familiarity the moment I saw her. She reminds me so much of Destiny as a child. Do you see it, Chris?"

Chris put his pipe on the ashtray and leaned forward. "Yes. It's uncanny."

The little girl would not be parted from Destiny. Even though she could not understand Italian, somehow Destiny knew what Angelica wanted. She sat with the child on her lap until Sarah commented on the late hour.

"She should be sleeping, Destiny. She's still recovering from her ordeal. Did you know she was found wandering in the Basilica of St. Peters? It's amazing she was able to survive at all. She's a remarkably resilient child. It seems she's taken quite a liking to you. Why don't you take her into your room tonight?"

"Yes. That sounds like a good idea," Brett said. "It's time we turned in anyway. It's been a long day."

Destiny rose and scooped Angelica into her arms. "We can't stay long, Mom. Perhaps just one night. We have—some things to take care of."

"I'm glad you came, sweetheart," Sarah said. "Maybe when you and Brett get settled, you'd consider—"

"Yes," Brett answered for the both of them while holding Destiny's eyes. "We'll gladly adopt Angelica. Looking at her, she could be our daughter."

Destiny sent him a grateful smile. He had read her thoughts. Her parents were getting on in age and she knew that the fostering was just a temporary measure until a suitable home was found for Angelica.

Sarah's gaze drifted to Destiny's ring. Destiny spoke before her mother posed the obvious question. "Isn't it beautiful, Mom? Brett gave it to me for Christmas. The ring belonged to his grandmother."

"I've never seen anything quite like it," Sarah said as she watched the sparkling gems.

"Well, I'm happy Angelica will have such a good home," Chris interjected with a smile. "If we can make a difference even in one child's life, then we've accomplished something truly wonderful."

Destiny suppressed a premonition that the home her father referred to would be something she could barely imagine. With each passing moment, the mission the voices spoke of no longer seemed so farfetched.

"Goodnight, Mom," Destiny said and kissed her mother on the cheek. "Night, Dad," she said, bending down to kiss him on the forehead while wafting away an aromatic cloud of pipe smoke.

Upstairs, Brett embraced Destiny and Angelica for a moment.

"Seems we have a ready made family," he said while he rested his cheek on the top of her head.

"So it seems," she answered. "Yet another piece of the puzzle that we'll gradually come to understand." She stood on her toes and kissed him. "Goodnight, Brett."

He waited until Destiny closed the bedroom door before he entered the guestroom. After he'd undressed and crawled under the blankets, he lay with his hands under his head and stared at the sleet covered window and wondered what the next day would bring.

Concerns buzzed through his mind, but they were overshadowed by tauntingly familiar memories of another place lingering just beyond the border of recognition and uncertainty. Focusing on the steady rhythm of icy snow ticking against the windowpane, he thought about their mission, the voices and where they would lead them next.

***

CHAPTER SEVENTEEN
December 27th, 2008

It was still dark when Destiny woke up. Just as she opened her eyes she heard the grandfather clock chime. Its mournful, resonant notes drifted up from the living room five times. She shifted, to find a little body curled tightly against her. Carefully, she edged away from Angelica. As she swung her legs over the bed, she glanced back at the child and gasped at a radiant white light that engulfed her. Its brilliance was so startling that it illuminated the entire room in an ethereal glow. "Why didn't I see this before?" she whispered. "This child is part of the link, but how? Why would they use an innocent little girl?"

"Because she is pure and because she is part of you," a voice spoke beside her.

She snuggled back onto the bed and pulled up the covers. "I knew her before. I felt the familiarity of her touch."

"Yes. Brett and you both knew her during your days with us. She is the blood of your blood. Only the purest and the most innocent could bring you the item she carries. She will give it to you this day when you must leave."

"Blood of my blood? So do I have a child on this other world? You talk in terms I don't understand. How much longer do we have to keep running? I'm beginning to feel like prey."

"Be patient, Destiny. You will understand everything at the appointed time. Now, you must continue your journey. You must succeed in opening the portal. It is humanity's only hope."

"So Altithronus will come to save us from destruction?"

"Only the ones who have not joined with the elementals will have that privilege."

"How will he know who to choose?"

"We have bestowed all people on Earth with auras so we can distinguish those that have not yet embraced evil. Those that hover between darkness and light will remain here on earth."

"My friends, my family, are they among the chosen ones?"

"You will see, my child. Nothing can alter the course of destiny now. Those that have joined the elementals have done so of their own free will. The evil seed that already festered in their soul has now bloomed; they are united with the entities that will attempt to destroy Earth."

Destiny felt a moment of sadness at his words. She thought of her two girlfriends and wondered about them. Would they be among the chosen ones? She could hardly imagine either of them as evil, but Brett had thought the same about his friends.

"Where do we go today?" she asked.

"You will be guided."

"The storm's severe. We can't travel the roads under such dangerous conditions. We'd be risking our lives."

"The storm has stopped and the roads will be cleared. Banish the doubts that still linger in your mind. You will leave today."

"I don't want to leave Angelica. Not now that you've told me she's part of me, I don't think—"

"She will be safe. You and Brett must continue your journey if you are to reach your destination on time. You have a long and difficult road to travel."

"But—"

"We must go now. Sleep, Destiny—"

"Please, I want to ask you—" she started but the voice echoed into silence. Quietly, she got out of bed and went to the bathroom.

Though she went back to bed and tried to sleep as the voice had suggested, it would not come. Too many questions and uncertainties churned in her mind. Who would be among the chosen? What was the portal? She tossed and turned, unable to silence the questions that plagued her. She willed the voice to come back to tell her more, but only silence greeted her.

The night seemed endless. She was glad when around seven she heard her parents get up. Angelica stirred in her arms and greeted her with a beautiful smile. She spoke to her in Italian and Destiny wished she could understand her, but the little girl seemed happy just to chatter. Destiny stroked the child's silken hair and listened to the musical sound of her voice.

At the sound of a soft knock on the door, Angelica jumped off the bed and rushed to open it. Brett caught the little girl in his arms as she threw herself at him. She shrieked with delight when he swung her high and carried her back to the bed. He sat on the side of the bed with Angelica on his knee and bent down to kiss Destiny. "Good morning. Did you sleep well?"

"Could have been better. And you?"

"Like a log."

"The voice spoke to me this morning," she said. "We have to leave today."

"What else did it tell you?"

"That we'll be guided. They didn't explain how, but our journey will be difficult." She chuckled dryly. "That much I think we figured out already."

"I wonder where the journey will take us," Brett said. "No more attacks, I hope. What about Angelica?"

Destiny momentarily lost her train of thought as she gazed into Angelica's fathomless eyes. "She stays here. The voice said she'll be safe. Brett, she's surrounded by the most beautiful aura. I saw it early this morning. It was like the way I remember sunlight in the spring. The voice also told me she's part of me, blood of my blood. It makes me wonder. But her aura, it's dazzling—"

"That's not surprising. She's so young and innocent."

"I hate to leave her now. She seems to have attached herself to us."

"If she's part of the plan, part of us, then she'll find her way. You have to learn to trust, Destiny."

She cast him a startled glance. "That's what the voice said."

Brett smiled. "Then we should listen to it."

She hungrily sniffed the air as an intoxicating aroma wafted from downstairs. "Pancakes. My favorite." She grinned at Angelica. "Let's get dressed. I'm starving."

"I'll meet you downstairs," Brett said.

After they dressed, Destiny took Angelica's hand and rubbed it on her stomach and sniffed. The little girl smiled and nodded. She followed Destiny down the hallway toward the stairs. Destiny stopped for a moment and listened at Lisa's door. She could hear the young woman moaning feverishly in her sleep and muttering unintelligible sounds. She was about to open the door when she felt Angelica's hand tug at her sweater. "Okay, little one. Let's go have breakfast first. I'll look in on Lisa later."

Once they arrived in the kitchen, Brett opened the door a crack to look outside. "It's finally stopped snowing. Why aren't I surprised?" he said and quickly closed the door again.

Chris sat down at the table and helped himself to a generous serving of pancakes while Sarah bustled over the old wood stove. "After breakfast, I'll go out to clear the drive."

"I'll help you," Brett said while he sat down. "What about the others, Sarah? How are they?"

"They spend most of their time sleeping. With the scourge taking its toll on their health, all I can do is give them soup, some herbs and hope for the best."

Destiny helped Angelica with her pancakes and then served herself. She glanced at her mother, worry for her lodgers evident in her eyes as she bustled about. "Come and sit down, Mom. We haven't had breakfast as a family for a long time."

"Yes, just wait till I pour coffee," Sarah said while putting a tiny bottle of maple syrup on the table.

Destiny's mouth watered at the sight of the stack of golden pancakes and the syrup. "Mom, this is a feast. Wherever did you find maple syrup?"

Sarah smiled conspiratorially. "You remember those markets they had a few years back before supplies really dried up? Well, I traded my eggs for a bottle. I hear it goes for up to a hundred dollars a bottle on the black market. I saved it for a special occasion."

Destiny carefully poured a trickle of syrup on Angelica's pancakes. The little girl gazed at the golden brown dribble with wonder. "I don't think she knows what it is," Destiny mused. She poured syrup onto her own pancakes and cut a small piece. "Mmm—delicious!" she said, enthusiastically chewing.

Angelica watched Destiny then carefully took a bite of her own pancake. The transformation was miraculous as she hungrily wolfed down the remainder. "Delizioso!" she repeated.

The others burst into laughter. "Whoa! Easy there!" Destiny said as the little girl devoured her breakfast with gusto. "Slowly. Remember to chew your food!"

"I have enough batter," Sarah said. "She can have as much as she wants."

Angelica smiled beguilingly as if she'd understood Sarah's words and drank her milk daintily.

Destiny soon polished off her own pancakes. "You know, Mom, I'd almost forgotten how good your pancakes are."

While they ate their breakfast and chatted, Destiny glanced at the smiling, relaxed faces around the table. *It's almost as if the outside world doesn't exist*, she thought. *Why can't it just stay like this? Why does everything have to change?* She pondered the journey ahead and tried to imagine what lay in store for them. The concept of herself as some kind of savior of the world was difficult to accept, yet each day brought new and more bizarre events that left her no alternative but to accept her new task.

After breakfast, the men went out to clear the drive, while Destiny helped her mother with the dishes. Angelica sat at the table nursing a second glass of milk. Now and again, she cast Destiny an enigmatic glance that belied her innocence.

"Mom, we have to go soon," Destiny said with a pang of guilt at the disappointment mirrored in her mother's eyes.

"So soon? I'd so hoped you could stay a few days this time. You had to rush off on Christmas day as it was."

"I know. I really wish we could stay but Brett has commitments. We'll be back soon," she promised.

"What time are you leaving? And how are you going to make it clear to Angelica that you'll be back?"

"We're leaving as soon as the driveway is cleared. I haven't figured out what I'm going to tell Angelica yet."

Destiny took the little girl upstairs to her bedroom and gave her one of her old dolls to play with. After she made the bed, she opened the drawer of her nightstand and took out a battered photo album. She'd had it since she was a little girl but felt it should stay at the farm until she had her own home. Considering what happened to her apartment, she was glad she made that decision. To lose such precious memories would have been the worst blow of all.

"Come take a look, Angelica. This is what childhood should be."

Angelica was enthralled with the doll but when she glanced up and saw Destiny leafing through the album, she jumped up and cuddled close beside her. Destiny's nostalgia blossomed as she listened to the child's squeals of delight, her eyes widening at the sight of grass, trees and colorful flowers. Photos taken at a charming petting zoo enthralled the little girl and almost brought tears to Destiny's eyes. *Will this child ever see such beauty again?* she thought as she gazed at the animals. *And to think we took all this for granted—*

"Yes, she will see it again, and so will you," a voice in her mind spoke.

Angelica gazed up at her suddenly and smiled as if she'd also heard the words. Destiny closed the album and stood up. Taking Angelica's hand, she said, "Come, let's go and see if the men are finished shoveling."

She glanced at the time and noticed how long she'd been busy with the little girl. "Angelica, why don't we go downstairs now?" Angelica would not let go of the album so Destiny let her take it along.

In the living room, Destiny peered through the window to find the men finishing up outside. "I'll be back in a moment, sweetheart," she said to the little girl who sat on the couch leafing raptly through the pages.

The pungent aroma of herbs greeted her as she opened the kitchen door. Sarah was busy ladling vegetable soup into four mugs. "Mom, that smells scrumptious. The men are almost done. I'm sure they'll welcome something hot."

"Yes, shoveling is today's way to keep in shape," Sarah quipped. "No need for boring gym workouts anymore." She set the mugs on a tray along with a bottle of herbal elixir.

"Would you like me to take that upstairs?" Destiny asked.

Sarah shook her head. "Why don't you keep an eye on the soup? You can season it a bit more, I made it bland for the others."

"Is it that bad?" Destiny said, reading the fleeting expression of sadness in her mother's eyes.

"I just think it would be better if I take it upstairs, Destiny. I don't want you to risk exposure, no matter how minimal."

"Where did you get the medicine?"

"This is a herbal drought I made up myself. Unfortunately, Dr. Moran had no medication to spare."

Destiny resignedly watched her mother leave the kitchen and turned her attention to the soup.

Soon afterward, Brett and Chris came into the kitchen. "The drive is passable now," Brett said while rubbing his hands. "Destiny, we have to go."

"So soon?" Chris complained as he sat at the table. "If I didn't know any better I'd think you two had a plane to catch."

"In a manner of speaking," Destiny said, wondering if the promised sign had appeared. She couldn't very well ask Brett in front of her parents. "Mom made soup. Let's have some before we go, Brett. We've got a long drive ahead of us."

Sarah returned to the kitchen, her face somber. "I don't know if they're going to last the day," she announced softly while ladling soup into mugs for Chris and Brett.

Brett gratefully accepted the mug of soup Sarah handed him and sat next to Chris. His face was blue from cold and he wrapped his numb hands around the mug to warm them while he inhaled the aromatic steam. "That's too bad, Sarah. I wish we could help somehow."

"Nothing much anyone can do," Sarah said grimly. "All I can do is make them comfortable until the end. I just wish you two wouldn't leave just yet. I worry about you."

Brett's eyes were inscrutable as he glanced at Destiny. "No need to worry, Sarah. We got here safely, and we'll get back to Vancouver safely. We'll get going as soon as I finish this." He savored a mouthful of soup. "This is wonderful. If your daughter's cooking is anything like yours—"

"She'll learn, just like I did. Destiny, why don't you go tell Angelica that you have to go? It's time for her lunch anyway."

Destiny sighed. She got up and returned to the living room and gazed wistfully at the little girl who had finally turned her attention from the album to some crayons and a coloring book. Kneeling beside Angelica, she looked into her serene blue eyes. "Angelica, we have to leave now."

The little girl regarded her with a serious expression. At first Destiny thought she would cry, but then a radiant smile lit up her little face and she nodded. She jumped up and scrambled upstairs. Destiny wondered if Angelica had understood and was about to follow when the little girl quickly reappeared. She held something tightly in her small hands and approached Destiny.

"Arrivederci," she said softly and with a smile held out the object she carried.

Destiny took it from her hands. It was an exquisite gold candlestick; its finely engraved base inlaid with rubies and emeralds. She felt its sudden warmth radiate through her body and wondered what significance the candlestick held. "Thank you," she said and held her arms out. "We'll be back for you, sweetheart, I promise. Arrivederci, Angelica."

The look in the little girl's eyes confirmed her comprehension. She pulled back for a moment and gazed into Destiny's eyes and nodded. "Si. Non prima di mezzanotte."

Destiny kissed the top of Angelica's head and wondered at the little girl's words. Somehow, she'd understood the Italian phrase—*not before midnight*—but what did Angelica mean?

When she heard the faint roar of the Jeep's engine, she gently disengaged Angelica's arms and with a sigh walked to the kitchen. While Brett had gone out to start it, Sarah insisted that Destiny take two thermos flasks filled with hot soup, a pack of sandwiches, snacks and a box of dried vegetables and fruits.

Brett came back in rubbing his hands. "It's freezing out there. We'd better get ready now."

After they put on their overclothes, Brett and Destiny said good-bye to her parents. Destiny saw emotion darken their eyes and struggled to keep the tears at bay. Sadly, she wondered when or if she would see them again.

"I'd rather you two had stayed until the worst of this weather was over," Chris said. "I don't think driving in these conditions is a wise decision."

"We'll be fine, Dad," Destiny said, though she wasn't at all sure how the roads would be. "I'm sure they've cleared and salted. I'll call you."

As they got into the Jeep a haunting cry resonated far above them. Brett looked up at the oppressive clouds and saw a speck circling against the blanketed sky. He strained to discern the shape in the wintry light. "You know, that almost looks like an eagle. That's rare for this time of the year and these conditions, and even more unusual that one of them would have survived."

Destiny gazed up at the sky. "I can't tell. It looks large enough to be an eagle." She opened the window and looked out to see her mother's face pressed against a cleared section of window and her father's shadow behind her. Deep emotion shook her for a moment. Instinct told her that she'd said goodbye to her parents for the last time—

Once they were driving, Brett spotted it keeping pace with them. "Look! It *is* an eagle. Do you see it circling above us?" He took his eyes off the road for a moment to watch the great bird dive toward them. Its majestic wings flapped gracefully as it descended and circled the Jeep. His feathers gleamed in rich shades of brown, complementing his resplendent crown of white feathers. Fiery yellow eyes peered knowingly at them.

"He's magnificent," Destiny said, awed by the proximity of such a beautiful creature. "I've never seen one close up. I didn't even think there were any left. I wonder if he's the sign."

"I don't know, but we'd better fill up at the next gas station or we won't be going anywhere."

She removed the candlestick from her bag and showed it to Brett. "Look what Angelica gave me. Isn't it lovely? It feels warm when I hold it and strange sensations flow through my mind when I close my eyes. I keep wondering about the purpose of all these objects. Why are they so important to us?"

"I'm sure the voice will explain it when the time is right."

They drove into the township of Chilliwack to fill up at a solitary service center. Brett was thankful he had his departmental gas card though he wondered how much longer he would be able to use it. It allowed him to take as much gasoline as he needed while ordinary qualified drivers were allotted a ration of five gallons a week. Under different circumstances, rationing would have single-handedly banished pollution and traffic far more effectively than any other means. As he inserted the nozzle he wondered about the bodies of his friends and if they had been discovered yet.

While Brett was filling up Destiny noticed something on the seat at the bus stop in front of the station. At first it resembled a bundle of rags, until she saw movement. She was shocked to see a very old woman rise from the bench. Heavily bent, leaning on a stick, the elderly woman stumbled through the snow. With consternation Destiny noticed her threadbare coat, bedraggled cap and bare, frail legs. The woman carried a small bundle in her ungloved hand. Destiny's heart filled with sorrow for the old soul.

Without thinking twice she turned around and pulled a blanket from the back seat. Opening the suitcase, she rummaged through the contents and pulled out a pair of socks and sweatpants Brett had packed. Her mother had supplied them with enough food to last them several days, so she took a package of sandwiches and a thermos of soup and headed toward the bus stop.

"Where are you going?" Brett shouted while taking the chains off the wheels.

"I'll be back in a minute," she called back over her shoulder.

He watched her and when he saw where she was headed, he smiled, no longer surprised by her kindness.

Destiny approached the woman. "Excuse me?"

The woman stopped and looked at her with intently. Her sallow face was weathered and resembled parchment. Destiny guessed her to be close to a hundred years old. Long gray braids hung over her stooped shoulders and the colorfully beaded band around her forehead indicated she belonged to an Indian tribe. She wondered why the old woman was out in the cold. "Are you hungry?" she asked and held out the thermos and the package of sandwiches.

Deeply lined, keen brown eyes scrutinized her before gnarled, arthritic fingers took the sandwich and thermos from her hands.

Destiny held out the blanket, socks and sweat pants. "Here. Take these. You really shouldn't be out in this weather."

The woman smiled and accepted them gratefully.

Destiny pointed to a church not far from the station. "If you go to that church and ask for Father Delancy, he'll help you," she said, glancing at the woman's battered ankle boots. "I wish I had a pair of shoes to give you."

"Thank you," the woman said with an accented voice. "You are Destiny."

"How do you know my name?"

"All of us that belong to the legion of light know your name. I was waiting for you," the old woman said. "My name is Brenda Whitehorse. The volcano destroyed my home and killed my family."

"I'm sorry. I wish I could be of more help."

"You have already helped more than you can imagine, Destiny. Please accept this." Brenda opened the ragged bundle she carried and took something from it. She dropped it into Destiny's hand.

Destiny looked at a star made from the purest opal she had ever seen. About two inches wide, it shone with rainbow iridescence and seemed to draw her gaze. A familiar tingling emanated from her ring as she cupped the gem in her hand. By now, she had become accustomed to the fact that the ring was far more than a piece of jewelry, but a powerful bond to her heritage.

"This is beautiful, but I can't possibly accept it. It must be extremely valuable."

"You must accept it. You'll need it," Brenda said firmly.

"Need it? For what?" Destiny asked while she gazed at the radiant star in her hand. When she looked up, the old woman had shuffled away. "Brenda, stop. What did you mean?"

Brenda glanced back over her shoulder. "I will see you soon, child. Be careful and follow the eagle. He is your guide. His eyes see everything," she called out and continued on her way.

Hoping the old woman would follow her advice and go to the church, Destiny hurried back to the Jeep. She noticed the eagle perched on a nearby fence, patiently waiting for them. Powerful talons securely gripped the post; his snowy crested head cocked toward her. His sharp eyes watched her inscrutably above his fearsomely curved beak.

Suddenly, he spread his wings. She heard their rhythmic beat as he soared into the air to circle above them. Clearly, it was to signal the continuation of their journey.

Brett finished filling the tank. Thankful that his fuel allocation card had not been canceled yet, he started the Jeep and waited for her. "That was kind of you, Destiny," he said while pulling out of the service station. "I doubt anyone else would have bothered."

"I guess I'm not like everyone else." She paused to watch the eagle bank close to the windshield before soaring once again into the sky. "I hope father Delaney will be able to help her. Strange, she also knew my name."

"It seems that we constantly run into people who know us. Perhaps we knew all these souls before we came to Earth," Brett commented.

"That's possible. But if they remember us, why don't we remember them? Maybe we didn't know them before. Indian people are known to communicate with the spirits. Perhaps she had a psychic vision. She gave this opal to me and said I'd need it," she said and showed him the star. "She also told me that the eagle is our guide."

He stared at the colors that shimmered like the surface of the sparkling lakes she remembered. "It's beautiful. Guess you'd better put it in the bag with the other objects," he said and grinned. "Pretty soon you'll need a suitcase if you gather any more." He gazed out the window thoughtfully for a few moments until suddenly he knew. "Destiny, you're right. These people, we don't know them. They were warned to expect us, perhaps in the same way that you were contacted, or maybe through dreams, like Bill Laguna."

She thought of the voices and the dancing spheres. "Of course, dreams would be the perfect medium for the Antiquitas to communicate."

The eagle's abrupt eerie cry drew Brett's attention. "Okay, he's flying west. I guess that means we head back toward Vancouver," he said as he watched the bird.

"It's hard to imagine that an eagle is our guide," she said, her thoughts still on her mystical guardians.

Brett nodded. "This is amazing. When I was growing up, I used to watch eagles and hawks through binoculars while on nature hikes, but to have one follow us, or lead us to wherever our destination lies, is a miracle. I wish I had my camera."

All the way to Vancouver, the eagle swooped down toward them soared again into the sky and flew steadily ahead in a consistent pattern. Watching it made the journey less tedious. Before they realized, they arrived in Vancouver. The ancient steam-clock on Powell Street, still intact though no longer functional, barely showed above the accumulated snow. The eagle swooped down and perched on it.

"He stopped," Destiny said. "Now what do we do?"

"I have no idea. Let's take a break. Maybe the voice will guide us." He didn't voice his concerns as he thought about the carnage in his apartment, but he suspected that by now an APB had been put out on him. He wondered silently how long it would be before they were apprehended and if the spheres could protect them from Earth's law—

***

CHAPTER EIGHTEEN

Sergeant Patterson of the Burnaby Police Force jumped up from his creaking swivel chair and banged his beefy fist on the desk. Papers scattered from the impact, his ruddy face slowly mottling as he vented his frustration. "Dammit!" he shouted. "We can't afford to lose another five men!"

Captain Garring sighed wearily from behind his desk. Double shifts, lack of sleep and the efforts of maintaining a semblance of peace in the city had aged him beyond his fifty years. His once brown hair was prematurely gray and severely framed the deeply etched lines of his face. Shadows circled his bloodshot hazel eyes echoing the darkness consuming his spirit. Cramped for hours on end within the dreary confines of the station, battling the never-ending war of shrinking manpower and morale, it took a supreme effort to deal with Patterson's rage. Though it shamed him to admit it, there were times when he felt like fleeing into the night when faced with an outburst from his officers. He forced himself to arrange the scattered paperwork on his desk and stared disapprovingly at the sergeant.

"Sit down, Patterson," he said with a distant, tense voice. "Making a scene won't bring those men back."

Patterson sank grumbling into the chair.

"I agree we can't afford to lose any more men but it's too late to do anything about it now," Garring said. "We've lost five good cops. Tomorrow we'll probably lose more. Anger will hardly help matters." He retrieved a manila file from his in-tray. "I've read your report. It seems unlikely that Young could have killed these officers alone. He must have had an accomplice. I also feel that the report is somewhat exaggerated in respect to the carnage described. What's wrong with you? This sounds like nonsense from some B-rated science fiction film."

Patterson's dark eyes flashed indignantly. "With all due respect, Captain, if you read the reports that came in from Vancouver, you'll find a similar scenario."

Garring sighed and glanced at the stack of reports forming a crooked pile on his desk. His head ached from the low intensity lighting and the stale air. Not even the background bustle of the station was a comfort to him anymore. "Do you have any idea how many reports I receive each day, Patterson? I barely have time to sift through the most urgent, let alone the lower priority—"

"I would hardly call the murder of five cops low priority!" Patterson bellowed. He reached for a battered manila folder lying on top of the stack and leafed through a sheaf of papers. He pulled one sheet out and handed it to Garring. "Read this, Sir."

The Captain glanced at the paper then reached for his glasses and read more intently. He shook his head as he scanned the text. "What the hell is this bullshit? More slasher stuff—what are we dealing with here? Some kind of demonic cult? You know Young quite well. Do you honestly think he had anything to do with all this? For God's sake! He's one of our best men!"

A trace of acquiescence flashed in Patterson's eyes. "I don't know, Captain," he said tiredly. "This doesn't sound like Young, but the two murder scenes tie in together and since the second incident occurred at his apartment, I think he can throw some light on the situation, unless he's been killed, too. Though I doubt it. Evidence indicates that he fled the scene."

Garring frowned and tossed the report aside. "Okay. Put out an APB out on Young. I want him brought in for questioning."

Without another word, Patterson rose from his chair and marched out of the office.

Garring pensively stared at the sergeant's belligerent pace, the slamming door finally bringing some peace. He glanced at the battery operated wall clock, the numerals almost invisible in the murky glow of the dimmed fluorescent lights. Behind him, a grimy window barely filtered the wintry light. He shivered despite the relative warmth of the room.

His arm shot out abruptly and angrily swept the quagmire of paperwork from his desk. "Shit!" he cried as it littered the floor. "It's all going to hell—and there's nothing we can do about it—"

The phone rang. He groped for it. Listening to the voice at the other end, his mood darkened even more.

"Yes, Mr. Barrows. Of course I'll cooperate." He slammed the phone down in fury. "What the hell! That's all I need. The damned government giving me orders—"

***

CHAPTER NINETEEN

Warmed by the Jeep's heater, Brett and Destiny drank some of the soup her mother had packed. Destiny sipped pensively as she stared at the wintry landscape beyond. "So where do we sleep tonight? Somehow I can't seem to work up that feeling of wanderlust. God, I wish we could just go home."

"I'd like nothing better," Brett said, "but remember, the voice told me that we can't ever go back."

"What difference does it make where we go? The elementals find us wherever we are."

"Which is why we have to stay a step ahead of them. The search for us is on, Destiny."

Except she doesn't know yet that we're not just dealing with the aliens and elementals, but also that the entire force will be after me by now, he thought. He turned the radio on and tried to find a station. Bursts of static periodically obliterated the words of a solitary newscaster.

"Yesterday, the mutilated bodies of five officers were—" Quickly he turned the radio off and glanced at Destiny to see if she had heard, but she was gazing intently at the eagle who had not moved from his perch.

"I wonder if the eagle was really our guide. It certainly seemed that way, but now he's just perched on the clock and the voice is silent. What do we do now?"

"I only know that we're collecting enough artifacts to open our own antique store. I could stand a hot meal. We should hang onto the food your mother packed for us in case we can't find a place to eat. How about you? Are you hungry?"

"That depends if there's even anything open."

"Let's just drive around Gas Town a little and see if we can find a place."

Gas Town was barely recognizable anymore as the tourist attraction it once was. Quaint shops were either closed down or reduced to snow covered heaps of rubble. They left Cambie Street and turned onto Water Street. Traffic was light, the holiday break between Christmas and New Year turning the city into a virtual ghost town. Only the soup kitchens and emergency shelters bustled with the huddled forms of street people.

Destiny's gaze riveted on a twisted form hacking violently in an alleyway. Though she did not want to look, somehow she felt compelled to observe the dark-clad figure. From the violence of the coughing, she knew it had to be a serious pulmonary disorder. She shuddered at the memory of one of her tubercular colleagues terminated from her job because of the threat her infected lungs presented to the entire staff. It was inevitable that the chameleon virus would eventually claim her co-worker. Brett's voice broke her train of thought.

"There's a little restaurant." He pointed toward a tiny coffeehouse perched between two condemned buildings. Though damaged, it seemed to be open for business. He found a spot to park the Jeep and commented on the pedestrians braving the weather. "Guess we're not the only hardy ones," he said with a grin.

Destiny felt sudden warmth emanate from the bag. She reached inside the towel and held the skull for a moment. It glowed intensely between her hands, its heat penetrating her gloves and commingling with the warmth of the ring. "Yes, that's where we need to go," she told Brett and quickly wrapped the skull in the towel again.

As they entered the restaurant, a quaint reincarnation of a 1950's malt shop, the rare sight of filled tables and lively conversation greeted them. A quartet of musicians huddled on a tiny stage at the rear churned out golden oldies and an appetizing aroma of food wafted from a functional kitchen. Destiny suddenly stopped and clutched the canvas bag close to her. Her gaze roamed across the tables and a variety of faces. She anxiously tugged Brett's sleeve. "Brett, don't you see it?"

"What did you say?" he yelled, trying to make himself heard above a belting rockabilly tune. "I see a table at the very back. Come on," he shouted and grabbed her hand to pull her along.

She looked in consternation at the fog of green auras hovering around the customers and the waitresses both serving and behind the counter.

Brett pulled out a chair for her. She shook her head at him but he didn't understand and pointed to the band. "This is great. Haven't heard live music in years! I wish I'd brought my guitar along, I'd join them."

Her gaze roamed over the four musicians. The colored stage lights powered by a small generator positioned behind one of the musicians obscured their faces. One played the guitar, while the others played drums, a saxophone and a bass. *What an unlikely quartet*, she thought. Three of the musicians were surrounded by brilliant green auras while the fourth, the trumpet player, was engulfed in shimmering mauve light.

She settled back onto the chair and stared at the young man. He was absorbed in his music and paid no attention to the customers. Resembling a hippie of the sixties, his bearded, longhaired appearance looked out of place among his clean-shaven contemporaries. Sable eyes gazed up at the ceiling as if he were in another dimension. She glanced at Brett. He watched enraptured, no doubt reminiscing about his past guitar playing days.

The trumpeter's slim, tapered fingers cradled the instrument like a fragile infant. As the ebullient song finally wound down, his eyes closed when he blew the last notes and slowly let the trumpet sink to his chest. Enthusiastic applause greeted the musicians as they stood and bowed in thanks.

Suddenly the trumpeter's eyes swiveled to meet her gaze. She noticed his frown and slight shake of the head and averted her eyes. It was a warning. Leaning toward Brett, she cupped her hand around his ear and said, "Brett, we're surrounded by elementals. Concentrate and see for yourself."

He looked at her with questioning eyes, then focused on the faces around him. His expression gradually darkened as understanding dawned. He started to get up, but when the trumpet player saw their attempt to leave, he shook his head and discreetly motioned Destiny to wait. She leaned toward Brett and told him, "the trumpet player's a messenger of light. He wants us to wait."

"Is that a good idea?" he whispered. "This place is like a viper's nest."

She nodded and looked away when a waitress arrived. Brett quickly perused the brief menu and asked for two vegetable stews. She returned with surprising swiftness and left two steaming bowls on the table. Destiny gazed dubiously at the unrecognizable ingredients and motioned Brett not to touch his. He understood and stirred it so not to arouse suspicion.

Feeling the energy shift around them, Destiny shifted uncomfortably. Suddenly her throat felt constricted, as though she was struggling for air.

The band stopped playing to take their break. They set aside their instruments and reached for drinks on nearby table, though the trumpeter periodically glanced their way. Destiny's eyes fixed on him as she toyed with her stew. She struggled against a rising panic that compelled her to flee from the restaurant and tried to maintain her composure.

The trumpet player reached inside his case and casually slipped something into his pocket. Obscured by a large speaker, he quickly scribbled something on a piece of paper and folded it. He picked up his drink and sauntered past their table. Bumping into it, he apologized and dropped the folded piece of paper by her bowl of stew. She waited until he passed before discreetly opening it. *Meet me outside*, was all it said. She slipped it to Brett under the table.

He read it and nodded. "Let's go," he mouthed and deposited some money on the table. Draping his arm around her shoulder, they wound their way through the crowded tables toward the exit. Though none of the patrons seemed to pay attention to them, Destiny felt an increasing apprehension as they approached the door. She flinched at the tangible wave of darkness gnawing at her back.

Overcome by a sudden sensation of choking, she pushed past

Brett and bolted out the door. Coughing and spluttering, she surged through the snow toward the Jeep.

"Destiny, wait!" he called, struggling to keep up. "What's wrong?"

They spotted the trumpet player hunched by the vehicle. Dressed only in a jacket, he was shivering and vigorously rubbed his hands together. Nervously, he glanced behind them to see if Brett and Destiny had been followed.

"I've been waiting for you, Destiny."

The feeling of evil that suffocated her in the restaurant eased and she finally caught her breath. "It seems everyone's waiting for us nowadays," she replied.

"That's to be expected since you're the chosen one. The elementals' forces are growing daily. All of them back there—"

"I noticed," Brett said. "What were you doing in there? It's obvious you don't belong with them."

"I joined the band a few days ago just to wait for you. I knew you were coming. My name is Daniel. I have something for you," he said and dug in his trouser pocket to withdraw a tissue wrapped object. It fit neatly in the palm of his hand. He held it out to Destiny. "Please, take it and leave immediately."

She quickly removed the crumpled tissue paper from the small object and set a miniature copper trumpet in her hand. "It's beautiful—an exact replica of a real trumpet. I'm curious. How did you know to give it to me?"

"It has been in my family for generations, handed down from father to son." Daniel said. "The legend passed on to us by our forefathers was that one day the chosen one would need the trumpet and until then, it was to stay in the family with the eldest son. We would know instinctively when it was time to relinquish the trumpet. The description of the chosen one was very clear. The legend also spoke of a magnificent aura. Such light surrounds you that it dazzles the eyes. You must never let the trumpet out of your sight. It's part of the key. You'll receive the final objects when you reach your destination." He glanced toward the restaurant. "Go now. It's not safe here."

Just as he spoke, a stream of people burst through the restaurant doors and flowed toward them like a pack of rabid dogs. They moved as quickly as the slippery conditions would allow—their silence unnerving. Though several skidded and fell and were trampled by the oblivious horde, no one uttered a sound. Above the mob, Destiny saw a churning maelstrom form. Ominous shapes writhed within, and for a moment, she thought she glimpsed the same flash of metal she had seen on their way to the farm.

"Get the hell out of here, now!" Daniel cried.

"Come with us," Brett said. "They'll kill you if they catch you."

"No. I can't go with you yet," he said, backing away from the Jeep. "Don't worry. We'll see each other again soon. Now go!" he shouted and darted toward an adjacent derelict building.

Brett and Destiny quickly piled into the Jeep. She hastily stuffed the trumpet into her bag while Brett started the engine. Flooring the gas pedal, it started with a roar. Tires skidded uselessly as the vehicle sashayed from the curb.

"Hurry, Brett!" she yelled, anxiously eyeing the approaching mob.

He spun the steering wheel into the direction of the spin and the Jeep straightened out. Destiny cried out as a body thudded against the hood and bounced lifelessly onto the road. Several men raced behind them with murderous expressions, their eyes vacant. They clawed mindlessly for the bumper while Brett struggled to control the vehicle. A force like the slap of a hand turned Destiny toward their pursuers. Her eyes rolled back as their images faded to a blur. The air around her began to roil and shift and cries of agony rose from the men whose flesh sizzled with each contact of the Jeep.

Smoke hissed angrily when one hurled himself at the spare tire and hung onto it. His body was dragged along the road, his screams echoing through the vehicle. Though the others fell back, he would not let go even as the contact with the tire seared the flesh on his face.

"Jesus!" cried Brett when he glimpsed the mutilated man in the rearview mirror. Glancing at Destiny, he realized his words hadn't penetrated her intense concentration and tried to focus on his driving, but nothing would mute the horror of the man's cries.

"Destiny, snap out of it! Let him go."

The dying man continued to wail, but gripped the tire with

supernatural strength. Destiny's head lolled as a searing white energy flowed from her and embraced the man.

Brett reached out and shook her. "Destiny, let him go!"

The Jeep fishtailed down Burrard Street. Destiny convulsed and grunted and turned in surprise toward Brett. The faceless man silenced and instantly crumpled onto the road, staining the snow a sickening crimson. Brett glanced in the rearview mirror and saw the pursuing mob stop around their fallen comrade. Some shook their fists and mouthed obscenities but none followed.

This time, Destiny did not fall asleep. She sat quietly in her seat and did not look back. It wasn't until they left the city to drive through Stanley Park that she finally spoke. Her hand snaked like a frightened creature toward Brett's arm. "Brett, what am I becoming?"

He swallowed. His throat felt tight and dry. "I—don't know. The voice spoke of powers. It seems that the elementals possess those powers too, but through the force of goodness, your power is purer and much stronger."

"I—I feel strange. Like I've been dreaming—"

Brett sighed. "You were in some kind of trance. Somehow, your power is channeled when you're in these states. It's incredible—it flows from you and nothing's able to stand against you."

Destiny listened silently. "It isn't going to stop, now or ever. As long as we live, they'll keep pursuing us." She stared bleakly at the ruined city. "I just want to go home. All I want is a normal life. I didn't ask for any of this! I don't want to be the holder of such awesome power or the one to open the portal. It's all so unbelievable. Who or what the hell are we supposed to be? Some kind of super beings?"

"Nobody asked for this, Destiny—not you, not me, not any sane person. But we can't go back. Too much has happened. You know that."

"Maybe we could go back to the farm," she said. "Just for a little while—"

"No!" boomed a firm voice.

Brett started at the intrusion and almost skidded.

The voice continued patiently. "Nothing must hinder your journey. If you return to the farm, all will be lost. Your mission must be successful."

"What mission?" Destiny cried. "I've asked you the same question so many times but I never get any straight answers. I don't want the damned mission! Nobody asked my permission. I don't want to be used like this."

"You are the chosen one, Destiny," asserted the voice. "You were selected before your earthly birth and you agreed to complete this mission. There can be no other. You must accept the responsibility of your decision."

"That's a heavy load for one woman to bear."

"You were aware of that when you assumed an earthly body."

"I only remember that Brett and I knew each other before, that we were happy. Why can't we go back to that place?"

"You will be happy again when you're home. Trust us."

"I'm human. Things have changed. I know only the here and now. I remember little of what was, except that there was none of this misery—"

"Earth's ordeal will soon be over. Tonight you must rest and prepare yourselves."

"Where can we go?" Brett asked. "No place is safe for us."

"The eagle will guide you. You must be strong to face what lies ahead. You must be strong—"

The voice faded. Destiny pulled the strap of the canvas bag off her shoulder and searched for the trumpet. It glowed softly in her hand as she removed it. "Pieces of the greatest puzzle of all," she said softly.

Brett suddenly craned his neck. "Look! The eagle's back."

The majestic creature soared above tall evergreens that stood naked and forlorn like huddled skeletons. Stanley Park was once a beautiful haven for city dwellers, but now it was nothing more than a barren wasteland. No more ducks waddled across the street; playful chipmunks were nowhere to be seen. Birds that had once chittered from the trees were long gone.

They approached Lions Gate Bridge. The choppy waters of Burrard Inlet, far below, battered the hulks of abandoned freighters moored at rat-infested docks. Slabs of ice drifted with the current toward open sea. The bridge had been damaged but crews had worked hard to repair it and traffic could now cross it on one side only. On the left side of the bridge the orange painted metal still lay in twisted heaps, large gaps attesting to vehicles that had crashed through to the frigid waters below. Brett stopped the Jeep. They waited while a lonely black van crossed the bridge from the other side.

Instead of leaving the bridge, it suddenly skidded to a stop across the lane, blocking their path.

"What the hell?" Brett muttered under his breath as the Jeep idled.

"Brett, get down!" Destiny shouted when the passenger window rolled down and a shotgun pointed at them.

It fired, barely missing them and ricocheted loudly off the bridge's metal gridwork. Brett slammed the Jeep into reverse and tried to steer the vehicle while he crouched as low as possible behind the wheel.

Focusing on the van, Destiny felt a familiar, detached sensation course through her body. Suddenly, the windshield shattered into a thousand fragments as a bullet whistled past her. Glass rained down on the dashboard and their laps. Her concentration momentarily broken, her eyes widened when she saw blood seep from Brett's temple. "Brett! You're hurt!"

"I'm fine," he shouted, wiping the shattered fragments off the dashboard. "Just a flesh wound. We've got to get out of here!"

Now she needed no concentration. Fueled by a burgeoning fury, she felt the power within her shift as she drifted into limbo. Her eyes rolled back. The energy roiled from her body and spanned the distance between the pursuing van. The shotgun violently bucked and backfired explosively, eliciting a piercing scream from the sniper.

The van began to swerve and bounced against the guardrail, spun and crashed into a girder. Brett rose from his crouch and turned the Jeep onto the bridge. He glanced into the rearview mirror and saw a woman bolt from the driver's side of the van. A hunched shadow remained in the passenger seat, its identity unknown. Destiny, still in her trance, rocked quietly, her eyes rolled back, lips moving soundlessly.

Brett grimaced when he spotted the woman withdraw a pistol from her coat pocket and pursue them with impossibly long strides.

Her wild, flame-red hair snapped like a banner behind her. A glimpse of her face revealed a startling beauty tainted by a twisted mask of hatred. Shots fired into the wintry sky until the weapon emptied its chamber. Her pace never varied even as the Jeep left her behind.

Using his sleeve to wipe the blood and sweat trickling down his face, Brett's eyes constantly darted to the rearview mirror. Outdistanced by the retreating vehicle, the woman hurled the useless revolver aside and howled at the sky like an enraged animal before continuing her pursuit of the Jeep. Brett shuddered at the sight.

Destiny emerged from her trance. Noticing Brett's eyes constantly flicking to the rearview mirror, she glanced behind and saw the woman. "No—" she whispered. " No more—"

Now it was becoming easier, her concentration honing to a fine point as she felt the power surge from her. A spectral wave of flame belched across the bridge deck, melting the snow in its wake. It enveloped the woman, and consumed her, her screams unearthly. Desperately, she rolled across the deck trying to extinguish the flames but it was no use. Destiny turned away and flinched when the woman flailed against the railing and disappeared over the side. "When is this going to stop?" she murmured.

Brett sighed. "It isn't."

Her eyes shifted to Brett's wound. Immediately, she rummaged through her bag and produced a towel. Gently, she dabbed at the wound then pressed the material against it to stop the bleeding.

"Wasn't that to protect the skull?" he said.

"The skull will be fine. It's yours I'm worried about."

Suddenly Brett braked. The Jeep skidded into a full spin and crashed through the wooden barrier blocking the other side. Destiny dropped the towel and covered her eyes, sure that the Jeep would plummet over the edge into the frigid waters below. "Shit, Brett! We're going over the edge! What the hell are you doing?"

"There's another van blocking our path. Didn't you see it?" he answered in too calm a tone. "It's okay. You can look now. We didn't go over, but whatever you do, don't move!"

Carefully, she opened her fingers and gasped at the harrowing view below. "We're hanging over the edge! Now what?"

Only his lips moved when he answered. "I don't know, but I see three men in the rearview mirror. They're coming toward us and they've got guns. One shove from them and we've had it."

"How the hell did they know where to find us?" she whispered. "Are their powers as strong as mine? Can they predict where we're going?"

"I don't know," he hissed, keeping his foot tight on the brake, "but we'd better think of something fast. Destiny, use your powers to at least frighten them off."

"But if I move—" she whispered the words barely audible above the protesting growls of the Jeep's engine.

"Concentrate—"

She closed her eyes and tried to focus but her thoughts strayed to the Jeep and the imminent danger they were in. Banishing her fear, she pictured herself as a beam of steel, powerful enough to support them, but flexible enough not to bend.

"Now would be a good time," Brett said.

"They won't push us over. They want me alive." As she spoke, she felt a gentle tug. She opened her eyes and with amazement noticed the Jeep slowly levitate and drift backward until it hovered over the bridge deck. "My God! I really did it! I had no idea what—"

"Destiny, they're right behind us—"

A gunshot sounded. They ducked when a bullet struck the bottom of the Jeep and ricocheted toward the men. One of them crumpled, mortally wounded. As the vehicle thudded onto the bridge deck, the other two advanced with poised weapons. Destiny's body began to tingle from the force of her concentration. The men cried out in anger when their guns flew from their hands and sailed over the bridge. One of the men cursed loudly in a foreign tongue and withdrew a knife from his belt. With a savage cry, he broke into a run. Suddenly, the eagle soared from the sky like a missile, his formidable claws gouging the man's face into bleeding ribbons.

"My God! Look!" cried Destiny.

Blinded, his screams echoing in the eerie silence, the man crawled away on his hands and knees. His accomplice, seeing the eagle flap toward him, scampered off. The eagle let out a piercing cry, swooped on the terrified man and sent him off the bridge before banking off into the sky.

Destiny sagged against Brett, who sat in stunned silence.

"It's over," he said after a while. He looked around to make sure there were no more elementals and seeing the coast clear, drove to the other side of the bridge.

"For now," she said tensely. With shaking hands she retrieved the fallen towel and dabbed at the blood that oozed from the flesh wound on Brett's temple.

After they exited the bridge and turned onto Marine Drive, she withdrew the towel to see if the bleeding had stopped and found the material heavily stained. "I think you need stitches, Brett. We should stop at Lions Gate hospital. I think parts of it survived and it's still open for emergencies."

Her fingers stroked his injured temple. She saw him wince and at the same time, felt an intense heat surge through her fingers. In amazement, she watched as her flesh glowed pink, the wound closing before her eyes. "I don't believe it," she said, staring at completely healed skin.

"Don't believe what? Is it that bad?"

"No—it's gone. The cut's completely healed." She brushed the smooth skin with her fingers. "There isn't even a scar—"

Brett shook his head in disbelief and peered at the wound in the rearview mirror. "My God, you're right." He cast Destiny a strange look. "Carrier of secrets *and* healer. What next?"

She suddenly looked out the window. "Look—over there—the eagle's heading up Taylor Way."

Brett slowed and turned onto Taylor Way, then followed the eagle onto Clyde Street. It flapped toward a nondescript motel harkening back to the sixties. The cheesy neon sign, Park Royal Motel, was not lit up, but it was intact. The majestic bird perched on it and cocked his head.

Brett slowed as they approached the motel. Seedy and decrepit, it had clearly seen better days, but it was unlikely they would find other shelter before nightfall. "Guess we'd better spend the night there," he said, pulling into a carelessly plowed parking lot. "Why don't you go in and register? I'm certain they have an APB out on me by now. I'll wait here, though, in case we need to make a quick getaway."

"Heaven forbid," Destiny said dryly as she climbed out of the Jeep.

A musty odor assailed her when she stepped into the dusty

office. The wood-paneled room smelled of age and decay. Scattered magazines on a battered coffee table were years out of date. She rang the rusted bell on the chipped counter and waited. A moment later, a paunchy, middle-aged man emerged from a back room. The manager seemed almost shocked to see her and nervously rubbed his hand through his sparse gray hair. Much to her relief, she noticed only a watery mauve aura surrounding the man.

"How many nights?" he asked as he eyed her.

"Just tonight."

"Folks heading out of the city?"

She nodded wearily. "Should have done it years ago."

"That'll be twenty dollars."

The manager nodded knowingly when she handed him the cash and asked no more questions. He seemed quite happy to have customers and gave her the key to a room. Waving Brett on, she went ahead to the room while he parked and took a moment to clear segments of the shattered windscreen from the vehicle's interior. Quickly, they hauled all their belongings into the pokey room. Brett, unable to relax with the Jeep in view of the highway, kept glancing out the window.

"Maybe you should park it around the back?"

Brett shook his head. "It'll be dark soon anyway. Besides, they would have been waiting for us already."

Destiny nodded. "The manager's okay. I have a feeling we'll be safe here. At least for the night." She sagged onto the creaking bed and set the canvas bag beside her. "I don't understand. If they need the information they think I have so badly, why are they trying to kill us?"

Brett fumbled with a primitive coffee machine. The granulated coffee and teabags were well past the use by date and were reduced to little more than aromatic dust. He cursed softly and tossed them into the trash. "It's me they want to kill. Not you. They probably want me out of the way so they can get to you easier, or so they think. What I can't understand is how they don't know how vulnerable they are against your powers."

Destiny opened the canvas bag and stared pensively at the skull and the other talismans. "There's a lot I don't understand either, Brett. Those men on the bridge—and the others—surely you noticed how almost nothing seemed to slow them down? Injuries that would have killed or seriously debilitated an ordinary person—" She shook her head. " This is all like a nightmare neither of us can wake from. In the space of a few days, our lives have been turned inside out."

Brett sat beside her on the bed and cupped her chin. Faint lines traced her eyes and a deep weariness shone from deep within them.

"I wish there was something I could do to make it all go away," he said. "But we both know that things are going to get even worse from now on. If I'm going to help you, we need our wits about us." He stared at their reflection in the dresser mirror; his eyes fixed on the spot where the bullet graze had miraculously healed. "Let's get some rest. We're going to need it."

Destiny moved to a rickety stand and opened her suitcase. She frowned at the array of clothing Brett had packed for her. She found enough jeans, sweat pants, sweaters, socks, but nothing to sleep in. "Brett, did you pack T-shirts?"

"Yes, a couple for myself, but I didn't think you needed any. You can have one of mine," he said and pulled one out of his duffel bag.

"You want to shower first?" she asked, stifling a yawn as she dug through an array of toiletries.

"Why don't you go first? You're exhausted. I'll tidy things up around here."

Destiny shuffled into the tiny bathroom and stood under the shower until the timer shut off. The murky water was barely warm, but it felt refreshing and invigorating. When unwelcome images began to float through her mind, she concentrated on scrubbing herself until her skin glowed. After winding her wet hair in a towel she slipped into Brett's shirt and emerged into a lukewarm room.

"Hot water?" he asked with a grin. He eyed her appreciatively. "Never knew a gal could look so sexy in a towel and T-shirt."

Destiny looked into his admiring gaze and felt a shiver run down her spine. "Lukewarm, actually, like the heating."

Brett impulsively stepped forward and embraced her. He rubbed her back with smooth, firm strokes. "Feel better?"

She shut her eyes and savored the warmth and closeness of his body. "Much better. I could stay like this forever."

"So could I," he responded as he held her close. He noticed her head sag against his shoulder. "But I think you should get to bed now. I won't be long."

She stepped toward the bed and suddenly swayed. Brett caught her and guided her. "You okay?" he said with concern.

"Yes—I think so," she said, gingerly pulling back the covers. She gazed at musty smelling sheets. At least there were no signs of bedbugs. Fatigue overpowered her repulsion so she slipped beneath the covers. "It felt like the floor lurched beneath my feet. I'm okay now, just tired."

Brett tucked her in. He glanced at the canvas bag piled with the luggage on the rack. "What should I do with your bag?"

"Bring it here. I want to keep it close by, just in case—"

He set the bag by the bedside table and quickly slipped into the shower. By the time he returned Destiny was fast asleep, the canvas bag tightly packed against her body. He stood and watched her under the peachy glow of the bedside lamp and bent to gently stroke her face. Planting a kiss on her cheek, he slid into bed beside her. Her warmth enveloped him like a glove, her weight a satisfying presence.

Uselessly, he tried to settle to sleep, but it would not come. He reached out with his hand and gently intertwined his fingers with hers. Tired as he was, he could not vanquish the disturbing images of the day's events as they replayed relentlessly in his mind—

Slowly, the images transformed until the walls melted away to reveal a frightening vision. Masses of people churned—their voices a frightened chorus. Above their heads writhed a massive black thunderhead. Sinister metallic shapes darted like shooting stars. Green mist funneled from the wraiths and probed the human crush below. Some embraced the hellish veil, while others repulsed it. Brett's eyes widened when he saw one of the phantoms close-up. It was an abomination beyond description, a demonic character reminiscent of a Bosch painting.

Within moments, an army of elementals emerged from the crowd. They turned on those who had resisted the darkness and viciously attacked them. Hooting as they groveled in the blood and entrails of their victims, they raised their heads and began to march in unison through the snow. Brett shuddered when an eerie, discordant chant rose from their lips, the dark anthem personifying the evil that sought them.

Slowly the image faded, but he knew without a doubt that the masses were marching toward him and Destiny. They were pursuing them with single-minded determination. His heart pounded from the disturbing vision. Too disturbed to lie still, he started to rise from the bed when the spheres suddenly appeared in the room. They pirouetted around him, humming their enchanting melody.

Gradually, the horror of what he witnessed drifted from his mind and was replaced by breathtaking scenery, platinum beaches, and majestic, snow-capped mountains. Two young girls frolicked in the azure waves lapping pristine sand. Both had waist length tresses of silver.

"Destiny and Angelica," he whispered. "So they did know each other before, but Angelica's now a child. How can it be?" The questions whispered in his mind, unanswered by the spheres that eased him into sleep and erased the fear of what lay ahead.

***

CHAPTER TWENTY

Commander Jeff Collier of the Canadian Armed Forces grunted as he slammed the phone down. "Next they'll ask me to walk on water," he muttered. He stared at his cluttered desk. "Where am I supposed to requisition choppers? And all for the sake of two fugitives, for God's sake—" He stabbed the intercom. "Brown, get in here," he said over the intermittent crackling. "Our esteemed superiors have ordered us on a mission."

Sergeant Brown entered a moment later and steeled himself as he glanced at his superior's angry expression. A stout, dour man sporting an iron gray crewcut, Collier reminded him of an indignant bulldog. Not once in the years he had served under the Commander had he ever seen the man smile nor heard him utter a pleasant word. "What's up, Sir?"

"Have you watched the news at all?"

"Whenever I can get anything."

"The government in its infinite wisdom has decided we should become involved in the apprehension of those two suspects wanted in the police slayings."

"Isn't that a waste of resources, Sir? I mean, two people hardly justifies—"

Collier gestured impatiently. "Seems the Prime Minister thinks they're some kind of terrorists. Apparently they've displayed an extraordinary ability to evade capture so far. The police have had no luck."

"Or they don't want to admit they've blundered," Brown said.

"That may well be," said Collier, "but unfortunately I'm in no position to argue. The Minister of Internal Affairs, John Barrows, has ordered me to muster the ground troops. Scavenge whatever heavy equipment you can get your hands on and organize supplies. Sources have reported the fugitives crossing Lions Gate Bridge."

Brown glanced through a frosted window at the dismal landscape beyond. "Look, Sir, we have enough to contend with without chasing a couple of—"

"I'm not going to debate this with you, Brown. Just get on with it. Understood?"

"Yes, Sir!" Brown saluted and retreated from the office.

Collier stared wearily at the sergeant's back. Sinking his head into his hands, he rubbed his throbbing temples while he tried to formulate a plan. Nothing would come, his fatigued mind balking at the thought of more problems to contend with.

A voice suddenly broke his half-hearted concentration. He shrank back in his chair as a dark green mist spiraled through the window Brown had looked through and undulated menacingly toward him. An arctic cold penetrated his flesh.

"Collier—"

Collier blanched. The staccato clicking gradually transformed into a raspy voice. Its soulless resonance echoed through the office. "Yes—?" he stuttered, his eyes fixed to the wraith that coiled around him like a malefic serpent. Collier flinched as he felt something like a slimy tongue flicker against his face and bit his lip to keep from screaming. Insectoid eyes flickered on and off like spectral headlights; their penetrating gaze boring through him. The creature's fleeting image teased him, the ominous flutter of wings at once near and distant. Collier heard the drumbeat of his heart.

"The woman we have told you about—she is the fugitive whom you must capture. Now is the time to deliver her to us!"

"She—she's the one?" Collier said, almost gagging at the fetid stench surrounding him.

"Yes. She carries the key to the portal. Do what you must to prevent her from reaching her goal. Do you understand?"

"Yes. What do you want me to do?"

"At all costs she must be taken alive. She travels with a man. Use him to get to her if necessary. He is of no consequence. Remember, she must be captured alive and uninjured."

"I understand."

"Your rewards will be beyond your imagination."

The voice faded as the creature contracted once again into a green mist and funneled through the window. Almost faint with terror, Collier gasped for breath. His face felt clammy, his flesh numbed from his contact with the creature. He wiped the slime trail from his face with the sleeve of his uniform.

Though the creature had converted him to darkness after the death of his wife and daughter, he could not get used to its random visitations. Despondent after the death of his family, he had intended to commit suicide when the awful voice had first spoken to him. The creature never revealed itself entirely, but rather seemed to enjoy taunting him with horrific glimpses of its alien countenance. To Collier, the creature personified the ultimate corruption. He had no desire to learn more about it, only that it promised that he would be united with his family again. All that it required of Collier was that he help recruit the people of Earth into legions of elementals. Tempted by the thought of unlimited power and wealth, he had surrendered his soul and became a conduit for the creature.

Now, the time had finally come to fulfill his mission and a gut-wrenching fear he had never before experienced suffocated him. He coughed and gasped for breath.

Another voice, one from the past, whispered in his mind.

"Daddy—help me—Daddy—"

"No!" he cried, clamping his hands to his ears. "You're dead. Leave me alone!"

"I will restore her to you," the creature's voice teased from a great distance.

"That's impossible!" Collier cried.

"Once we possess the key, nothing is impossible."

Collier recoiled from the force of the voice, the promises too unbelievable, his fear combating his greed.

"If you abandon us now, you will suffer a fate beyond the comprehension of man."

"No," said Collier. "I won't fail."

"Good. Now, organize your men and pursue this woman."

The voice finally vanished. Collier shuddered. He took a deep breath and reached for the phone. Grim resolution crossed his face while he dialed the number and waited for the other party to answer. "Captain Garring? This is Commander Collier. Look, I just received a call from John Barrows. I need to ask you a few questions—"

***

CHAPTER TWENTY-ONE

Urgent knocking at the front door startled Chris as he adjusted the makeshift aerial above the television. Sarah, absorbed in her knitting, cast a curious glance at her husband, the strident knocking relaying a distinct sense of urgency.

"Who the hell could that be at this hour?" she said.

"Don't know," replied Chris while hurrying to the door, "but they'll wake everyone in the house at this rate. The last thing our sick guests need is to be so rudely disturbed."

A tall, dour looking man overshadowing a severe young woman dressed in baggy gray overclothes, waited on the porch. Both looked as if they had spent far too much time in the cold and the tone of the woman's voice reflected their mood.

"Mr. van Kampen? I'm agent Marian Woolley and this is my partner, George Degen. We're from the Internal Security Division of the Vancouver police. We'd like to ask you some questions." She produced a badge and flashed it at Chris. Her partner remained silent, his stony eyes scanning the area beyond the open door.

"Internal security?" Chris asked dumbfounded. "What would they want with us?"

"May we come in?" Degen asked.

"I'm sorry. Yes, come in," Chris said, reluctantly ushering them inside. Turning to lead the unexpected guests into the living room, he noticed Angelica at the top of the stairs. Standing quietly, she held onto the railing and shook her head, her blue eyes serious beyond those of a child.

Chris shifted uneasily beneath the intensity of her stare. Discomfited, he reluctantly showed the agents into the living room. Only the crackling fire penetrated the heavy silence as they scrutinized the cozy room.

"Sarah, these are agents Woolley and Degen from Internal Security. They want to ask us some questions but you'd better go and see to Angelica first. Their loud banging woke her up."

"Internal Security?" Sarah asked with an arched brow.

"Your granddaughter?" Agent Woolley asked.

"Eh—yes. I'd better put her back to bed. If you'll excuse me—" Sarah rushed off before anyone could protest.

Chris motioned the two agents to sit down and sat down in his easy chair. "What would you like to know?"

"Sir, we want to talk to you about your daughter, Destiny van Kampen," Woolley said. "We'd prefer to wait until your wife returns."

Chris bristled. "Destiny? I can assure you my daughter wouldn't be involved in anything questionable."

Sarah returned to the living room and sat on the couch. "She's settling down. Now, how can we help you?" she asked, looking both agents squarely in the eye.

Chris marveled at Sarah's composure.

"We'd like to ask you some questions about your daughter, Mrs. van Kampen," Degen said.

"Exactly why would Internal Security be interested in our daughter?"

The agents glanced at each other. Woolley asked the first question. "Was your daughter adopted? We tried to locate records of her birth but none were available."

"I'm surprised you would even ask such a question," Chris said. "You know perfectly well that most pre-war records were destroyed. The hospital where Destiny was born was one of the many razed by the earthquakes and the government buildings in Victoria were destroyed."

"Sir, are you the natural father?" persisted Woolley.

Chris's face flushed a deep scarlet. "What kind of a presumptuous question is that? Of course I'm her father!"

"You're sure of that?"

"Chris, calm down," Sarah said. "Look, agent Woolley, if you're implying that I slept with someone else then there's always DNA testing to corroborate—"

Woolley's tone became conciliatory. "I'm sorry. No, we're not implying that. But we must ask if anything unusual occurred before or at Destiny's time of birth?"

Sarah's expression grew thoughtful as a distant memory surfaced of the night she had first seen the spheres and tried to wake Chris. Her mind drifted to the peculiar mist that had funneled into Destiny after her birth.

"Mrs. van Kampen, you look distracted. Are you all right?" Woolley asked.

"Yes, I'm fine," she said in a thin voice.

"Agent Woolley's question seems to have disturbed you, Mrs. van Kampen," pressed Degen. "Did anything happen that we should know about?"

Sarah composed herself. "Nothing happened. It's been a long time since I've had something pleasant to remember that's all. Frankly, I find this interrogation offensive. Destiny is a decent young woman and you'd be better off spending your time pursuing real criminals."

"I don't doubt she's a decent young woman," Woolley said softly. "But I do feel you're not telling us something."

Chris rose irritably from his chair. "Unless you have a warrant I suggest you leave at once—unless you can explain the reason for these questions."

"Very well," Degen said. "We have reason to believe that your daughter and her boyfriend are terrorists. They've killed five police officers in addition to wounding and killing dozens of civilians and are currently on the run. We really need to question your daughter."

Sarah suppressed a shudder as she looked into the man's cold gray eyes. "This is nonsense!" she cried, half rising from the couch. "Terrorists? My daughter involved in a killing spree? Just what exactly is your agenda, Agent Degen, because this sounds like some concocted story to me."

Chris bolted toward his wife and tried to comfort her. "Easy,

Sarah. Don't let them upset you. These allegations are nothing but bullshit!"

Woolley saw Sarah's eyes fill with tears of rage and realized that the old couple was undoubtedly ignorant of the situation, but time was of the essence if they were to capture the fugitives.

"I know this is difficult to believe, Mrs. van Kampen," she said soothingly. "For now, we simply want to bring your daughter and her boyfriend in for questioning. There may be extenuating circumstances we're unaware of, and if we're to clear them of suspicion, we must speak to them."

Chris's voice shook with barely concealed anger as he turned toward the agent. "Dammit! Our daughter was conceived in this house! If you're searching for a killer, then you've come to the wrong place. Go on! Take your accusations and get the hell out of here!"

Woolley and Degen woodenly stood up to leave, but Woolley, glancing toward the mantelpiece, casually strode over and perused a silver-framed photo of Destiny. "Do you mind if we take this?"

Sarah flew toward her. "Yes, I do mind. That's a family heirloom."

"I promise we'll return the picture," Woolley said. She quickly slipped the backing off, removed the photo and slipped it into her pocket. When Sarah didn't take the offered frame, Woolley placed it gently on the table. "I realize the photo is very precious to you."

"You've got no right—" Chris started to say.

"Mr. van Kampen, we have every right," interjected Degen. "Your daughter and her boyfriend are murder suspects."

Chris took a threatening step toward Degen. "I'm warning you! Get out of my house!"

Woolley tugged at Degen's arm. "Let's go, George," she said as they walked toward the door. "We have the photo." She lowered her voice. "We won't get anything out of them anyway."

"I think we should bring the woman in for questioning," Degen muttered. "She's obviously hiding something."

"I agree, but we can bring her in later. I doubt they're going anywhere." Woolley turned toward Chris and Sarah. "We're sorry to have disturbed you," she said and flashed them a smile. "If your daughter does contact you, we'd appreciate it if you told her that it would be in her best interests if she surrendered. Like I said, all we want to do is question her and her boyfriend. It would best for everyone—" The implication lingered in the air. "We'll be in touch with you later."

They had barely stepped outside when Chris slammed and double locked the door. "Who the hell do they think they are coming in here and harassing us like that!"

Sarah stood in the hallway, her face ashen. "I'm going upstairs to check on Angelica," she said, unsuccessfully trying to quell a burgeoning fear for Destiny.

The little girl was still awake. Her eyes fixed on Sarah as she approached the bed. Sarah smiled and sat beside her. "It's okay, sweetheart. They're gone now."

Angelica's delicate hand touched Sarah's cheek for a moment and a brilliant smile lit her face as if to comfort her foster mother. Sarah felt a lightening of her spirit. Within a moment, the little girl nestled into her pillow and fell asleep. Sarah softly stroked her silken halo of hair and reluctantly retreated from the bedroom. She trudged wearily down the stairs, her mind roiling with questions and concerns about Destiny's birth.

Returning to the living room, she sat next to her discarded knitting. Chris was busy fiddling with the aerial, the television picture a stubborn haze of snow.

"Chris—"

"Yes, Sarah?"

"There's something I have to tell you. I should have told you long ago, but I was always afraid you'd think I was crazy."

"Everything is crazy nowadays. I don't anything would amaze me anymore," he said laconically. "By the way, I heard about those murders on the news and that the search is on for Brett and Destiny. I didn't want to tell you because I knew you'd worry yourself sick."

"Destiny couldn't have had anything to do with that," Sarah stated firmly.

"No. I would think not. And Brett is a police officer. Not the type to do a Bonnie and Clyde."

Sarah nodded. "Yes, I felt good about Brett as well. Chris, about Woolley's question—something did happen before Destiny was born, and again during her birth."

"Let me go and get a bottle from the root cellar. I think a glass of wine would do us both good right now. You seem pretty shaken."

Sarah nodded silently. Years ago, their grapevines had produced lush fruit and they had made their own wine. Now that the vineyard had withered, they opened a bottle only rarely. Chris had clipped the dead vines to the root in the hope they would sprout again, but the soured soil had become as barren as moon dust, killing even the hardiest weeds.

"I'll go and check on the others," she said.

Her thoughts roiled while she ascended the stairs. Softly, she opened the door to the bedroom Lisa shared with Candy. Despite her mother's serious illness, the withdrawn little girl refused to be parted from her and lay quietly asleep. Sarah's eyes fell to Lisa's motionless form on the bed. A shudder coursed down her spine as she approached. Bringing the oil lamp closer to Lisa's face, Sarah struggled not to flinch when she saw that the young mother was dead. Her sunken eyes gazed sightlessly at the ceiling, angry purple blotches marking her inflamed skin. What was left of her once beautiful mahogany hair clung from her scalp in scraggly patches.

Sarah stifled a gasp and steeled herself against burgeoning tears. *Another child without a family,* she thought. She did not even begin to know how they would deal with Candy. Swallowing to ease the tightness in her throat, she pulled the sheet over Lisa's face and gently picked Candy up. The little girl stirred and stared at her with sleepy eyes, but did not call out for her mother.

"It's okay, little one," Sarah whispered, softly stroking Candy's cheek. "I'm just going to put you in Angelica's room while I give your mother some medicine."

The little girl lay like a limp doll in Sarah's arms while she carried her to Angelica's room. As Sarah quietly opened the door and approached the bed, Angelica's eyes opened and rested on Candy. With a sublime smile, she pulled back the cover and made room for the little girl. Sarah could barely stifle a gasp when she set Candy down on the bed. The child actually turning to meet Angelica's gaze, nestled beside her and smiled timidly. Reaching for Candy's hand, Angelica squeezed it and gently tucked the little girl beneath the covers.

"Buona notte," she murmured when Candy's eyes closed.

With tearful eyes, Sarah withdrew from the room and softly

closed the door. The lamp trembled in her hand as she approached the bedroom the two elderly men shared. She took a deep breath and opened the door. In the bed by the window, Mr. Cheltam tossed feverishly, muttering gibberish. Sarah felt his forehead. He too burned with fever, his weight loss rendering him little more than a skeleton. Mr. Mead lay still, his breathing shallow. She felt his pulse, the faint heartbeat erratic. Biting her lip to quell a wave of sorrow, she tucked the blanket around the old man and quickly retreated from the room.

With a heavy heart she went back downstairs and sat quietly before the fire, the crackling of the wood a soothing tonic as she wiped her eyes with a handkerchief. Despite the sorrow she and Chris had endured over the years, she could never get used to the inevitable horror the scourge inflicted.

A clock chimed from the kitchen announcing the lateness of the evening. While she waited for Chris, Sarah thought about that night and the day Destiny was born. *Could it be?* she wondered. *No, surely they must be wrong. What happened was strange—and even stranger that I got pregnant after so many years—*

Chris returned with the wine. After uncorking it, he poured them each a glass. "Drink up. You look quite pale."

Sarah took a generous sip. "Chris, it's Lisa. I'm afraid she's gone."

He blanched. "Oh, God—I'm so sorry. You did your best for her," he said, quickly hugging her.

She sagged against his chest, her voice breaking. "I don't think the men will last the night, either."

Chris looked at her with glistening eyes. "No one could have done more than you, Sarah. You know that." He sighed and shook his head. "But still, I had hoped that at least Lisa— I'll build a coffin for her tomorrow."

"I'd hoped it would never come to this," she said. "And those agents harassing us like that—what's become of our world?" She sipped the rich, ruby wine and felt it soothe her shattered nerves. Staring at the half empty glass, she wistfully recalled the special dinner she had cooked the night she announced that she was pregnant.

"Chris, do you remember the day I went to see Dr. Allan?"

"Like yesterday," he said with a faint smile. "And the delicious dinner you served that night before you hit me with the news."

"That night, I saw the lights."

He frowned. "Lights?"

"You remember—our bedroom suddenly filled with colored spheres and then I heard voices. I tried to wake you, but you wouldn't stir."

"Why didn't you tell me?"

"I did. You said it must have been a dream."

His eyes grew distant as he recalled the event. "Oh, yes, I remember now. I thought it was caused by your excitement at being pregnant." He paused and stared at Sarah. "So what *did* happen at Destiny's birth?"

Slowly, she told him. When she mentioned the mist that had funneled into Destiny, Chris frowned.

"So now you think our daughter is some kind of supernatural being?"

"I don't know, Chris. How else can you explain what happened? I wasn't imagining it."

"Surely you don't think Destiny could have anything to do with the killings?"

She shook her head vehemently. "No. Of course not. But if she's possessed by something—"

"Possessed by what? For God's sake, Sarah, Destiny was always such a loving child and she's grown into a caring, wonderful young woman. Not exactly the pedigree of a psychopath."

"I know. But those strange things did happen. I didn't want to tell the agents."

Chris drained his glass in a single gulp and poured another. "I don't know what to think about what you've just told me. I guess there are still things that can surprise me after all. Let's keep this between ourselves in case anyone else comes to question us." He glanced at his watch. "Anyway, it's late and it's been a difficult day. Let's go to bed. I think we need to pray for our daughter."

"Yes," Sarah said softly. "Destiny's in trouble and there's no way we can help her except pray for her safety."

Just after they'd gotten into bed and clasped hands to pray together, the bedroom door opened slightly. A chink of brilliant light appeared as Angelica slipped into the room. Moving like a shimmering cloud, she crawled beneath the heavy quilt and silently placed a small hand on each of their foreheads. They barely glimpsed her serene expression before they fell into peaceful and profound sleep.

Angelica's face beamed as she curled like a kitten between them, the light from her presence bathing the room in an ethereal glow—

***

CHAPTER TWENTY-TWO

Huddling deep into their collars to avoid the biting force of the wind, Woolley and Degen trudged through the drifting snow to the helicopter waiting in the field beyond the barn. Degen frowned as he peered at the hulking shape almost obscured by the deteriorating weather. When they had arrived, it had landed far enough away from the house so not to alert the van Kampen household, but if conditions continued to worsen, they would be grounded.

Woolley cursed softly under her breath. "Shit. Last thing I want is to get stuck out in the boondocks."

Degen nodded and drew further under his parka. "Barrows isn't going to be pleased."

Woolley snorted derisively. "The word isn't in his vocabulary. But I think it's safe to assume the woman is protecting her daughter, even if she doesn't know the whole story."

"I doubt a dutiful daughter would call home to report the latest killing spree."

An orange clad figure emerged from the chopper and anxiously waved them on. Woolley and Degen labored more quickly through the snow, their breath misting from the effort.

"Frank's getting antsy," Degen said, his voice almost drowned by the wind.

The chopper began to rev as the pair plowed toward the open door. Woolley glanced backward to check to make sure they hadn't been followed, but saw nothing suspicious. She sighed heavily when the pilot, a wiry, heavy-set man, helped her into the chopper. Her mind churned with disappointment and frustration. The questioning had not gone well. She'd so hoped that the girl's mother could have given her a clue, anything at all. Clearly, the woman was protecting her daughter, but it was unlikely either she or her husband knew anything. Fifteen years in the service had honed her senses like a lovingly carved piece of scrimshaw and the old couple simply did not fit the profile of conspirators.

More questioning might have softened their resistance and perhaps provided a few more clues so she could divert Degen's attentions, but she and her partner were under orders to proceed immediately to their superior and the team assigned to pursue the two felons.

Degen clambered in and slid the door shut behind them. The din of the ascending chopper all but obliterated their words when it lurched sickeningly from the ground. Woolley shook her head and leaned over to whisper into the pilot's ear. "Patch me through to government headquarters. I want to speak to Barrows."

The pilot called out repeatedly. Static burst explosively from the radio. He shook his head grimly as he peered into the swirling leaden skies above the control panel. After several fruitless attempts, he finally received a crackling response.

"Mr. Barrows?" Woolley shouted into the mike. "This is agent Woolley. I'd like to question the parents again before we proceed."

Static preceded a curt voice. Degen shook his head as though anticipating the reply. "We don't have time to waste coddling senior citizens, agent Woolley. Proceed as planned."

"But Sir, I'd like to at least—"

"Did you obtain a photo of the suspect?"

Woolley mouthed a silent curse.

Degen shrugged and cast her a knowing look.

"Yes," she shouted.

"Then proceed as ordered. After we apprehend the suspects, we can bring the parents in for questioning."

Woolley's response was cut off by another jarring burst of static. She handed the mike back to the pilot and hunkered next to Degen as best she could in the confined space. Moisture from their boots and parkas pooled onto the floor. The chopper swayed dangerously, the din of the rotors muted against the rising storm. A surging curtain of white blotted the view and cocooned her with an unpleasant sense of claustrophobia.

"This thing going to get us back in one piece?" Degen asked nervously.

The pilot grumbled. "Must be nice for Barrows, keeping his ass warm with our so-called leaders while he leaves the dirty work to us. You might want to tell him that not even I can defy physics. We shouldn't be out in this fucking weather. It's not like these babies are rolling off the assembly line anymore."

Woolley shifted uncomfortably as something dark and sinister loomed before the window of the helicopter. Breathing relief that it was only a tree, she turned her thoughts to the old couple and the young girl watching from the top of the stairs. Even in that brief moment of eye contact, the child had touched her in a way she could not explain. She considered the old couple, trapped by a hostile world and fearful of their only child. Hugging herself tightly, she tried to banish the feelings of sympathy and remorse that threatened to overwhelm her. Degen must not see where her sympathies lay—not now—not yet—she had to play along just a little while longer—

***

CHAPTER TWENTY-THREE
December 28th, 2008

Beyond the limited view from the grimy motel window, dawn cast its anemic light onto the dreary, snow-scoured landscape. The room was chilly; the heating operational for only two hours in the evening and it had long since evaporated within the poorly insulated room. Wrapped in a moth-eaten blanket pirated from the closet, Destiny stood before the window and watched a solitary car cautiously thread its way along the highway. The occupant, a faceless dark shape represented what she, her hopes and dreams had become—an inconsequential blot on a planet about to be consumed by its own folly.

Warm hands brushed her shoulders. Brett's presence infused her with a sense of well-being, his scent a familiar friend. She closed her eyes and leaned into his embrace.

"You know," he said, his eyes roving the desolate landscape, "despite everything that's happened, I always thought the world would find a way to pull through. I never thought it would come to this. The end is something you see in a movie or read in a book. It scares the hell out of you, but when you leave the theater or close the book, the fear is gone like a bad dream."

"This is no movie, book or dream, Brett. It's that bump in the night that used to terrify you as a child, that lurking monster you knew was hiding under the bed—all our fears have been realized."

She turned suddenly and gazed into his eyes. Running her hand through his tousled hair, she noted how the lines on his face had become more firmly etched. She extended her finger and felt the warmth of a tear trembling from the corner of his eye.

Their lips met in a searing kiss—the intensity of the contact releasing a floodgate of emotion. Clinging to each other, they waltzed toward the bed in a slow-motion ballet. With a sense of urgency borne from a place beyond mere need, beyond loneliness and fear, they tumbled together on the bed in defiant celebration of the darkness around them. Fueled by an energy that fused them together, their limbs intertwined, their bodies moving as one until only their urgent cries broke the leaden silence.

Afterward, they lay quietly in each other's arms. For at least a little while thoughts of their difficult quest and the misery beyond the motel door was forgotten in the passion of the moment.

Brett gently nuzzled her ear. "Thanks for this gift, Destiny. I'd forgotten what it was like to be close to a woman. You've awakened feelings that I thought I'd never experience again. You don't know what your love means to me."

She smiled and stroked his cheek. "Feelings that we apparently have experienced before. And if my love means as much to you as it does to me, then I do know. At least now, if we have to leave this world behind, we'll take something precious with us—"

"It is time to leave," the voice spoke as they lay entwined on the tousled bed.

Brett looked around with a start. Destiny sat up and turned to the direction of the voice with a calm demeanor. "So soon?" she said reluctantly. "All we wanted was a little time together."

The gently vibrating voice swirled around her. "You know by now this is your path. Your time together will come. Soon."

"Yes—we know."

"The struggle will not go on forever, Destiny. You must have faith. But there can be no turning back now. You and Brett must continue. It is time—time—time—"

She scrambled up unwillingly. Looking at Brett, she said, "Brett, hold me in your arms for just a minute longer in case we don't get another chance."

He sat up and embraced her. Their lips lingered before breaking away. "You didn't even blink at this unwelcome interruption," he said with a grin.

She smiled. "You can get used to anything after a while."

"Your smile is more than enough compensation." Reluctantly, he rose from the bed and began to dress. "Then let's get moving. If there's anything I've learned from these voices, it's that trouble isn't far behind."

The haunting cry of the eagle pierced the silence. Destiny gasped at its proximity.

"Our guide calls," Brett said. He walked to the window and drew back the threadbare curtain. His eyes widened when he spotted the Jeep. "My God, he's perched on the roof waiting for us."

Destiny hurried to the window. The magnificent bird peered obliquely at them with fiery golden eyes. He fluttered his wings in acknowledgment of her presence.

"He's beautiful," she said.

"I think he's also in a hurry," Brett said, his gaze fixed on the fearsome talons gripping the Jeep.

"Give me five minutes," she said and quickly disappeared into the bathroom with some hastily grabbed clothes.

Brett reluctantly drew away from the window and fiddled with a tiny black and white television perched on the dresser. "Wonder if this antique works," he muttered, turning the ancient knob.

A snowy, distorted picture emerged from a single channel. The gender of the newscaster was determined only by the masculine voice.

"—is now in full force in the Vancouver and North Vancouver areas. Suspects Young and van Kampen are wanted in connection with the recent slaying of five police officers in Burnaby, the killing of one patron of a Vancouver restaurant and the wounding of more than a dozen others. They are also suspect in the killing of several civilians on Lions Gate Bridge. The suspects are armed and extremely dangerous. If anyone has any knowledge of their whereabouts, please call the number shown on your screen. Do not attempt to approach or apprehend them, but report their location immediately."

Brett frowned and turned the set off.

"I'd like to hear the rest of it, Brett," Destiny said, emerging from the bathroom.

"Look, I—"

Her eyes remained fixed on the blank screen. "Turn it back on."

"Destiny—"

"We need to know what's going on."

Reluctantly, he turned the television back on. A barely distinguishable artist's rendition of them appeared on the snowy screen but faded quickly to the site of the restaurant incident.

"They can't know about the incident at Li's shop yet or the numbers would have been higher," Brett said. A vaguely familiar female reporter spoke with a group of people milling about outside. The reporter's voice droned as she interviewed the spectators.

Destiny listened in horror to the fantastic stories concocted about them. The whole incident was magnified into something so diabolical that the truth seemed tame. They were now believed to be members of some demonic cult who used drugs to endow them with superhuman abilities. She shuddered and thought about the thugs at Li's shop. "Maybe Li took care of them." Her blood chilled when she recognized one of the musicians in the crowd. "Brett, look at—"

"Yes, I see Daniel. He's no doubt acting as a decoy for us. At least we have friends. Let's listen to what he's saying."

Daniel's strangely wooden voice rose above the poor picture as he recounted what happened in the café. "Couple of strangers, tweakers," he asserted, "came in here with an attitude and then all hell broke loose. We tried to get them out but they both went crazy. No place safe anymore—no place— Don't look anything like those two on the pictures—"

"Thank you," the reporter said, returning her attention to the camera. "Just to recap, the search for the suspects has—"

"Well, he tried," Destiny sighed, watching the angry crowd argue Daniel's story. "I hope he's going to be okay. We're going to have a hell of a time if the Internal Service is after us," she said tightly. "What do you know about them?"

"Not as much as I wish I did. They're a high clearance division, mainly dealing with matters of national security, a lot like the American CIA or FBI, I'd say." He glanced at his watch. "Anyway, we'd better get going. The manager looks like the type who would sell his own mother for a price. I'll go out to the car to grab some of the food your mother packed and then we'll go."

He returned carrying the whole box. "I didn't know what you wanted, so I brought it all."

Destiny rummaged through the box and removed as much as she thought they could carry. The rest they tried to eat rather than waste. Afterward, they gathered their gear. "I'm worried about my parents, Brett. If they've seen these reports, they'll be frantic." She stared longingly at the phone.

"Not a good idea. That one isn't working anyway. I checked."

"What about your cell phone?"

"Too easy to trace with my police channel. We might as well raise a red flag."

They both heard the eagle's impatient flapping.

"Time to go, Destiny. I know you're worried about your parents, but we can try calling them from a safer place. Every minute we waste means a greater chance of capture."

Hurriedly, they loaded the Jeep. The eagle flapped majestically into the wan daylight and circled slowly. In the eerie, almost preternatural silence, his haunting cry was almost the stuff of a surreal nightmare, rather than the horror-edged reality Brett and Destiny had become used to.

"I wish we could ditch the Jeep," Brett said as they clambered inside. I know there's an APB out on us and this monster is so easy to spot."

"Why don't we switch plates with that car over there?" Destiny interrupted, pointing to an abandoned car parked by the garbage skip.

He hesitated. "If someone sees me from the road—"

"You see any traffic out there? Park behind the car. How fast can you switch plates? We're probably the only business the manager's had in weeks. I doubt he'll say anything."

Without a word, he turned and rummaged for tools he kept in the back. He gave them to Destiny and slowly drove toward the abandoned car. Satisfied no one was watching he parked behind the rusted relic. A desultory wind rattled a battered tin can along the garbage-infested parking lot.

"Get behind the wheel in case someone shows up," he said.

She nodded and slid behind the steering wheel as Brett got out. Brandishing his tools, he quickly removed the original plates from the car and replaced them with the Jeep's. A few moments later, he got into the vehicle and started it, the eagle a solitary mascot in the leaden sky.

"Relic's been there for years by the look of it," he said. "I'm surprised no one's living in it."

"Judging by the trash piled in that skip, I think that's the least of the manager's worries," Destiny said, wrapping a woolen scarf around her face to conceal her features.

The eagle swooped down, circled for a few moments then flew over the motel toward the back. Brett shook his head. "Where does it want us to go?"

"There's a driveway beside the motel, Brett."

He turned the Jeep and drove slowly around the motel to the rear parking lot. "It backs onto the Capilano River," he said and stopped. "Looks like we're going to have to get out and follow it on foot." Grabbing the canvas bag, he slung it over his shoulder and got out of the Jeep followed by Destiny.

They sank knee deep into the snow as they entered the skeletal forest and headed toward the river. "I seem to remember a scenic walk beside the river," Brett commented. "It leads to the inlet."

The eagle flew ahead. Every now and then it perched on a branch or a rock in the middle of the raging river and watched them with sharp eyes to make sure they followed. Their progress was slow, the deep snow hampering them. Beside them, the river gushed, sending its polluted waters toward the inlet. Gusty wind tore at the withered trees. Several collapsed under its force and tumbled to the snow below dragging dead branches with them as they fell. The sounds echoed eerily through the silent morning. Perched on a large boulder in the center of the river, the eagle soared into the sky when a tree trunk came crashing down upon the rock. Its protesting squawk startled Destiny.

"Brett, it's like we're tramping through a bizarre story book world. Where's the good fairy to rescue us?"

He stopped for a moment. "Yes. All that's missing is some fire-breathing dragon confronting us."

"Don't speak too soon. I see shadows everywhere," she said while rubbing her gloved hands.

"It's only the trees. I don't think there's anything out here besides us."

She shivered. Somehow, she knew that danger lurked everywhere. Just because they weren't accosted this time didn't mean they were alone. She unconsciously touched the ring beneath her glove. "There are people out there. I can sense them but I don't think they're a threat to us right now."

Finally they spotted the seawall, or what was left of it and beyond it, the choppy water. They stopped. Just near the mouth of the river, the carcass of an Orca whale partially covered by snow lay rotting on the shore. Brett helped Destiny climb over some fallen tree trunks and pulled her against him. "Well, here we are. Now what?"

"Look! The eagle's flying toward that freighter," she pointed out.

"I see that. Looks like an old wreck to me."

"There are people aboard. They're watching us," she said and stepped forward. "I can feel their eyes on us."

"Careful, Destiny. We don't know what's beneath this pile of snow."

Quickly she stepped back into the circle of his arms. They stood silently, watching the eagle and the freighter. Suddenly there was movement. A rubber dinghy was lowered from the side of the boat and small figures climbed down a swaying rope ladder into it.

The small orange dinghy bobbed up and down on the choppy water, the rowers obviously fighting against the swift currents. When it got closer, Destiny spotted three people inside. One of them waved to attract their attention.

Monolithic slabs of dirty ice drifted lazily down the inlet. Once, its polluted waters were tainted a dirty green. Now, it was brown, murky, the waters resembling congealed blood. A bedraggled seagull perched sullenly on a slab, its features misshapen. Destiny wished she had some bread to toss to the pathetic creature. Legions of bloated, dead fish floated on the rank water, the stench enough to make her retch. The carcass of a solitary seal lay sprawled on a chunk of ice, its flippers spread in mute supplication.

She shuddered at the dismal scene. The sight of dead wildlife affected her more than the destruction of the cities. To strip the air, land and sea of their kingdoms was the most heinous crime. It was an outrage beyond description, a precious heritage plundered by the dubious stewardship of man.

Destiny noticed that the seawall where it crossed the river had caved in, blocking all access to the Indian reservation beyond. A solitary standing totem pole indicated that this once was Indian Territory. Other poles lay fallen around it, their painted faces barely protruding from the snow.

They turned to survey a sorry collection of derelict and abandoned vessels. Long ago, sleek yachts had sailed these waters. The rusted remains of a fishing boat rose from the water. Garbage and bird carcasses floated on the oily surface. A bell tolled mournfully from an unseen masthead.

"It's like a graveyard here," Brett mused.

"This whole place stinks of death," Destiny said. "What the hell are we doing here?"

Brett glanced at the eagle perched motionless atop the bow of a badly listing freighter. "Maybe we're supposed to escape by boat, but we can't travel the inlet. The ice would rip the hull apart in seconds. And where would we even find a decent vessel?"

They watched the dinghy approach slowly. Finally it reached the seawall and one of the rowers threw a rope toward them. Brett hesitated to catch it until Destiny told him, "It's okay Brett. They're surrounded by light."

He caught the rope and pulled until the dinghy reached the sea wall. Carefully, they stepped closer. The two rowers were men. They wore fur hats suggesting they came from a Slavic country. The third person was a woman.

"It's safe, Brett," Destiny said. "I see no green auras, only the purest mauve light around them all."

He gazed entranced at the woman. "I wonder who she is? She looks almost as if she's from royal lineage."

Destiny nodded and appraised the woman. Though her clothes were tattered, she could see they were of superior material. The mixture of deep blues and greens sang above the somber winter shades of her comrades. A turquoise shawl was artfully draped around her shoulders. Her mane of shimmering black hair crested to her waist. Feline eyes with a Slavic slant regarded them with benevolence and understanding, the corners of her full lips raised in the slightest smile. The woman's eyes danced, her face lit as if she was overjoyed to see them.

"Welcome," she said in a melodious, accented voice. "My name is Isha. My people and I have waited long for this day."

"You speak English," Destiny observed. "Where are you from?"

"When the darkness came, we fled Eastern Europe. I was a noblewoman in my land. Now I am the same as my people, the soul of the earth. We have traveled far and braved many storms to find you." Isha raised a slim, graceful hand and held out a glittering object. "Please, take this. It belongs to you."

Destiny stepped closer and while Brett held her hand to stop her from falling into the water, took a miniature, jeweled coronet from Isha's hand. A constellation of precious gems sparkled at her. The coronet fit inside the palm of her hand and glowed with silken warmth. Regarding the priceless object, she smiled almost in recognition. "Thank you, Isha. Is there anything we can do for you?"

"No. We have done our work. You must take the coronet and keep it safe. We will meet again." Isha glanced over her shoulder. "Go quickly now. Your pursuers are not far behind."

She covered her head with the shawl. Without a further word, the men pulled the rope back into the dinghy and the two silent, stone-faced men started to row back to the freighter.

Destiny and Brett exchanged glances. "Looks like we have another talisman to add to our collection," he said. "I hope we're not going to be carrying the crown jewels around with us."

The eagle cried out and flapped from his perch on the trawler. "Guess it's time to go," Destiny said. She and Brett backtracked along the river. The great bird circled until they returned to the Jeep. Soaring into the sky, it led them back to Taylor Way toward the Upper Levels highway then carried on toward Horseshoe Bay. The numbing wind chafed their faces as it blew through the broken windshield.

"It's heading toward the ferries," Destiny said. "Surely we're not meant to go there? I don't even know if any are even running anymore."

"I guess we'll find out when we get there," Brett said.

As they passed what had once been British Properties, an elite settlement built against the side of the mountain, they had to drive on the other side of the road. Most of the beautiful homes and buildings lay heaped at the bottom of the mountain, the dismal sight now smothered by snow.

The eagle did not fly into Horseshoe Bay. Instead it veered to the right and flew above the Squamish highway. Brett frowned. Severe rock and mudslides and a collapsed bridge had closed the highway some time ago and though crews had been working steadily, he doubted they could get through.

"I guess we're headed toward Squamish," he said, following the eagle.

A toppled road sign warned of treacherous conditions. They had not driven very far when they stopped at the yellow barriers blocking the highway. "Dammit! I thought as much. The highway is closed."

"No. You must continue," the voice spoke around them. "You cannot stop."

"The highway's closed," Destiny answered. "We would need a jump jet to get over this."

"Open the barrier," the voice commanded.

"Look, the conditions are dangerous," argued Brett. "The bridges aren't safe and rock slides snow could easily—"

"The bridges are passable. You must continue. You have no option. Open the gate."

The voice receded into a jarring echo. Brett and Destiny glanced at each other. "Can we open it?" she asked.

"Either that or we crash through it." He got out of the Jeep and approached the barrier. He yanked at it and at first it wouldn't move, but then it slowly lifted. The heavy metallic barrier barely budged and he had to use all his strength to lift it to an upright position. Despite his efforts, it would not stay upright. "I can't hold it!" he shouted to Destiny. "Drive through!"

She nodded and after scrambling into the driver's seat, gassed the Jeep through the opening. As she passed, Brett released the barrier. With a worried frown he studied the highway. Covered in ice and snow, its hairpin curves would present a terrific hazard even without the rocks that could be concealed beneath the snow. So far they'd managed without the chains, but now he doubted that even with chains the Jeep could get through the mounts of snow on the highway.

It took a while for him to put the chains back onto the tires. His fingers were numb from cold and two of the chains kept slipping. Finally, he managed to secure the last chain on the front tire. He had to rub his numb hands before he was able to drive. Glancing at Destiny, he reached out to clasp her hand for a moment.

"Somehow I feel this is the final segment of our journey," she whispered when the Jeep surged forward.

"I feel it too," he said.

She stared at the jagged profile of the mountains beyond. "Whatever's waiting for us is out there." Glancing back at Brett, she noted his apprehensive expression as his eyes scoured the hazardous terrain.

He nodded. "Somewhere—" he murmured.

***

CHAPTER TWENTY-FOUR

They made little progress. Severe conditions and the possibility of concealed rocks beneath the innocent blanket of snow forced them to drive so slowly that the speedometer barely crept above zero. The eagle would soar ahead then return as if to check on them, his resonant cries urging them to hurry.

"I think cross country skiing would have been faster than this," Destiny said, hunkered against her seat from the cold blowing in through the missing windshield.

"In this snow?" Brett said. "You've got to be kidding. We also have no idea how far we have to go. We might as well enjoy the comfort of the Jeep while we can. I doubt we'll be able to negotiate the highway if the conditions get any worse."

Destiny stared at the bleak undulation of snowbound mountains. "It's difficult to imagine the scope of destruction hidden beneath all that snow. The landscape looks almost serene."

Brett nodded. "Maybe it's best that we can't see what's hidden below. We've seen enough horror to last several lifetimes."

She gazed out of her window at the Howe Sound far below. Somehow the topography seemed altered, suggesting that land shifts had occurred. Islets dotted the water and the Sound was narrower than she recalled. To their right, sheer cliffs flanked the highway. Natural springs that normally trickled steadily down their walls had transformed into craggy icicles.

"I don't know about you, but I'm starved," Brett said. "I think there's a lookout point just ahead. We should stop and eat something." Carefully, he pulled off the road. "I'll have to switch off the engine. We can't afford to waste gas as I'm sure none of the stations will be open on this route."

"Then let's hurry before we freeze," Destiny said while she dug in the box for sandwiches. "Running the heater's a luxury we can't afford. I wonder if the soup Mom packed for us is still warm. I think I'll have some anyway," she said and opened the thermos. "It's lukewarm. Do you want some?"

"Sure. Anything to keep up our strength."

They ate in silence, each lost in thought. Destiny observed the peaceful serenity of the snow-flanked mountains while Brett focused on the arduous trek ahead of them. She was about to sip the last of her soup when a timpanic rumbling shattered the silence.

"What the hell was that?" she said, anxiously looking around.

"Look at the eagle!" Brett said.

The great bird squawked loudly and descended with frightening speed. It skirted the Jeep, soared and swooped down the highway as the ominous rumbling approached.

She watched the eagle with growing concern. "Is that thunder? It doesn't feel like an earthquake."

Brett frowned, cracked the window open slightly and cocked his ear. "Shit!" he cried and started the Jeep. His soup sloshed over the cup as he reversed crookedly onto the highway and fishtailed forward on squealing tires.

Destiny's soup spilled onto the floor. She clutched the armrest with white knuckles. "What the hell's wrong, Brett?"

He gripped the wheel and forced himself to stick to a safe speed. His eyes frequently darted to the mirrors, though the poor visibility revealed nothing.

"It isn't thunder and it isn't an earthquake. It's the sound of vehicles. Lots of them."

The eagle loomed like a specter ahead of them. It buzzed the Jeep and circled impatiently as if urging them to hurry.

Destiny turned to peer at the road behind them. "How far behind do you think they are?"

"It sounds like they're big vehicles. Maybe army transports.

Their trucks and Jeeps can move through anything. What I'd like to know is how they tracked us."

"The elementals must have spotted us at the pier. Isha warned us they weren't far behind."

The Jeep slowly gathered speed. Destiny's heart leapt to her throat when they skidded around a corner and hovered precariously over the edge of the road. Dislodged snow cascaded to unseen depths. "Brett, you're driving too fast!" she cried. "Slow down!"

He pulled back and forced himself to slow down. Slowly, Destiny exhaled. She glanced at the Howe Sound and its rocky shores a harrowing distance below. The skeletal barrier of trees visible through the snow flanking the mountains would hardly block their fall if they careened off the road.

"I know," he said, grimly gripping the wheel. "But it's the only way to put distance between them and us."

"Wait— I hear something," she said. She wound her window down to look out. Dark shapes hovered menacingly in the wintry sky above. "My God, those are choppers and they're right on top of us!"

"I hear them," Brett said. "But we're almost at Britannia Beach. We can hide there."

She tried to picture the area in her mind. "Where?"

"I don't know. We'll worry about that when we get there. The highway widens up ahead. Hold on."

He drove as fast as the hazardous conditions would permit. The force of the wind blowing through the broken windshield stung their faces. Destiny noticed the eagle had disappeared and became concerned by its absence. She closed her eyes wishing for it to return and felt herself sinking, her body suddenly weightless as if she were floating in her mother's womb. The ring pulsed beneath her glove, imbuing her finger with almost searing heat. All sound disappeared, all sense of where she was—

Suddenly, transformed into the eagle, she dove through the frigid air, her arms spread out like great wings. She swooped and turned—her body sleek and powerful. Skimming the great expanse of snowbound terrain, she spotted them. Several convoys crawling slowly along the Squamish Highway—trucks, Jeeps and tanks. Two rumbling snowploughs preceded the procession. Brett's Jeep was little more than a speck barely a mile ahead. Helicopters circled above like swarming bees.

"Destiny?"

For a moment she thought she'd tumble to the ground when voice interrupted her, but it was Brett's voice, its warmth guiding her back to the Jeep.

"Sorry. Brett, I just had the strangest experience."

"What happened?"

"I saw everything through the eagle's eyes. I soared into the sky and saw the convoy following us."

"What are we dealing with?"

"Looks like the entire Canadian forces. Every vehicle you can think of. They're about a mile behind us."

"God—" he muttered as he tried to speed up.

She sank back into her seat, still overwhelmed by what she had just experienced, and hoped they could stay ahead of the convoy.

Dusk fell early within the frigid embrace of the mountains and by the time they arrived at Britannia Beach, it was almost dark. Once, Britannia Beach was a tourist attraction. A large, deserted lot used as a vehicle depot for the mine rose from open land that had once housed fruit and souvenir stands. An avalanche of massive boulders had demolished the small native Indian stores at the back of the property.

Brett's eyes scanned the area for a hiding place. To the left were the train tracks running beside the waters of the Sound. The wharf was also gone. Choppers buzzed behind them like angry hornets, their flanks aglow with spotlights. Voices obscured by the wind bellowed warnings from speakers. Brett was surprised they'd not yet opened fire. *If they opened fire, they could kill Destiny and they want her alive*—he thought as a blinding spotlight skimmed past them. He glanced at the mountain that had housed the mines. There were no signs left to indicate that a mine had ever existed, the mountain's face now deeply gouged.

"Brett, there's no place to hide."

"There has to be. If necessary, we'll ditch the Jeep and run for it."

"And then what? Rollerblade?"

"What else do you suggest? At least on foot we have a better chance of hiding."

"If only we had cross-country skis," she mused wistfully.

Darkness fell swiftly and ushered a bone piercing cold. The rocky shore of Britannia Beach was a fathomless black smudge against the misty gray snow. Destiny felt like she had fallen into an abyss as Brett turned off the headlights and drove slowly onto the empty property. The spectral outline of rubble fronting a snowy clearing was the only evidence of the historic mine structure that had once graced the side of the mountain and drawn many tourists. Twisted railway tracks protruded from the snow like insect antennas.

Brett's mind churned. The choppers fanned out behind them and they systematically swept the area with their spotlights. He realized that under such bitter conditions it would be impossible to continue without food or a vehicle. If they ditched the Jeep, they would be stranded and at the mercy of their pursuers, and he had no doubt what the outcome would be.

"Destiny is the key," the voice suddenly said, startling them both.

"How?" she asked, staring into the darkness.

"You must act quickly. Concentrate on the land. Focus your energy. There are many unstable areas prone to rockslides and avalanches. It will take the elementals hours to clear the road."

"But what about the choppers?" Brett asked. "They're carrying enough hardware to turn this place into a crater."

The voice spoke to reassure them. "We will take care of them. Now hurry. Turn the Jeep around and face south. Destiny, you are the conduit. Use your gift. It is your birthright. Envision on the skull, embrace its strength from your mind."

Brett made a sloppy U-turn and faced the Jeep into the direction they had just come.

Destiny blanked out the idling sound of the engine and focused on the dark rise of mountains beyond. She felt a prickling sensation against her skin as the air around her began to shift slowly. Her vision clarified sharply when she spotted a rumbling convoy descending on the ribbon of road entering Britannia Beach. Preceding them were two modified snowploughs resembling belligerent scorpions.

"They've even got tanks," Brett murmured. "I didn't think they had the resources."

He had barely spoken when the choppers congregated above them and immersed them in a pool of blinding light. Shielding his eyes, he ducked instinctively. "Destiny! Do something now, before they open fire!"

She sat motionless in the pool of light and stared unblinkingly toward the convoy, oblivious to a voice blaring from a bullhorn. "You're under arrest. Step away from the vehicle and keep your arms above you at all times—"

The activity was detached, remote, the approaching convoy nothing more than the annoying activity of ants disturbed by water. Destiny imagined the skull, envisioning its warmth with her mind's eye. As the air continued to ripple around her, her eyes rolled in her head and she fell back against the seat.

Brett, shielding his eyes from the blinding spotlight, glanced up at her through his fingers. Two of the pursuing helicopters descended to land while the others pinned the Jeep in their spots. Turbulence from the rotors created a maelstrom that rocked the vehicle and sent debris flying like missiles.

"Destiny!" he cried, his voice barely audible. "We're out of time!"

A swirling miasma of colors engulfed her as energy surged through her body. Each experience was different, each more intense until she became attuned to the phenomenon resident in the depths of her mind. Uttering a soft moan, she shuddered and went limp. A moment later, a tremendous din rose above the drone of the choppers. The mountains trembled, paused and let loose a tremendous rockslide that buried the highway. Brett gasped as he watched the face of the mountain disintegrate.

The choppers abruptly veered away and headed toward the scene of the disaster. Darkness overwhelmed them once more. In his mind, he heard the screams and cries of the trapped men. He glimpsed faces, caught the movement of hands frantically scratching at the prison of dirt and rubble. Destiny, still in her trance, stared vacantly at the sky.

A howling wind rose from the direction of the wounded mountain. Groaning an unearthly bass, it violently swatted the approaching choppers. Their engines whined as the pilots struggled to maintain control, but the gale was so powerful it snapped the rotors and sent them hurtling into the ground. Severely damaged, the choppers spluttered, jerked and hopped through the air like wounded grasshoppers. Brett turned away when they slammed into the mountains and exploded into a fireball that rained onto the slide area. Many of the voices he had heard in his mind silenced abruptly.

Destiny snapped into consciousness, her eyes wild and staring. "My God—" she muttered. "I was in a place full of colors, like an ocean. I could see the stars from a great distance. The power was everywhere. It was amazing—"

She stared around her as though seeing the area for the first time. Suddenly, she turned toward the shattered mountain.

Brett sat beside her and took her hand. A tear silently rolled down her cheek.

"Did you hear them?" she murmured.

"Yes. I heard them."

"I—this wasn't what I expected. I didn't think I'd become some kind of—exterminator."

The voice boomed around them. "Destiny, you must learn to accept that your mission is for the greater good. Now, you must continue. The elementals have been delayed but reinforcements will come. Not far beyond the bridge is a small café. It is abandoned. You will be safe there for the night."

"Wouldn't it be better if we kept moving?" Brett asked. "They could easily get more choppers up here."

"No. You need to rest. You will be safe. They will not risk harming Destiny for fear of losing the knowledge and the power she carries."

"Then they know about it?" she said.

"The leaders do. It is imperative they capture you alive. Otherwise they are doomed. They cannot harm you."

"Then why are they coming after us with the big guns?" Brett asked.

"They merely want to frighten you, to coerce you into giving up. They will not kill you, Destiny, but Brett can be used to get to you."

"I don't remember volunteering for hazardous duty," he muttered darkly.

"Neither did I," Destiny whispered.

"Remember, Destiny, you must learn to trust. We have told you this many times. Do not doubt your path."

The voice receded into the wind. For a long time, Brett and Destiny stared at the ruined mountain and drank in the silence.

Brett reached out and felt the coldness of her hand. "You okay?"

She nodded. "Whatever that means anymore."

He sighed and started the Jeep. The sound of the engine seemed intrusive as he turned and drove toward the small bridge. He knew of the café the voice had mentioned. Often, he had often stopped there for coffee and a burger on his way to Whistler to go skiing. A pang of remorse stung him when he thought of the simple pleasures he had taken for granted. The memory of his skiing trips was a token from a different lifetime.

The Jeep crept carefully over the bridge, then up the hill. He glanced at the gas gauge and wondered where they would find fuel to fill the half-empty tank.

When they arrived at the summit of the hill, the café and a scattering of houses were cloaked in darkness.

Emotionally and physically exhausted, they got out of the Jeep. Destiny clutched the canvas bag containing her precious cargo against her chest. She trudged wearily through the deep snow and waited while Brett carefully approached the boarded-up door of the cafe. Surprisingly, the boards fell off easily, as though they had been pried off before and carelessly replaced.

"Looks like someone's beaten us to it," he said.

She sighed tiredly. "Why would they bother to put the boards back up then? The place is deserted—I can sense it."

He shrugged. "Maybe someone was using the place as a shelter and didn't want anyone else poking around."

Once inside, they couldn't see anything. Brett felt his way around trying to remember what the interior looked like. He felt a table and dragged it over to the door. After jamming it tightly against the door to barricade it, he turned and took Destiny in his arms. He felt her trembling and held her tightly.

"It's going to be okay. You heard what the voice said. They won't harm you. If anyone should be worried, it should be me."

Destiny brushed his cheeks with her lips and moved aside to

set the canvas bag on a table. "Don't worry," she said in a peculiarly detached tone. "I won't let anything happen to you."

He stared at her, blinked, and looked again as a faint glow emanated from her eyes and winked out—

***

CHAPTER TWENTY-FIVE

Brett blinked again, but the fleeting glow in Destiny's eyes had vanished. He shut his eyes and rubbed them. *Keep a grip, Brett*, he told himself. *This is no time to lose it—*

"Smells musty," Destiny said, tiredly plopping onto a chair.

"Whoever the visitors were are long gone," he said. "At least we don't have to worry about rats. Let me see if I can find some candles. I feel like I'm blind."

"Won't the light give us away?"

"They always know where we are, so it hardly matters. The voice said we'd be safe, so let's start listening to it."

"I could do with something to eat."

"Is everything we brought with us gone?"

Destiny nodded, then realized Brett couldn't see her. "Almost. Mom didn't anticipate a prolonged siege."

By now, Brett's eyes had become accustomed to the dark. He could distinguish a vague shape of the counter and felt his way around it. When he brushed past the cash register, something heavy tumbled over. The noise startled him. His groping fingers closed around a large flashlight. He was almost afraid to press the button in case the battery was dead.

A bright beam of light pierced the darkness. "Destiny, I'm going to look for something drinkable."

"Can you see a bathroom anywhere?"

He shone the light around and found a doorway leading to the rear. Peeking into a short corridor, he panned the flashlight back and forth and spotted a restroom at the end. "Through here."

He lit her way until she closed the door and heard her grumbling and groping around in the dark. Satisfied she was all right he stepped into a compact, adjoining kitchen. A quick search of the cupboards and fridge revealed nothing, the contents obviously scoured by the previous visitors. He almost tripped over a cardboard box covered by a moldy piece of canvas. Only the rattle of glass prompted him to look and he was quite surprised to find two small bottles of orange juice. Slipping them into his pockets, he continued toward a door with a broken lock. The hinges protested loudly when he leaned his weight against the door. It opened up into a pantry.

Though he realistically expected to find nothing, he still felt a pang of disappointment as he panned the flashlight across shelves laden with decimated flour, rice and cereals bags. The outline of empty cans, jars and boxes rose from the dust-caked shelves. Whoever had been here before had been painstakingly thorough. He was about to leave when his flashlight caught the faint glint of foil on the floor. Tucked in the cobweb-draped corner by the door lay a handful of battered energy bars, perhaps dropped or simply overlooked by the scavengers. He scooped them up gratefully and brushed them off.

"Destiny?" he called, turning the flashlight toward the bathroom.

"Out here."

He found her rummaging through the canvas bag.

"Dinner is served," he said. Setting the flashlight on the table, he produced an energy bar and a bottle of orange juice. They carefully divided the last of the food—the meager meal consisting of some dried fruit and some strips of jerky.

Silence ensued while they consumed their meal.

"I had no idea how hungry I was," she said, washing the energy bar down with the last of the juice. "Even this is a treat."

"We need to keep our strength up if we're going to stay ahead of the mob," Brett said. He peered into the darkness around them. "If anyone's listening, perhaps some soup or stew next time please?"

She shivered. "I'm freezing. Has the temperature dropped or is it me?"

"It's the higher elevation. Let me get the blankets from the Jeep."

"Be careful."

He returned a moment later. They wrapped themselves in the blankets and settled down in some chairs. Brett found himself glancing at Destiny's eyes as if to confirm what he had seen before was merely his imagination. Her face was spectral in the tenuous glow of the flashlight, her expression troubled.

"You're very quiet. What's on your mind?"

"I was wondering what happened to the eagle. Did you notice he disappeared when it got dark?"

"Perhaps that was as far as he was meant to take us."

"I can't help wonder how close we are now. I feel as though something's waiting for us."

He shrugged. "Whatever it is, we face it together."

She smiled weakly and reached for his hand. The simple contact was enough to reassure him.

"Don't you feel at all overwhelmed? Look what I've put you through. Hell of a price to pay for a roommate—"

"Well, you did save me on advertising costs. Besides, you heard the voices. You, well— I mean we, have to learn to trust. We've gotten this far despite some pretty harrowing odds, so we have to believe we'll reach our goal."

"Goal—" she echoed. "Funny to think the word once meant mundane stuff like graduating from college or finding a job. Now it's turned into a life and death struggle not only for us, but for everyone, and we're still not even sure what this goal is."

"It can only mean survival at this point," he said. "There simply aren't any other options." He rose and stretched. "Anyway, I'm going to look for somewhere for us to sleep."

She watched the beam of light from the torch disappear as he explored the rest of the café and shivered at the intense cold teasing her flesh. Alone in the darkness, her thoughts drifted to the pursuing convoy and all the men who died as a result of her actions.

"And it's only the beginning," she whispered, the shimmer in her eyes like the reflective gaze of a cat as other images suddenly appeared—glimpses of frightened hordes, pushing, shoving, trying to wrestle through the snow toward a solitary refuge. Roiling green clouds fueled by the essence of unimaginable evil hovered over the multitude, taunting, urging them on. The cavalcade of spectral faces shifted from human to demonic as many faces were transformed by the darkness released from their souls.

Like the dreamlike scenes from a surrealistic film, the images merged into a hellish montage. She glimpsed other countries, identified by a glut of tongues or a familiar landmark that had somehow survived the holocaust of recent years. The world languished in its death throes, its cry of agony echoed in the tormented voice of humanity, clearly understood by Destiny.

Her hands flew to her throat in response to the horde that seemed to close in on her, suffocating, cutting off her breath. She gasped for air—

Brett shone his flashlight on her kneeling figure. Her distended eyes starkly contrasted the pallor of her face. He dropped the flashlight and rushed to her side. "Destiny! What's wrong?" he cried, his panic rising. He seized her by the shoulders and roughly shook her limp form. "Destiny! Breathe, dammit!"

She gasped for air, her lungs wheezed in protest as she fought the malevolent presence that threatened to overcome her.

Brett's fingers scrabbled through the canvas bag and grasped the skull. He shoved it against her chest and watched its glow suffuse her body. A wraith of amber light entered her mouth. Slowly, her breathing returned to normal, her glazed eyes glancing up at him with recognition.

"Brett—" she whispered. "It was horrible. The whole world— I just saw the world dying—"

He gathered her in his arms and tried to still the shudder that coursed through her body. "I know. Each time the visions get worse."

"I felt a darkness beyond description. It wasn't of this earth, Brett. It was monstrous."

"But this was more than a vision. Something attacked you just now. I couldn't see it, but I could feel it."

"Thank God for the skull." Tiredly she clutched it and nestled against Brett's chest. "I feel like I'm becoming something I don't want to be, that I've lost control of myself and my life."

"You need to rest." He arranged the potato sacks he had found and guided her toward the makeshift bed. "Lie down. Keep the skull close. It will protect us."

They settled on the sacks and got as comfortable as they could, huddled in each other's arms. The skull glowed softly between them, its luminescence a comforting beacon that embraced them with its warmth.

***

CHAPTER TWENTY-SIX

Commander Collier climbed out of his battered army Jeep. Weathered beyond his years by handling too many crises with too few men and supplies, his impatience was permanently mirrored in his flinty eyes. He waved imperiously to Sergeant Brown seated in the transport behind. "Get your men out here and start cleaning up this mess," he barked. "Where the hell are those choppers headquarters promised us?"

"Damned if I know, Sir," the sergeant replied as he hustled, his chapped face all but obscured by the heavy fur trim of his parka hood. "The weather probably hampered things. Okay, men! Let's get to work!" he yelled at a group of conscripts huddled in the rear of a transport.

Collier grimly watched the men clambering off the truck. The icy wind made his eyes water as he mentally assessed his troops. Gaunt, underfed, poorly trained, they were the best recruits the worsening city conditions allowed and that was being generous. Most still healthy enough to serve had long fled. Their loyalty and patriotism long vanquished by the struggle of daily survival. Not even a guarantee of steady pay, food and health care was enough of a temptation.

His lips curled in disdain as Brown directed the men to various points along the barricaded highway. Boulders and dirt from the avalanche created a hazardous peak effectively blocking the route.

"We'll need to dynamite, Sir," Brown told the commander.

"Then get on with it. We've lost enough time as it is. We have to capture those two alive at any cost."

The rumble of heavy equipment distracted Collier. He glanced further along the convoy to see a pair of somewhat ramshackle bulldozers coughing to life. Even working nonstop, it would take them hours to clear the debris left by the detonation. He shook his head. Despite his repeated requests, he had been unable to requisition any more heavy equipment from the metropolitan areas, though he had no doubt Barrows would be the first to blame him for delays.

"Don't worry, Sir," Sergeant Brown said. "The scouts reported back to me. They've spotted a faint light moving around in a café just beyond the bridge. It's probably a flashlight. They won't get far."

"Good. Make sure you radio the men to take them alive if they try to leave the café," he said brusquely. "I want no fuck-ups, Brown. Understood?"

The sergeant jumped to attention. "Yes, Sir!"

Collier climbed back into the Jeep. He wiped the condensation from the window and leaned back against the seat. Muttering to himself, he contacted headquarters on his short-wave radio.

"Patch me through to Barrows."

"Sir, the lines are jammed and—"

"Dammit, cut through if you have to—" Collier said and waited impatiently.

A burst of static preceded the steely voice of an older man. "Commander Collier? I hope you have good news for me."

Collier frowned. "I'm sorry, Sir, but so far the suspects have eluded us. A landslide destroyed most of the convoy and we've had to call for reinforcements. As you can imagine, our resources are strained to the limits—"

"I'm not interested in hearing excuses," Barrows said. "I want facts."

Collier sucked in his breath. "Frankly, Sir, I'm not sure if there are any answers here. The suspects—well, they seem to be impervious to capture. There was an incident last night while the helicopters had them surrounded. It was unlike anything I've ever seen. As our men were about to apprehend them, all hell broke loose. First the mountain collapsed onto the convoy, and the choppers—each one was destroyed before they were able to return—"

"Yes, I heard about that. Any explanations?"

Collier's eyes narrowed. "It's the woman. I'm convinced of it. She's—different."

"We know that already, Commander."

"You know what I mean, Sir."

Faint crackling distorted the signal. "Then you must make certain she's captured as quickly as possible. I don't need to remind you what's at stake here."

"I know perfectly well what's at stake here, Sir."

"Good. Then proceed as discussed. Keep me informed. We must apprehend those suspects, understood?"

The signal faded into a background hiss. Collier switched off the radio and scanned the skies for the promised choppers. "Government lapdog," he muttered. "Damned suits don't have a clue what it's like out here." He gazed thoughtfully at the barrier blocking the highway. Even with dynamite, it would take too long to get through. He studied the surrounding landscape and wondered if an alternate route was feasible. Surely a few of his men could get through the rugged terrain? The two scouts keeping the café under surveillance would need backup if past encounters with the fugitives were any example. Quickly he radioed them.

"What's going on there?"

"Nothing, Sir," came a distorted voice. "The light went out. There's no sign of movement. No indication yet that we've been spotted."

"Well, even they have to sleep sometime. I'll send backup. If anything happens, let me know right away."

He shouted at Brown, who was busy supervising the placing of the explosives. The sergeant came trudging through the snow—his gait cumbersome in the heavy military overclothes.

"Sir?"

"Assemble a team of four men, Brown. I want to try and navigate through the mountains. We can't wait for the blasting."

"But, Sir, the charges are already in place."

"Then continue. But I want a team assembled as soon as

possible, preferably with some experience of climbing. It won't be easy, but if we can get some men through to apprehend the suspects, the choppers can go directly there. We can't let the suspects slip away again."

"What about the water, Sir?" said Brown. "Maybe the men can skirt the shore."

Collier walked to the edge of the road and stared down at the Sound. The water resembled a dark puddle of spilled ink as it wound lazily toward the sea. He glanced at the huge boulders littering the landscape and pursed his lips. It would be a dangerous trek, but still—

"The café isn't that far away, maybe a mile. Barring any unexpected incidents, the team should get there in about an hour. Very well, Sergeant, take care of it. One way or another, we're getting to that café. And find out where those damned choppers are!"

Almost two hours had elapsed before Sergeant Brown contacted Collier. "Sir, the suspects are in the café and everything appears quiet but our men can't get near it."

"Why the hell not?" Collier barked, impatience and anger a dull throb in his head.

"We've tried several times but we can't get beyond a few feet of the place. There seems to be some kind of protective barrier around it."

"Then blast through it," cried Collier with disgust. "Use your brains, man. Take them while they're asleep!"

"Sir—"

"You heard me!"

"But, Sir, we attacked with everything we had! None of our weapons managed to penetrate the barrier. We've even tried hand grenades. Everything bounces off. It's like an impregnable wall."

"Then stay there until we get through. Don't let them leave that café!" The transmissions crackled. "Did you hear me? Brown—"

"Yes, Sir!"

"And take the woman alive! Understood?"

"Yes, Sir!"

Collier leaned forward and banged his head on the steering wheel. "What the fuck—bouncing grenades—invisible walls—" he muttered in exasperation. "Where the hell are you?" he suddenly shouted. He balled his fists and gazed up at the somber sky. "Why can't you give us the powers to break through? Why are theirs so much stronger? I thought you had the mightiest army! You promised—"

While he stared bleakly into the darkness, a writhing green mist materialized and insinuated into the vehicle. Regretting his outburst, Collier's anger transformed into terror as the mist cocooned him in a spectral web. Choked by rising panic, he struggled to stifle a scream when the creature throbbed against his flesh like a pulsing organism. A staccato clicking filled the Jeep. Collier blanched, the rearview mirror reflecting a mask of terror as wispy filaments snaked across his face and teased his eyes, ears and nostrils. Slowly, deliberately, they encircled his neck and tightened their grip. "I'm sorry— I didn't mean to be disrespectful—" he stammered.

"Be patient," the creature murmured, the words a raspy sibilance. "Soon you will have all the powers you longed for—and more."

Collier squirmed as the filaments released their tenuous grip. "But—but the woman is thwarting our every move. We're helpless against her."

"The battle will soon be won. Our time is near. The woman will be yours."

"What if she opens the portal before we have a chance to—"

"She will fail. Our armies are gathering now and are preparing for the final battle."

"We—we have to reach the portal before her," Collier muttered.

"And I have told you she will fail. The woman carries the key. Once you take it from her, events will follow their preordained course. She will be a hindrance no longer."

Collier swallowed convulsively as the creature slowly receded into a mist and funneled out of the Jeep. It drifted toward several men placing dynamite and encircled them in a malefic green veil. He sagged against the seat and exhaled with a shudder. The creature had brought him little comfort. Time— It told him they had time, but how did it know? No one knew the right time. They wouldn't know—not until they had the key—and what the hell did the key look like? At first he thought it was a disc or some kind of microfilm, but now he knew it was something quite different. Yet the voice refused to tell him what the mysterious object was. The voice had said only that he would be told after they captured the woman.

Leaning his forehead on the cold steering wheel, the unpleasant sensation of the filaments still lingering on his skin, he waited anxiously for the call from Brown confirming that the team had apprehended the suspects.

***

CHAPTER TWENTY-SEVEN
December 29th, 2008

Their sleep was restless and filled with inexplicable images and sounds. The pile of potato sacks made an uncomfortable mattress and stank of must and damp. Throughout the night they tossed and turned, their senses attuned to the slightest noise. Destiny's murmuring awakened Brett more than once. The last time, she spoke in a sharp, guttural tone. It took a moment for his groggy mind to register that she was speaking in different tongues, none of which he recognized. He listened until fatigue pushed him back to sleep.

Dawn's anemic light woke Destiny. She stretched and grimaced, her body a mass of aches. In the paleness of day, the café revealed itself to be a simple mom and pop operation. She glanced at Brett and saw his eyes flutter open. "I'd do anything for a shower right now," she said while carefully putting the skull back into the bag.

"And me," he said tiredly. "I feel as if I'm wearing ten pounds of potato dirt."

She bent down and kissed him on the lips. "Did you get any rest?"

He hesitated. "I'd have preferred the Hilton."

"My dreams were filled with more of the visions I had last

night," she said. Suddenly her head swiveled toward the door.

"What's wrong?" he asked, quickly rising to his feet. His hand brushed his weapon.

"We're not alone."

Brett cautiously approached a window and carefully peered through a slat in the blinds. The stillness of the deserted landscape beyond was so jarring he felt he was looking at a movie still.

"My God!" His eyes began to discern the sinister shapes of abandoned weapons and spent shell casings littering the snow. "Destiny, you have to see this—it's like a battle was waged out there." His confused glance fixed on the undamaged Jeep.

She stared apprehensively through the slats and paled. What she surveyed looked like a mock battlefield. "Jesus—" she whispered. "What happened here? I can't believe we never heard anything."

Brett shook his head. "The military must have sent in a task force and we slept right through it? So why aren't we in custody? With that arsenal they should have leveled the building." He strained to peer through the slats. "I don't like this. Where the hell is everyone?"

Destiny shuddered and withdrew from the window. "They're out there—maybe three or four men."

"Elementals?"

She shrugged. "Yes. I hardly think anyone else would bombard us like this."

Brett scanned the immediate area and the deserted highway beyond. The rocks and fallen trees provided endless hiding places.

A fiery glow suddenly illuminated the walls around them. They turned in unison and stared in disbelief as a gibbous light emanated from the canvas bag.

"The skull," she said.

They glanced at each other. She slowly approached the bag and gazed into the kaleidoscopic colors. Without fear, she removed her gloves, reached inside and clasped the skull. Her eyes fluttered in response to an intense warmth that coursed through her flesh.

Brett moved toward her as she was enveloped in a diaphanous veil of color that insinuated through and around her like an ocean current. "Are you okay?"

Fixing her eyes on the skull, her expression suddenly became vacant. "The way is clear," she murmured in what Brett recognized was Italian, then again several times in various other languages. He overcame his fear and approached. With an awestruck expression, he gazed into the bag to see Destiny's hands merged with the glowing skull. A ribbon of light emerged from the eye sockets and spiraled to the ceiling. Continuing her recital in strange tongues, as though making an announcement to a distant audience, he watched the other talismans shimmer with almost dazzling intensity.

A voice suddenly boomed around them. Brett started. Its resonance echoed off the walls and broke Destiny's trance. The beam of light winked out and her eyes fluttered. She withdrew her hands from the still glowing skull.

"Yes?"

"The path of escape is clear. Blow the trumpet. Its sound will not disturb the pure. Those who wait for you will not be able to withstand it."

"Joshua brought the walls of Jericho down with the sounding of his trumpet," Destiny murmured.

"Yes, and so will you bring down the elementals who await you outside with the sounding of this trumpet. We have shielded you against their assault, but now you must go. The way is clear—the way is clear—"

The voice faded to a whispering resonance.

"Brett, get our stuff ready. I need to use the bathroom before we leave."

"Okay. Let me just take a quick look around in case I missed anything last night. Who knows if we'll find food or shelter after this."

Entering the small bathroom, she shuddered. Last night in the dark, she couldn't really see anything. Now, in the dim light, the bathroom was filthy, the toilet stained and cracked and the water a murky brown. Holding her breath, she quickly relieved herself, then waited while Brett searched the café. After a few minutes, he returned with a solitary, dust caked bottle of orange juice and a forlorn box of raisins.

"Better than nothing," he said almost apologetically.

While Brett gathered their gear, Destiny removed the tiny

trumpet from the bag and lovingly cradled it in her hand. It emanated a gentle glow and bathed her palm with comforting warmth. Resolutely, she approached the window. Brett followed, his hand hovering above his weapon.

She carefully peered through the slats. For a moment, she imagined she saw a shimmering haze like glittering constellations surrounding the café. The vision abruptly disappeared. Movement flickered beyond the huge boulder. She knew without a doubt that the elementals were planning to move on them at any moment. Focusing her thoughts, she brought the little trumpet to her lips and blew. No audible sound emerged but within her mind she could hear its angelic resonance. She blew again while her eyes fixed on the boulder and the enemy she sensed beyond.

"It plays the same tune as the music box," Brett said wonderingly.

"Yes, but according to the voice," she said, she slipping on her gloves, "the elementals can't bear the sound of it."

Several bloodcurdling cries rose from the direction of the boulder and the fallen trees next to it. "Let's go!" she cried to Brett and grabbed the canvas bag.

They burst through the door and sprinted toward the Jeep, their breath misting from effort and the stabbing cold. Screams continued to pierce the air, echoing through the mountains, bringing a shuddering chill to Brett as he tried to imagine what was happening to the hapless men. The absolute silence afterward only augmented the nightmarish cacophony and despite everything they had endured, he felt a moment of pity for those who were sucked into the dark realm.

They jumped into the Jeep. It roared to life when Brett floored the gas, the tires crunching over shells and other debris. He drove as fast as the icy conditions would allow. Though Destiny continued to look behind, no one pursued. She shuddered and turned to face the road ahead, glad to be away from the dismal scene.

The vehicle labored up the hill. Brett noticed that the snow got deeper the farther they drove until even the four-wheel drive had trouble handling it. "Under normal conditions, we'd be in Squamish in fifteen minutes."

"How long do you think it'll take?"

"At the rate we're moving, at least two hours, assuming the convoy doesn't catch up with us first."

"I wonder if there'll be a welcoming committee waiting for us there."

"Unlikely. From what I heard on the news in the past, most of Squamish was destroyed during the last quake. It's probably another ghost town."

Destiny sighed. "How's the gas?"

"A bit less than half now. We'll be screwed without the Jeep, but where we'll find gas is anyone's guess. My allotment's probably been canceled by now anyway."

"I thought you said we should trust the voice? You don't sound very confident."

Brett shook his head. She reached out and stroked his cheek. "I do trust them, but I'm just worried," he said, giving her a sideways glance. "Some strange things have been happening—"

"Strange? Like what?"

"Well, when you were holding the skull back in the cafe, you began speaking in tongues. And last night—your eyes—at first I thought I was imagining it—"

She turned away and stared at the bleak landscape. "I—remember, but I thought it was part of the vision. I didn't realize I was manifesting."

"You're changing, Destiny. We both are. I can hear and see things now. Not as well as you, but I think we're both evolving into something else."

She sat back in the seat with a pensive expression. "Evolving? Or devolving into what we supposedly were?"

He shrugged. "It's mystifying. I've always had an open mind, but never in my wildest dreams would I have believed something like this was possible."

On impulse, Destiny reached for the radio. Nothing but static burst from every station she tried. "It's gone—everything we knew. Our last link with humanity— Everything—" she said wistfully and turned the radio off. "Will we ever see it again, Brett?"

He reached out to squeeze her hand. "I honestly don't know, Destiny. All we can do is keep going. Your strength is amazing; it sustained me when I felt like surrendering. If there's ever been a guiding light in my life, it's certainly been you." Quickly he withdrew his hand to grab the steering wheel.

She felt encouraged by his praise and the trust he placed in her. "You know, Brett, as we're driving it's almost as if I can hear the whisper of time slipping by with the wind."

He didn't answer her, the answer apparent to both of them.

Suddenly he swerved to avoid an umbrella; buckled and distorted like the world around them it tumbled forlornly in the wind.

"Besides my powers, I wish I had psychic abilities as well. Then I could figure out the elementals' agenda."

"I suppose the voices already know," he said. "It's probably enough that they're here to guide us."

They drove in thoughtful silence. Every now and then she turned back to see if anyone followed, but her senses already confirmed that there was no one behind them.

***

Almost two hours later they arrived in Squamish. On the left, what was once a MacDonalds restaurant was now a pile of rubble. The golden arches and the huge yellow M stood like fallen monuments to the spot where the fast food restaurant had once stood. Only the red and white bucket emerged from the nearby ruins of a Kentucky Fried Chicken outlet. The colonel's smiling face leered in a grotesque parody of normalcy.

At the main intersection, the traffic lights were nothing more than stumps in the snow. Brett looked to the left where the city of Squamish and its small shopping center once stood. All he could see was water, the town consumed by the ocean. The small harbor, once teeming with life, dozens of fishing boats, yachts and sailboats moored at the wharves, was gone. Several shattered boats lay on dry land as if tossed like discarded toys. Half buried by snow, their broken masts attested to the pummeling forces they had endured.

Tightlipped, he continued on toward Garibaldi Highlands, a suburb of Squamish. He wondered what was left of it, knowing that half the mountain had disintegrated and the houses nestled against it were all buried. The main suburb lay in a valley. He hoped that with a bit of luck, something might have survived there.

Destiny stared grimly at the surrounding ruins. She had sensed no one would be waiting for them, and found her abilities honing with each passing day. Unfortunately, with it came a painful awareness of the suffering endured by those that had lived here. She wondered how much more her empathy would increase. Would she soon be capable of hearing the heartbeat of humanity itself?

The Jeep plodded tiredly through the almost unsurpassable snow to a host of sinister clanks and rattles. Lush forests that once flanked the highway were now reduced to barren wasteland with no sign of the wildlife that had once inhabited it. Far in the distance, Destiny thought she saw fleeting shadows. "Brett, I don't know what it is but I see movement all over the place. It's like the darkness is converging on us. I don't think they're human. The shadows are ghostly, almost like—"

"Entities," he said grimly. "Or perhaps demons. Every aspect of darkness is manifesting itself."

After more than an hour's drive, they entered Garibaldi Highlands. Isolated houses still spotted the countryside. Brett searched for signs of life, smoke from a chimney, the movement of a car, anything to indicate there were still people in the area.

When they approached the main intersection, he noticed with relief that the small shopping mall still stood along with a crudely repaired service station. With the gas gauge now hovering at less than a quarter, he had no choice but to fill up if they were to continue. He hoped what little cash he had on him would suffice; to attempt to use his allocation card would only be inviting trouble.

With difficulty, he veered right onto Garibaldi Way. When he entered the gas station's lot he realized it was closed. A sign near the cashier's door indicated alternate days of operation. The remaining pump was locked.

He looked around to make sure he was unobserved before he discreetly broke the lock. Muttering a silent prayer that the fuel tanks would not be empty, he inserted the nozzle into the Jeep's tank. The nozzle spluttered, hissed a few times, then with relief, he heard the gush of liquid. Quickly he pumped the tank full of gas.

Destiny had gotten out to stretch her legs and stood beside him. "Looks like they've restored some power here. I see lights."

"Maybe something will be open in the mall," he said glancing across the street. "See that apartment complex across the street? I know it well. A friend of mine used to live there. It's a miracle it survived at all, although I notice some pretty bad cracks in the structure. If we park in the rear lot, the Jeep won't be easily visible from the main roads and we can walk across to the mall to see if anything's open."

"I only saw a few cars in the mall parking lot."

"Yes, I know, so we'll have to expect the worst. But let's check it out anyway."

They got back into the Jeep. Brett drove around the block to the back of the apartment building. Most of the spots were vacant so he picked a spot tucked beside an overflowing garbage tip. Ever vigilant, they hurried from the parking lot. As they plowed through the snow toward Garibaldi Highway, Destiny noticed the movement of curtains in one apartment. She tugged Brett's sleeve. "Someone's watching us. What if they call the police?"

"I doubt it. The remaining tenants are probably not used to seeing much activity around here, though we'd better not waste too much time just to be safe." They lumbered through the piled snow toward the mall entrance. "We'll hit the food places and go."

Banks of snow flanked the poorly cleared parking lot. A few lights shone from inside the mall as they entered though virtually all of the stores were closed. Walking past empty storefronts, their footsteps echoed eerily. Of all things, Destiny found the lack of muzak most unnerving. "This is the smallest mall I've ever been in. Ten steps and you're on the other side."

Brett grinned. "It's a small town. Look down there, Best Foods is open, and it looks like the drugstore in it is, too."

"Wonder how well stocked they are."

"Right now," he said, "I'd settle for dog food."

They strolled casually into the market. Only one cashier was working and the store was deserted save for a couple of customers and a pair of surly guards that watched carefully for shoplifting. They eyed the couple with suspicion.

The young woman behind the cash register smiled. "Hello."

"Hi," Destiny said with a smile as she noticed the pretty blonde's shimmering pale mauve aura. "Do you sell hot food?"

"Yes. We have a government licensed soup kitchen at the back."

"We should have brought the thermos," Destiny said wistfully.

"Brett glanced at the guards. Despite the other customers, the men seemed unusually interested in them. "That sounds great," he said, drawing Destiny away. "Thanks."

Few items stocked the shelves, and there was almost nothing in the cooler sections. Brett bent close to Destiny's ear as they headed for the soup kitchen.

"Did you notice anything about the guards?"

She nodded. "Both had faint green auras, but they aren't a threat."

She immediately stiffened though when she caught sight of the swarthy, middle aged woman manning the soup kitchen whose green aura snaked around her like a noxious fog. Brett noticed Destiny's change of expression and struggled to retain his composure as he approached the counter. Destiny pretended to inspect a meager display of canned goods nearby.

"Can I help you, Sir?" the woman asked, a stony expression on her plain, doughy face.

Brett mustered a smile. "We'd like some soup, please. Large servings."

The woman eyed him for a moment before carefully ladling some kind of vegetable soup into two plastic containers. "I'll have to charge you for four servings. Government mandate."

"That's okay. Smells good."

While handing Brett the soup, the woman's eyes flicked to Destiny. "That'll be ten dollars."

He winced at the gouged price but said nothing and paid. Thanking the woman, he quickly guided Destiny away. Neither of them saw the woman duck into the back.

"She's one of them," Destiny said.

"Did you see her aura?"

"Yes. The darkness was so strong within her it was like feeling hands tightening around my neck."

The guards cast them a pointed look when they left the store. It was all Brett could do to keep from breaking into a run. His hand drifted to the weapon clipped around his belt until they were out of sight. Once outside, he grabbed Destiny's arm.

"Hurry, let's get the hell out of here. This doesn't feel right."

They sprinted across the road, the snow hampering their escape. Destiny suddenly felt compelled to turn around. From behind the mall, a security vehicle emerged and slowly made its way across the parking lot.

"Brett, look!"

"I see them. I had a feeling by the way they were watching us, they'd show up."

They scrambled down the driveway of the apartment building and piled into the Jeep. Just as Brett reversed, a group of elementals appeared out of nowhere and blocked their exit. Destiny gasped at their misshapen bodies and hate-filled faces.

"Jesus—" Brett muttered.

"They're barely human," Destiny said. "What the hell have they become?"

She shuddered when one of the elementals paused to sniff the air like an animal. The man, his features barely recognizable beneath a horrible encrustation of his face, uttered a garbled cry and lunged toward them.

"It's like they're no longer of this Earth," Brett said tightly. He floored the gas pedal and struggled to control the vehicle as it skidded down the driveway. Undaunted by the speeding Jeep, the man veered across Brett's path. Brett swore and swerved to avoid him but could not steer away in time. Destiny winced. The man seemed to stare directly at her a moment before he vanished beneath the wheels. A single, garbled scream emerged when the Jeep rolled over him with a sickening bump.

Destiny stuffed her fist in her mouth to keep from crying out. Brett managed to straighten the Jeep and continued as fast as he could. Even in four-wheel drive and equipped with chains, it had difficulty negotiating the icy conditions. Fishtailing into the road, Brett glanced at the security vehicle, its tires spinning uselessly in the snow. One of the guards was ineffectually firing at the eagle.

Destiny glanced back at the creatures crouched by their fallen comrade. Silently, they rose and stared at the retreating Jeep.

"My God, Brett—" she murmured.

"He came straight for us," Brett said tightly. "There was nothing I could do."

The eagle veered suddenly toward the Jeep. It banked gracefully and headed toward the highway. "It's flying north again," Destiny said with a quavering voice, the ghastly image of the man's death still branded in her mind.

Brett turned right on the highway but the poor conditions kept him from speeding much more beyond a crawl. Remembering the soup that she had mindlessly hurled into the Jeep, Destiny was relieved to find the containers intact. She guided Brett's cup to his lips while he drove. The soup warmed and revitalized her. Suddenly, her ears pricked. Though she did not immediately hear anything, she kept turning around.

"Now what?"

"Something's coming."

He glanced into his mirror but saw nothing. "Choppers?"

She nodded. "Reinforcements."

Brett pointed to the sky. "Look, the eagle's turning toward Whistler."

"Then Whistler it is," she said.

She continued to look behind as they drove for a grueling three hours. Occasionally she thought she glimpsed dark shapes hovering in the distance, but the advent of yet another storm front had sharply reduced visibility. Whether she actually saw anything was now irrelevant, she sensed the approach of danger as clearly as if a beacon flashed in the sky.

Brett turned a hairpin curve and braked to avoid the obstacle looming ahead. The Jeep skidded toward the edge of the ravine. Gripping the wheel with white knuckles, he fought to control the vehicle. He exhaled tightly when the Jeep halted mere inches from the edge and stared in disbelief.

More than a landslide, the obstruction was as though the entire mountain had shifted directly in the path of the road. He angrily slammed the steering wheel.

"Well, this is fucking marvelous. What do we do know, ignite thrusters for liftoff?" He peered into sky. "So how about some help here?"

Destiny gazed thoughtfully at the obstruction. "It would be a long hike, but we could probably continue on foot. How far are we from Whistler Village?"

He irritably shrugged. "I have no idea. All the signs are gone. At the speed we've been traveling, maybe we're three quarters of the way."

"If we stay here, they'll capture us."

Brett glanced at her and noticed the calm resolution in her eyes. Feeling foolish at his outburst, he nodded. "Let's get our gear."

They got out of the Jeep and sunk to their knees in snow. With a melancholy glance, Brett gazed at the vehicle and thought of the long trek ahead of them.

"They'll have no choice but to send choppers now."

"Conditions permitting," she said. "If they want us that badly, they'll have to blast through this mountain or continue on foot like us."

Brett scanned the dull, empty sky. "Our guide seems to have departed. Wonderful. We'll need a team of Ghurkas to find our way now." Quickly, he drank the rest of his soup and threw the empty thermos on the front seat of the Jeep. "We'll have to settle for whatever's left in our packs." "All that's left is some dried fruit, so don't eat it too quickly," Destiny said. "We have a long trek ahead of us."

They hiked clumsily, the cold and the effort forcing them to stop often to rest. Destiny suddenly stopped and looked around. "Brett—" she whispered.

He halted and turned in time to see a pack of silver wolves materialize from a rock formation. Some of them growled softly as they watched the humans with liquid eyes. Brett clutched Destiny's arm. "Back up slowly," he mouthed.

She remained motionless and stared at the wolves. At least a dozen, they did not advance but just stood and watched them, their breath forming clouds of steam in the frigid air as they panted. All the time they maintained eye contact with Destiny as though trying to convey something to her.

Suddenly the pack shifted and fell to the side. A great white wolf appeared, his luxuriant coat blending almost completely with the pristine snow. Gracefully, he loped toward Brett and Destiny, his ice blue eyes never wavering as he regarded them.

Gazing into the wolf's intense eyes, recognition spurred Destiny. "It couldn't be," she murmured. In her mind she glimpsed a fleeting vision of a playful pup. "My little companion—is it really you?"

The wolf yipped and wagged his tail in reply. Destiny smiled and stepped forward. She held out her hand. "Welcome, old friend. It's been so long since we played together—"

***

CHAPTER TWENTY-EIGHT

Destiny and Brett remained motionless as the great beast sauntered toward them. Beyond, his court silently watched, motionless, their breath rising in a white mist. The wolf silently approached, his fathomless blue eyes steadily fixed upon them.

Destiny could not help but admire the creature. In the flesh, he exuded a mesmerizing power and beauty that could never be captured in a photo. Whatever doubts she had that this was her friend from the past quickly evaporated. An assured calmness settled within her—a knowledge that this beautiful animal was the puppy she once knew. Aware of Brett's tension, she slowly reached out and clasped his hand. He started at the contact, but gradually felt his demeanor relax as her confidence flowed through him.

The wolf stopped to gaze at them for a moment. Only a thin, reedy wind disturbed the eerie silence, the cold a sharp knife stab in her sinuses. Transfixed, Brett regarded the surreal scene before him. The wolf cocked his head sideways in a curiously assessing motion. Sidling up to Destiny, his luxuriant tail wagged like that of a friendly dog. He yelped softly and gently nuzzled her extended hand. She smiled with delight when he began to lick her hand, the warmth emanating through the leather.

Suddenly, he jumped up against her, his weight almost knocking her off her feet. The wolf stood a head taller than her as he rose on powerful hind legs, his huge paws planted firmly against her chest.

She felt his hot breath on her face and unconsciously held her own. He licked her face several times, then fell back to the ground in a single, graceful motion. His eyes searched hers as though trying to communicate with her.

He strode away and looked back inquisitively, only to return when they did not follow.

Brett finally dared to speak. "I think he wants us to follow him."

"He's our guide," she said. "He won't harm us."

Moving slowly, they started to follow the wolf. The animal yelped playfully, his tail wagging. He skillfully navigated the snow and forged a path to make their progress easier. His white coat blended so completely with the snow they had to watch carefully not to lose him.

Far behind, the attendant pack followed. Their lush silver fur contrasted sharply against the snow, so they were easily seen.

The white wolf led them to an avalanche site. Trees and rocks jutted from the collapsed mound of snow, the effect like a crushed wedding cake. With amazement, they watched him crawl through a barely visible hole near a shattered tree. When Brett and Destiny did not follow after a moment, he returned and patiently waited for them before crawling into the hole again.

"He wants us to follow him into that hole," Brett said.

She frowned. "I don't like the look of it. What if the snow caves in?"

"The snow's pretty hard, almost frozen. I don't think the wolf would lead us anywhere dangerous. I'll go first."

She watched him crouch down low and follow the wolf into the hole. Aware of eyes on her back, she turned to see the wolf pack sitting in a semi-circle behind her. Their fur glistened in the sharp gray light.

"He's dug a tunnel," Brett called back to her. "It's okay. Come on."

Recalling her fear of elevators, claustrophobia threatened to overwhelm her even before she crawled into the hole. The tunnel was so confined that the canvas bag clutched tightly in her hand scraped the ice as she dragged it along. She heard a muffled sound behind her and almost immediately, the tunnel darkened alarmingly. An unpleasant sensation pressed against her when the comforting light faded. "What the—" she murmured, anxiously peering around in the encroaching darkness. "Brett?"

"Keep going, Destiny. The tunnel definitely leads somewhere."

Almost in response, the wolf barked. The timber of its voice echoed reassuringly around her. She felt her burgeoning panic subside and continued along the narrow tunnel with more confidence.

Measuring her pace, she sagged with relief when she noticed the reassuring glow of light in the distance. The final segment of the tunnel narrowed and forced her to wriggle through some tight spots. She felt the numbing pressure of snow against her shoulders but managed to keep her fear of the confined space at bay. When she reached the tunnel exit, Brett held his hands out to her and pulled her out into the welcome light.

Breathing heavily, she fell against his chest and relished his warm embrace. They watched intrigued as the wolf quickly dug to conceal the hole.

"The pack didn't follow," he said. "I think they buried the hole on the other side. That's why it suddenly got so dark."

"They're covering our tracks. I think we're in good hands here."

He retrieved what little remained of the orange juice and gave it to her. "We need to get some decent food into us soon. With all this exertion, we've burned whatever calories that soup gave us."

Gulping down the tangy liquid, she nodded and handed him some dried fruit. "What I'd do for something warm right now, even a cup of clean water—"

They paused long enough to catch their breath and continued their trek through the barren winterscape. Brett had no idea where they were going as they followed the wolf. There was nothing to indicate they were near any resorts and the topography of the land was drastically altered from what he recalled of the area. He and Destiny exchanged glances, but said nothing. Laboriously, they tread through the snow.

She stopped and called out to Brett. The wolf yelped at her impatiently.

He turned. "We have to keep going, Destiny."

"Brett, look," she insisted, pointing west.

He shielded his eyes. Snow had begun to fall again. Huge flakes resembling strips of lace drifted slowly down from the blanketed sky. In the distance he saw specks through the drifting veil of snow. They were no more than dark wraiths against the light background. He recognized the elementals and turned to Destiny. "Elementals," he said. "They're following us but keeping their distance."

"Yes, I can feel it," she said and at the wolf's urging, continued on, her eyes periodically drifting to the wraiths that shadowed their every move. "I wonder how far our pursuers are behind us—"

***

CHAPTER TWENTY-NINE

The Jeep leading the convoy stopped abruptly before the devastated mountain flanking the highway. Hours had been lost dynamiting and plowing through the last avalanche at Britannia Beach, and now, an even larger obstacle lay in their path. Collier swore in exasperation and climbed from the vehicle. The rumble of the idling convoy rose starkly as he crunched his way toward the landslide. The abandoned Jeep stood forlornly in the snow, the interior bare, save for a discarded thermos that revealed no clues. Snow began to fall and left a powdery dusting on the floor and seats. He paced around it, examining it as though expecting an answer. Sergeant Brown came scuttling up, his expression dismayed in anticipation of Collier's customary backlash.

"This is turning out to be a goddamned conspiracy," Collier grumbled, spitefully kicking the front tire. "If I didn't know better I'd say this was planned."

"They're only one man and woman," Brown said. "Luck's been on their side so far, but it's bound to run out. Shall I call in the demolition team?"

Collier stared wearily at the leaden sky and shuddered. "Fucking cold. Always so fucking cold—"

"Sir?"

"Call them in. I want this cleared before dark. And go over that Jeep again. They left that thermos. Maybe they left something else behind, anything to give us a clue. Any news from the teams?"

Brown shook his head and ineffectually wiped at the frost clinging to his sandy moustache. "Not since the first check-in, Sir. They should have radioed at dawn to report their positions."

Collier closed his eyes. "Tell me this isn't another screw-up, Brown. The suspects could be miles away by now."

Brown stared at his boots. "I could send another team—"

"No. Let's get this damned landslide out of the way. Time's running out."

The whine of an approaching Jeep caught Collier's attention. He frowned when it parked at the front of the convoy. A man and woman emerged and lumbered toward them.

Retrieving her badge, agent Woolley flashed it at Collier. "Sir, Agents Woolley and Degen from Internal Security. John Barrows assigned us to this case in a supervisory position. We need to know your progress regarding the suspects. Captain Garring and Sergeant Patterson of the Burnaby police will join us shortly to help in the search, as they know Brett Young. Unfortunately, they were delayed in Britannia Beach when one of their Jeeps slid off the road and got stuck."

Sergeant Brown reflexively saluted and hurried away when he noticed the thundercloud expression forming on Collier's face.

"I might as well tell you I was ordered to cooperate with you. Since when do Internal Security and the police interfere with military operations?"

"Since national security has become compromised to the point of a breakdown. Sir, I don't have time to argue political agendas. If you wish to file an official protest, feel free to contact John Barrows. The suspects are more than terrorists; they may possess enhanced abilities caused by the chameleon virus. This could be a potential—"

Collier barked derisively. "Enhanced? Bullshit, that's what I call it! You really expect me to believe that we're dealing with a pair of Area 51 renegades here?"

Degen's wooden expression barely shifted as he addressed Collier. "Perhaps you can explain why two lightly armed suspects have evaded you so successfully?"

Collier's eyes narrowed. "Lightly armed is conjecture on your part, Agent Degen. Has it occurred to your elite organization that the suspects may have help? Or possess technology we're unaware of? The world may be one fucked-up place at the moment, but one thing I haven't seen is the emergence of some super race capable of paranormal abilities, enhanced or whatever the hell you want to call it. The suspects are probably highly trained terrorists. Considering the general breakdown of resources, it's amazing we've gotten as far as we have."

Woolley's eyes drifted to the abandoned Jeep and the snow that was churned up immediately around it. She moved toward it and examined the surrounding area. A moment later, Collier and Degen crunched toward her.

"I don't see any tracks leading away from the Jeep," she said. "How is that possible, Commander?"

Collier snorted. "My men are working on it, Agent. Or are you going to suggest the suspects levitated to a higher plane?"

Woolley's eyes flashed with anger as she turned to face Collier. "Are you always such an arrogant son of a bitch? Look for yourself if you don't believe me. How do you explain the churned snow around the Jeep? It looks almost as though any tracks have been deliberately concealed. I'm pointing out the obvious here, not metaphysics."

A tense silence passed between the three. Degen flashed Woolley the 'I told you so' look reserved for awkward types like Collier. Collier grumbled and stalked off as far as the churned snow extended. Woolley and Degen followed a short distance behind.

"Guess he has to see the obvious with his own eyes," Degen said.

Anger still suffused Woolley, flushing her, despite the cold. "It's as they've disappeared into thin air," she said, pointing to a smooth area a few yards ahead. "Look. You can see where the snow is completely undisturbed."

Collier paused when the churning came to an abrupt end. He stared beyond at the untouched snow, then glanced back at Woolley and Degen before trudging past them with a curt attitude.

"My men are setting up explosives. Maybe we'll get some answers when the landslide is cleared. In the meantime, I suggest you stay out of my way."

Woolley and Degen watched Collier return to the convoy. Sergeant Brown approached him in typical lap-dog fashion.

"His head is so far up his ass it's amazing he can see where he's going," Degen commented dryly.

"Probably doesn't like a woman in his face," Woolley said. "No doubt disturbs the testosterone levels around here."

Their heads swiveled up at an approaching drone. Squinting against the stark light, they spotted a modest armada of makeshift planes and a pair of ancient choppers in the distance.

"The cavalry approaches," Degen said.

Woolley shook her head. "My gut tells me it's going to take a lot more than surplus to capture these suspects."

Degen sighed. "Then we'd better get to work—"

Woolley walked away from the men and retrieved a pair of binoculars from her pocket. Placing them against her eyes, she scanned the area. Far in the distance, the elementals spread like a dark stain upon the road. They emerged from the mountains, negotiating the hazardous terrain without concern for their safety. Several slipped and fell, their cries ignored by their companions. The sound echoed eerily. "My God, they're getting closer," she murmured. "How the hell can I stop Collier? Time is running out. I need help— Destiny must get there first!"

Degen startled her out of her musings. She reflexively retrieved her weapon and aimed at his chest. "Jesus, Degen. Don't creep up on me like that!"

"Take it easy, Woolley. Who were you talking to? Or have you developed a habit of talking to yourself?"

If I wasn't surrounded by so much evil, I'd shoot you, you son of a bitch, Woolley thought. She felt very much alone, her task seemingly impossible as long as they were surrounded by the military. Collier must never get close to Destiny. She had to prevent it at all cost, even if it meant sacrificing her own life—

"I was saying that I'm starving. Coffee would sound good right now. Any left in the thermos?" Quickly she holstered the gun and walked away from him. The green aura surrounding Degen was growing stronger every day, the taint penetrating her with its corruption. Despite her efforts, it was becoming increasingly difficult to work among the elementals. She silently wished she had not been chosen for this task.

Degen eyed her suspiciously as she retreated. He concentrated but saw no aura at all around the woman. *Strange*, he thought. *She should at least have some kind of aura, even the faintest to give us a clue as to her loyalty.* He made a mental note to mention it to Collier the next opportunity he had to have a few civil words with the man. Instinct prompted him to be cautious, the animosity between himself and Collier merely a ploy to fool any potential spies among them—

***

CHAPTER THIRTY

Like automatons, Brett and Destiny churned through the numbing snow. Immersed in their own pace, they kept their eyes on the white wolf. Effortlessly, almost gliding through the snow, he created a path for them to follow. The pack silently materialized behind and followed closely. Apart from some stiffness in her calves from trudging through the snow, she felt no fatigue, her energy remaining surprisingly constant. Nor did Brett show any undue signs of exhaustion, a near miracle considering the intense cold, their constant flight, minimal food and sleep. She wondered if changes were taking place in her mind, her body, apart from her abilities which had already surfaced, that steeled her to an ordeal that would have felled ordinary people by now.

The echoing sound of distant thunder boomed far behind them. They paused, the sound of encroaching humanity almost an intrusion into the breathless winter silence.

"They're blasting through the mountain," Brett said. He shifted the weight of his bags and turned toward her. "How are you doing?"

Destiny hefted the canvas bag to her other arm. She glanced inside and gently touched the skull. It glowed momentarily at the contact.

"We have a long way to go. Let them try to follow."

The wolves yelped once to urge them forward. They turned and trudged at a constant distance from them. At length, the white wolf turned sharply and led them to the shelter of a skeletal forest. She shuddered at the eerie sight of the denuded trees; their tortured limbs raised to the dun sky like supplicating hands. Only the snow-laden branches offered them shelter from airborne visibility.

She stopped at the sound of a soft growl behind her. Turning slowly, she froze when she saw a huge grizzly approach, his shaggy brown coat shaking as he lumbered toward them. "Brett—" she said calmly. "Brett, stop—"

He stopped and turned toward her. The wolf bounded past before he could speak and greeted the bear by nuzzling its great wet nose. The bear growled in response and butted the wolf playfully. Circling, the pair mock charged and smelled each other, the wolf's tail wagging as though greeting an old friend.

"I've never seen or heard of anything like this," she said.

"That's because it's happening only now," Brett said. "Look over there—an elk."

She gazed in awe at the magnificently antlered animal placidly watching them from the naked trees. Its liquid eyes flashed as the wolf and bear approached it. Gently, it lowered its head and rubbed its formidable antlers against the coats of the wolf and bear. The wolf whimpered at the elk, which nodded in turn.

"I don't think we'll be alone again," Destiny said. The trio suddenly stopped and turned to look at them, then continued to lead the way.

It was late afternoon when they approached the resort town of Whistler. They had followed the trio without stopping and had barely approached the ruins of a half-buried ski chalet when they heard the staccato drone of a helicopter.

Brett grabbed Destiny and pulled her beneath a felled tree trunk partially buried by snow. Huddling together, they listened tensely to the circling chopper. Nearby branches crackled from the force of the rotors. When the sound of the chopper receded, Brett ventured a peek. Beyond, the white wolf and his pack stood quietly, the pack a distance away, waiting and watching. The bear and elk had vanished like mist into the landscape.

Venturing out a bit further, Brett calculated the distance between the trees and the ski chalet. It was within easy distance, but without the cover of trees, they would be clear targets against the snow.

"What's happening?" Destiny asked.

"We've got company. We'll have to wait till dark. No way we can get to the house before then."

They waited beneath the shelter of the trunk for dusk to fall. The wolves serenaded them in the distance, their harmonizing mournful yet beautiful. The eerie song lulled them into a false sense of security and gave them an opportunity for some badly needed rest.

The chopper circled relentlessly, its spotlight illuminating the phantom forest. Though the spots skimmed the chalet several times, even Brett could see that the heavy, undisturbed snow cover belied their presence and seemed to finally convince the chopper pilot they were not hiding there. He let out a sigh of relief when the chopper finally veered off to the North.

He gently nudged Destiny and whispered in her ear. "They're gone. Let's get moving. There's enough clearance on the porch for us to access one of the windows or the door."

"I was almost starting to get comfortable," she said, crawling from beneath the trunk. "Amazing how you adapt to conditions you would have thought intolerable."

He grinned. "The survivalists have nothing on us."

Supporting each other, they plowed through the deep snow. The slight incline made their progress more difficult but they eventually reached the chalet. Mounting the sagging porch stairs, they tested each step carefully before proceeding. At length, they reached a front door hanging askew on its hinges. Brett kicked it in. Snow showered them as they stumbled into the inky, musty interior. Destiny grimaced at the rank odor.

"We could do with a few open windows in here."

Brett set his bags down, switched on the flashlight and panned it across what appeared to be the living room. The beam of light rested longingly on a fireplace still stocked with wood.

"Don't say it," she said, eyeing the box of matches resting on the mantelpiece. Her gaze flitted across an array of knickknacks and framed photos, the carefree, smiling faces staring back at her from days long gone. On the corner of the mantle stood a small, carved wooden box. She picked it up and opened the lid to find souvenirs of the millennium celebration inside. Coins, mementos and a number of family photos filled her with nostalgia as she recalled the wonderful fireworks she and her parents watched that night. Even then she had nurtured hope that somehow in the new century, humanity would find its way, that it would truly usher a better, brighter era.

Reluctantly, Brett turned the flashlight away from the fireplace and panned the remainder of the room. It was surprisingly untouched, attesting to the suddenness of the avalanche. He crossed the hardwood floor gingerly. Though floorboards creaked alarmingly, none gave way. "I think we're safe for now. This place is sturdier than it looks."

"Let's check out the kitchen," Destiny said, setting the canvas bag on the floor. "If they had to get out that suddenly, there might be food left behind."

They almost raced each other as they quickly inspected the remainder of the chalet. The still-functioning bathroom distracted them long enough to attend to nature. They continued their explorations, small, cozy rooms and beds covered with thick down quilts tempting them. One of the bedrooms at the rear of the chalet had partially caved in. Brett could barely open the door as something was wedged against it. He shoved hard and finally managed to step into the room. Before he could warn Destiny, she followed him. He heard her gasp when she saw the object lit up by the flashlight.

"My, God, Brett! I wonder if he's one of the people in the pictures I just looked at or just a drifter looking for shelter—"

Protruding from the boards and posts that partially covered the bed was the torso of an elderly man. One of his arms was extended, the limb twisted in a grotesque plea for help. Pale eyes surrounded by a frame of white frozen lashes stared sightlessly up at the icicles hanging from the battered ceiling, the man's blue color attesting to the intense cold. His gray hair and moustache resembled a miniature forest of icicles. The man's mouth was frozen open in a silent scream, his body hunched beneath a stiffened, bloodied quilt.

Brett quickly turned the flashlight away from the gruesome sight and urged Destiny out of the room.

A shudder shook her body. She heard Brett tug hard at the door to close it. "Jesus, Brett, did you see the expression on his face? I've never seen such terror."

"Yes. I saw," he said grimly. "Try not to dwell on it. He's obviously been dead for some time. Right now, we need to find some food."

"Yes. Let's inspect the kitchen," she said, desperately trying to erase the disturbing image from her mind. Though she tried to concentrate on the thought of food as she followed Brett, she found even now it was difficult to steel herself against the horrors she witnessed.

The welcome sight of the kitchen at the rear of the chalet banished the shock of finding the frozen body. Brett peered through the door first, suspecting that the snow cover would be heaviest at this part of the chalet. Though the roof was sagging and snow pressed firmly against the windows, the structure seemed sound.

"Let's get what we need and get out. This part's holding for now, but I wouldn't want to hang around too long. Look at what happened to that bedroom."

Destiny slipped past him and headed for the fridge. She was almost afraid to open the door. In the flashlight's milky glow, no surprises awaited, though the shelves were disappointingly barren save for a few bottles of water.

"The fridge is empty. Obviously, no one has lived here for a while. Whoever that was must have been someone looking for shelter," she said, quickly removing the water. "Maybe we'll find something in the cupboards."

Her search through the cupboards proved more fruitful and produced an unopened box of crackers, a small jar of strawberry jam, a can of soup and a couple of cans of condensed milk.

Brett found himself growing suddenly quite hungry as Destiny collected her booty and hustled it along with some crockery back to the living room. Once again, they eyed the fireplace.

"Brett—"

"No way."

"But—"

"Dammit, Destiny, they'll see the smoke. Besides, the chimney's probably blocked. We can't take the chance."

She sighed and pried off the jam lid with a knife and hacked at the soup can with the can opener she found in one of the drawers. It was difficult, her fingers were stiff from cold and the frosty can didn't help. Finally she managed to lift the lid and gingerly stabbed at the sludgy contents. "Soup's on."

They ate the almost frozen soup by the glow of the flashlight. Nothing but crumbs remained of their meager meal, yet to Destiny, the sweetness of the jam spread thickly on the stale wheat crackers was the ultimate gourmet feast. They drank the condensed milk and shared a bottle of water between them. Feeling restored, they sank onto the couch and quietly held each other.

"What next?" Brett asked, idly stroking the fur-trim of Destiny's parka.

"A good night's sleep in a proper bed would be nice. Also some warmth. It's freezing in here."

"I wish we could stay. It would be the perfect—"

The sound of yelping caught their attention. They scurried from the couch and peered through the curtained window. The wolf pack jumped and frolicked in the snow. Their forms were dark shapes against as they erased their steps to the chalet. Brett's gaze was drawn to the almost invisible presence of the white wolf standing quietly beyond the pack. His icy eyes were fixed on the window.

"I see him," Destiny said, reading his thoughts. She turned to Brett and took his hand. "Come. Let's get some sleep. We'll be safe now."

He nodded and followed her to one of the small bedrooms. Snuggled together beneath the covers, they instantly fell into a deep slumber. The wolves abandoned their play and lay in a semi circle around the chalet to keep watch.

The white wolf remained motionless. He stood sentinel and silently surveyed his wintry domain. The only movement was the occasional turn of his head to gaze at the distant lights sweeping the brooding sky. He raised his head and emitted a single, piercing howl before turning his attention once again to the chalet.

***

With a gleeful cry, young Destiny plowed through pristine snow that sparkled like crushed diamonds. Her father had built her a sled and she happily pulled it behind her as she trudged toward the slight hill on their property. She hummed a tune, one that had become quite familiar to her.

After she reached the crest of the hill, she sat on the shiny red sled and gazed at the snow-covered flats below. When the spheres appeared, she embraced them in her thoughts. Soft tinkling music accompanied her humming as she lay on her belly on the sled, ready to slide down. She whizzed down the hill and felt exhilaration surge within her. All too soon she landed on the flats. Suddenly, she spotted a dog. Quickly she scrambled up and sat on the sled. "Here, puppy," she called, holding out her small gloved hand.

The white pup merged with the snow and trotted toward her with fluffy, wagging tail. "Nice puppy," she said softly and patted his luxurious coat. He licked her face, his icy blue eyes gazing deeply into her own. Destiny smiled when she felt an intense warmth course through her body. As she reached to embrace him, he suddenly raised his head and howled, then vanished like a specter into the snowbound landscape.

The spheres danced around her, their serenade filling her with joy. She climbed off the sled and lay in the snow. Swiftly her arms and legs moved to form snow angels. When she was done, she jumped up to inspect her handiwork. Smiling, she looked at the spheres as if seeking praise. They hovered around her and briefly caressed her. She smiled and reached out to touch her friends.

CHAPTER THIRTY-ONE
December 30th, 2008

A chorus of howling startled Brett and Destiny from their slumber. At first disoriented, Brett groped for the flashlight as he scrambled out of the bed and rushed to the living room window.

Destiny followed, disgruntled at having been woken from a restful sleep and peered through the curtain. "What's going on? They're agitated about something, but what? I don't hear any choppers approaching."

Darkness pressed against them. They discerned motionless shapes on the snow. A creaking step drew their attention to the porch. She gasped when she saw the white wolf barely a few feet from the front door. He yelped softly and lowered himself.

An image flashed through her mind. In that fleeting moment, she glimpsed a white wolf pup, its glacial eyes fixed on her as she ran her hand through its luxuriant coat. The sun blazed from an impossibly turquoise sky, the unfamiliar buildings around them bleached white above an azure sea lapping against a picturesque fishing harbor. Distant voices murmured, familiar yet unintelligible—

For a moment, she dwelled on the bizarre vision. It was as if she had been shown a page out of time, a glimpse into her childhood. The image seemed unreal, the presence of a wolf in such a setting an anachronism. Yet—somehow she knew the wolf had been her companion in another place, another time.

Dawn's anemic light kissed the sky and cast misshapen silhouettes against the snow. Brett touched her shoulder, banishing the vision.

"Look," he whispered.

Her eyes quickly acclimatized to the twilight. The white wolf now sat with his pack. Beyond, the grizzly and elk stood side by side accompanied by a host of wildlife she not even thought still existed.

"Am I hallucinating?" she said. "Over there—is that a lynx? And behind the bear, is that deer I see?"

"Take a look at the tree," Brett said.

A great spotted owl perched on the twisted branches of a tree. Even from a distance, she sensed the intensity of its stare. A shudder of recognition coursed through her. She shook her head. "I thought they were all gone. I thought there was nothing left."

"There are more in the distance, but I can't make out what they are."

Destiny stepped back.

Struck by the strangeness of her voice, Brett turned to stare at her in the obscure light.

"What is it? What have you seen?"

It was also suddenly clear now that the wolf had taken this form to be her companion. A thought entered her mind, *Antiquitas—perhaps all the animals out there were their protectors, the guardians of her people.*

"I don't know—" she murmured. "A vision, perhaps a memory of the wolf as a cub and me as a child. It felt like a long time ago." Her head swiveled to the animals in the forest. "You know, it's almost as if—" Her words trailed off.

Brett followed the direction of her gaze. "As if what?"

"We haven't seen the spheres recently."

"Well—maybe they are the spheres. Maybe they've become more than voices."

They looked wordlessly at each other.

"Of course," she said. "The vision I just had filled my mind with voices from the past, the voices of the ancient ones. They've assumed these forms to guide and protect us."

"Why didn't you tell me before?"

"It all sounds so bizarre. The Antiquitas have been the guardians of our people for millennia. They gave us the skull and bestowed its power upon my ancestors."

"Look, I've believed you up till now and that hasn't stopped," he said thoughtfully while watching the animals outside. He allowed his mind to go blank and for a split second shared Destiny's vision. "You're right. They're not mere animals, but something far greater."

Grateful that Brett's powers were increasing, she nodded. "Yes. And they've been there for us many times without us realizing it. It's time to go now."

A sound behind them shattered their moment of tranquility. They spun around. Three creatures hovered in the hallway, their cilia-covered, insectoid bodies almost four feet in length.

"My God," Destiny yelled, reflexively backing away.

Brett stepped in front of her, the revulsion clear in his face as he regarded the creatures. "What the hell are they?" he muttered. "Move back slowly."

"They must be the Eletarii. But how did they get here?"

"I'll be damned if I know."

Her mind suddenly swam for a moment, all sound ceasing as she heard the voice.

"Behold the creatures that covet Earth."

She stared in revulsion at the aliens. A sextet of limbs supported their scaled, segmented bodies. Wings flared from beneath bottle green carapaces, their bulbous heads cocked as they regarded her. Rows of tiny red eyes glared like those of a malevolent spider while their fearsomely hooked mandibles clicked in a semblance of language. It was hard to imagine they could possess enough intelligence to travel through space, let alone try and capture a whole world.

Brett noticed her glazed expression. He shook her arm. "Destiny, snap out of it!" He grabbed her hand and instinctively, reached for his gun and fired.

One of the creatures hissed and lunged at Brett. The bullet passed harmlessly through the hideous specter.

It's not real!" Destiny cried.

A distant roar overpowered the agitated hissing of the other creatures as they slowly advanced.

"Avalanche!" he shouted. "The gunshot set it off. We have to get out of here!" He grabbed Destiny by the hand and yanked her toward the door. A deafening roar resonated throughout the silent landscape. Quickly scooping up their gear, they scrambled outside, the white wolf sprinting off to lead them to safety.

"Hurry or we'll be buried alive." Pulling her, nudged on by the animals, they trudged through the snow. The timpanic din vibrated the ground beneath them. Destiny's heart hammered at the thought that any moment tons of snow could crash down on them.

The bear materialized before them and gave her a mighty shove that sent her flying through the air. As she landed, the snow broke her fall but she still felt its jarring impact. Brett landed next to her with a soft grunt a moment later. Scuttling to their feet, they watched in awe as the powerful avalanche obliterated everything in its path, snapping the tall trees like a mighty fist smashing matchsticks. Its destructive force barely missed them. A cascade of snow and rock decimated the chalet.

Brett stood and brushed off his clothes. "Jesus, that was close! Destiny, are you okay?" he asked, pulling her up.

She nodded; her gaze fixed on the destruction. "So now we've finally seen our adversaries. I've always believed that other life exists in the universe, but who could imagine that such creatures would actually invade Earth?"

The voice responded close to her ear. "Hunters exist throughout the galaxy. They are drawn to the scent of the weak and reek of blood."

"They're abominations," she said.

"Which is why your mission is so critical. They have conquered other worlds. We cannot let it happen to our people. Whatever they have become, they are still our brothers and sisters."

She nodded as the voice faded, her fear giving way to a feeling of resoluteness.

A few feet ahead, the wolf barked and bound toward them with a wagging tail. The other animals remained motionless and watched.

Destiny smiled. She crouched to pat the wolf on his head and scratched behind his silken ears. "You know me, don't you boy?" The wolf nuzzled her affectionately. She savored his warmth and for the first time, she could distinguish a brilliant white aura around him. "Where are you taking us today, old friend?"

He yipped softly then padded away and stopped to check if they were following. As they followed, the owl fluttered from the tree and soared ahead of them. The wolf pack and the other animals kept pace from a distance.

Falling into step that by now was becoming almost automatic, Brett scanned the surroundings. He heard no sound except the crunching of snow and the whispering wind and wondered if the search for them had been abandoned. Rather than feel reassured by the pervasive silence, he became concerned.

The wolf continued to lead them into the deep wilderness that Brett knew would be difficult to search with limited resources. Destiny was unusually silent and her faraway gaze told him she was in a place that never saw cold or snow. Occasionally, he glimpsed touching the ring beneath her glove as if to seek reassurance.

Their trek took them through some fairly rough terrain. Many times they were obliged to climb over boulders or thread through the remains of great tracts of forest, though not once were they hampered by fatigue.

As the skies brightened to the usual gray shroud, a whining resonance echoed in the distance. The wolf pricked his ears, studied the sky then turned to Brett and Destiny. Glancing up, they glimpsed a metallic flash. Their eyes met. Though neither spoke, they knew that it was not a plane they saw. They peered up at the sky waiting for a clearer view, but the sighting had only lasted seconds. Brett silently shook his head as he tugged Destiny's hand and they continued on their trek.

A moment later they rounded a slope and emerged at Whistler. The popular ski resort had disappeared, the once booming village buried under an avalanche. Were it not for the glimpses of cars and buildings poking through the snow, they could have quite easily missed the resort completely.

Brett stopped and stared at the carnage. "My God. It's like an enormous hand flattened this place. Have you ever been to Whistler, Destiny?"

She shook her head. "No. My parents never skied and while I was at college, I was too busy studying or practicing with the swim team. I always wanted to go, but by the time I had the chance, the war came and most of the resorts were either destroyed or closed down."

"I used to come here a long time ago," he said, wistfully staring at the remains of the road. "That street— I used to stay at a lodge there. I remember drinking hot toddies around the fireplace—"

Destiny reached for his hand and looked up at him. A hundred memories flashed through his eyes as he surveyed the decimated resort.

"It's always the small things that get us, isn't it?" he said. "Even more than the cities and countries, it's those special places, those little things that meant so much to us and can never be replaced."

Gazing at a pile of snow-covered rubble a bright flash of red caught Destiny's eye. She walked toward it and yanked at a piece of torn cloth. A battered doll surfaced, its face scratched and gouged— its eyes hollow sockets. A stab of pain pierced her when she thought of Angelica and Candy. Would their toys, once her own, litter the ruined earth as sad mementos of mankind's folly?

The white wolf barked impatiently and agitated in the snow. Brett reluctantly moved on behind Destiny, glancing a last time at the resort. Behind them, the pack of silver wolves darted playfully. She looked at them, envious of their freedom. *No one left to hunt you down,* she thought. *You're free, as you should have always been.*

They lapsed into thoughtful silence as they continued their arduous trek. Destiny's glance occasionally strayed to the owl circling ahead of them. Winding their way through infinite wilderness, time no longer bore any significance. The worries of city life that had once consumed her every waking moment were as remote as the sun beyond the eternal cloak of cloud. Today, now, consisted only of snow, ice and phantom forests. If it were not for those who pursued them, it could almost be the landscape of a surreal dream.

She paused to drink some water and handed the bottle to Brett. The animals paused like a still-life scene. "Where do you think we are?"

"Somewhere between Whistler and Pemberton. At this rate, we're going to see the entire province on foot."

"I don't think so. Somehow I feel we're getting closer." Her eyes misted and the landscape around her disappeared. The outline of streets crammed with cars and a multitude of people superimposed the snowy vista. Screams echoed, great cities collapsed beneath the onslaught of the elementals. Skies the color of pitch roiled with spectral clouds that spewed thunder and lightning upon the multitude. The world's greatest exodus had begun, the elementals fighting to prevent those who had not sold their souls from gaining access to the portal first.

"I just had another vision of the exodus," she said, her face pale and drawn. "Or should I say vision of hell."

The white wolf became agitated before Brett could reply. His tail wagging, he turned his head to make sure he and Destiny followed. The animals fell in around them as they continued on their journey.

They had not traveled far when the wolf suddenly stopped. He raised his head and howled, indicating danger. Destiny joined Brett. "Wonder what's wrong?" she asked, her breath almost crystallizing.

Brett gathered her close. "Look, over there," he said, pointing.

A sled, pulled by a team of huskies, moved painstakingly toward them. She noticed the malevolent green aura surrounding the driver, who constantly cracked a whip across the huskies' backs. The dogs yelped, jumped and tried to pull harder, their frantic barking echoing throughout the silent mountains and valleys. As they approached, she realized it was not an echo she heard. Moving out of the circle of Brett's arms, she turned around. "Brett, look behind us!"

Another sled approached from the opposite direction. It slid with ease over the snow, the dark clad figure on the sled not wielding a whip, but using only his voice to encourage his team of huskies. Both sleds seemed to head straight for the couple. The wolves gathered around Brett and Destiny to protect them.

"Let's get out of here," Brett said, pulling her along. "Somehow I don't think they're the welcoming committee."

They trudged on. She glanced behind to see both the sleds on a collision course and stopped abruptly. "Brett, look!"

As soon as the sleds converged, a vortex of light erupted from the ground and enveloped the two men. The first, surrounded by the green aura, attempted to beat the second driver with his whip.

The aura of the second man rose like a mauve beacon as it spiraled around him, shielding him from the stinging blows of his adversary. A crescendo of aggravating barking rose from the huskies. The terrified animals broke free from their reins of the first man's sled and scampered off.

Brett and Destiny recoiled and watched the vortex transforming into a perfect orb of radiant light. Emanating energy like a newborn star, it embraced the two men battling within its fiery heart. Destiny felt the earth shake as though its bowels had been torn asunder. Around them, the animals watched guardedly, the silence a stark contrast to the upheaval behind them. Suddenly, the second driver threw his head back and uttered a guttural cry. With preternatural strength, he seized his adversary's whip and cracked it across the man's head. The man emitted the horrific squeal of a wounded animal and tried to sidle away, but the light's blazing core instantly consumed his body and the sled.

Uttering another guttural cry, the second driver cast the whip into the heart of the light. The white wolf howled as it receded and winked out. Only a solitary, battered sled remained as evidence of the frightening encounter. Breathing heavily, the driver slowly stepped from the sled and approached them. Destiny stared at the sturdy, dark haired man; his icy blue eyes identical to the white wolf.

"You're the chosen ones," he said. "I've traveled far to find you. We must hurry."

Brett and Destiny looked at each other.

"We must reach the final destination," the man continued. "Get on the sled and you can ride the rest of the way. I will walk and lead the team. The elementals are not far behind."

***

CHAPTER THIRTY-TWO

Collier tried to contain his anger at the demolition team's sluggish progress. Pacing back and forth, his jaw clenched tightly, he muttered under his breath as he surveyed the men. The first batch of explosives had failed to ignite and now the team fussed like a group of demented chickens in their attempts to set up another batch. Snowploughs and teams had cleared some of the landslide, but there was simply too much for the old ill-maintained machines to handle. He knew they would be lucky to make any appreciable headway by dusk. Although he had repeatedly radioed for more backup and supplies, he knew reinforcements were unlikely. At any moment he expected an angry call from Barrows, or those insufferable agents —

Though Agents Woolley and Degen had silently departed after the first demolition attempt failed, Collier still rankled at their intrusion and resented the fact that they might find a way to apprehend the fugitives before him. His men found no evidence in the Jeep that might at least provide a clue about the suspects. No doubt Internal Security had better resources, but he would rather push the Jeep over the cliff edge himself than give those government interlopers any assistance.

He found himself staring at the bustling demolition team, their bright orange winter gear so reminiscent of a night three years earlier. Though he tried to shove the unwelcome memory back into the recesses of his mind, he could not prevent the young girl's bloodied face from peering at him once again, her glazed eyes beseeching as they stared from the crushing embrace of the collapsed building.

Collier caught his breath. Orange-clad rescue workers sifted through the rubble day and night in the search of survivors, but the quake's fury was swift and merciless, trapping sleeping residents in the maw of a high-rise already compromised by previous quakes. His wife had pleaded with him to move, but he had greater concerns in dealing with a horde of chameleon infected refugees that stormed a medical center and held the staff hostage—

"I'll deal with it when I can," he told her more than once, his posting as chief of rescue operations often taking him from home days at a time. "The center's the only one for miles. We have to protect it." Though he saw the concern in his wife's eyes, he chose to ignore it.

Collier shuddered. How many times had he recited that litany, until the quake hit, and suddenly it was too late to deal with anything. His wife and daughter were among the casualties, crushed when the unstable upper floors collapsed into the lower levels. The sandwiched floors were reminiscent of the notorious freeway collapse in San Francisco back in the late eighties as his team frantically searched the compressed debris. Only Jennie's face was visible from a painfully narrow gap, her eyes—those beautiful green eyes forever gazing into the surrounding darkness, her hand reaching for his—

He had worked like a madman to free her, but could not quite reach her grasping hand. The team, occupied with other victims, was already stretched to the limit, their equipment inadequate for the daunting rescue. Water dripped from an unseen location, the odor of gas a nagging reminder of the danger they all faced. His gloves, badly worn from friction, ended up discarded as he dug through the debris with bare hands until the flesh was raw and bleeding. But even as his fingers closed the distance to Jennie's hand, the light died in her eyes, her hand dropping like a felled bird into the dust.

His scream echoed through the rubble until his voice hoarsened and the team had to forcibly drag him away from the entreating fingers of Jennie's motionless hand. Even now he could hear still hear that damning drip that echoed through the devastated building.

Collier gasped at the memory. The Eletarii had promised him that once he had fulfilled his mission, Jennie and his wife would be restored to him. But would they also erase the horror of that moment? Could they possibly ease the pain? And after so long, how could they restore two bodies crushed beyond recognition? It had been days before the demolition crews could even clear the debris—

"Sir?"

Collier started at Sergeant Brown's intrusion. Hurriedly wiping away an incipient tear, he turned gruffly to his aide.

"Yes?"

"We received a transmission from Internal Security. Seems one of their choppers is searching the mountains beyond Whistler."

"Damned busybodies. I can't believe that bastard Barrows would authorize such interference—"

"The fugitives aren't believed to be in the Whistler area any longer, Sir."

"Well, what else is new? Any word from the teams?"

Brown hesitated. "No, Sir. At this point, it seems likely—"

"Yes, yes, felled by two lone terrorists, I know."

Brown glanced at the demolition team. One of them raised a red flag and began waving it. "Sir, the demolition team's ready."

Collier glared at the men. "This had better work. We've no more time for dicking around."

He and Sergeant Brown retreated to the convoy, now parked a safe distance from the landslide. A moment after the all clear was given a tremendous explosion rocked the landslide. The earth juddered from the force and sent debris skyrocketing into the air. A triumphant grin lit Collier's face as the snowploughs and dozers prepared to tackle the piles of rocks and debris caused by the explosions. If they worked nonstop, they could have a path cleared by daylight.

The clearing continued through the night. Men and machinery forged a rough path through the debris and finally linked with the undamaged portion of the highway. By the following afternoon, the last of the convoy crawled over the crest of the rock-strewn road and proceeded in the wake of the snowploughs.

Collier knew that since the suspects were now on foot, they could hardly be far ahead of them. How they even survived without food or supplies was a mystery. Yet somehow, some way, they managed to stay ahead of them and find a way to hide under impossible conditions.

He kept in constant contact with the search helicopter but so far the suspects had not been spotted. Either they had help or they were remarkably skilled, as they consistently seemed to defy both capture and the harsh elements. The forests were stripped, the bulk of resorts and villages destroyed by avalanches. Even a small animal could easily be spotted against the snow.

Reports crackled from the radio, most of them false sightings. Choppers had spotted a pack of wolves near the decimated Whistler resort and several cougars loitering around abandoned chalets. Impatience teased him as the convoy crawled along the highway past the mines. He could not fail. The suspects, particularly the woman, had to be apprehended, but it had to be done his way. The meddling by Internal Security was beyond his control. Barrows was not yet swayed to the ways of the new order. He was especially suspicious about agent Woolley, who somehow did not display an aura. It was unusual and he began to wonder if she was in league with the suspects. If so, she could be a dangerous adversary.

He could not allow that to happen at any cost. The elementals were growing in strength each day, the conquest of nations and the subjugation of their populations almost complete. The knowledge possessed by the suspects could not come to fruition. He trained his binoculars on the convoy behind him and searched for any sign of the two agents. The glass was fogged. He breathed on it and rubbed the lenses with his gloved fingers. Again he searched for the agents, Woolley in particular. It was important he contact Degen. Although he had radioed his men to keep an eye out for the agent, no one had sighted him. He mentally berated himself for not speaking to Degen earlier about eliminating Woolley.

He sighed and stared at the rumbling snowploughs, his thoughts returning to the suspects. They obviously had powers, though he did his best to debunk any such rumors from spreading. His men were weak, afraid, and ready to believe anything, but he still required the normal function of the military organization to further his own needs for the moment. When the time came, they would be easily conscripted into the new order.

***

Woolley rubbed her hands to get the blood flowing again. Though Collier believed her and Degen gone, she'd retreated to the rear ranks to remain out of sight.

Under the pretence of questioning refugees that steadily trickled from the wilderness, she kept a constant vigil on Collier and the progress of the demolition teams. Most of the men were ready to abort the seemingly impossible mission. Among them she discerned many green auras, but also faint hues of mauve. Tension was growing among the troops. She wondered how long Collier could keep his men under control if the road was not cleared soon.

The only food available to the men was what they had left of the scant rations a helicopter had dropped. Some had been careful with their rations, but those left without food had resorted to attacking those with meager supplies. Several times she stumbled across the body of a soldier killed for probably nothing more than a mere energy bar. Clearly, the tenuous order that Collier maintained would soon surrender to chaos once conditions and despair worsened.

She pricked her ears at a distant rumbling. Though she knew about Collier's requisition for backup, she hoped they would not be available, but there was no mistaking the distinctive sound of approaching land vehicles and choppers. She suddenly knew that the government must be desperate to plunder already scarce military resources.

The ominous drone of engines echoed through the hushed mountains. Above it all she heard the sound of distant shouting, as if a multitude advanced toward them. The exodus had begun—

Degen suddenly approached the Jeep where she sat. "What the hell are you doing, Woolley? Headquarters is wondering why you're wasting time questioning refugees."

"Don't interfere, Degen," she snapped. "You'd be surprised what people might know. Someone might have seen the suspects."

"Like this rabble would know anything," he countered, disdainfully eyeing the smattering of bedraggled refugees milling around a campfire. "Anyway, I want a word with you. You told Collier that we were leaving, yet here you are questioning people? What are you really up to?"

She winced as Degen pulled her out of the Jeep and dragged her behind the shelter of a nearby mound of snow. "Let me go! Who the hell are you to dictate how I do my job?"

"No more games," he spat. "You think you had us fooled, but I know what you are now—a traitor." He grinned dangerously, his countenance transforming into something Woolley did not recognize.

Fearlessly, she held his gaze. She felt his gun poke her in the ribs and didn't flinch. Strength flooded her suddenly, stemming from the knowledge that she had to thwart Collier. He and his followers had to be prevented from reaching the final destination and securing it for the elementals before Destiny's arrival. The dreams had warned her of the coming conflict and had imparted the knowledge she would need for her task. She had also been chosen not to display an aura. Her dreams, if they were indeed dreams, had also told her that the aliens, aided by the elementals, had one purpose only, to conquer Earth and prevent the opening of the portal.

She shook her head to clear her mind for the battle ahead. The knowledge gave her the strength and inspiration to face the grueling task ahead. However, it was not her place to question; it was her duty to proceed.

Degen wavered for a moment beneath Woolley's steadfast gaze. She seized her chance and brought her knee up hard between his legs.

He howled, doubled in pain, his hands clutching his crotch. "You bitch! I should have—"

She quickly knocked the gun from his hand and drew her weapon. The shot could barely be heard through the din of the approaching reinforcements. Gazing down at her partner, she felt a moment of pity at what the man had allowed himself to become.

Sighing, she bent down to retrieve his last rations and gun. She stuffed them into her pockets and straightened. It was time to pursue Collier. It would not be long before the troops would be able to scale the mountain blocking their path.

She stumbled through the churned up snow and almost tripped over the body of a soldier crumpled near the wheels of a stranded Jeep. His eyes gazed silently at the leaden sky, the blood from a gunshot wound to his temple a frozen trickle. The driver had also been shot. Summoning all her strength, she yanked the dead man from the vehicle and climbed into the driver's seat while, grateful for the brief opportunity to rest. The engine started with a roar and soon it plowed through the snow.

Carefully, she negotiated the tracks left by other vehicles. The Jeep crawled along, but it was better than walking. Grimly, she looked at the gas gauge and saw that the needle hovered on empty.

Barely a mile later, the vehicle ran out of gas and spluttered to a stop. Desperately, she searched it for a spare gas container, but found none. With a sigh she got out and continued following Collier on foot, remaining far enough behind so that she would not risk being seen. Shading her eyes, she looked behind her. The multitude inexorably converged upon the road. Stumbling, falling, fighting to get ahead, they approached with the determination of an army of ants.

She trudged through the snow anxious to infiltrate Collier's troops, but found herself caught in the wave of advancing elementals. Above, the skies transformed into a lurid glow, the grayness split to reveal churning black clouds stabbed with flashes of green. Among them, she glimpsed the metallic flash of ships that bore the same insectoid countenance as their occupants. Automatically, she put one foot before the other, her heart pounding to the rhythm of her thoughts, *stop Collier—stop Collier—*

Occasionally, she glimpsed a mauve aura among the seething mass of humanity. Like hunted prey, those that had not embraced the darkness scrambled to save themselves from damnation. A latticework of lightning pierced the skies followed by timpanic explosions of thunder. It was as if the heavens themselves revolted against the alien onslaught.

Darkness fell, but the crowds pushed on, dragging Woolley along with them. So far, she had escaped injury by mimicking the madness around her to avoid detection—her purposefully incoherent cries and rambling enough to convince those around her. Fear compelled her as she glimpsed faces transformed by the darkness, the spark of humanity extinguished from their eyes. She silently prayed that she would have the strength to reach her destination.

The encroaching dusk seemed to fold in on itself. She gasped when she felt the air sucked from her lungs and dove for cover beneath a partially rotted log. Even as she crawled to safety, a deadly hail the size of golf balls rained from the sky, transforming the mob into a screaming frenzy as they sought cover. The unearthly rattle was deafening even against the cover of snow. Several mortally wounded elementals fell around her, their bodies ruthlessly pummeled by the hail.

The onslaught lasted only minutes, yet it seemed like hours while she cowered inside the log. Finally, an awful silence punctuated by the moans of the wounded and dying prompted her emergence into the hellish scenario of a battlefield. Nauseous from the reek of blood and the sight of mangled bodies illuminated by the lurid sky, she averted her eyes and quickly trudged through the snow to continue her mission.

Collier's men were slowly making progress along the blocked road. Cursing softly under her breath at the loss of the Jeep, she considered her options in stopping him. A gunshot from close range would take care of him, but she would undoubtedly be killed by the elementals before she could hope to get away.

Gunshot—the thought jarred her in its simplicity. She glanced at the snow-laden mountains ahead. Devoid of the protection of trees, a disturbance would easily shift the heavy mantle. Briefly, she wondered why the hail had not loosened the snow, but she didn't waste time pondering the question. Retrieving her gun, she took cover behind a nearby boulder. Before she had a chance to fire, a sinuous green mist materialized before her. Her limbs locked in terror. The apparition slowly approached, its multiple eyes glittering as they held hers.

Suddenly, its clicking transformed into words she could understand. They insinuated into her thoughts, lulling her with a seductive mantra that promised her riches beyond her imagination. The voice teased her, its cadence numbing her mind and weakening her grip on the gun.

She gasped and felt her will draining away—then from somewhere deep in her unconscious mind, another voice, its resonance as pure and clear as a bell, called out to her. It infused her with strength, the power rushing through her body and surging into her fingers. As though snapping out of a trance, Woolley turned to the creature and raised the gun. It hissed angrily and retreated.

Steadying the weapon with her left hand, she aimed above the creature and fired at a particularly heavy overhang until the clip emptied. A faint smile of triumph lit her lips as a soft, distant rumbling transformed into a deafening roar—

***

CHAPTER THIRTY-THREE

The sled driver, who had introduced himself as Joseph Milligan, steadily followed the white wolf's trail. Progress was measured like the hypnotic pulse of a metronome, the crunching of snow a discordant tune. The surrounding animals moved in phantom synchronicity and halted as the sled did. The wolf stopped abruptly, sniffing and silently staring ahead causing the team of huskies to almost collide with him. Trudging beside the sled, Brett almost stumbled, his attention on the near collision. He glanced to where the wolf was intently staring.

"Another resort?" Destiny said, her cheeks now a burnished pink from the cold. She rubbed her hands more from habit, the freezing conditions seeming to affect her less and less. Turning to survey her escort, she found all eyes fixed on her. The wolf pack pawed at the snow, the younger animals frolicking and mock charging each other. Above, in a gnarled tree, the owl flapped his wings.

Brett shook his head and scanned the immediate area. The white wolf remained motionless except for the subtle twitching of his ears.

"I'm not sure. The area has changed so much I don't know what's over that ridge. He suddenly cocked his ear. "Listen."

She frowned upon recognizing the distant drone of a chopper. "Damn! They're sweeping the area. It'll only be a matter of time before they come this way."

"Maybe we should—"

Brett's words were interrupted by a stampede of softly yelping silver wolves. The animals surrounded the sled and Brett, and forcefully jumped up against them, their heavy paws almost forcing them onto the snow. Brett, Joseph and Destiny tried to maintain their balance, but could not resist the powerful creatures. "What are they doing?" Brett shouted when one young female nudged him playfully.

Destiny tried to scramble up but found her attempts thwarted. Glancing at the white wolf, she glimpsed the unmistakable message in his eyes. "Brett— I think I understand. They want to conceal us so that if the chopper comes this way, whoever is watching will think it's only a pack of wolves."

He shrugged and nodded to the young wolf. "My friend here isn't about to let me go anyway," he said, the animal nuzzling him. "Nice and warm though."

The white wolf yelped softly and moved on. Immersed in the pack, they moved with difficulty through the deep snow. Obliged to discard the sled, Joseph concealed it beneath a bank of dead shrubbery. The distance to the ridge seemed endless and being so closely surrounded by the wolves and huskies was almost suffocating, but the sound of the approaching chopper compelled them to continue. They inched forward until they reached the ridge, their progress tiresome through the dense snow.

"You okay, Brett?"

He grunted a response from his living cloak of warm fur. "There are better ways to get a workout. Good thing our gear is waterproof."

She smiled, amazed that despite their situation, he managed to retain his sense of humor.

"Just think," she said. "People used to spend time and money working out in gyms to stay fit."

"I'll take an hour on a cross-trainer any day."

At one point, the chopper approached so closely they clearly heard the whirring of its rotors. A turn in direction would reveal the wolf pack. As if sensing their urgency, the wolves bustled more quickly as they traversed the ridge and approached a slope. The snow was smooth and undisturbed by rocks or trees and Destiny realized that no human had trekked this way for years.

Gently descending with their escort, Brett and Destiny suddenly found themselves among thick, verdant shrubbery. They collapsed against each other and panted for breath. Satisfied that they were concealed, the wolves withdrew.

"This is amazing," she said, gingerly reaching out to touch a lush green thicket peppered with bright red berries. "How can this be alive?"

Brett glanced around at the berries hanging from the bank of thickets. "At this point, nothing surprises me. Maybe there's a Hilton around the corner after all."

They had barely caught their breath when the white wolf appeared. He lowered his head and approached Destiny. Running her hand through his thick, silken fur, she was struck once again by the image of a young pup by her side. A name grazed the borders of her memory, but it would not come. The wolf licked her hand with a rough tongue, the contact against her ring ushering a pleasant tingling through her flesh.

"I never knew they could be so tame," Brett said.

Destiny smiled. "We know each other. Or knew— I see a familiar place in my mind but I still can't identify it."

He turned sharply. "A place—like an island?"

"You didn't tell me about any such visions—"

"I didn't know what to make of it. Lately I've been seeing glimpses, but with everything going on, I haven't had time to really think about it. And I'm not sure if they're visions or memories."

"I'm certain it's our home, or world—wherever it is we came from, Brett. Doesn't it feel familiar? It's more than just a sense of déjà vu. After all, the voice did say our memories would surface."

He rose to stretch. The escort of animals grazed contentedly among the shrubbery, the sight filling him with a sense of peace. Destiny stood and leaned against him, accompanied by the white wolf. She rested her hand on his head and watched the animals feed.

"This is how the world should be. Not the hell we've been plunged into. When did it start to go wrong?"

Brett placed his arm around her shoulders. "Maybe we have to learn some hard lessons to regain what we lost."

"We need a second chance. Some of us have tried to make it work. It's not right that all of us should suffer."

He turned to her, his eyes searching hers. "It still can. I believe that more than ever."

Their lips brushed in a gentle kiss. The white wolf yelped and gently gripped Destiny's hand in his mouth.

"Time to move on, it seems," she said as the wolf pulled her along. "Joseph!" she called behind her. When there was no answer, she turned around to see the sled driver sitting quietly, surrounded by his dogs, beneath a tree. "Joseph, we've got to keep going."

He smiled. "I know you do. But I can't go any further. My task is complete for now. We will meet again, soon. Be assured your journey's almost over. Continue now; you will be safe."

Destiny hesitated until Brett called out to her. "Destiny, we've got to get moving. The wolf is becoming restless!"

The great beast snorted and pawed the snow, then reached for her hand. Reluctantly, she turned away from Joseph. Silently, she and Brett followed the wolf, their amazement growing as the shrubbery transformed into a lush wood, the thriving, fragrant trees forming a verdant canopy above their heads. Moss and pine needles softly cushioned the dusting of snow on the ground, the living forest an anachronism to the destruction around them.

Suddenly, Destiny stopped and listened.

"What's wrong?" Brett asked urging her on.

"Listen. Hear that rumbling?"

"Sounds like another avalanche. Probably caused by all the commotion behind us. Come on, let's keep going."

As they continued to descend, they abruptly reached a clearing overlooking a steep slope. They stopped and gazed down at Emerald Lake. In the depths of the icy winter, the lake should have been frozen. Instead, steam rose in spectral drifts from the brilliant green water, creating the effect of a thermal pool. Majestic mountains embraced the lake, their flanks dotted with lush evergreens. Further down the slope, they noticed that there was virtually no snow, the heady fragrance of pine intoxicating. Even the temperature was somehow warmer; the bitter winter chill receded to a pleasant spring-like mildness.

They gazed at the shores beyond. An oasis of endless green

forest surrounded the shimmering lake.

"Look," Destiny said and pointed up at the sky. "Is it my imagination or do I see the faint glimmer of pastel colors peeking through that gray blanket?"

Brett gazed up. "Yes, I see it—like the hues of a sunset. They're moving, almost as if they're coming toward us."

Destiny let her eyes wander back to the lake and inhaled deeply as she gazed at the wondrous sight below. "It's an oasis. Amidst all the destruction and misery, it's a miracle a place like this still exists."

"I've heard of Emerald Lake," Brett said, abstractedly petting the young female wolf that had playfully approached and now nuzzled him. "But I never would have believed it survived—or—maybe it didn't survive. Maybe it was recreated just for us as part of our mission, a final step toward the opening of the portal."

She gazed at the lake's mirror clear surface, the shimmering vision resembling the perfectly cut facet of the gemstone it was named after. Steam writhed from its limpid surface and embraced the trees with a lacy veil. The effect was magical and she experienced a sudden longing to climb down to its shores and immerse herself in the warm waters.

The white wolf sat beside her and regarded the water. For a moment, she saw the lake reflected in his eyes. Rising, he wagged his tail, yelped and moved in the fashion that she now recognized as their sign to follow.

Brett frowned and watched the wolf descend the steep slope. The pack waited behind them as if to urge them on. Their progress was slow but facilitated by numerous rocky outcroppings and sturdy shrubbery that served as convenient hand and footholds. From time to time, the owl would circle and hooted in encouragement. Destiny noticed that though the sound of the chopper had receded to a distant point, it never completely disappeared.

Darkness fell just before they reached the shoreline. Destiny noticed that only the wolves and the owl accompanied them now, though she could not actually recall when the other animals had departed. The voice picked up her thoughts and answered the question.

"The Antiquitas acting as your guides have departed from their animal hosts. Fear not, they will find sanctuary until the dark days have passed."

Her concerns about the animals answered, she gazed longingly at the emerald water. It shone with a luminescence that illuminated their path and reminded her of the glow of fireflies on a sultry summer evening. On impulse, she removed her gloves and stuffed them in her pocket. Nostalgia overwhelmed her as she kneeled and swished her hand in the water. She cupped some and drank it, its pure taste like the sun and sky. "Mmm—delicious. And warm enough to bathe in."

"That sounds almost as inviting as a hot shower," Brett said, kneeling beside her to drink.

Restored by the refreshing water, she suddenly noticed a glint coming from the shallow depths. At first she thought it was the reflection of her ring, which sparkled pinpoints of blue and green, but when she moved her hand, she realized the glint emanated from another source. Intrigued, she bent to reach for it, the warm water soothing her skin like a loving caress. "Brett!" she called, peering more closely. She noticed the glimmering outline of something half concealed by the mud.

The intriguing glint beckoned as she groped for the object. Her fingers closed around it and felt its firmness. Suddenly, the gleam of gold filled her vision.

"It's a key!" Triumphantly, she lifted it from the mud and handed it to Brett.

"Another talisman—" he murmured, staring at a magnificent key carved in baroque style. Gemstones like tiny faceted eyes twinkled from its intricately embellished flanks. Warmth radiated from it and penetrated his hand.

"Now we have only one more to find," she said and reverently took it from Brett's hand. Placing it in her pocket, she turned to find the wolves sitting quietly along the shore. Perched on branch, the great owl flapped his wings and with a hoot, soared off into the sky.

"We're almost there—" she said, the expression in their eyes knowing. She gazed up at the mountain they'd just descended. The highway they had crossed far above now seemed an eternity away.

As if a spell had been broken, the wolves suddenly rose from their haunches and approached the water. They lapped thirstily and led the way along the rocky shoreline. Destiny was constantly tempted by an intense desire to go for a swim, but realized she would be easily visible on the water's glassy surface. Suddenly, the white wolf jumped onto a huge boulder and disappeared among some shrubbery.

Brett frowned. "Now where did he go?"

The wolf's head appeared from between the shrubbery, then disappeared again. "You know the drill by now," she said.

"Wait here," he said. "I'll check it out."

He climbed the boulder, then hunkered low and struggled with the branches to follow the wolf. "It's okay," he shouted after a moment.

The wolf had burrowed through enough branches to create a viable path. Destiny crawled into the dense green mass and followed Brett's voice. The soft mossy soil cushioned her movements and exuded a pleasant, earthy aroma as they slowly wound their way up the incline.

After climbing a fair distance, they arrived at a rocky ledge and paused outside a narrow entrance to a cave. The wolf's head appeared at the opening. He barked once and vanished. Brett and Destiny hunkered through the opening and followed the animal, their way lit by a ghostly illumination. Drawn by the distant susurration of water, they were unprepared for the sight awaiting them as they stepped into a large cavern. A luminous glow emanated from translucent walls resembling faceted shards of crystal. The dazzling effect reminded her of a hall of mirrors. Her eyes scanned for torches, candles, but saw nothing. Brett approached a huge crystalline altar rising from the center of the chamber.

Destiny stared in awe. "It's warm in here," she said, her words echoing off the walls. She approached Brett and dropped the bag to the ground. "Not the worst place to spend the night."

She noticed his concentration on the altar and glanced at it. Cut from a huge hunk of crystal, it reflected glimmering veins of ruby, amethyst, emerald and sapphire. The altar's facets sparkled with a constellation of tiny pinpoints—the effect bathing the chamber in magical light. Her ring seemed to shimmer in response. Seven curious inscriptions etched the altar's surface. She touched them and immediately withdrew her hand.

"What's wrong?" Brett asked.

"Feel it."

He gingerly touched the smooth surface and rubbed his fingers along the strange symbols and indentations. "It's almost a pulsating warmth, like a living entity."

"That's what I thought."

They stared at the inscriptions. Inlaid with a mosaic of semi-precious stones, their evocative shapes were reminiscent of hieroglyphics. "Look at the symbols," she said. "A skull rests in the center and radiating around it are points for the crown, star, key, vial, trumpet and candlestick."

"But there's one more," Brett said, his finger tracing the outline of the remaining inscription. "This one resembles a half moon. Daniel said we would find the last of the talismans when we reached our destination, but where could it be?"

"I don't know, but it's bound to turn up somewhere. Maybe it's hidden somewhere in the cave."

She retrieved the skull from the bag and carefully placed it into the central indentation. "It fits perfectly. Like the missing piece of a jigsaw puzzle."

"Look at the wolf," Brett said.

She followed his gaze and saw the wolf perched majestically on a broad ledge high above them. He had vanished after leading them into the cave and had reappeared like an apparition. His eyes gleamed in the suffused light and bore into hers. The chamber melded into a brilliant light as the wolf's eyes transformed into a blazing azure sky.

Destiny felt faint for a moment. Embraced in limbo, her mind transported her to another place, another time. She gasped as she felt the warmth breath of the sun against her bronzed skin. The pungent odor of the sea wafting from a white sandy beach, the roar of distant waves a droning serenade. A white wolf pup frolicked at her side, its intense blue eyes gazing at her with a knowing expression.

"It is almost time, Destiny," the voice said softly.

"Destiny? Destiny, are you all right?"

Brett's concerned voice shattered the vision. She started and stared blankly at him.

"Did—you say something?"

"You were in one of your trances."

She turned away and withdrew the other talismans from the bag. "I know what we have to do," she said, placing the music box beside the skull.

"Do you know where the other talisman is?"

"No, but let's search the cave. If we've reached our destination, it has to be here."

Shortly after they started to search, a rustling noise drew their attention to the cave entrance. The wolf pack filed into the chamber and was settling in a protective circle around them.

"Guess we're definitely in for the night," Brett said. He turned and inspected the walls. In the suffused light, they emitted an almost phosphorescent glow. "You notice anything unusual about this place, Destiny?" He ran his hand along the surface. "The walls are too uniform to be a natural formation—and look at these facets. It reminds me very much of—"

"A diamond," she said. "Yes, I noticed it, too. It's almost as if we're in an ice cave, but it's not ice. It's like a crystal chamber."

"Where do you think it came from?"

She shrugged. "I don't know. From the glimpses I've seen it might very well not be of this world."

Venturing toward the rear of the cave, they stopped when the glassy floor sheared off abruptly. They peered into the dimness and noticed a gurgling stream about five feet in width. Warm, emerald water flowed beneath them. Steam rose and wafted through the opening, the briny odor oddly reminiscent of the sea. She felt a sudden pang of nostalgia as she inhaled the familiar aroma.

"I guess we've found a place to bathe," she said, kneeling toward the water.

"About time," Brett said. "No one here but the wolves and us."

She crouched and dipped her hand into the water. It rushed soothingly against her fingers. Images flashed through her mind of happier times, a time long buried in the forgotten recesses of her mind in a place unknown to mankind.

A vision emerged of a scene very similar to this one, except there were many people happily bathing in the stream. She moved among them, smiling and speaking in a foreign tongue. An older couple approached and greeted her. She watched the man helping his wife into the water. Destiny understood now that the stream contained healing powers of great magnitude.

A young girl called to her. Dressed in a flimsy pale pink gown, golden bands draped crossways over her budding breasts, the diaphanous material waved like a banner behind her. Joyfully, she approached Destiny and fiercely hugged her. A silken mane of silvery blond hair hung to the girl's waist. *My sister—* Destiny thought, overwhelmed by a sense of affection and recognition.

"Are you getting in?" Brett asked.

His voice startled her, causing her mind's eye to close. The vision had vanished but with sudden clarity she knew the girl was Angelica, her younger sister from the other world she belonged to.

"I'm wondering about my parents and Angelica," she said.

"So am I. In here it's like the world beyond doesn't exist anymore, but I'm sure they're fine," he said, taking her hand in his for a moment. "Soon, this nightmare will all be behind us. I'm still not sure what's in store for us, but somehow I know we'll see them again."

"Will we, Brett? Will our lives ever be normal again? Is that possible after everything that's happened?"

"I'm sure of it," he said reassuringly, though he did not meet her eyes for fear they would mirror his own doubts.

"I can't wait until midnight tomorrow has passed. But I wonder about this portal I have to open. What powers will I unleash? What will happen? Will it be over or just beginning?"

"I guess we'll find out then," he said. He stared longingly at the gurgling water. "So how about joining me for this long awaited bath?"

***

CHAPTER THIRTY-FOUR

During her few days with Chris and Sarah, Angelica had learned quite a bit of English. An adept student, she picked up the language remarkably fast. Sarah was amazed, the child's fluency indicative of a great gift. Even as she mounted the stairs, she could hear the child mumbling phrases to herself.

"Angelica, would you like a sandwich?" she asked, stepping into the Destiny's room.

The little girl raised her head from one of Destiny's old books. "Egg sandwich?" she answered with an enthusiastic smile. "Yes, please, Aunt Sarah!"

Sarah smiled at the child's delight. The chickens laid two eggs the day before and Angelica treated the event like it had been an historical occasion. She watched the hens with reverence and delighted in holding the still warm eggs in her hand. Sarah could only imagine the conditions that the child must have endured to be so enthralled by something as simple as a pair of newly laid eggs.

Angelica set the book on the bed and trotted after Sarah, who paused to check in on little Candy. Asleep in Angelica's room, the child's expression reflected a serenity that belied her mother's recent death. Her tiny hands clutched a bedraggled teddy bear that her mother had given her as a Christmas present, its moth-eaten fur spilling the last of its stuffing. Sarah suppressed a surge of hope that the child might yet overcome her withdrawn condition.

"Come Angelica," she said. "We won't disturb her." An appetizing aroma of apple pie wafted through the house as they made their way to the kitchen. Chris fiddled endlessly with the television in an attempt to obtain a decent picture, his muttering competing with the static intermittently shattering the transmission.

Angelica skipped into the kitchen and sat expectantly at the table. Sarah chuckled and removed the eggs from the fridge. "Angelica, I don't know if you understand, but there are others in this house who have need of a few bites of protein. How about if I make an omelet?" she said while breaking the two eggs into a bowl. She added some powdered milk, a little bottled water and started to whisk the mixture.

Chris suddenly called from the living room. "Sarah, take a look at this. Brett and Destiny are on the news!"

She frowned, handed the whisk to Angelica and quickly rushed into the living room and shut the door behind her so the little girl would not hear Brett and Destiny's names. The picture was so snowy it was almost impossible to distinguish the male newscaster.

"—possible sighting of the suspects in the Squamish area. Commander Collier of the Special Forces Brigade reports that they're closing in and expect—"

Sarah paled. "I don't believe it. They're treating Brett and Destiny like terrorists. What in God's name could they have done to provoke this?"

Chris shrugged. His expression drawn, he watched the report from his armchair. Though a cheerful fire crackled, the atmosphere was laced with fear and tension as they watched silently.

"I don't know," he said, feigning calmness. "It must be a case of mistaken identity. What else could it be?"

"What else, indeed," Sarah said, sighing wearily. Two photos of the suspects appeared on screen and she recognized the photo of Destiny that Agent Woolley had commandeered. "We've lived through so many horrors, but this is the worst of them all. It's almost like the military is looking for scapegoats."

"They probably are. I wish the weather would lighten up a bit. I need to bury our dead," Chris said somberly. "I can't imagine Brett and Destiny being out there in this intense cold."

"Neither can I, but clearly they're surviving somehow," she said.

Her expression darkened as she turned to the frosted window. "I wouldn't worry about our dead. It's so many degrees below freezing, the caskets should be safe in the shed for a while."

"Yes, but it seems indecent to just leave them there."

The living room door opened unnoticed behind them. Angelica stepped inside and glanced at the picture of Destiny on the screen.

"Destino," she said and smiled broadly.

Chris and Sarah turned to face the child and wondered at the glow on her face as she walked slowly to the screen and touched Destiny's image. Though her lips moved no sound came from them.

"Yes, that's Destiny," Sarah said, her throat constricting.

Angelica ran toward Sarah and flashed her a brilliant smile. "Egg sandwich?"

The sight of the child's beaming upturned face brought a reluctant smile to Sarah's lips. Angelica reached out and clasped Sarah's hand, her grip firm and warm. Sarah put an arm around the child's shoulders and led her to the kitchen. "Let's go fry that omelet. You can help me," she smiled, hoping that Angelica would not sense her anxiety about Destiny and Brett.

***

CHAPTER THIRTY-FIVE

The invitingly warm water shimmered as Destiny and Brett shed their bulky winter clothing and jumped in.

Brett gasped when his body made contact with the steamy water. "Christ, that's hot! It's like jumping into a spa."

She shut her eyes and sank into the soothing water. As it was only chest deep, she reclined against the crystal wall until only her face was visible. "This is bliss! I'd forgotten what it was like to be warm."

"I'd forgotten how many aching muscles exist in the human body," he said. "No doubt we'll get an anatomy lesson out of this."

She opened her eyes and grinned. Despite Brett's complaint, he too lay stretched on the smooth base until only his head was visible. His steam-plastered hair gave him a boyish look, his hand idly splashing the water.

Carefully, slowly, she slipped from the side and waded toward him. Grabbing his arm, she pulled him off his support and sent him tumbling into the water. Spluttering and coughing, he shot up like an indignant water sprite and spat a geyser from his mouth. Destiny, doubled over with laughter, could barely stay upright in the gurgling water.

"This calls for extreme measures!" he cried, and clumsily charged after her.

Giggling like children, the pair tumbled around in the water. "It was time you had a bath anyway," she challenged as Brett playfully dunked her. "You need it!"

"Speak for yourself! I didn't notice any deodorant packed in your bag."

The white wolf shifted his position on the ledge and watched them with interest. Intrigued by the shouts and cries, the pack also approached and sidled slowly toward the stream to observe the humans' peculiar play. One of them gingerly stuck his paw in the water but quickly withdrew it. Overcome by curiosity, one of the cubs overbalanced and tumbled into the water. The others yelped worriedly. A large silver female bounded over to investigate.

Brett quickly grabbed the struggling cub and lifted it from the water. He deposited the wriggling and yelping animal on the ledge. The mother immediately licked its wet fur and nudged her offspring away from danger, but not without first casting a grateful glance at Brett.

Destiny waded beside him and draped her arms around his waist. "Did you see that?"

He nodded, a thoughtful frown furrowing his forehead. "Yes."

"Maybe this was a chance to make up for Murphy."

He turned and looked into her eyes. "Or maybe this was a chance to appreciate what I have when so many others have nothing."

She ran her fingers through his wet hair and traced a pattern along his cheek and jaw line. Their eyes held each other for a moment before their lips met. Compelled by the urgency of their situation and an unspoken need, they clung to each other and stumbled against a smooth ledge. Their lovemaking was brief but fierce as they splashed like beached fish, their action a defiant fist raised against the circumstances that had cast all they knew into madness.

Spent, yet elated, they crawled from the water and retrieved a blanket from one of the bags. Huddling together, they sat contemplatively and dried in the warm, humid air.

A resonant, grinding noise from the altar drew their attention.

"Now what?" she said, their moment of tranquility shattered.

"I don't know. But I suggest we get dressed."

They donned their clothes reluctantly; grateful at least to be free of their bulky overclothes. Moving cautiously, they approached the altar and stared in surprise at an open compartment at the base of the great crystal. A glimmer of color shone from within.

Destiny hesitated before reaching inside. Her fingers sank into a luxuriant length of cloth that almost melted at her touch. Woven from a material she did not recognize the fabric shimmied with exquisite softness. Iridescent colors shone with rainbow brilliance. She handed it to Brett.

"It's so light," he said.

"It's beautiful," she said, peering further into the compartment. "But, wait a minute—there's more inside."

She exclaimed softly and retrieved a shimmering white gown. A mere wisp of diaphanous fabric, the texture gleamed like the finest silk. The shoulders were gathered and held together by golden clasps studded with midnight blue sapphires. She silently ran her fingers along the gems that echoed the deep blue fire of her ring.

The next item she retrieved was a matching cloak. It was made of a heavier material almost like cashmere and shone a royal blue. Accented by gold-braided trim, the pattern matched a slim belt that she presumed was an accessory for the gown.

"This is remarkable. I feel like I've won a shopping spree."

She gently withdrew garments more suitable for a male. A sapphire blue tunic edged with gold braid complemented a matching cloak. Last of all she pulled out two soft blankets and two pairs of intricately embroidered slippers. "As in Rome do as the Romans?"

Brett set the length of shimmering fabric on the ground and examined the unlikely wardrobe. Destiny stared transfixed at the blue cloaks.

"The sky—" she blurted. "Does it remind you of—?"

Brett shook his head almost in disbelief. "Yes—it does."

"This is all exquisite, Brett, but hardly suitable for conditions outside. Do you think we're meant to wear these?"

He laughed. "They would be fine for a costume party but not sub-zero temperatures."

"They are rather romantic. You would look like Caesar."

"And you like Cleopatra, no doubt."

"We'll have to ask the voice the next time it speaks to us what the wardrobe represents," he said. "For now, how about catching up on some sleep?"

Destiny shook her head. "Not right now. I want to enjoy the peace and quiet for a while. Tomorrow we may have to travel farther to find the remaining talisman if we don't find it here."

Brett folded the gown and robe and piled them neatly onto the blanket. "Why don't you just lie in my arms and we can talk?"

"Can we eat something first? I feel faint from hunger."

He frowned. "We've got only one energy bar left. Guess we'll have to forage roots for dinner."

They sat on the blankets and shared the energy bar. Finally, the warm interior and tranquil environment lulled them to drowsiness. They lay on the blankets and curled into each other's arms. Closing their eyes closed, they were unaware of the warm light that enveloped them. Ethereal voices resonated throughout the cave and echoed off the walls. One of the wolves howled softly in accompaniment. The white wolf watched from his perch until the two humans slept soundly. Then he, too, lay down. His head resting on the edge of the ledge, he did not sleep but kept his eyes riveted on the slumbering humans below, watching—waiting—

***

CHAPTER THIRTY-SIX
December 31st, 2008

The frolicking cubs woke them the next day. They bounded across Destiny and licked her face, then rolled over onto Brett while they played and nipped each other.

"Guess that's our wakeup call," he said, rising and stretching to a chorus of scuffling paws.

Destiny yawned and got to her feet. "I'll fill the empty water bottles from the stream. That should—" She stopped and sniffed.

Brett, noticing her reaction, looked around curiously. "Is someone reading our minds?" he said wonderingly.

She turned toward the wolves. Huddled around the base of the altar, they yelped softly and moved away to reveal a number of objects in the open compartment. She did not need to see them clearly to recognize the smell of fruit.

"Oranges—" she said, gleefully descending on the compartment. "Brett, come and look at this—there are bananas, grapes—my God, peaches! I haven't seen one in years! Look at the size of them! I've never seen anything like it!"

"At least not on Earth, perhaps," he commented while examining a bunch of deep violet grapes. He took a banana from the compartment and held it up to her. "Have you ever seen orange bananas before?"

"Not unless they're a mutated variety." She grinned and popped a luscious grape into her mouth. "Well, I don't care where it comes from. It's food and tastes like the nectar of the gods!"

They knelt beside the compartment and gorged themselves on the delicious offerings.

"I'm not asking any questions," he said, biting into a plump, juicy peach. Pink fluid exploded from the flesh and trickled down his chin.

Destiny glanced at the white wolf, now seated with his pack by the stream. He watched her with inscrutable eyes. "Thank you," she said, peeling a ripe banana.

The wolf nodded imperceptibly in acknowledgment.

They gorged themselves on the fruit until only a few skins and pits remained.

"Now I know how Robinson Crusoe must have felt on his desert island," she said.

"Maybe this was meant to be a refuge for us, perhaps a haven from the storm."

"I wish we could stay here, but I don't think we will. I have a feeling we've come to the end of this part of our journey—don't you?"

He nodded. "I've felt that way since we got here—like the closure of a chapter in our lives."

Her expression grew pensive. "I keep wondering how Mom and Dad are coping—and the others. They've been through so much. The last thing I wanted is for them to suffer. You know, suddenly I feel guilty. We're sitting here gorging ourselves on this fruit, surrounded by relative luxury while they—"

He sighed and drew her to him. "I know it's hard, but your parents are resilient. They've had to manage all these years and were better prepared than most to face this crisis. Besides, they have Angelica. I don't believe her arrival was any coincidence."

"No—neither do I. Angelica's part of this, and I'm convinced she was sent here to help my parents. In fact, I wonder how many others, just like us, are here on this world."

Her gaze suddenly shifted to the water bottles vibrating on a nearby rock. Despite a faint, eerie resonance rising like the tinkling of crystal, the wolves sat undisturbed around the cave mouth.

"What the hell is that?" Brett said, anxiously looking around. "Quake?"

"No. Listen—it almost sounds like voices."

He rose. "I'm going to take a look outside," he said as the resonance increased to a gentle susurration.

"I'll come with you. Something's happening. I can feel it."

Together, they approached the cave mouth. The white wolf watched them, but the pack made no move to allow them through. Destiny's hair began to halo from static electricity. Behind them, the stream vigorously splashed and the water bottles rolled off the rock and rattled to the ground. Brett touched her arm and recoiled when a tiny blue spark emanated from the fabric of her clothes.

As they stepped back from the cave mouth, a shimmering white light engulfed the cave. The air crackled and reeked sharply of ozone. Sparkling blue pinpoints formed a constellation that swirled like a newly formed galaxy. Brett and Destiny groped for each other and held on tight. Beneath their feet, the ground swayed and rocked.

"What's happening?" he cried.

Destiny squinted into the spectral maelstrom. "It's starting!" she shouted. At the same moment she felt fabric billowing behind her in the wind. She gasped and noticed that both she and Brett were now clad in the elegant blue clothing. Brett brushed his hand against his billowing cloak, the gold braiding glinting. The gown's fabric felt sinuously alive against Destiny's flesh as it swirled around her in a sapphire cloud. The ring radiated a sensuous warmth against her finger.

Before them, the cave walls vanished to reveal the mist-enshrouded lake gleaming with emerald luminescence. The chorus of a thousand voices rose like an eerie sirocco and echoed in countless tongues. Spectral faces loomed from the shore and surrounding slopes, some bathed in light, others cloaked in roiling darkness.

"They're here," she said. "It's time to open the portal."

The haunting melody of the music box suddenly filled the air. Brett and Destiny turned to find the talismans aglow on the altar. The skull blazed with a radiance that almost forced them to look away. On the wall behind the stream appeared what looked like a wheel, its center an emerald of enormous dimension. A ballet of glowing orbs surrounded it. The wheel rotated slowly, the emerald bathing the cave's interior in an eerie green light. Its radiant center beckoned the eye like the nectar-laden stamen of an exotic blossom. As Destiny gazed into its shimmering heart, glimpses of another world, her world, teased her.

She turned and half-walked, half-drifted to the altar. The white wolf loped to her side. From the corner of her eye she saw Brett's hand reach to stop her, but she shook his hand away. "It's all right. It's beginning. I have to do this."

Taking a deep breath, she reached out and placed her hands on the skull. The feeling of dizziness was no longer a concern as she understood that she would experience a transition to another world. An intense, electrical contact coursed through her body. Her head fell back and her eyes rolled in her head. The white wolf howled when she began to rapidly utter sentences in a foreign tongue. A brilliant azure sky burst through the translucent cave walls and bathed her in delightful warmth. She opened her eyes and gazed at sunshine dappled hillsides flanked with lush vineyards and orchards. The song of countless birds and the heady fragrance of flowers filled the balmy air.

She reached for the white wolf, now a playful cub. He pranced and nipped at her fingers. Standing near a wind-scoured cliff, she gazed at a jewel-like harbor below. Gossamer sailed boats bobbed on an indigo sea. The distant roar of breakers was punctuated by the raucous cry of seabirds. Children frolicked on a pristine beach dotted with shimmering, light-reflective parasols. The outline of a nearby island rose like a camel hump; its verdant cliffs dotted with bleached white villages.

Behind her rose crystalline buildings and spun sugar towers. A gong chimed—the resonant tone peaceful and meditative. People strolled quietly, their features strong and handsome. They were at once familiar but different, the language one of the mind as well as the spoken word.

Following a mosaic path toward the idyllic city, a sense of belonging suffused her. Fountains played, spilling their rose colored water into delightful pools filled with exotic fish. Birds resembling swans but with multiple sets of wings and flame gold eyes glided on the transparent surface. The wolf frolicked around her and yelped as she explored.

"Alaya."

The name, for it was a name she recognized, drew her attention. A masculine voice called from a courtyard ahead. The face was hidden by the shadow of a brilliant scarlet creeper, but the voice was strangely familiar. Flashes of blue moved with him.

"Alaya."

"Destiny."

The vision began to fade when someone called to her by her Earth name.

"Destiny."

She blinked and the vision of the island vanished. The white wolf silently gazed at her as she turned to face Brett.

"You started to fade," he said, his expression etched with concern. "It was like you were about to step into a different dimension."

She affectionately petted the wolf's head. "I went home, Brett. Our home. It's becoming so clear now. Soon, we'll be there. Our Earthly life as we knew it, is over—"

***

CHAPTER THIRTY-SEVEN

Vancouver roiled in its death throes as an infernal light seared the sky and cast a bloody light on the city. The clouds parted, revealing a fleet of ships that descended from the conflagration and hovered above the fleeing masses. Fueled by the faceless terror concealed in the winged vessels, the last semblance of normality crumbled while a desperate populace sought escape.

Besieged by armies of elementals and chameleon infested the few remaining services ground to a halt, plunging the city into darkness and despair. Vehicles littered the roads and highways like corpses as the exodus veered toward a place that existed only as a vision.

"The lake!" rose a universal cry. "Sanctuary waits at Emerald Lake—"

Above, the fleet of ships directed the panicked crowds like dogs driving a herd of sheep.

Screams penetrated the endless night, the cry of children a soul-wracking litany. The ferocity of the winter was no match for the terror that prodded Vancouver's desperate survivors into the jagged snow-capped mountains beyond. The snow was dotted with dark shapes huddled in blankets, overcoats or anything that would give them warmth.

In the struggle to reach Emerald Lake, human fell upon human, the last traces of sanity crumbling like wave-tossed sandcastles.

Mothers abandoned screaming babies, young people left their children or parents behind. Humanity raced against the last minutes of the world, the finishing line—a place known only as a sanctuary. No one knew where or how the rumors about Emerald Lake had started, only that their destination awaited them in the distant mountains.

An eerie green mist funneled from the ships and cocooned selected groups from the mob. They raised their arms entreatingly to embrace the darkness that consumed their souls, their cries welcoming the diabolical baptism. Emptied of the last vestiges of humanity, their souls forfeit, the possessed fell upon those hovering between belief and unbelief, between the darkness and the light.

Like an approaching dawn, an orb of radiant light scythed a path through the newly turned elementals and embraced a group of chosen ones. Impotent against the benevolent power, the enraged elementals stumbled back into the shadows. The light retreated with its precious cargo. As the frightened people reached safety, the orb winked out like the afterimage of a flashbulb.

The elementals raged as they tried to pursue the refugees, but it was useless. United, the chosen ones were stronger. Turning their faces to the churning skies, the elementals hungrily inhaled the aura of their dark benefactors hovering above until they lost all semblance of humanity. Their faces transformed into hideous masks displaying their basest instincts, their darkest desires. If necessary, they would die in their quest to reach the portal—

***

Sarah and Chris sat quietly in the darkness before the crackling fireplace. Candles flickered from the tables, the power long since cut and the generator reserved for a few hours a day. Holding hands, they stared at the blank face of the television, the terrified voice of the newscaster still echoing in their minds as the broadcast terminated abruptly.

"I wish we knew what's happened to Destiny and Brett," Sarah said, thoughtfully staring at a flickering candle. "I feel so strongly that our time has come—that everyone's time has come."

Chris affectionately squeezed her hand. "We've had more years than many. Good, memorable years. And maybe—maybe it's best not to know too much."

She turned toward the clock ticking on the mantelpiece.

"It's almost midnight," Chris said. "Should we wake Angelica and Candy?"

"No need. Look, by the door."

Angelica stood the doorway. Clad in one of Destiny's old flowered nightgowns, she resembled a cherub. She held little Candy by the hand. The normally withdrawn child gazed steadily at Sarah. A smile played on Angelica's lips as she and Candy ran to Sarah and climbed onto her lap.

Sarah choked back a sob and fiercely hugged the girls. Angelica had become the saving grace in their lives. Candy struggled out of the embrace and sat on the floor by Sarah's feet. She reached down to stroke the child's russet curls and marveled at the renewed life shining from the little girl's eyes.

Chris got up to look out of the window. He scraped the ice off until he had a clear spot. His frown reflected the fear in his eyes. "My God—look at the sky. It's like the very heavens are on fire. Wait— I see something. It looks like a squadron of fighters. No—they're not planes. They're not like anything I've ever seen. Sarah, come and see!"

Sarah lifted Candy from the floor and sat her on the other knee. She gently rocked both girls on her lap. "I don't need to see anything. I can feel the end approaching. It's almost time."

The clock on the mantelpiece started to strike twelve. The chiming echoed eerily through the silent room. Without a word, Chris embraced his wife and the two children. Eyes closed, they sat locked in each other's arms until the final chime faded away. A feeling of disembodiment overcame Chris.

"Sarah," he said softly.

Sarah buried her head against his shoulder as she too was overcome by a sense of disorientation. The floor swayed beneath their feet like a ship at a sea. Fear tightened her chest until a small hand reassuringly squeezed hers. Sarah opened her eyes to look into Angelica's serene face and glimpsed a countenance older than the eons themselves.

A shimmering light oozed from the darkness and engulfed

them. They felt themselves drifting into a kaleidoscopic veil of sound and color. Voices whispered, and Sarah felt a wonderful lightness enter her spirit when her gaze rested on the spheres that had visited her so long ago. Two of the spheres hovered beside her, Brett and Destiny's faces reflected in their luminous depths. Sarah nudged Chris. He nodded as he, too, gazed at the spheres. Destiny's smile was brilliant, her eyes full of love—beckoning, urging them not to be afraid. Embraced by indescribable warmth, buoyant in a sea of love and compassion, they soared above the wounded earth.

***

CHAPTER THIRTY-EIGHT

The din of hell abruptly shattered the serenity of Destiny's vision. She and Brett turned and faced the translucent walls of the caves. A cacophony of voices, screams, and the whirring sound of chopper rotors shattered the tranquil silence of lake. She approached the tenuous wall of the cave and reached out to touch it. Her hand wavered as it passed through.

Beyond, speckling the slopes, a teeming mass of humanity surged toward them.

"Look at them," Brett said. "They're like lemmings mindlessly seeking the edge of the cliff."

She scanned the throng and found every race, every nationality represented. Auras in every hue of mauve and green glowed like incandescent mist. "They're coming—the light and the dark ones. People that once lived together as communities have become adversaries. Families have been torn apart, friends are now enemies."

"What about the last talisman?" Brett said, casting a glance at the altar. The skull shone like a miniature sun. For a moment, he thought he saw the outline of eyes peering from the orbits. "Surely we need it to complete our task."

The white wolf rose when the pack agitated around the cave mouth. Brett and Destiny watched as they heard something stealthily scuttle through the tunnel. A flurry of motion preceded the appearance of the eagle. The great bird hopped inside, cocked its head and glanced sideways at them with a knowing expression. Something glittered in its beak. Spreading his wings, he gracefully soared toward Destiny and dropped the item onto her outstretched hand.

The white wolf barked in acknowledgment as the eagle flapped toward him and perched on the ledge. Holding up a golden object resembling a miniature sickle, Destiny swallowed away the lump in her throat. Carefully she wiped dirt off the blade and withdrew the golden key from her pocket. For a moment, she stood transfixed and stared at the remaining talismans. "Everything humanity has experienced has led to this moment, to these objects I hold in my hand."

She turned to the altar and fitted the blade and the key perfectly into the last inscriptions then embraced the skull with her hands. For several moments her hands melded with the skull, her body a mass of dazzling light that merged with the brilliance engulfing the altar. All seven talismans and the skull vibrated and glowed with an intensity that illuminated the entire cave.

The white wolf jumped down from the ledge and padded toward her. Gently, he tugged at her gown. Destiny emerged from her trance and stumbled after it to the mouth of the cave. She grabbed Brett's hand and pulled him along. "Are you afraid?"

He shook his head. "Not as long as I'm with you."

When they stepped out of the cave mouth, the surrounding shrubbery had disappeared. They stood on a bare rock ledge and gazed in awestruck wonder at the lake glowing infernally below. Tongues of fire darted from the churning, steaming waters. A tremor beneath their feet echoed the growl of thunder from the skies. With a timpanic roar, a fireball exploded through the clouds, its fiery wake crackling like lightning. A murmur of terror rose from the multitudes as it plummeted to the lake.

Strangely unafraid, Destiny watched its approaching reflection in the turbulent waters. It cut a brilliant swathe through sky, its veils of flame draping the mountains like a mantilla. Anticipating an enormous impact, Brett reached for her, but even as his hand made contact with her arm, the fireball dissolved into a pool of molten gold when it touched the water.

"It's like fireworks," she gasped, entranced by the constellation of golden streamers spiraling into the depths of the lake.

They watched silently until the light show winked out. After a moment, the lake began to churn violently. Vortices sporadically appeared on the surface, creating a mass exodus from the shores. Again, she felt the land shift beneath her feet. Brett's mouth opened, then closed, words failing him as a brilliant light emanated from the bowels of the lake.

Emerging like a specter from the depths, a translucent sphere rose majestically. Surrounded by a cloud of glittering particles, leaving a cascade of bubbles in its wake, the vision appeared to Destiny like something from a mystical dream. She watched the hues transformed from crystal brilliance to a prismatic glow. Suddenly, the waters parted as the sphere broke the surface and levitated slowly into the air. A balmy wind whipped from the lake, transforming the surface into a stormy sea. Cries and entreaties rose from the land.

Shielding their eyes, Brett and Destiny gazed up at the phenomenon that glowed like the sun and shifted like a living entity. It hovered momentarily, then slowly began to rotate until it elongated into a ribbon of color. A hush fell over the land as the color stretched like taffy into a shimmering rainbow. It arced toward Brett and Destiny until it formed a perfect bridge to the ledge.

The celestial bow penetrated the rock and filled the cave with breathtaking iridescence. The glittering cloud drifted over the rainbow toward the cave. A slight rumble shook the ledge beneath their feet. Brett placed an arm around Destiny's shoulders. They turned at the sound of an avalanche and watched unalarmed as the rock's face crumbled, the stone evaporating into fine dust. Slowly, the mountain opened like the petals of a flower to reveal a huge, glittering crystal chamber shaped like a diamond. Colors danced off its facets, mirroring the rainbow's brilliance.

Now that the shrubbery was gone, the opening no longer resembled the mouth of a cave but instead a perfectly symmetrical door.

Hesitantly, Brett and Destiny stepped through the opening. The rainbow extended into the interior of the chamber and settled on the wall just above the stream, bathing the altar in jeweled brilliance. Vapor wafted from the stream as the rainbow forged the outline of a shimmering stairway the texture of polished marble. The steps steadily ascended to a golden bow and a pair of sickles forming an arch at the summit. Two figures materialized beneath the arch, at once human, yet something else, their tenuous features shadowed by mist.

Through billowing, diaphanous robes of cerulean blue, the sentinels gazed at the surging throng of humanity converging down the flanks of the mountain. The masses pushed and shoved in their struggle to reach the arch at the summit of the stairs. Silently, the sentinels regarded the naked desperation of the damned; their shouts and voices in countless languages rising like the cries of wounded birds. Stragglers, still down by the lake, battled to ascend, the weaker brutally mown down by those determined to let nothing stand in their way.

Brett's arm tightened around Destiny shoulders. Locked in their embrace, they returned to the ledge where the rainbow shimmered beyond. She shielded her eyes and gazed up at an infinity of stars. "Look, Brett!" she shouted and pointed.

He followed her gaze and looked in wonder at the moon and stars that was hidden until only a moment ago by the endless cloak of cloud. The sky was so perfectly mirrored in the water that it was impossible to tell which was a reflection. The lake continued to steam and hiss, geysers of steam spurting high into the air.

As they watched, a luminous glow began to form on the celestial bridge. Brett's gaze drifted toward it, his astonishment growing as the glow shifted into a vaguely human form. Suddenly, a tall, graceful figure materialized. He nudged Destiny, but she had already seen it.

Stepping out of the circle of his arm, she moved forward to greet the figure.

"I have come," the familiar voice spoke in her mind. Thousands of voices joined in a jubilant chorus. "It is he! Altithronus has come—it is he—"

"Altithronus!" Destiny shouted in joy and recognition.

The white wolf suddenly appeared beside them. She felt his wet nose against her hand and bent to pat him, but he turned and headed for the kaleidoscopic bridge.

They watched him trot away, his tail wagging in expectation as he crossed the bridge toward Altithronus and sat beside him.

The eagle emitted a haunting cry and soared off to perch on his left shoulder. A pearlescent halo shimmered around the trio.

Recognition filled Brett's mind. Memories surfaced of words of wisdom, a voice filled with kindness, compassion, eyes that were compelling, a face, yet faceless, an imposing figure, an individual of infinite mercy who had led them so long ago. The voice entered his mind. Carefully he listened to the words.

"Ascend the stairs, but do not pass beyond the arch. You are no longer of this world and if you step onto Earth's soil, you will remain with the damned and suffer their doom. You and Destiny are the greeters. You will guide the chosen onto the bridge and direct them to me. Go now."

Destiny and Brett turned simultaneously. Her eyes were large and luminous as she looked at Brett. "He spoke in my mind."

"Mine too," he said and held out his hand. When they entered the chamber, they paused for a moment before the stairs. Together they climbed the shimmering steps and joined the pair of sentinels.

Tongues of darting flame illuminated the two sickles flanking the arch. Beyond the barrier, a horde surged forward, many of them deformed beyond recognition by the chameleon virus and the darkness within them. They moved like a mindless tide, their cries a terrifying ululation as they stormed the arch. Charging like spooked animals, they trampled those that did not move quickly enough. Desperately they tried to grasp the radiance above them. Destiny winced. One after another was brutally flung back, their bodies thudding on the rocks. A haze of static electricity shone blood red when yet another swarm of elementals followed, the stink of fear and disease a noxious fog.

"Free your powers, Destiny," a voice spoke in her mind. "The path must be cleared for the chosen."

She stepped into the radiant arch. From the deepest recesses of her mind came the knowledge. Shutting her eyes, she felt an incredible force surge from her body.

Brett watched an ethereal light surround her. She pointed to the sea of angry, twisted faces. The mob fell back as if scorched; their furious cries rising in protest against a shimmering path of light that steadily pushed them back.

Only the chosen ones could penetrate the shield her powers

had created. Tentatively, they emerged from the shadows; their eyes fixed on the glowing arch. Protected from the murderous hands straining to seize them, a swarm of humanity followed the path engulfed by a communal aura of mauve. Above the screaming crowd, the green mist writhed, vicious streaks of lightning illuminating the flanks of the alien ships.

The damned screamed and attacked in unison, many jumping off the sheer cliff face to try and reach the stairs from the mountainside. Their efforts were useless, the huge crystal oblivious to their assault.

Outraged by their inability to reach the stairs, the throng rolled, tumbled and slid down the mountain toward the boiling lake. Some writhed on the steaming shores while the infernal waters consumed others. Geysers tainted with blood exploded into the sky but never reached the radiant bridge.

Destiny swayed as she emerged from her trance. While turning to descend the stairs, she glanced at the silent sentinels, their faces ever shifting. Below, Brett waited anxiously, his hand outstretched.

"Destiny—you have to see this."

She quickly joined Brett but was unprepared for the sight that greeted them from the ledge. Looking down at the tumultuous lake, she shuddered at the floating armada of skeletons. She could not believe the beautiful, placid lake she had drunk from had become a cauldron of death. Yet for as many killed by the turbulent waters, more elementals surged in a human tidal wave as they sought the stairway. Men, women and children trampled and maimed each other in their panic. She watched as one man physically picked up a screaming woman and lifted her high above his head. He threw her into the lake, her flesh disintegrating before Destiny's eyes, leaving only a floating skeleton. Her heart ached for humanity, for what Earth had become. These people had been her people for twenty-five years. And now, what was left of them could not even be described as human— The clamor echoed in her ears, the timbre of agony beyond description.

"It is time, Destiny."

She gazed up at Altithronus, who stood benevolently watching from the bridge. "You must guide the chosen through the arch. This darkness is not for your eyes."

Nodding, her heart still bleeding for the calamity around her, she took Brett's hand. Together they returned to the chamber. Glancing once more at the blazing altar, they ascended the stairs until they flanked the sentinels at the arch. Beyond, a legion of chosen waited on the shielded path.

Suddenly, a familiar voice rose above the din. Destiny peered into the milling crowd, her heart dancing when she recognized the antique dealer, Bill Laguna.

"Destiny!" he cried as he approached, bedraggled, weary but joyous.

Smiling, she reached out and clasped Bill's hand. "Come," she said, guiding him through the arch. Leading him down the stairs and out to the ledge, she squeezed his hand. For moments, they gazed at the waiting Altithronus flanked by his proud mascots.

"I've dreamt of this moment so often," he said. "The vision sustained me all these years."

"Go, my friend," she said, guiding him onto the bridge. "We'll meet again shortly."

A miraculous transformation occurred as Bill slowly approached Altithronus. His back straightened and his gray hair reverted to a mop of unruly brown hair. He gazed in wonderment at a cloud of shimmering particles reaching to embrace him. As he watched, his body transformed into the strong physique of a young man. He held up his hands in joy and gazed at the firm flesh devoid of age spots and prominent veins. His pace quickened until he broke into an easy jog, eager to reach the promise that his eyes beheld.

Altithronus murmured something as Bill passed. With an expression of joy, Bill followed the arcing rainbow to where it disappeared into the lake, its heart untouched by the surrounding violence.

Destiny gazed at Altithronus. He now held a parchment scroll in his hands, but the colors from the glowing rainbow obscured his face. Clad in the same blue garments as their own, she glimpsed a platinum mane of hair cascading over his broad shoulders.

As she returned to the arch, she met Brett coming down the stairs guiding the Chinese merchant. The ancient man, his hands hidden in voluminous sleeves, nodded when she passed. His eyes radiating untold joy, he descended with the sprightliness of the youth that would soon be his.

Reaching the sentinels, she witnessed their sickles abruptly descend. Somehow, one of the elementals managed to penetrate the arch and tried to enter. It was a young woman, not much older than Destiny. In her arms she clutched an emaciated infant. As the sickles touched her head, she slowly turned to dust before Destiny's eyes. She shuddered and looked at the squalling infant that lay between the two sentinels on the first marble step amidst a filthy pile of blankets.

The sickles remained poised. Destiny surged forward and grabbed the bundle. She clutched the baby to her breast, thankful that it was spared. The cacophony from the elementals beyond the shielded path rivaled the roar of the ocean and pressed against her until she felt she would scream from the horror of it.

"It is good to feel sorrow," a voice spoke in her mind. "Mankind will suffer much in the days to come. Bring me the child and return to lead the others onto the bridge."

Time slipped into a curious limbo as Brett and Destiny guided countless numbers through the arch and onto the bridge. Among them was the young musician, the refugees from the harbor, the sled driver and the old Indian woman who transformed into a beautiful young woman as she crossed the bridge.

Eventually, Destiny no longer needed to guide the chosen. Emboldened against the darkness writhing only feet from their path, uttering words of gratitude and jubilation, they eagerly flowed through the arch and descended the stairs to the bridge. When the flow trickled to a stop, she felt a pang of anxiety in her heart that neither her parents nor Angelica had appeared. She nodded to Brett, who guided the last few down the stairs.

"I'll be waiting for you," he said.

The mass of humanity surging along the path to the arch pushed, shoved and trampled one another to break through. Even as she watched, those bearing the last vestiges of humanity transformed into an ugliness beyond description. She noticed several arms penetrate the force that restrained them and waited for the throng to burst through.

As the barrier began to fade, a woman stumbled through the arch. Dirty, disheveled and panting from exertion in her effort to reach the arch in time, Woolley greeted Destiny with a weak smile. Their eyes locked for a moment. Destiny nodded and touched the woman's shoulder.

"Hurry," she said to Woolley. "Your task is complete. You've done well."

Woolley eagerly descended the stairs. Destiny turned to see four figures appeared on the path—a man, woman and two children. Her face lit with a beaming smile. She rushed forward and held out her hands.

Angelica and Candy were the first to step through the arch and threw themselves into her arms. She hugged the little girls and watched her parents follow. "Mom, Dad, I'm so happy you made it!" she shouted so they could hear her above the infernal din. Dumbstruck by their manner of transportation, astounded to see Destiny and shaken by the spectacle, Chris and Sarah, their eyes constantly darting to the hatred emanating beyond, could only nod.

Fueled by utter hopelessness, the throng finally broke through the barrier and stormed the arch. Time and time again the sickles descended, but they did not deter the desperate that hoped they would be the ones spared.

Destiny grabbed the little girls by the hands. Motioning her parents to follow, she hurried down the stairs toward the bridge where Brett waited. He took the children and guided them across. Angelica clasped Candy's hand and together they skipped along the transparent veil of colors toward Altithronus. Candy reached up to touch Altithronus, then with a joyous cry moved toward the embrace of the lake. Destiny watched Angelica stand silently before the imposing figure, unafraid, her small face expectant. She laughed with delight when Altithronus placed his hand on her head. For a moment, a golden glow concealed them, the shimmering cloud concentrating on only the girl. As he withdrew his hand, Destiny no longer saw a child, but an exquisite young woman—her sister.

Angelica turned and nodded as though reading Destiny's thoughts. *You know now why I came*—she whispered in Destiny's mind. *My powers, our family's power, manifest through the Antiquitas, shielded you and your Earth family until the moment you would open the portal.*

But why were you sent to Rome? Destiny replied. *Why weren't you here with us?*

Angelica smiled. *The holy relic I brought to you bore the essence of humanity's goodness. Its light would safeguard the path of the chosen. And now, sister, I must go.*

Destiny nodded tearfully as her sister moved toward the water. Chris and Sarah watched awestruck, their eyes darting from the transformed Angelica to the formidable Altithronus, but when Destiny turned to beckon them, they stepped without hesitation onto the bridge and approached Altithronus. Watching the years peel from them, like the skin of a fruit, she watched them with joy.

"It is done!" a voice boomed. Its resonance echoed through the mountains and drifted to the legions of elementals.

The desperate wailing increased, but the commanding voice overpowered them. "It is done!"

Brett took Destiny's hand and guided her onto the bridge. Altithronus waved them on, the motion of his hand releasing the bridge from the ledge. As they stood by his side, the rainbow retracted into the lake, moving them with it. Below them, the entire lake had once again transformed from an angry maelstrom into a serene mirror, a flawless emerald.

When they reached the gleaming surface, they looked back once more. The crystal chamber lurched and with a thunderous crack, the mountain embraced it once again, concealing the chamber beneath its rocky surface. The land crawled with a solid mass of lamenting humanity that sought the arch with anguished cries.

The sentinels vanished in a misty haze moments before the arch and stairs crumbled beneath a massive avalanche that swept the face of the mountain clean.

"It is time," said Altithronus, his words echoed by the bark of the wolf and the flapping of the eagle's great wings. He reached to affectionately pat the wolf's head.

For the first time, Destiny and Brett looked at him closely. He was tall, much taller than Brett was who stood at six foot four inches. Framed by long platinum hair, his beautifully sculpted features melded into a thousand different faces within a mere glance. His eyes reflected the depth of the sea and sky and were filled with love, sorrow and infinite wisdom.

He rolled the scroll and slid it back into a golden tube, which he placed into the folds of his billowing robes. With a contemplative expression, he turned to Destiny and Brett. "The power of the Eletarii and the elementals is great," he said with a gentle voice of forged steel. "But greater is the power of good. Do not underestimate the might of the armies that will take on the battle to save what is left of this Earth. Our work here is finished for now. We must leave."

Destiny gazed into the water's glassy surface. As she stared into the limpid depths, the image of a fabulous crystal city mirrored from the surface. She gasped in recognition and reached out for it. Though it seemed within arm's reach, the transparent waters were fathomless, the city merely a reflection of their past and their future. Brett's hand sought hers. They turned for a moment to find Altithronus and his mascots gone. The bridge retracted into the water. The moment had almost come for them to move on.

Their last glimpse of earth would be engraved forever in their minds. Fearsome shards of lightning split the tortured skies until it seemed like the universe had cracked like an eggshell. The spectacle framed the alien fleet as it descended toward the lake and its minions. Until now, neither had spoken. Their hands clasped together, they watched with awe and sorrow the destruction of humanity and the planet that had been their adopted home all these years—Earth.

Altithronus' voice beckoned them. The water churned as the alien fleet sharply banked toward the water. A panel slid open on the underside of each ship, revealing a series of indentations resembling gills. They flared an electric blue and fired a disruptor wave in an attempt to thwart the retreating bridge. Though silent, the weapon scythed a path of devastation through land and flesh alike. It whipped the lake once more into a frenzy. The water surged toward Destiny and Brett with a frightening roar.

Destiny felt a thrill of terror at the approaching tsunami. Brett's hand snaked to grasp hers. The wave crested, and for a horrible moment seemed suspended between the earth and sky. Destiny shut her eyes as it exploded above them in a thundering torrent.

Have no fear—echoed Altithronus' distant voice.

She opened her eyes and stared in astonishment at the curtain of water cascading harmlessly around the bridge. Close enough to touch, she felt only the coolness of the rushing plume.

"Brett—look at this. It's amazing."

He cautiously raised his head and looked around in wonderment. Extending a finger, he gingerly probed the column of water. It shimmied and bowed under his touch, but did not dissipate.

"It's like we're in the eye of a hurricane," he said. "It can't touch us."

The raging water boiled into the lake, the ensuing turbulence no impediment as the rainbow bridge gently merged into the water. Destiny glanced once more at the sky before she surrendered to the liquid depths. It enveloped her body in a warm cocoon and closed over her head.

Her mind slowly numbed as the last horrors embedded in her memories were purged. She felt a mildly disorienting sensation followed by a powerful suction that pulled her into the brilliant embrace of light—

***

CHAPTER THIRTY-NINE

The avalanche trigged by Woolley killed most of the troops and barely missed Collier. Of the men who survived, all had either defected or embraced the elementals. Blind with rage, Collier trudged across the mountain of snow blocking his path. "Where is the power you promised me?" he screamed to the sky. "How can I serve you when you won't help me?"

His anger was drowned by the encroaching multitude. Swept away by the human tide until they crested the peak overlooking Emerald Lake, he began to feel the power of the elementals and eagerly opened himself to it. Above, the alien fleet loomed like birds of prey, the ships eerily silent above the mayhem. Immersed in the surrounding violence, he half-scrambled, half-slid down the mountainside, oblivious of those he trampled in the process. Muttering incoherently, he trembled from the fury that consumed him at his failure to prevent Destiny from opening the portal. Now he faced a punishment that instilled him with terror.

Pushing his way through the throng seething beyond the shielded path, he was determined to break through and approach the arch, but when he saw the sickles descend and destroy several others, he quickly stopped. The woman, the sole obstacle blocking his goal, stood beyond it. A hatred unlike anything he had ever experienced surged through him as he glimpsed her guide so many through the arch. The sight sickened him. If he could somehow get through, maybe there was still a chance to stop her—

He pressed toward the path but found himself held back. His bloodshot eyes widened when he recognized a figure moving along the shielded path toward the arch. Charging the barrier like an enraged bull, he pounded at it, inciting those around him to do the same. Despite the bitter cold, an unnatural heat flushed his body. "You bitch!" he cried, violently bouncing off the barrier. "You were one of them all the time! I should have killed you when I had the chance!"

Woolley turned. Dirty and disheveled, her face marred by cuts and bruises, she flashed a victorious smile and gave Collier the finger. "You made your choice!" she shouted. "Now live with it."

Uttering an outraged roar, Collier leapt at the barrier. An older man he had trampled rose and viciously attacked him. An agonizing scream rang out from the scuffle. Woolley averted her head. Glancing over her shoulder, she noticed that only a few chosen remained behind her. She hurried her pace and stepped through the arch, her heart skipping a beat as she gazed at Destiny and understood her mission was now complete.

"Hurry," she said to Woolley. "Your task is complete. You've done well."

Wounded and half-blind with rage, Collier kicked aside the semi-conscious body of the older man aside and watched Woolley disappear through the arch. An elderly couple and two children followed her closely. Ghostly silence descended on the crowd as the shielded path slowly faded from sight. A moment later, pandemonium erupted when the sentinels vanished along with the arch. Above, the alien fleet approached, eliciting a mass cry of terror.

Echoing the celestial battle, the mountain groaned under the onslaught of a tremendous avalanche, the earth trembling convulsively. Those that remained stormed nothing but rock, their screams piercing the din. Finding no refuge, no sanctuary in the unyielding rock, they turned upon each other until blood drenched the dirt.

Collier fled before the madness could claim him. He wept bitterly at his failure to procure the key. Though he tried not to look at the raging skies, he could not blot out the din hammering in his ears. In the distance, he glimpsed the rainbow bridge recede into the water. Desperately, he tried to control his descent, but in his haste almost fell to his death. Oblivious to the pain of his scraped hands, he continued to climb down to the lake. For a moment he glimpsed a figure on the bridge. Surrounded by a radiant halo, he could not discern its features, yet something about its imposing stance sent a thrill of terror through him. He cringed like a beaten animal and hid among the bodies littering the muddy shore.

"You have failed me!" a voice hissed next to his ear. Collier cowered behind a rock but the voice resonated painfully in his mind. "Please—don't punish me—" he begged. "I tried my best, but the woman—"

"Spare me your sniveling! The weakness of your species is a disease unlike any we have seen elsewhere. Now get up off your knees! Gather reinforcements and destroy the mountain. The chamber containing the altar and the keys must be found if we are to sever the link to our adversaries and claim this world as ours."

Collier struggled to his feet. Already the multitude was beginning to descend upon the lake, some of them careening into the water in search of the elusive rainbow. Above, peals of thunder echoed the celestial battle, the moon and stars obliterated by an advancing bank of bloody clouds that cast a hellish light onto the land. A bitter wind howled an eerie ululation, raising the hackles on his flesh. The fleet descended and fired their weapons, destroying everything in their path. Collier gazed at the deadly blue waves devastating the land and shuddered.

He reeled when an emaciated older man stumbled into him. "Get the fuck away from me!" he shouted pushing him aside. The man cried out in a foreign tongue and struggled weakly as he fell in the mud. Enraged, Collier kicked him into unconsciousness.

"So—you are not completely beaten," mocked the creature. "Now, gather yourself and help me claim this Earth as our domain. Declare your position as leader of the new order before it is too late. Go now."

Shaking from rage and fear, Collier pushed his way through the panicked mob and laboriously scaled the mountain. Hands reached for him as if to hinder him, but he shook them aside. Ignoring his pain-wracked body, neither a pleading voice nor tearful eye deterred him from his grim quest. When he finally reached the summit, a strange calmness replaced his exhaustion. Clambering onto a large rock overlooking the lake, he turned to the crowd and began screaming.

"People!" he shouted, his voice carrying above the din. "Calm yourself! Listen to me!"

He repeated the command until the uproar gradually subsided and it stilled into eerie silence punctuated only by the occasional sob. Faces devoid of hope watched him with fearful eyes, their bodies wasted by starvation and disease. A peculiar odor of corruption wafted from the mob, emanating from beyond the flesh. The fleet hovered above, their weapon stilled.

Satisfied by the crowd's obedience, Collier continued with more confidence. "Hope is not lost." He glanced at the fleet and heard a fleeting cacophony of clicking in his mind. A new sense of power and confidence surged within him. "The overlords and I will lead you! Together, we'll find the portal and open it. It's there—we saw the mountain claim the chamber. We'll dig for it until we find it. Unlimited power will be ours! Come with me and I'll lead you from the darkness. It's not too late for us!"

A tentative murmur whispered through the crowd as his words were passed from one to another.

Collier surveyed a myriad of expressions and realized how easy it would be to manipulate them. Weak and desperate, their souls already tainted, they would willingly follow anyone who promised them relief from their misery. "Do you hear me?" he cried, his oration booming like a zealous evangelist. "Those sheep followed the wrong side. They'll find nothing but damnation! Didn't you see them fall into the lake? They're all gone, drowned, lost to their so-called visions. Don't be led astray. Follow me and find salvation."

He paused to survey the effect of his words. "Who will join me?"

"I will!" Sergeant Brown, suddenly emerging from the crowd, yelled. His face bloodied and his uniform in tatters, he joined Collier.

Collier smiled coldly and stared at the sergeant who had been one of the first men to desert him. In his mind, he imagined a gruesome punishment for the betrayal. Brown scrabbled toward him, followed by a contingent of others.

Within a moment cheers broke loose. A human tide surged forward. The people shouted, danced and hugged each other, oblivious of the ships above. As the multitude assembled below the rock, Collier raised his hands. He glanced down at the hellish vision mirrored in the lake and smiled.

"Within the chamber lies the key to power and riches beyond your imagination. The universe beyond the portal is ours for the taking. Come with me now!"

***

CHAPTER FORTY

Vaguely, Destiny felt her fingers slip from Brett's grip. A spiraling sensation reminiscent of a roller coaster ride filled her with a pleasant thrill of exhilaration. Descending through a twilight world of darting, phosphorescent shapes and pulsing ripples, she felt a childlike wonder as the phantom images passed through her extended hand. Her hair haloed around her, her body buoyant. Suddenly, her descent slowed until her feet touched a resilient surface.

Smiling, almost giddy, she turned to look for Brett. He stood a short distance behind her, his eyes wide with wonderment. A luminous amoeba-like creature slithered by, casting his features in dayglo splashes of aquamarine. He stared entranced at his vaguely glowing flesh.

"Where are we now?" she asked

"Look, it's one of the spheres!" he said.

She turned. A translucent sphere bobbed toward them, its surface gleaming with soap bubble rainbows. She tentatively reached out to touch it. A mild tingling coursed through her flesh, her fingers slipping through the fragile membrane.

"Come, my children!" a voice boomed from within.

They stepped through the sphere and entered a magical domain of misty, dancing lights. The familiar tune of the music box softly echoed around them, surrounding them with peace and tranquility.

An almost narcotic aroma of wildflowers eased their apprehension.

"Welcome. This has been a moment I have long awaited."

They looked into the direction of Altithronus' voice. The misty lights cleared to reveal him comfortably reclined on a cushion-strewn couch, a jeweled goblet in his hand. A sweep of exotic flowers flanked the couch, the glimmer of a thousand candles winking like earthbound constellations. He smiled in welcome. His hair cascaded down the shoulders of his blue robes, his distinguished features exuding a powerful yet comforting aura.

"This is the beginning of your journey, the exploration of your memories, which must now fully surface. Come and sit with me, drink from this goblet and you will understand how you came to be on Earth."

Destiny and Brett sank onto on a pile of silken cushions facing the couch. She drank first from the goblet, the richness of the ruby wine a warm caress on her tongue. As she sipped, the tension drained from her body until an exquisite sensation of contentment filled her. Watching Brett with half-closed eyes, she handed the goblet to him. He drank, his expression mirroring the same sense of contentment. Settling further in the luxuriant cushions, a glimmering veil of firefly lights enveloped them. Each slowly expanded into a small sphere, each an individual slideshow of events in their lives. Slowly, they remembered—

"After we had chosen to undertake our mission, you transformed our bodies into pure energy," Destiny said.

"First we implanted the embryos within the hosts," replied Altithronus. "Then the energy was funneled in the form of light into your infant bodies. Your Earth parents were excellent hosts but unfortunately the parents we chose for Brett did not fare so well. The father abandoned the mother soon after Brett's birth. Unable to cope, she left the newborn infant at a hospital entrance and fled. Shortly afterward, the baby was placed with foster parents."

Destiny nodded as the recollection came. "The Antiquitas wanted us to be born as Earth children so that we would know them as our people. When we agreed to undertake this mission, we knew that we would not remember our origins until the appropriate time. But what I don't understand is why you simply didn't warn the governments of Earth about the elementals? If the Antiquitas were so powerful, why couldn't they help?"

"Your subconscious memory of Nirvana always remained," Altithronus said. "You were aware even though you did not understand. We were a primitive race before your ancestors discovered the skull. When the Antiquitas appeared to them, this began a transformation that would lead to many changes on Nirvana, including the gradual dispersal of the original tribe into separate nations. Though they remained under the dominion of Zamphirus, interaction became limited to general matters of state. Eventually, the people of Zamphirus ventured to the stars. Upon discovering Earth, we felt a particular kinship to this world. A small group expressed the wish to remain there. Because there were so many similarities to Nirvana, they integrated easily with humanity and taught them the knowledge imparted by the Antiquitas. Unfortunately, through the fullness of time, this wisdom was cast aside in favor of those who deified technology."

"And nothing could be done to stop this?" Brett asked.

"Our ability to communicate with our brothers and sisters on Earth diminished as the centuries passed. Despite our efforts most turned away and began to seek the way of life that eventually caused their downfall. Only a few receptive minds remained opened to the influence of the Antiquitas. They nurtured the knowledge and passed it through the generations to their descendants who were your guardians on Earth. The Antiquitas warned us that Earth was at risk and out of concern for our sister colony, we, and the guardians, watched events closely. Unfortunately, we did not expect the situation to deteriorate so rapidly. We were aware that Eletarii scouts discovered Earth during the time of the second Great War during the last century. What we did not expect was how easily they corrupted many of the chosen in positions of power whose influence had the ability to shape history— and which ultimately allowed the Eletarii to learn of our intervention. By then, virtually all of humanity had lost the ability to access the collective memory and seek the guidance of the Antiquitas. The rest, of course, speaks for itself in the grim chronicle of events that led to the final conflagration."

"I see," Destiny said. "Even before all this happened, I often wondered why the people of Earth have always been so prone to violence. Endless wars, despotic regimes, nothing but strife and bloodshed in every corner of the globe—"

He paused, his expression thoughtful. "Even though our powers are considerable, we cannot change the course of predestined events. We could intervene to help Earth battle the invasion of the Eletarii, but we could not prevent the creatures from ultimately seeking to conquer worlds beyond their own frontier. Our role is to balance good and evil in the universe."

"What a legacy we've inherited," Destiny mused as she watched another sphere drift by.

"It's difficult to believe that humanity is our kin," Brett said. "After everything we've been through on Earth, I couldn't imagine a race less like the Nirvanans."

"The potential for enlightenment is always there," Altithronus said. "It is only when one no longer listens to the heart, to the wisdom of the ages, that darkness sets in."

Thoughtful silence ensued. Destiny smiled and pointed to several spheres lazily drifting by. "Look, Brett, there's Angelica, my sister. And there are you when you were a boy! Your name is Nadiro."

"I was thinking about the palace," he said. "I remember when we assembled to learn of our mission on Earth. You were—you are, Alaya."

"My parents!" Destiny suddenly cried when the reflection of two much loved faces drifted by in the spheres. She watched their regal countenances, her father tall and handsome, her mother possessing sublime beauty.

"Your real parents," Altithronus said.

For a moment her face clouded. "How will my Earth parents react to this?"

"While on Nirvana, they will not remember you as their child, only as a revered princess. Later, when they have been prepared to return to Earth they will be able to accept the circumstances of your birth and understand it. "

"And my sister?"

"Only the purest of children could salvage the candlestick from the Basilica. We waited seventeen years after your birth on Earth to send Angelica to Earth. She had to be born to an Italian family not far from the Basilica. At the age of eight, she was ready to bring you the candlestick. As the second princess it was her right. When she volunteered, we accepted. She is now as she was when you left."

"No wonder I felt so drawn to her. And my parents—how are they? I've been away so long—"

The spheres slowly faded as memories burst into full bloom. Destiny felt a thrill of foreboding even before Altithronus spoke.

"Alaya, I am sorry to tell you that we face yet another crisis. Your parents are not on Nirvana. An alien race whom we believed to be in distress betrayed our trust and abducted them."

Stunned, Destiny could only stare mutely at Altithronus. "I—don't believe this. What happened? How is such a thing even possible?"

He looked at each before responding. "A few months ago, we received a message from the Klatrians in the form of an automated distress call repeating on all frequencies. Despite their preoccupation with the situation on Earth, your parents authorized a response. Claiming themselves victims of a catastrophic occurrence that shifted the orbit of their planet, the Klatrians appealed to us for humanitarian aid."

"And my parents believed them?"

"There was no visual contact, so your parents requested corroborating evidence. When the Klatrians provided astronomical data of the event, apparently a violent orbital shift caused by a cometary impact to a sister planet two Nirvanan decades ago, they agreed to provide assistance by establishing a supply route with the Klatrians. Though they claimed to have developed some self-sufficiency in their radically altered environment, the severe climate and widespread destruction of resources was hindering their efforts to secure the survival of their race. We did not realize that in the meantime, they had been infiltrating Nirvana."

"Forgive me, Altithronus," Brett said incredulously. "But I find it impossible to believe they could have arrived on Nirvana undetected. We're talking about an advanced society. I can't imagine an alien race would be able to simply waltz into your own backyard."

"We are highly advanced, Brett, but not impervious," he replied. "Unusual patterns of meteorite activity in our vicinity suggest that the Klatrians might have used cloaked ships to reach Nirvana, though we have yet to find evidence of such vessels."

"They must have been hidden or sabotaged."

"We have assumed the same. Of greater concern was the discovery that our visitors were not what they seemed. Even with our powers, we could not detect them because they were artificial life forms designed to impersonate us. We can sense a soul, but not circuitry."

"They were able to blend in that well?" Brett asked.

"The resemblance is startling, with one exception. They cannot tolerate prolonged exposure to our atmosphere. Those we managed to capture died before we could interrogate them, even though some of their injuries were not severe. When our scientists performed autopsies, they discovered a self-destruct mechanism integrated into the controlling circuitry."

An image from an old science fiction series unwittingly popped into Destiny's mind. She shook her head in disbelief. "Artificial life forms—what do these Klatrians want? Why did they take my parents?" A sob caught in her throat. "How do we even know they're still alive?"

"Though we have received only infrequent transmissions from the Klatrians, we do have confirmation that your parents are unharmed. It appears they wish to negotiate for what we cannot give them—the skull. They do not appear to realize that only Nirvanan royals can activate it and benefit from its powers. Even if it were possible to bestow such a capability on them, they would probably kill your parents anyway."

"So we don't even know who or what we're truly dealing with," Brett said. "What about probes? Surely there's a way to determine the nature of the Klatrians. The artificial life forms are no indication if they're meant to look like us."

Altithronus looked momentarily uncomfortable. "Your parents were in the process of planning such a mission when they were abducted. The event occurred a few days before I was to leave for Earth, while I was involved in the Melding ceremony."

"My God," Destiny murmured.

Brett's head swiveled toward her. "What does this mean?"

"It is an ancient tradition known only to the royals, Brett," Altithronus said. "The Melding is a ceremony adjuncts to the

Antiquitas like myself undergo each century to reinforce the bond between the flesh and spiritual. It is a process I will undertake until I am ready to appoint a Nirvanan successor and join the Antiquitas in a final ceremony known as the Ascension."

"It also involves complete immersion into a transcendental state," Destiny added. "The only time Altithronus would be technically unreachable. And with my parents and the Antiquitas so involved with Earth as well—"

Brett frowned. "How convenient. Too convenient, in fact. What's wrong with this picture?"

Destiny swallowed hard and looked into Altithronus' fathomless eyes. "Earlier you mentioned 'betrayal.' Is it what I think you meant?"

He nodded.

Blinking back tears, she reached for Brett's hand. He clasped it with a stricken look.

"Someone they trusted?" she whispered.

"It would have to be someone close to the royals, someone clever enough to play both sides to their own advantage by revealing enough, but not everything about the skull."

"Do you have any idea who the traitor is?" Brett asked.

The word hung heavily in the air.

"We have not yet identified them, but considering the circumstances, it is clear that complicity was involved."

"What I don't understand is why my parents didn't use their powers to prevent their abduction," Destiny said. "How could they have been so vulnerable?"

"This could have happened only if your parents were completely unaware of the threat. Therefore until we apprehend the perpetrator and learn what happened, we must assume they were taken by surprise or somehow overcome."

"What can we do?"

"Without a royal ruler, we cannot activate the skull and therefore cannot utilize its powers. Now that you have returned to us, you will need to assume the throne and rule in your parents' absence."

"But the skull remained on Earth."

"No, it did not. It is already safely in its place in the star temple on Nirvana waiting for you to embrace its full powers."

"I don't understand why the Antiquitas sent the skull to Earth. Without it, Nirvana was unprotected."

"Once the royals have initially activated the skull, the power remains with them forever. The same will apply when you assume temporary rule of Nirvana and activate the skull. We know the skull's energy is linked to the crystal mountain where it was discovered so long ago. Somehow this energy can be directed into infinity. Normally, distance and location present no issue, but in the case of your parents, we believe they are incapacitated to prevent them from accessing the skull."

Destiny shuddered at the chilling import of his words. "Incapacitated—how?"

"From the last transmission we received from the Klatrians, it appears your parents are being kept at a subconscious level, probably as a means to control them."

"Mind control—" she murmured. "Then whoever the traitor is has at least suggested enough to make the Klatrians suspicious of my parents."

"Suspicious of their abilities, yes, but not the full extent. Remember, such a revelation would leave the traitor no bargaining power."

"We're talking about my parents! Not some damned game of poker!"

"This sounds like something from the days of the Cold War," Brett said.

Destiny paused to take a deep breath. "I'm afraid for them, Altithronus."

"Do not despair. The Klatrians will not risk losing what they covet so much. Your return to Nirvana will pave the way for their rescue."

She sat in silence while her mind churned from the glut of events. "And what of Earth in the meantime? There is still so much to do there. What of all the people transported through the portal? Will the cultural diversity cause a problem on Nirvana? Will we face even more discord?"

"No. They will not remember their origin until the time comes to prepare them for their return to Earth. Until then, they will integrate into our culture in every way."

"What happens next?" Brett asked.

"When we arrive, your bodies will automatically adapt to Nirvanan physiology. You will remember and know everything you have experienced during your years on your adopted planet so you may direct the battle raging on Earth. When the elementals have finally been conquered and their stain wiped from the land, reserves of the chosen we have brought to Nirvana will be returned so that the cleansed Earth may be reborn."

"When will that be?"

"In human time, about a decade. We cannot predict exactly how long the transition will take. A child by the name of Piper was born thirteen Earth years ago in Alice Springs, Australia. She will play an important role in the restoration of the planet upon your eventual return."

"Is she also from Nirvana?" Destiny asked.

"No, she is human. But she possesses superior intelligence that will make her a critical part of Earth's new order. She is the descendent of our original colonists, a gifted child bearing the best traits of both worlds. Before the cataclysm that devastated Australia, she was already known as a prodigy. Though she has lost her family and suffered greatly, she possesses an indomitable spirit. She will be a great leader and asset to you."

"If she's is so important, why did you leave her on Earth? Isn't she vulnerable to the elementals?"

"Her presence is vital there. She is equipped with the intelligence and skills necessary not only to ensure her survival but to prepare for humanity's renaissance."

Destiny grew pensive. "Are the Klatrians in league with the Eletarii? Is this all part of some horrible conspiracy?"

"No, they are yet another enemy. The Eletarii's domain borders the void of space. They seek to expand their territory by subjugating other races through the corruption of mind and spirit. Like parasites, they feed on the host until nothing remains of the individual, then they claim the conquered world as their own. Ultimately, however, humanity will recognize the elementals for what they are—a scourge far beyond the disease that ravaged Earth. To defeat the elementals is to defeat the Eletarii. Without their loyal minions, they cannot maintain control of Earth. Therefore once the elementals have been defeated, a wonderful renaissance will transform the planet you knew as your home."

"How can the remaining few conquer the elementals?"

"As you are aware, a solar flare will soon erupt that will cause great disruption on Earth. Our scientists know of it, but cannot provide an exact date. Chaos will ensue, but those remaining will come to understand that the true power of the elementals is the darkness that thrives within the human spirit. They will form a spiritual bond that will ultimately defeat the enemy. As I told you before, there are those who retained the characteristics of our original colonists. Woolley was one example, as were the guardians to the keys. We recruited those we knew would play a critical role in assisting you. When the time is right, we will send the chosen back to Earth to help repopulate and infuse our ways once again into the new world. The merging will forge a stronger race. You and Brett will accompany them to oversee the process."

"What about the crystal chamber? The elementals will do everything in their power to blast the mountain and unearth it."

"No alien or human will ever reach the chamber. It is encased in Demurion, a Nirvanan metal. Its properties are similar to the force that protected you in the cafe. Nothing can penetrate it. It will remain embedded in the mountain until your return to Earth. Now, in view of our imminent return to Nirvana, I must ask if you would prefer to be known by your real names or the ones you have adopted on Earth?"

"I'd like to remain Brett. I'm used to it now," he said.

"I may use both for the time being," Destiny said. "At least until the conflict on our worlds are settled."

"Good. Now it is time to continue our journey. Please close your eyes and rest."

"Altithronus, before we continue, there's a piece missing from the puzzle in my memories that never surfaced. The talismans, why were there so many? Why couldn't I simply be told what and where they were?"

Altithronus gazed at her and saw in her eyes the same strength and resolution borne by her parents. "The Antiquitas were the only ones who knew which talismans were chosen to become the keys to open the portal. In anticipation of the Eletarii's planned dominion over Earth, we devised a plan. The Antiquitas placed earthly objects where the elementals were unlikely to find them. Some were entrusted to loyal guardians such as the Chinese merchant and the musician. When your journey began, the Antiquitas made sure you would retrieve the objects. Only the skull, ring, music box and the vial originated on Nirvana. However, only the royals could activate the skull, and then only the combined power of the skull and the talismans could open the portal."

Destiny gazed at the ring sparkling on her finger. "How was it that I could open the portal if I haven't ascended the throne yet?"

"The Antiquitas allowed you the power to activate the skull because of the unique circumstances of your mission. The fate of Earth depended upon your success. However, the full scope of the skull's power will be yours once you have ascended the Nirvanan throne. But, Princess, we must continue our journey. Are you ready now?"

"Yes," Destiny said quietly while reaching for Brett's hand.

A susurration like a distantly murmuring ocean filled the sphere and embraced them in shimmering pinpoints of lights. Gently, it ascended from the lake bottom. As they drifted through outer atmosphere, Destiny glimpsed an armada of bobbing spheres transporting the chosen to safety. Though grateful to see their successful retreat, she felt a stab of remorse as waves of alien ships closed in on Earth. *Like jackals closing in for the kill*—she thought. Rising further into the embrace of stars, she gazed down at Earth. Shrouded by a bloody ring of mist, the planet retreated like a scattered billiard ball. Gradually, she felt herself drifting into a serene void that gradually vanquished the pain, anguish and uncertainty roiling within her.

Cast by the solar winds, they drifted in a dream-like state within the tenuous shell of the sphere, the only sound the distant pulse of the universe. Aware, yet unaware, Destiny gazed at the gauzy palette of stars and nebulae that jealously guarded unimaginable wonders and horrors. Abstractedly, she shifted on the strewn cushions. Beside her, Brett drowsily surveyed a chaotic mushroom cloud nebula that bled an incredible spectrum of colors found only in a hallucinogenic vision.

A subtle flash of light drew her attention. She turned sluggishly in time to catch the fleeting afterimage of Altithronus before it faded away. In the ever-shifting dimensions of the sphere, she found herself able to view all angles at once. Altithronus was gone—had he indeed ever been there?

She mused at his remarkable disappearance only until a cluster of planets appeared around a bright yellow sun. Fully emerging from her trance, she gazed at the spectacular sight. At first, she thought one of them was Earth, but when the sphere drifted closer she realized it could not be. Her adopted world had become a distant memory, some of them precious, some dark. The good she would cherish, when Earth smelled of flowers and spring rain and the sun shone on a world still untainted. Her soul was filled with wonder and delight now that she knew she was going home, but her heart would always be torn between two worlds—

One planet stood out among the others. Much larger than Earth, it orbited about halfway from the sun. The armada of spheres bobbed toward it like a school of exotic sea creatures. Vast indigo oceans embraced verdant continents interspersed with sparkling lakes, sprawling desert terrain and towering mountain ranges. Her fingers reached out for Brett and found the warmth of his hand. He smiled, sat up and looked around. Puzzlement briefly crossed his face.

"Did I miss something? What happened to Altithronus?"

Destiny gazed at the their idyllic home below. "I think he'll be waiting for us."

Embraced by radiant sunshine, the sphere descended with dizzying speed through an intensely blue sky. Though the other spheres landed before them, she saw none in their general vicinity. Below, a familiar camel-backed island rose from an indigo sea. Fishing boats dotted a harbor overlooked by bleach-white homes perched on windswept cliffs. Anticipation spurred them as the sphere dissipated and they found themselves on the ivory sands of a beautiful shell strewn beach. The effect was magical, surreal, and filled Destiny with an intense sense of peace. A balmy breeze ruffled her hair, the aroma of flowers strong on the air. She smiled at Brett, who stood gazing at the wondrous scenery beyond.

"I know this place so well—" he murmured.

She squeezed his hand. "I know."

Warm powdery sand cradled their feet as they made their way toward a lush jungle bordering the beach. The thunder of the surf accompanied them until they entered a dense wall of foliage. Exotic birds called from the trees, their jewel like feathers vying with resplendent blossoms clinging from vine wrapped branches.

Destiny inhaled the almost narcotic aroma. "Could Nirvana be the paradise we imagined to be on Earth?"

Brett paused to sniff the satin yellow petals of a bell shaped flower. "Maybe it wasn't a myth after all."

A clearing appeared as they stepped through a bank of trees bearing a peculiar gourd-like fruit. Clouds of gossamer insects flitted about—their murmuring not unlike bees. Brett and Destiny paused to regard the fluted pink marble columns of a large temple magnificently adorned by colorful frescoes and carved hieroglyphics. Wind chimes tinkled from unseen nooks, lending a magical quality to the scene. Fountains cascaded from tiered levels until they emptied into a rectangular reflecting pool fronting the temple. Multiple-eyed fish darted through the crystalline water, their blue and gold finnage trailing like veils as they swam through floating scarlet lilies the size of footballs.

Destiny approached and brushed her hand through the deliciously cool water. A juvenile fish paused to tentatively nibble her finger. Her ring reflected a shaft of sunlight striking the water, the colors shifting as she withdrew her hand. A brilliant emerald shone from the heart of the ring, the diamonds and sapphires cresting like a wave around it. She gasped at the transformation and ran her finger across the flawless emerald.

"We're home," Brett said.

"Yes. At last, you are home," echoed a resonant voice.

They glanced toward the magnificent golden temple doors. Altithronus stepped forward to meet them, his warm smile reflecting the joy in his eyes. His blue robes shone in the dappled sunlight as he approached.

"Welcome, my children," he said, grasping their hands.

Destiny gazed into his fathomless blue eyes. "I hadn't realized how much I missed this place."

"We have all been waiting for this moment," he said. "It has been and will be a difficult journey, but you are finally here. Come — the others are waiting."

Brett and Destiny glanced at each other while they followed Altithronus into the temple, their footfalls light on the polished marble. Assembled around a cloth-draped altar of fruit and flowers, faces that they instantly recognized watched them with emotion as they approached. They were all present — her Earth parents and all the chosen ones who had given her the talismans.

Tears blurred her vision as she regarded the familiar faces. Ageless, perfect, they gazed at her with the loving demeanor of family.

"Welcome," said one young man whom she knew as Brett's younger brother.

Staring at the blue-clad young man he had not seen for so long, Brett felt a powerful sense of love and recognition. Beside him stood his parents and siblings, all aglow in their prime.

"Mashan, my brother, I'm so glad to see you—"

The young man nodded with a smile. "I should hope so. I've missed your company. You've been gone far too long. Remember how we used to race each other to the lighthouse? You always bragged about how strong a swimmer you were."

Brett's parents stepped forward. Bronzed and golden-haired, their faces were alight with joy as they embraced their son.

Destiny watched, her heart laden with sadness. Her parents should have been here to greet her — instead, she faced a task she was not quite ready for, the ruling of Nirvana and the seemingly daunting rescue of her parents.

The assembled group extended their hands and smiled. Brett and Destiny fell into the communal embrace, each experiencing the shared memories of days long gone and the anticipation of what was to come.

"There's so much to do," she said as she turned to Altithronus.

He gently clasped her hand. "Yes, but you have both been gifted with the power to build a new world. Wisdom and patience reign in your hearts, as is fitting for those whose task it is to lead the people of Nirvana. Until your parents return safely to us, you will guide those who already reside here and those who are chosen to return to the healed Earth. Through your unique experiences, you will be able to forge the mold of tomorrow."

"It sounds beyond the capability of mere mortals," Brett said.

"Abandon such a notion, Brett, for you will find nothing beyond your capabilities. You are no longer mere mortals. You never were. Now, we must start the matrimonial ceremony. It has been postponed long enough and you cannot rule this world unless you are joined."

Brett turned to Destiny with a smile. Though they now remembered their vows of betrothal and the postponement when they accepted their missions on Earth, she could not help but fear for her parents. Excitement, longing and sorrow filled her heart as she reached out to clasp Brett's hand.

***

CHAPTER FORTY-ONE

Holding hands, Brett and Destiny followed Altithronus and the others as they left the temple. A contingent of guards appeared and followed from a discreet distance, their eyes constantly scanning the surrounding jungle. At length, the retinue dropped a short distance behind and began a melodious chant. It halted abruptly when they emerged into a grassy clearing. Destiny paused and stared in wonderment. Before her, the crystal city she had seen reflected in the lake stretched before her like a living fantasy.

Towers and minarets rose like fragile blown glass flowers from behind a translucent wall surrounding the city. The great crystalline gates, once always open, were now closed. Guards flanked both sides—the sight strange for a city that had only known peace. She realized that many questions needed to be answered, but was most disturbed by the Klatrian infiltration of Zamphirus. That they were apparently assisted by one of her own people galled her, and try as she might, she could not fathom the reasoning behind such a betrayal. For an endless moment she stood staring at her home, her mind clouded by the absence of her loved ones.

Overwhelmed, she stepped forward, her gaze transfixed by limpid waterways winding through the city amidst verdant expanses of parkland. Even as she watched, a distant gong sounded the opening of the huge gates, their brilliance highlighted by the sun that sent prismatic ribbons dancing across the walls. Figures emerged through the gates and approached a temple flanking the entrance to the great city.

"Magnificent—I appreciate Nirvana's beauty now more than ever," she murmured.

"Behold the great and wondrous glory of your heritage, Destiny and Brett. Your people await you," said Altithronus.

"While we were still on Earth, I saw this place," she said. "But not in my memories."

"You were allowed glimpses, but not in detail until we felt the time was right. It is important that you embrace your kingdom with the heart and mind you have now."

He glanced at Brett and Destiny. "But let us continue now. The ceremony must be concluded by sunset."

The chanting retinue continued along a sloping path toward the monument. A faint susurration rose from the city, which Destiny recognized as cheering. She felt Brett's grip tighten on her hand when they approached the star temple, a sculpted crystal masterpiece comprising an angled view of the galaxy illuminated by a blazing core.

Altithronus stopped before an altar set beneath the monument. Carved from a single crystal and bearing gleaming veins of precious stones within, it was an exact duplicate of the altar in the cave. Set in the wall behind, an emerald wheel surrounded by glowing orbs began to rotate and flooded the area with shimmering light. Destiny suddenly realized that the emerald in her ring was an exact miniature of the wheel. The retinue silenced and assembled around them while the guards retreated to a respectful distance. Beyond, a multitude of blue clad figures rapidly approached, their heads adorned with floral garlands. Music from a harp and a variety of stringed instruments drifted languorously on the breeze.

Altithronus knelt and withdrew the crystal skull from a concealed compartment. He bowed his head and whispered a few words before placing it on the altar. The skull glowed softly as if welcoming them to Nirvana.

He clapped and the chanting resumed. More and more people flocked around the temple, their combined voices resonating in the air. "Brett and Destiny, the skull awaits your joining. Embrace it so you may be united, so that you, Destiny, may rightfully take your place as ruler of Nirvana." His eyes fell to Destiny's ring. Grasping her hand, he held it within his own. "Embrace as well this ring, the symbol of the unity between Nirvana and Earth. Let the diamond reflect the sun and stars, the sapphire the sky and sea, and the emerald the green of the land. Wear it always as a bond between our worlds."

They approached the skull. It blazed with a radiance neither had ever seen as they placed their hands upon it. The glow bathed them in ethereal light and infused their minds with ancient secrets and future wisdom. Destiny closed her eyes and savored a sense of elation. She felt Brett's presence beside her and relished the familiar comfort it gave her.

Altithronus raised his hands and chanted loudly in an unfamiliar tongue. At first she did not understand the words, but then she realized that he was reciting wedding vows. Automatically, she and Brett followed as if the exchange had been rehearsed.

Joy sprang to her heart when Angelica appeared. Dressed in shimmering folds of blue and gold, she smiled brilliantly and presented them with two garlands of lacy pink flowers. "Let these be a symbol of your eternal union," she said, winding the garlands around their wrists. She handed a third garland to Altithronus.

Heady fragrance entered their nostrils, reminiscent of jasmine but much stronger. They embraced and kissed. According to Nirvanan customs, they were now joined forever.

A loud cheer rose from the onlookers as Altithronus threw a handful of the pink blooms over the heads of the newlyweds. From the altar, he produced the silver inlaid vial and touched their forehead with the sacred oil of the Antiquitas. Wafting a subtle scent of spice and wood smoke, it was an extract derived from a rare flower found only on the precipices of waterfalls surrounding the crystal mountain.

"Out of respect for your parents, the wedding celebrations will be postponed until they return so they may partake of this joyous occasion," he intoned. "Now, go, my children. Mingle with your people. Zamphirus, capital of Nirvana, awaits you. Heed the wisdom of the skull. It will guide you and your descendents through the generations."

Her gaze was inexplicably drawn to a woman and two men

lingering by the trees. Though they cheered with the crowd, something about their eyes set them apart from the others. Cold and unblinking, their gaze seemed fixed on herself and Brett. Instinctively, her hand reached for Brett's. As if sensing her scrutiny, the trio began to weave through the crowd toward them.

"Brett," she murmured. "Over there—by the trees—"

He turned and glanced where she was staring. "Who are they?"

"I don't know—but there's something strange about them—"

A group of boisterous children stumbled across the trio's path. The children, immersed in play, clasped hands and formed a circle around the group. Caught in a sunny area, the trio acted uneasily when the children began to sing a song.

Destiny turned to speak to Altithronus, but he had left to mingle with the crowd. "Find Altithronus," she said to Brett. "I think they—"

But even before Brett could turn away, a scream pierced the air. The crowd silenced and turned to the children, now scrambling away from the trio in terror.

The distressed woman fell to the ground and began to convulse. Her companions knelt beside her, their agitation increasing as she began to claw at the angry red welts marring her face. The men grabbed her and unceremoniously dragged her toward the shelter of the trees where she panted and gasped for breath.

An uproar emerged from the crowd. "Klatrians!" they shouted in unison.

The word hammered Destiny's ears. A furious group of onlookers charged the trio. "Brett!" she cried, still stunned at the horror she just witnessed.

Abandoning the writhing woman, the men bolted, but managed only to flee a few yards before the hostile crowd surrounded them. The guards pushed their way through and split up to seize the men and the struggling woman.

Altithronus' voice boomed through the air. The agitated crowd parted as he approached the woman. Brett and Destiny quickly followed, but Altithronus raised his hand and motioned them to stop.

"Behold the face of the enemy," he said, gazing solemnly at the woman's hate filled eyes. Like a shedding snake, strips of reddened skin peeled from her face, revealing raw, brownish flesh below. Her panting erupted as harsh gasps.

Beyond, her companions, now trapped in the sunlight, also struggled for breath.

"Evil begets its own punishment," Altithronus said. "For all the treachery the Klatrians have committed against us, for all the technology they have subverted for their own dark purposes, the simplest thing defeats them—prolonged exposure to our atmosphere."

Destiny stared in revulsion at the Klatrians. The thought that her parents were in the hands of such heinous creatures, filled her with terror.

"Take them away," Altithronus ordered the guards. "We will deal with them later."

The crowd roared as the contingent bore the Klatrians away to the city.

"So this is the face of the enemy," Brett said. "A mirror of ours."

"Not quite. Their appearance is merely an illusion to conceal the evil within."

"I dread to think what their world must be like," Destiny said. "And what my parents must be enduring—"

"Your parents are strong. They will survive."

Brett pensively watched the retreating guards. Angry citizens hurled abuse at the Klatrians and more than one attempted to attack them. The guards reluctantly fended them off, their unwillingness to act aggressively toward their own people evident by their halfhearted actions.

"They knew we were here," he said. "They must have been watching us."

"They have grown bolder," Altithronus said. "But we have also become more vigilant to their presence. Our scientists are working to isolate the properties of our environment to determine exactly what triggers the self-destruct mechanism within their bodies. This will provide us with a powerful weapon. Such tactics are not our chosen way, but sometimes in battle, you must do what is necessary." He paused. "But now, let us put this incident aside. Today is your homecoming." Turning to the crowd, he raised his hands. "Let us rejoice!"

They moved from the temple with Angelica at their side and gazed at their people. All the chosen ones who had preceded them on the rainbow were waiting. The crowd roared in jubilation and swarmed Brett and Destiny. Swept away by the wave of adulation, they could only laugh when they began to recognize faces. Yet even as they welcomed those who had been close to them, Destiny could not help but think of her natural parents.

Brett noticed her distracted expression. "Don't worry, we'll find a way to bring them home."

She nodded. "It's just that after everything we've been through, to finally come home to this— I want so much to see my parents, to hear their voices—"

"And you will. Never doubt that for a moment. Remember what I told you. As long as we're together, we can face anything. You'll see your parents again."

Destiny smiled. Suddenly, a pair of faces she scarcely recognized loomed before her. Her mouth dropped in amazement as she regarded her Earth parents. Youthful, but not young, wise, but not ancient, they bore the same regal timelessness as the others. Beside them, little Candy laughed delightedly and skipped around them, her animated face and shining eyes a miraculous transformation.

Brett thoughtfully watched Destiny hug her Earth parents. Joyfully, she bent to kiss the little girl. Sarah, her lovely auburn hair a burnished glow in the sunlight, ran a smooth hand lovingly against Destiny's cheek.

"How lovely you look, Princess."

Destiny smiled, though a slight twinge of pain gnawed at her heart. All these years she had known these people as her parents. They had wiped her tears, soothed a bruise and tended her through illness. Now, she had become just their Princess. "Thank you, Sarah," she said, vainly trying to control a moment of intense longing.

Overcome with emotion, Chris turned to Brett, who stared distractedly at a range of distant mountains. "We were honored to attend the ceremony, Brett. It was very moving. I know in my heart you and Destiny will be great leaders who will help vanquish the Klatrians."

"Yes," Brett said, "We'll do our best for Nirvana and those other worlds that need our guidance."

Destiny turned to him. "Brett?"

He started at the inquisitive sound of her voice. "What? I'm sorry. I was just—"

She followed his gaze to the mountains. "You have that feeling of foreboding, too? It's as if something is waiting for us."

Brett nodded. His expression was momentarily somber despite the jubilation of the crowd—many now filing into the temple to pay homage to the skull. "The knowledge in my mind is like arriving in a foreign country. There's still so much more to explore."

"And other challenges to meet," she said, her gaze fixed on the skies where somewhere on a hostile world her parents waited to be rescued. "So this isn't Eden. We are in a world where strife still exists." She turned and pulled the others into an embrace. "But our past on this world will become our future. We'll face all the tasks before us, no matter how daunting. She paused, her attention momentarily distracted by a dark speck in the sky. It vanished into the horizon before she could identify it. "We stand on the shoulders of those who came before us. We are united. We stand strong."

"Nirvana," Brett said. "We are home."

***

AUTHOR BIO
DIANA KEMP-JONES

It's said that some people have their heads in the clouds. In the case of science fiction author, Diana Kemp-Jones, her head can be found beyond this world into the realm of stars somewhere to the left of Alpha Centauri.

Born in Toronto, Canada, to a British father and Greek Cypriot mother, Diana was an imaginative only-child prone to creating fantasy worlds. In early elementary school, her talent for writing materialized in the guise of gruesome short stories such as the "Goushy Green Eye-ball." Inspired by the original Star Trek series, her love for science fiction later displayed itself in epic length stories for her English composition class. Though Diana's family immigrated to the US when she was a young girl, a passion for travel took her to Canada, Britain, Scotland, France, Greece, Cyprus and Israel during and after her college years. She eventually moved to England where she lived and worked for several years. A course with the London School of Journalism rekindled her long simmering interest in writing and prompted her to purchase her first, primitive word processor. Having explored and subsequently discarded the realm of more traditional jobs, she returned to the States and devoted herself to pursuing her true path as a writer. An admitted eccentric, Diana is an ardent swimmer, animal lover and fan of ethnic cuisine. Her surroundings are a rather bizarre mix of Art Deco, modern and Southwestern generously interspersed with chaos and clutter. Glow in the dark stars vie with Star Trek memorabilia. Books spill from cabinets onto the floor. A telescope lurks in the office closet. A prolific writer, Diana invites visitors to browse her varied repertoire of published and forthcoming books.

"I've been told by some that they think I'm not from this world," says Diana with a wry smile. "They may have a point. I never did fit into the normal scheme of things."

Write to Diana at scifidi@aol.com

Visit her website at http://www.dianakempjones.com

***

AUTHOR BIO
MARTINE JARDIN

Do I live in a fairytale world? A world that only exists in books?
On the contrary. I'm very realistic and walk this earth with two feet firmly planted on the ground. However, we all dream and therefore bury ourselves in books that speak of magical love, solutions to broken relationships, fantasy, science fiction, the mysteries of history, futuristic worlds and adventure. We imagine ourselves as the hero or heroine in these books. We get so absorbed in the story, that we almost live it.

I was born a writer. According to my mother, I scribbled when just a toddler and hid all the pencils on her by stuffing them in between the seams of armchairs. As soon as I learned the alphabet, I wrote stories, and I've written ever since. I won some short story competitions at the age of twelve. When I was seventeen, I wrote short children's stories and illustrated them for a magazine. I am published overseas. I've written stories for Playboy. Current publication is Shadowed Love, Picasso Publications.

During my career as a wife, mother and then single mother, I wrote many stories by hand. After my children grew up, I started writing seriously again and put all these stories into book form, writing my first complete novel by hand until my son convinced me to tackle the computer.

My daughter urged me to start submitting my material.

I was gifted with many talents. My hobbies are gardening, sewing, embroidery, knitting, painting, drawing, and many other crafts. But writing is my main talent and whenever I can, I now concentrate fully on it.

During my younger years, I traveled extensively and have lived in several different countries. For the past 28 years I have lived in beautiful British Columbia, Canada where I share a home with my son.

Write to Martine at martinejardin@home.com
Visit Martine's website at http://www.martinejardin.com

***

WATCH FOR THE NEXT VOLUME IN THE DESTINY SERIES

NIRVANA

Faced with the responsibility of ruling Nirvana and overseeing the battle to restore Earth, Brett and Destiny face their greatest challenge—to rescue her parents from the Klatrians and subsequently defeat the hostile race.

In league with a Nirvanan traitor, the Klatrians threaten to kill her parents unless she surrenders the skull. As part of a daring plan, she and Brett offer themselves as hostages in order to infiltrate Klatria and destroy the menace presented by Vark, a leader descended into the realm of madness who will stop at nothing to save his dying world.

***